*To all who served in Vietnam*

*Let love and faithfulness never leave you;
bind them around your neck,
write them on the tablet of your heart.*

—PROVERBS 3:3 NIV

# Table of Contents

## Part One

| | |
|---|---:|
| WELCOME TO HELL | 1 |
| HELL HATH NO FURY | 11 |
| ROCKET CITY | 19 |
| MUD, MOSQUITOES, MILDEW, AND MORTARS | 29 |
| A LIGHT IN THE DAMPNESS | 37 |
| NO SECOND CHANCES | 47 |
| SEMPER FI | 57 |
| TISSUES, TEAPOTS, AND GARDENIAS | 69 |
| BULLIES AND HEROES | 85 |
| A DIAMOND AND A CROSS | 93 |
| BEAUTY FROM ASHES | 103 |
| QUI NHON | 111 |
| LAM SON | 121 |
| UNTIL TOMORROW | 131 |

## Part Two

| | |
|---|---:|
| ROAD TO THE FUTURE | 145 |
| BILL | 155 |
| CATCHING UP | 165 |
| THE GRAND TOUR | 173 |
| THE WOODCARVER | 183 |
| WHEN PAST AND PRESENT MEET | 193 |
| REUNION | 203 |
| THE ACCIDENT | 211 |

| | |
|---|---|
| DISCOVERY | 219 |
| SEMPER FI | 229 |
| REVELATION | 239 |
| STEVE'S STORY | 247 |
| SECOND THOUGHTS | 255 |
| FIRE | 265 |
| THE WORLD ACCORDING TO EVIE | 273 |
| FAMILY REUNION | 285 |
| ANGELA | 293 |
| JONAS | 303 |
| A DECISION AND A CONFESSION | 313 |
| GABE | 321 |
| STEVE | 329 |
| ACKNOWLEDGMENTS | 341 |
| ABOUT THE AUTHOR | 343 |
| BOOKS BY MICHELE HUEY | 344 |
| CONTACT INFORMATION | 345 |

# Part One

# Vietnam

# 1970–1971

*"There is a land of the living and a land of the dead and the bridge is love, the only survival, the only meaning."*

—THORNTON WILDER
*THE BRIDGE OF SAN LUIS RAY*

CHAPTER ONE

# WELCOME TO HELL

*August 1970*

Somewhere over Saigon I realized my rebellion could very well cost me my life.

Something—loud—screamed past, then the jet jerked up into a steep climb, leaving my insides at the lower altitude and my forehead stunned after colliding with a flying book. Instinctively I folded over, my head between my knees, pressing the book against the back of my head. Not that it would do any good if we crashed. Or exploded in the sky.

"We're flying on our side!" Mickie screamed.

I peered past my seatmate. Yep, there was the ground, looking for all the world like a lush emerald paradise—except for the yellow tracers shooting past.

"SOBs're shooting at us!"

Gear stashed on the overhead racks tumbled about the crowded cabin. Images of flag-draped coffins flashed in my jet-lagged brain. *How many nurses did they say were killed so far? I should have listened better.* Peanut butter-flavored bile from what I managed to get down earlier burned my throat on its way to my mouth.

"Nuttin' to be 'fraid of, chillun," a deep male voice drawled over the sound of glass shattering. "That's jes' Charlie's way of welcoming y'all to hell."

Bubba. The son of a Washington bigwig headed for his second tour who, for the past twenty-four hours, had sickened us with gruesome stories. I was fed up with that fake Southern drawl—and his dirty jokes about women. Some lifers thought they could get away with anything.

"Shut up, Bubba," a shaky voice said. "This ain't funny."

Bubba's mean laugh exploded in the cabin. "It'll be over in less time than it takes for you to puke."

Thirty seconds later—a mere half minute of jerking and twisting, an eternity of gut-wrenching terror—the plane leveled out. The humid air reeked of vomit, sweat, and aftershave from smashed cologne bottles—and the stench of fear.

"Is anyone hurt?" The calm voice of the head stewardess, a pert blonde, sang over the moans and nervous titters. Pushing my hair behind my ears, I leaned back and closed my eyes. My heart throbbed in my throat. *One year. Three hundred and sixty-five days. Oh, dear God, what have I done?*

"I didn't know the VC was that close to Saigon." Mickie's trembling voice pulled me back from the brink of the abyss that threatened to swallow me. "I thought nurses were supposed to be in safe areas."

A sickening greenish hue tinged her olive complexion. My best friend since first grade pulled her untamed dark brown curls into a ponytail with shaking hands.

"Stupid Army!" she muttered, twisting a hair band around the mass. "Making us wear dress greens. I'd like to use one of these asinine heels as a weapon right now."

Taking her cue, I swallowed my fear.

"Don't you dare take them off!" I said, wagging my finger in her face. "In this heat, you'll never get them back on, and you'll have to hopscotch across the tarmac all the way to the building. And I'm not carrying you."

Mickie's Italian brown eyes gleamed with mischief. "You think maybe one of these fellas would?"

I rolled my eyes. The trembling inside abated. A little.

In the aisle a flight attendant shoved a scuffed duffel bag on the rack above our seats. My fingernails cut into the soft leather of the book that had collided with my forehead. I glanced down. A Bible. "John Andrew Dempsey" was inscribed in golden script in the lower right corner. *Must belong to a chaplain.* I scanned the rows of green uniforms, but none of the two hundred fifty GIs crammed in more seats than the modified commercial stretch jet was built to hold looked like a chaplain. Too young. What did a chaplain look like anyway?

"This is Captain Novak," a strong voice sounded over the intercom. "Due to the welcoming committee we encountered on our approach to Tan Son Nhut, we've been diverted to Long Binh, where we'll land in just a few minutes. Nurses, you'll wait in the building for your orders. Soldiers, your cattle trucks will arrive sometime today and take you to your bases. The temperature is a balmy twenty-ninety degrees Celsius—that's eighty-four degrees Fahrenheit—the humidity eighty percent, winds calm, and the local time is 0900 hours. Ladies and gentlemen, welcome to Vietnam. Good luck and *vaya con Dios.*"

*God be with you. God—if there is one—certainly wouldn't grace his presence in this hellhole, that's for sure.*

"I can't find my shoes."

I twisted around. Diane, the Navy nurse, was frantically reaching under her seat. Her bleached bouffant hair lay askew, her once crisp white uniform wilted and wrinkled.

"Darn, I shouldn't have taken them off. Hey," she yelled, straightening up and looking around, "anyone see a pair of white nurse's shoes?"

No one paid attention. Diane's panicky eyes met mine. I bent over and checked under my seat. Candy wrappers, cracker crumbs, and paper, but no shoes.

"Lookin' for these?"

I straightened up and turned, dread filling me. Bubba held Diane's shoes inches from her nose. Relief washed over her face as she reached to take them, but his meaty, hairy hand jerked back.

"Not so fast, honey. Don't I get a reward?"

Twenty-plus hours of faulty air conditioning, too many sweating bodies, no sleep, and continual jibes from this jerk and his ilk were more than enough to push me over the line. So what if his daddy had connections? Shoving the Bible at Mickie, I released my seatbelt and stepped into the aisle, shaking knees and all.

"No." I snatched the shoes and handed them to Diane. "You don't."

Bubba smirked. The soldier's mocking gray eyes met mine briefly, then dropped down to the open neck of my shirt.

"Don't what, honey?"

I eyed his sergeant's stripes. "You don't get a reward. And don't call me 'honey.'"

"You got spunk, girlie. I like that. Let's see what else you got under there." He tugged at the top button of my shirt.

Guffaws filled the air. Furious, I pulled myself up to my full five-feet-eleven inches and leaned toward him. My nose was less than an inch from his—close enough to detect the whiskey. The pale eyes I glared into flashed surprise, then a cold anger.

"Remove your hand, Sergeant."

He yanked my shirt. The top button popped open.

"What are you gonna do about it, *Lieutenant*?" he sneered.

"The Army," I said in a voice that carried through the cabin, "taught me that I'm an officer, a nurse, and a lady. The officer gave you an order, the nurse has seen more behinds than you, and the lady will slap the smirk off your face."

More guffaws.

"Ha! She told you!"

"Hey, Sarge, you met your match!"

Bubba's face flooded crimson.

"Sergeant." I narrowed my eyes. "Your hand."

Releasing my shirt, he about-faced and maneuvered the narrow aisle to his seat.

"Forget something, Sergeant?"

The voice came from several rows in front of me. I turned. A lanky frame—about six-four, I guessed—unfolded from the cramped seat and stepped into the aisle, two silver bars on the epaulet on his shoulder. A captain. All talking and laughing stopped.

"Sergeant." His calm, firm tone left no doubt this man brooked no defiance.

"What?" Bubba's belligerent tone surprised me.

"Last I checked," the captain said, "a lieutenant still outranks a sergeant."

Bubba snorted. "She's just a broad."

Anger flashed in the captain's eyes as he took a step toward the back of the plane. His cheek muscles twitched.

"Wilcott, get your sorry carcass up here. *Now*. You're already in hot water for your insulting behavior and blatant disrespect toward a senior officer. I'll be more than happy to add insubordination to my report."

"Okay, okay, I'm coming."

Bubba rolled out of his seat, swaggered down the aisle, and perched in front of me. He snapped to attention in a stiff salute, hatred emanating from every pore of his body. I shivered.

"You better hope you never end up in her hospital," the captain said. "Now get back to your seat."

"Yes, sir."

"And keep that foul mouth of yours shut."

Respect registered on the GIs' youthful faces. I nodded my thanks to the captain, then slipped back into my seat. I waited until the quivering—not from fear, but from anger—subsided and the mumble of conversation resumed, then I turned to Mickie.

"I wish he wouldn't have done that," I whispered.

She handed the Bible back to me and nodded. "We can take care of ourselves."

"It's not that." I stared out the window as the plane began its descent, anxiety knotting itself in my stomach. The Bubba incident wasn't over. "I just made one more enemy."

An indefinable stench accompanied the tidal wave of heat that rolled though the open cabin door. As the jet engine whined down, groans, yawns, and soft thuds filled the humid air as soldiers heaved overstuffed duffel bags over their shoulders.

"Hey, watch it! You almost hit me with that thing."

"Sorry."

"Hurry up. I gotta pee."

"Army's motto."

"What—'I gotta pee'?"

"Hurry up and wait."

"Funny."

"Man, my knees hurt. I feel like I've been locked in position for twenty-four hours."

"Suck it up, soldier. It ain't gonna get any better."

Their banter failed to disguise the nervousness, though, as they shuffled toward the front of the plane, boots scuffling across the metal floor. While Mickie and I waited for the mass of humanity in the aisle to thin out, we gathered our paperbacks, magazines, and puzzle books, and stuffed them into our totes.

"Good thing I brought my iron. My hair must look like I was on the wrong end of a lightning bolt," Mickie said, cramming her garrison cap atop the frizz. "Couldn't they have prepared us better?"

"Nope." The captain's voice in the aisle next to us cut into the commotion. "You have to experience it to understand it." His tone grew lilting. "Like love."

I didn't know which embarrassed me more—his words or my idiotic blushing. Hoping he didn't notice my red face, I forced my lips into what I hoped was a polite smile.

"I suppose a thank–you is in order, Captain, but, really, your intervention was unnecessary. I am perfectly capable of taking care of myself."

His eyebrows shot up. "Oh, I see. Miss Women's Lib in the flesh—excuse me, maybe I should say *Ms.* Women's Lib?"

I bristled. I hated Ms.

"*Lieutenant* will do, thank you," I said, fighting a strange mixture of annoyance and pleasure. I scanned the cabin, avoiding his eyes. "Do you see the flight attendant?"

"Up front. Anything I can do?"

I held up the scuffed leather-covered Bible. "I ended up with this when we tried to land in Saigon. It belongs to—" I glanced at the name—"John Dempsey."

His brow wrinkled briefly, then his eyes lit up and his face broke into a grin. He held out a broad hand. "I'll take it."

I pulled it back. His expression registered surprise . . . then amusement.

"Don't you trust me, Lieutenant?"

With those laughing blue eyes, teasing smile, and sandy crew cut, he was, hands down, the handsomest guy I'd ever seen. My heart flip-flopped.

"Oh, for cryin' out loud," Mickie said, snatching the Bible out of my hands and handing it to the captain.

My cheeks burned. "I just want to make sure I follow protocol."

"Don't pay any attention to Vangie here," Mickie said, a seductive smile spreading across her pixie face. "Thank you for what you did back there, Captain." She held out her hand. "Second Lieutenant Michaelena Molinetti. My friends call me Mickie."

He gave a curt nod to both of us. "Welcome to Vietnam, Lieutenants Molinetti and—"

My heart fluttered as his glance swept the front of my blouse—for my name plate, I realized. Flustered, I groped for my jacket and held it up, name plate facing him.

"Blanchard," he said, rubbing the stubble on his chin. "French?"

I had a sudden, desperate need to say something smart, something cute, but instead I nodded stupidly.

"Vangie your nickname?"

"Short for Evangeline."

*Of course he knows your name's Evangeline, stupid. You just showed him your name plate.*

"Evangeline. A name too beautiful to chop up."

He didn't just *say* my name, "Evangeline." He caressed it. I melted. My heart never flip-flopped like this, not even when I was with Bill. *Calm down*, I scolded myself. *Breathe deep*. The muggy, stifling air I inhaled jolted me back to reality. What was I thinking? I'd heard about wartime romances and affairs. I wasn't about to become another emotional casualty. I summoned my frostiest smile.

"I prefer Lieutenant Blanchard, if you don't mind, Captain." I pointed to the Bible, then gestured to the front of the cabin, where a handful of soldiers waited to deplane. "Don't you think you'd better hurry?"

The soft glow faded from his eyes. He shook his head.

"The Bible's mine," he said, turning to go. "Thank you for returning it."

I watched him grab his duffel bag and step to the front of the plane. I took in the broad shoulders, the slender hips, the long, lithe legs—and squashed a yearning that took me by surprise.

"Lucky you," Mickie muttered, her gaze, also, on the receding form of Captain Dempsey.

I stretched out of the cramped seat, folded my jacket over my arm, and pulled the thick strap of my duffel bag over my shoulder. "Why's that?"

"You didn't notice? Or are you being stupid on purpose?"

"Oh, come on, Mick. Guys take one look at my five-feet-eleven-inches and that's that. They like the petite, cute ones like you so they can feel manly."

Mickie hunched over and shuffled into the aisle. "I saw the way he looked at you."

I stepped back to let her go first. "You see everything through those lovelorn eyes of yours, dear friend. The next time—if there is a next time—he'll be fawning over you like they all do."

Mickie shook her head. "Not this time, Vange. There's chemistry between you two."

"I nearly failed chemistry, remember?"

"Ha! *You* almost fail anything? That's a joke." She swiped her jacket across her glistening forehead. "I don't feel like arguing. Let's get out of this heat. You think that building is air-conditioned?"

CHAPTER TWO

# HELL HATH NO FURY

Half an hour later six nurses—five Army and one Navy—crowded into the ladies' room of the Long Binh mess hall.

As the others chatted and introduced themselves, I splashed tepid water on my face and neck. *Sulfur. Everything smells like sulfur.* Pulling a hand towel out of my tote bag, I let the soft terrycloth linger over my nose. A wave of dizziness washed over me. I shut my eyes, listening, but not listening, to the chatter spinning around me, guessing at the accents to keep from passing out.

"All I want is a hot shower." *Diane.* Who still couldn't get her heels on. She'd crammed her swollen feet into a pair of loosely laced tennis shoes. "Let them write me up," she'd said.

"Not me. A bubble bath would be heaven right now." *Southern. Texas?*

"Heaven would be any place but here." *New York.*

"Wonder if the chow in this joint is half decent." *Mickie.*

"Hope it's better than the crap they fed us at Fort Sam Houston." *Midwest—Chicago?*

"It isn't." *New York again.*

"At least we had grits there. Ya'll like grits?"

I opened my eyes. The room spun around me. I grabbed the sink and bent forward, taking a deep breath.

"Are you all right?" New York asked, peering into my face. Concern poured from her dark brown, almost black eyes.

I nodded. "I just need something to eat."

"And a soft bed. I know." She draped a slender arm around my waist. "Come on. It'll be a while before the nursing supervisor gets here. She was waiting for us in Saigon. She drove to Tan Son Nhut from here to meet us."

"Bureaucracy at its best," Mickie said, grabbing her duffel bag. "Let's see what the grub's like. I'm starved."

New York, whose name was Nancy, was right—the food here was worse than at Fort Sam. I sipped the tea and tasted sulfur. Stifling a gag, I bit into the toast. It was cold. Mickie, who sat next to me on my left, shook a bottle of ketchup over her plateful of scrambled eggs, her appetite none the worse from the jostling over Saigon. A can of cola, dripping condensation, sat on the table to the right of her plate, a mug of coffee to the left. I eyed the soda. Mickie pushed it to me.

"Keep you from starving," she said, shoveling a forkful of eggs into her mouth.

While I sipped the cola—even at this early hour, it calmed my stomach—I listened to the table conversation, which centered on duty stations. Until the nursing supervisor arrived and gave us our assignments, I had no idea where I'd end up. More than a dozen evacuation and surgical hospitals were scattered throughout the country. I dabbed my forehead with a scratchy brown paper napkin. *Someplace where it doesn't feel like a blast furnace.*

"My cousin was at the Seventy-First after he got wounded," said Chicago, whose name was Judy. She'd opted for the toast, too. Her shoulder-length auburn hair, straight like mine, was tied in a ponytail at the nape of her swanlike neck.

"Where's that?" asked Diane, who'd managed, with a teasing comb and half a can of hair spray, to puff up her hair once again.

"Pleiku. Up in the mountains, near the Cambodian border in II Corps," said Nancy, who sat next to me to my right. "Cooler than anywhere else in this hellhole."

"Ya'll know anyplace with a beach?" drawled Texas, her dishwater blonde hair fashioned in a short bob.

"Cam Ranh Bay, in II Corps along the South China Sea," Nancy said. I glanced at her epaulet. She didn't have a butter bar, like the rest of us second lieutenants. Hers was the silver of a first lieutenant.

"Wonder where that hunk's stationed," Texas said.

Judy rolled her eyes. "Lucy, is that all you think of—men?"

Lucy giggled. "Of course. Don't you?"

I sat up. "What hunk?" I asked, unsticking my elbow from the plastic tabletop.

"Captain What's His Name—the one who sent Bubba the Bully packing," Lucy said.

"Oh, Captain Dempsey's taken," Mickie said, winking at me.

I nudged her discreetly. *Don't you dare!*

Chatter erupted around the table. "Taken? Is he married?"

"I didn't see a wedding ring. I checked."

Someone snickered. "Like that matters."

Mickie took a gulp of her coffee, grimaced, then spit it back in her cup. "This stuff is awful."

I let out my breath.

"I've never met him, but I hear Seth Martin's quite the heartthrob," said Nancy. She seemed more relaxed now.

"Who's Seth Martin?" Lucy asked.

Nancy glanced at her. "Dust Off pilot. A real legend in these parts."

"What's Dust Off?" Diane asked.

"The call sign of the Army's medical evacuation helicopters," Nancy said.

Judy poked her fork at her eggs. "How do you know all this stuff?"

Mickie leaned forward and turned to face Nancy. "Didn't you board in Hawaii?"

Nancy nodded, smiling for the first time. "I'm just getting back from R & R. I've been in-country six months already."

The chatter around the table hushed.

"Wow," Lucy said. "Six months. Where are you stationed?"

"I was way up north in I Corps, at Quang Tri, but I'll spend the rest of my tour here, at Long Binh."

"What's Eye Corps and Too Corps?" Mickie asked.

I stifled a giggle. Nursing a hangover from still another party prior to leaving for Travis AFB, Mickie had slept through that part of orientation and never bothered to ask me what she'd missed.

Nancy gave her a you've-got-to-be-kidding-me look. "South Vietnam," she said with a sigh, "is divided into four military divisions, according to location. I Corps, where Da Nang is located, is the farthest north, while IV Corps is at the southern end, in the Mekong Delta."

Lucy leaned across the table, her face resting in her hands, her elbows on the table in front of her. "Screw the geography lesson. Tell us about this legend."

"Best pilot in 'Nam," Nancy said, stirring her coffee. "One time the enemy fire was so intense, the ground troops told him to get out. But Captain Martin refused. 'Not without your wounded,' he said. He made it back—with a shattered windshield *and* the wounded men."

"Is this hero-hunk available?" Lucy asked.

Nancy shrugged. "He keeps his personal matters private. Many have chased him, but no one's caught him."

The clap-clap of high heels approaching halted the conversation. A trim, petite woman, her graying hair cropped short under her garrison cap, stepped briskly to the table. A gold oak leaf decorated the epaulet of her crisp uniform. The nursing supervisor.

Chairs scraped the wood floor as we stood, shoulders arched back, rigid fingers brushing our sweaty foreheads.

"At ease." She placed a clipboard on the table and lifted her glasses, which hung on a gold chain around her neck, to her shiny nose. "I'm Major Hunter. Starting from the lieutenant to my immediate right, identify yourselves, going counterclockwise around the table."

As each of us gave name, rank, and serial number, Major Hunter checked the sheet on her clipboard.

"With the exception of Lieutenant Walters, who will report to the Naval Support Hospital at Da Nang, and Lieutenant Richards, who will remain here at Long Binh, the rest of you have your choice of duty stations. We need nurses everywhere," she said, peering over her glasses. "Lieutenant Blanchard?"

*Mickie and I haven't even talked about it! Where did they say it wasn't so hot?*

"Pleiku," I blurted.

Major Hunter nodded and scribbled on her sheet. "Lieutenant Molinetti?"

"Pleiku."

Lucy and Judy chose Cam Ranh Bay. The screen door bumped shut. I shot a quick glance out of the corner of my eye. Captain Dempsey's lanky shadow moved along the wall. Major Hunter continued her instructions.

"You'll have your in-country orientation when you get to your duty station, where you'll receive your gear—flak jackets, helmets, firearms, et cetera. Lieutenants Dixon and Grady, you'll take a bus to Cam Ranh Bay. Hopefully it'll get here before the war ends. Lieutenants Blanchard and Molinetti, you get to ride in a Dust Off chopper. It turns out that one of our pilots has just returned from the States with a brand new Huey. Captain Martin said he'll be ready to leave at 1300 hours." She glanced at her wristwatch. "That's in about three hours. If you're thinking of having lunch, I advise you to make it light. Very light. Ah, here's Captain Martin now."

Captain Seth Martin, local legend and heartthrob, strode across the floor to the table. Mickie snickered. I bit my lip.

For the man who came into view was none other than the man I thought was Captain John A. Dempsey.

Three hours later, I stood on the steamy tarmac, aching feet spread apart, arms folded across my chest, glaring at the broad-shouldered back of Captain Seth Martin.

"You lied to me," I said. "Sir."

Dressed in his Army-green flight suit, he tossed another duffel bag into the Huey.

"I didn't lie."

"Will you please stop what you're doing and turn around and face me? I don't like talking to backs."

He heaved another bag into the chopper and glanced at the sky.

"In fifteen minutes we need to be airborne. Before it decides to rain," he said, turning to face me. "Make it fast, Lieutenant."

He was so close, I smelled his aftershave—and my heart did another flip-flop. Which made me even angrier.

"You told me your name was John Dempsey."

Captain Martin rested his long fingers on his hips and tilted his head, a slow, lopsided grin spreading across his face. Amusement gleamed in his eyes.

I scowled. "Don't laugh at me."

"I'm not laughing at you."

"Your eyes are."

"I'm smiling at your overreaction to a simple misunderstanding."

"Why did you tell me your name was John Dempsey?"

He shook his head slowly. "I never told you my name was John Dempsey."

I poked his chest with my index finger. A tingle went up my arm—and straight to my heart. "You told me the Bible was yours. The name on the cover was John Dempsey. What was I to think?"

"You added one plus one and came up with zero. Rule number one for survival: never assume anything."

"Then why is John Dempsey's name on the cover and not yours?"

Captain Martin lowered his arms to his sides and stared at something behind—beyond—me. Sadness, like a cloud shadow, passed over his face.

"JD gave me his Bible the night before he was shot down. He knew." Anger tinged his words. "They all know."

I pushed my hair behind my ears to cover my awkwardness. "I'm sorry," I said in a soft voice. "Sorry that you lost a friend and sorry that I accused you without getting all the facts. I . . . I don't know what came over me."

Anger flashed across his face. His cheek twitched. "It didn't take long." His voice sounded strangled.

"For what?"

"Get out, Evangeline, get out now! Shoot yourself in the foot or get pregnant. This place sucks everything out of you—your health, your mind, your dreams, your life. Get out while there's still time."

CHAPTER THREE

# ROCKET CITY

We arrived at the Seventy-First Evacuation Hospital in Pleiku after a noisy but blessedly brief flight from Long Binh. The deafening roar of the rotor blades and the din of the engine made conversation difficult. Not that I wanted to talk. I was too exhausted. And scared. Captain Martin's words, as much as I tried to push them out of my mind, volleyed through my thoughts, threatening to pierce every idealistic, patriotic bubble that had bolstered me since the day I signed up. Not that I was that idealistic. Or patriotic. I was just angry.

As we lifted off, his words—and his stern look—churned up the fear I'd fought to keep down. Who did he think he was, telling me to maim myself to get out of doing the job I came to do? So what if he was a local hero? He should know better. By the time we landed, I was so spitting mad at Captain Seth Martin, I was out of my seat the second he shut off the engine.

"Hold your horses, kemosabe," he shouted. "Stay put until the rotors slow down. You wouldn't want those long raven tresses of yours all tangled up."

"But—"

"Sit!"

Mickie yanked me back down onto my seat.

"What's wrong with you?" she mouthed.

"Nothing," I mouthed back, staring out the front window. Red dust swirled in the wash of the slowing rotor blades, in the steamy waves undulating off the tarmac. Or was the dull ache behind my eyes affecting my sight?

"I thought it was supposed to be cooler here," Mickie said, her voice still in talk-louder-than-the-rotors mode.

Captain Martin twisted around in his seat and grinned. "Cooler, yes. Cool, no. Welcome to Pleiku, ladies."

Pushing open his door, he hopped out of the chopper, then shoved open the sliding back door next to me. I ignored the hand he extended and jumped out on my own, stumbling when my ankle buckled on the hard surface. I would have landed on my can or my face, but he grabbed my arm, steadying me. Before I could break his hold on me, a mud-splattered Jeep screeched to a stop beside us. Grinning behind the wheel was a short, stocky soldier with a boonie hat jammed on his head.

"Ah, your limo, ladies," Captain Martin said, stuffing our bags into the back. "Sergeant Campbell will take you to your living quarters."

With that he gave a curt nod and strode away. *Well, that's that.* I settled in the back of the Jeep after Mickie claimed the front seat. Our first stop was headquarters, where we signed in and collected our gear: helmet, flak jacket, boots, fatigues, and .45 caliber pistol with ammo.

"A lot of good this'll do us, considering they never taught us how to use it," Mickie said, dropping her gun on top of the growing pile.

"Nurses don't need to know how to shoot," I said. "We're here to save lives, not take them."

In the distance a shell exploded.

After meeting Major Lennon, the Seventy-First's nursing supervisor, we crammed our gear into the Jeep and climbed in. I gripped the bottom of my seat as we zipped across the base, passing guard towers, tanks rumbling across the compound, and dozens of metal Quonset huts and wooden buildings with corrugated steel roofs, all covered with red dust. In the distance artillery and mortars sounded continuously.

"Artillery Hill, also known as Arty Hill," our escort said, pointing to a smoky mound in the distance. "Where all the racket's coming from."

"I never realized this place would be so noisy," Mickie shouted above the din.

Neither had I. I knew we'd be in a war zone—the entire country was a war zone—but I'd assumed hospitals would be situated in quiet places.

By the time "Soup," as Sergeant Campbell preferred to be called, deposited us at our hooch, I'd been awake for close to forty-eight hours. The dull ache behind my eyes had escalated into a throbbing headache—a giant rubber band tightening around my head. My entire body felt heavy, like I'd just gotten out of a swimming pool. All I wanted was a shower and a comfy bed. I'd caught a few winks sprawled on my gear, my head on my duffel bag, arm over my eyes, at Travis AFB waiting for our flight in-country. Forget sleeping on the plane. Too noisy, too much movement. Good thing Major Lennon had given us twenty-four hours to settle in before reporting for duty.

Hooch Number Three, our home, was a fifteen-by-forty-foot shack, the third in a row of identical wooden buildings. Soup helped us lug in our stuff. Two of the seven six-by-ten cubicles were unoccupied. Mickie chose the one painted a bright yellow—with paint filched from the air base, Soup said. My room, two doors down, was "puke green." The red dust was everywhere—on the walls, the metal bed, mattress, the wall locker, the wooden floors. I ran my finger across the windowsill. All I wanted was to drop into bed, but how could I sleep in such filth? Maybe I could find a bucket and rag and swab the place down. I wasn't about to unpack my clean clothes, let alone lay on that dusty mattress.

I poked my head out the doorway. Hearing Mickie's voice, I headed to her room. She sat on her bed chatting with a short, thin girl with damp auburn curls, who gave me a tired smile when I stepped in.

"You must be Vangie," she said, holding out her hand. "I'm DeeDee Stewart."

"DeeDee's from Oklahoma," Mickie offered, patting a spot on the bed beside her. Did I imagine it, or did a puff of red rise from the mattress? "Come on. Take a load off."

I shook my head. "I'd love to—really, I would—but I want to get unpacked and settled in." I turned to DeeDee. "Do you know where I can get a bucket and some soap?"

"Cleaning supplies are in the latrine next door. But I wouldn't bother," she said in a voice that sounded resigned. "You can't scrub it out."

An hour later I'd wiped everything in my cubicle with cold water. Hot water, apparently, was a luxury not to be had. After I dumped out the reddish water and put the bucket back in the cleaning closet, I returned to my cubby to unpack. My clothes felt damp as I placed them in my locker, so I left the door ajar. Then I put the sheets, also damp, on the musty smelling mattress.

By the time I was done, my clothes, which I'd worn for two days, were soaked with perspiration. Grabbing a towel and my bath bucket, I headed for the showers, peeking in on Mickie on my way. She lay snoring on her bare mattress, unpacked bags and gear scattered on the dust-covered wooden floor.

After a cold shower I headed back to my room, feeling somewhat refreshed. The hooch was quiet, with most of the nurses either on duty or sleeping. My nightstand looked bare with only a windup alarm clock and my journal. I hung my towel over the open locker door, then collapsed on the bed. Pulling the sheet over my middle and the pillow over my head, I gave in to the exhaustion. Nothing bothered me. Not the suffocating heat. Not the lumpy, musty mattress. Not even the rumbling of artillery in the distance. I closed my eyes.

*I sat on the grass, my neck arched back, enjoying the fireworks exploding overhead. Bill's arms wrapped around me. I leaned back against him, wondering why his cologne smelled like sulfur. Another explosion as red, white, and blue sparkles mushroomed above us. The ground shook. I twisted around, but it wasn't my high school sweetheart that held me. It was Captain Seth Martin.*

"Incoming!" The shout pierced my dream. "Vangie, get up! We're under attack!"

*Whistle. BOOM!* The windows rattled. I jolted upright.

"Here!" Mickie jammed my helmet on my head and thrust my flak jacket in my hands.

"To the bunker! Now!" an unfamiliar voice shouted.

Mickie and I scrambled to the bunker behind the hooch, where we huddled, clutching each other and trembling, with several other nurses. I squeezed my eyes shut. Maybe it would help if I pretended I was on a ride at Kennywood or in a theater watching a scary movie.

"What was that?" Mickie screamed. "I felt something creepy scurry by my feet."

"Just the rats." I recognized the voice as DeeDee's.

"Rats? Oh, God, please no," Mickie moaned, clutching me tighter. The nausea finally got the best of me. Twisting around, I shoved her away, doubled over, and retched.

"You'll get used to it," a resigned voice said.

When the explosions finally stopped, we waited a full fifteen minutes before returning to the hooch. A layer of fresh red dust covered everything in my room.

"You all right?"

*No. I want to go home.*

Two nurses stood in the doorway. They'd been in the bunker with us. The willowy blonde smiled. "Welcome to Rocket City," she said. "I'm Sarah Devine."

Her companion, a brunette with dimples, waved. "I'm Beth Phillips. Hey, we're heading over to the mess hall. Want to come?"

"Is it safe?" I asked. "Aren't we on red alert?"

Laughing, Sarah stepped to me and draped her arm around my shoulders. She was nearly as tall as me—about five-foot-nine.

"Honey, we're always under an alert. I don't even wear my helmet and flak jacket half the time anymore."

"You learn to live with it," Beth said with a dismissive wave of her hand. "Ignore it as much as you can. If you don't, nothing'll ever get done. And you'll go bananas real fast."

Light flashed in the night sky outside my window, accompanied by a dull thud.

"Will there be any more?" I asked.

"Once they rocket us for the night, that's it," Sarah said. "Usually."

Beth nodded. "Come on. You must be hungry."

On the way to the mess hall, I noticed Mickie and I were the only ones wearing our helmets and flak jackets, even though the sounds of war reverberated through the evening. Was it ever quiet here? An earsplitting whistle whizzed by overhead. Mickie and I dropped to the ground, our arms over our heads. Beth and Sarah burst out laughing.

"I don't see what's so funny," Mickie said, getting up and brushing herself off. "We could've been killed."

"I thought you said they were done for the night," I said, pushing myself off the broken pavement.

Beth shrugged. "Maybe they need more target practice."

How could they could be so . . . casual . . . so . . . cavalier . . . in the face of death? I tried to act nonchalant, but inside I was terrified. I'd never last a whole year.

At the mess hall, I made a cup of tea. It didn't taste like back-home tea, but at least I could drink it out of a real cup and it didn't taste like sulfur. A dark-haired soldier strode to the table, pulled out the chair next to Sarah, then casually draped his arm across the back of her chair. Her face glowed as she leaned close to him. I glanced at the captain's bars on his epaulet.

"Who's the guy?" Mickie asked Beth, nodding towards them.

Beth took a sip of her soda. "Sarah's fella, Dan. Cobra pilot. They're engaged. They're getting married after their tours are over."

The loneliness hit like the mortar attack. Maybe I shouldn't have broken up with Bill. At least then I'd have *somebody*. As it was, the only letters I'd get would be from Mickie's family, and that at the insistence of Mickie's mother.

"What's a Cobra?" Mickie asked.

"It's a gunship. Dust Offs are medical evacuation choppers, so they aren't armed. The Cobras accompany them and provide firepower and protection while the Dust Offs pick up the casualties."

While I nibbled on crackers and sipped tea, several other nurses and a couple of doctors came to the table and introduced themselves. They seemed happy to see us. "New blood," they said. Their warmth made me feel welcome, and I found my loneliness and terror subsiding. If they made it, I could too. I'd just have to take it one day, one minute, at a time. For the first time in my life I realized I had no promise of tomorrow, of even another hour. It was a sobering thought.

"Evening, ladies. I see you've settled in." Captain Seth Martin pulled out the empty chair next to me and sat. I tried to drum up the anger I'd felt earlier towards him, but I couldn't. Instead a feeling of warmth and joy coursed through me. I was about to smile a greeting when another explosion shook the building. The next thing I knew, he was pulling me across the room. Shoving me down against the wall, he dropped down beside me, put his arms around me and covered me with his upper body. Another blast. The building shook. I cringed closer to him, feeling his heartbeat, his breath on my face.

"I didn't hear the whistle," I said.

He pulled me closer, his lips against my ear. "When you hear the whistle, the rocket's going past you."

"How long will this go on? All night?" I said, vainly trying to push my hair up under my helmet with trembling fingers.

He pushed my stubborn hair out of my eyes and smiled. "You'll get used to it," he said.

"So I'm told, but I'm not so sure."

Ten minutes later—if it even was ten minutes—everybody was sitting at the tables, acting as though nothing had happened. Seth sat beside me, sipping a cup of coffee.

"Are you stationed here?" I asked, noticing the ripple in his cheek as he swallowed.

"My unit, the 283rd MDHA, is based here," he said.

"MDHA?"

"Medical Detachment Helicopter Ambulance."

I glanced at the shield-shaped, dark blue patch on his uniform shirt. White wings against a pale red cross outlined in white. I read the stitched letters.

"How did you get the name 'Dust Off'?" I asked.

"Back in the early part of the war, the guy who helped get the program started picked it out of a call sign book. Dust Off described our mission better than Gun Runner or Bandit."

"How?"

"When choppers land, the prop wash from the rotor blades blows dust everywhere. Especially during the dry season."

I remembered the red dust swirling when we landed and nodded.

"Back then, Dust Off was the call sign only for the Fifty-Seventh, but in time the entire medical evacuation program became known as Dust Off."

"But it's more than a call sign," Sarah added, squeezing Dan's arm. "It's a symbol of hope."

"That's right," said a soldier sitting across the table. "When you're lying in the jungle, wounded and wondering if you're gonna make it to your twentieth birthday, the sound of that chopper and the sight of that bright red cross give you something to hang on to. That is, if Charlie don't shoot it down."

"Shoot what down?" I asked. "The chopper?"

Seth nodded. "To the VC, those red crosses are nothing but targets."

I gasped. "The red cross is an international symbol. The Geneva Convention—"

"Means nothing to them."

I was amazed. "You mean they actually shoot down medical helicopters?"

"And fire mortars at hospitals."

How little I really knew of the war. I'd never heard of Dust Off until I landed right smack dab in the middle of the war zone. I knew that choppers brought the wounded to the hospitals, but that's as far as it went. Now those choppers suddenly became personal. They had a name. Those wounded soldiers, those pilots and their crews, all had faces. The papers back home gave only gruesome body counts and reports that made our side look bad.

Another explosion rocked the building. What sounded like chunks of concrete rained on the metal roof. As we scrambled back to the wall, I wondered if I'd make it out alive.

CHAPTER FOUR

# MUD, MOSQUITOES, MILDEW, AND MORTARS

My first week on the job was a blur. We worked twelve-hour shifts, but showing up half an hour before my shift in the surgical unit began and staying half an hour after made things easier. Wounded soldiers were brought to the 450-bed hospital one after another, wheeled on gurneys from the helipad fifty yards away—close enough that I could hear the roar of the Hueys' rotors through the Quonset hut's walls. For a fleeting moment I'd wonder if it was Captain Martin's chopper. If I'd been assigned to the ER, I could have seen who was out there. But the ER meant triage, and I didn't want the responsibility of deciding who would live and who would die.

Working in the OR wasn't what I expected, but then I don't know what I expected, really. To stand in a pristine room and slap instruments in the surgeon's hands, monitor vitals, start IVs. I wasn't prepared to be scrub nurse *and* assistant surgeon in a flimsy metal building sectioned off into six operating cubicles by shoulder-high cabinets. Where we constantly battled not only death but the ubiquitous red dust. Where, during the monsoons, crimson mud seeped through the cracks in the walls and across the floor as we worked, sometimes on our knees during a rocket attack, to save lives. But then, nothing could have prepared me for 'Nam. By the end of the first week, I was frustrated with my ineptitude—and sensed the others in the OR were more annoyed than I. What I learned in nursing school didn't apply here. Walt Greene, the thoracic surgeon I worked with, sensed my panic after we nearly lost one soldier we were working on.

"Lieutenant, why don't you take a break?" he said in his calm voice. I searched his eyes for anger, disappointment, accusation, but all I saw above his mask were kindness and sympathy. "I'll finish up here."

"Are you sure, Dr. Greene?" I asked.

"Go," he said, turning his attention back to the young man on the table. "Just be back in fifteen."

I nodded, feeling like a child sent out of the classroom for misbehaving. I glanced around, sure everyone in the OR had witnessed my shame and disgrace, but no one paid attention. I slipped out quietly behind a nurse wheeling a covered gurney to the morgue next door and dropped on the first bench I saw. Every muscle in my body screamed with fatigue. My feet hurt so bad I wanted to cry. My brain was numb. I was hot, sweaty, and dirty, and, after five twelve-hour shifts, a hundred miles past exhaustion. When was the last time I had a good night's sleep? The unrelenting mosquitoes, the ear-piercing shrill of the mortars, the pervasive stench of mildew, the hopelessly damp sheets, the suffocating humidity, the stubborn red dust, all conspired with the VC to keep me awake around the clock. How on earth would I last an entire year? Putting my elbows on my knees, I dropped my head in my hands and closed my eyes. *Just a few minutes . . .*

Something cold and wet on the back of my neck jerked me awake. My cheek felt wet. Where was I? *Omigosh!* I sprang to my feet. "What time—"

A hand pulled me back down. "Sit down, kemosabe."

How embarrassing! Had Captain Martin seen me slobbering in my sleep?

"I need to get back in the OR. Dr. Greene—"

"Said to tell you he's done for the day. Here." He put the can of cold soda on the back of my neck again. "This'll help."

It did feel good. I leaned back against it. "Thanks."

"No problem." He pulled another can of soda out of the pocket of his flight suit and handed it to me. "When was the last time you had something to drink? Don't answer. I can see you're getting dehydrated. Easy to do when you're running around like a chicken with her head cut off fourteen hours a day."

"There wasn't time," I said, checking my watch. I'd slept twenty-five minutes.

"Well, kemosabe, take the time. You're no good dead."

I still felt the sting of being sent out of the OR like an errant child. "I'm no good alive, either," I muttered, "so what difference does it make?"

He took the can from my neck and put it on the bench beside him.

"Turn sideways."

"Why?"

"Because, Lieutenant Blanchard, you're going to be the recipient of one of my famous shoulder massages."

I wanted to argue, but the massage sounded good, and I liked the idea of those strong hands caressing my shoulders.

"Ouch!"

"Lots of knots. One little session won't be enough. I'll have to schedule you for a full half-hour session, at least. How about today after your shift?"

"I can't."

"Why not?"

"Because all I want to do is go back to my hooch and crash."

I also wanted him to keep massaging my shoulders, but the noise of a chopper taking off outside jerked me back to reality. I twisted around.

"Thanks for the massage, Captain. I'd better get back to work."

I was close enough to notice a dimple, barely perceptible, on his left cheekbone right below his eye. I reached out and ran my fingers across it.

"That's an unusual dimple."

"Little League. Got kissed by a baseball. And found out why a black eye is called a shiner. Took three days for the swelling to go down."

"How awful!"

He chuckled. "Sure helped my batting average, though."

"Blanchard!"

Major Lennon, the nursing supervisor, hustled up to the bench, carrying a clipboard, which she shoved at me.

"Help Captain Martin get his supplies. Then you're done for the day."

I pulled myself to my feet. "But I've another hour on my shift."

"We're covered. Go get some rest. Soon enough there'll be a push, and so many Mas-Cals you'll be on your feet three days straight."

"But—"

"No 'buts,' Blanchard, get a move on. Just be back here at 0600 sharp."

Nodding at Seth—a sliver of a smile tugging at her lips—she spun around and hurried away.

"You didn't," I said, folding my arms across my chest and spreading my feet apart.

He stood, his grin lopsided. "What's that? Your battle stance?"

"You did . . . I'm so embarrassed . . . how can I do my job . . . I don't need anyone protecting me!"

"Settle down, kemosabe. All I did was request help restocking my medical supplies. It seems you're the only nurse available." He leaned over and pulled the clipboard out of my hands. "So let's get on with it, so you can go back to your hooch and crash."

And crash I did. Dropped on the damp, musty bed as soon as I stepped into my cubicle and slept through supper. I awoke still heaped on top of the scratchy wool blanket in my smelly fatigues, clutching my helmet and flak jacket. Swatting a mosquito, I rolled over and grabbed my alarm clock. Its glowing dials told me it was just after midnight. The day's sweat still on my body wouldn't make for a comfortable night, but then, with the mosquitoes, mildew, and mortars, it was never a comfortable night. I tried to summon the energy to take a shower.

Outside an explosion rocked the building. "Phooey with it," I muttered, shoving my helmet, flak jacket, and pillow under the bed. "I'll take one in the morning."

A day later Mickie, freshly showered and made up, stood in the doorway to my cubby. "You coming, Vange?"

I'd just gotten back from the mess hall and had a list of things I wanted to get done before I called it a day. My first week finally over, I had two blessed days off before my next shift—the night shift this time. Mickie worked the swing shift in the medical unit, which housed patients with malaria, typhus, pneumonia, dysentery, and hepatitis.

I shook my head. "Thanks, Mick, but not tonight." I emptied my laundry bag on the bed.

"What are you doing?"

"What does it look like I'm doing? Sorting my laundry."

"Why?"

"Because that's one less thing I'll have to do tomorrow."

"Why don't you let the hooch maid do it?"

The pile of green fatigues was growing. "She has enough to do. I can do it myself."

"That's her job, silly. Do you plan on spending all your free time alone, in this box? You'll go nuts for sure."

I gave her a wry smile. "I'm already nuts. I was nuts when I let you talk me into this."

"See? That's why you need to get out and have some fun. Come on, Vange. We're going to the Officers' Club." She sidled up to me, put her arm around my shoulder, and whispered in my ear, "Maybe Captain Martin will be there."

I left the laundry for the hooch maid.

As Beth, Sarah, DeeDee, Mickie, and I made our way to a corner table, I was tempted to scan the crowd, but I kept my eyes in front of me. I didn't want Seth Martin, if he was around, to think I was looking for him. The Jackson Five blared from the speakers. Sweat and musk hung in the smoky air. My eyes burned.

"What'll it be, ladies?"

Major Greene, sans scrubs, grinned down at us. "My treat."

I ordered a cola. I wasn't used to drinking and didn't want to embarrass myself. Let Mickie be the social butterfly. Walt returned, hoisting a tray with our orders, and, with a flourish, placed each of the glasses, dripping with condensation, on the table in front of us. I sipped mine and knew right away it contained more than cola. Well, I could nurse it all night if I had to.

"Thanks, Walt," Sarah said, wrapping a napkin around her glass.

"Where's Dan tonight?" he asked, plunking down next to me.

"Got called out about an hour ago," she said.

Walt peered at his watch in the dim light, sipped his drink, then turned to me. "By the way, if you taste something a little extra in your soda, blame Chas. The bartender. He likes to keep things hopping. Speaking of which—like to dance?"

"Yes, as a matter of fact, I took ballet in junior high."

A look of confusion flashed across his face, then he burst out laughing. I wondered how he could still laugh, after what he had to do all day.

"Let me rephrase that," he said, putting his soft hand on top of mine. His wedding ring glinted. "Will you dance with me?"

I shook my head, slipping my hand out from under his. "You're married."

"And madly in love with my wife. But what does that have to do with dancing with me?"

"I . . . I just don't feel right dancing with a married man."

How awkward! This was the surgeon I worked with. Now he'd be upset with me for acting like a prude. And I couldn't—wouldn't—ask to be assigned to another doctor.

He smiled—a tender smile like my father gave me when I was being stubborn. "If it eases your conscience, Lieutenant, I ask all the nurses to dance with me at least once."

"That's right," said a husky voice behind me. "It's a tradition. Dance with the man, kemosabe."

My face heated up. Taking a sip of my drink, I flashed my brightest smile at Walt. "I wouldn't want to break tradition, now, would I?" I held out my hand. "I'd love to dance with you, Dr. Greene."

Walt was quite a dancer. I learned later that he and his wife had danced in competitions back home and had won a number of awards. And that he was one of the few who remained faithful.

When we returned to the table, Seth had taken the seat next to mine and was chatting with Beth. He pulled my chair out for me as Walt whisked Beth away for another round on the dance floor. Honestly, I didn't know where the man got his energy. I scanned the crowd for the rest of our group. Mickie was at the bar, flirting with one of the doctors, and Sarah and DeeDee were at the jukebox. Seth and I were alone at the table. I took a few long sips from my drink, which the melting ice had watered down. Swirling around the packed room in the heat and humidity had churned up my thirst.

"That wasn't so bad, now, was it, kemosabe?"

"Why do you call me that?"

"That's what Tonto called the Lone Ranger. You remember the TV show when we were kids? About the masked man who galloped around the Wild West, righting injustices? Like you did on the plane when you stood up to Wilcott."

I stifled a giggle. "How romantic! I remind you of the Lone Ranger."

He reached over and gently moved my hair back, away from my eyes. "It means 'faithful friend.' I think it's rather appropriate, Evangeline."

The way he said my name sent a thrill through me like I'd never felt before. It was like a caress. Then he leaned forward, so close I could smell his aftershave. I closed my eyes, waiting for the kiss that never came.

"Attention! Attention, everyone!"

I opened my eyes. The shout from the doorway silenced the room. My heart dropped.

"Mas-Cals on the way in. We need everyone, I repeat, *everyone,* at the hospital. *Now!*"

CHAPTER FIVE

# A LIGHT IN THE DAMPNESS

The next three days blurred by. We worked nonstop, snatching sleep when we could on benches, on the floor in out-of-the-way corners, wherever we could drop for a few minutes. After the first twenty-four hours, I stopped wishing for a shower and clean clothes. The only thing that mattered was the man on the table.

I found one soldier's high school prom picture stuffed in his breast pocket. Flipping it over, I read the smeared ink: "Ron and Lizzie, May 9, 1969." My gosh! Barely out of high school, nineteen years old at most. *Dear God,* I prayed as we prepped him for surgery, *I know I don't pray much, but would you see to it that he gets home to Lizzie? Please?* For the first time since my father died, I hoped God was real and that he heard me.

Over the three-day push, I turned into a caffeine junkie. Strong black coffee—hot, lukewarm, cold, it didn't matter. And can after can after can of soda—anything that kept the exhaustion at bay. Sandwiches sent from the mess hall sat on a tray in the break room, but I didn't have much of an appetite. I didn't think I ever would again. When the last man was wheeled to post-op, I plopped on the bench in the hall to rest my aching feet before cleaning up our surgical cubicle. Mickie, who'd worked the ER during the push, dropped down beside me. Her curly bangs clung to her glistening brow, her brown hair a mass of frizz.

"Have you heard about Dan?" she whispered, handing me a can of my favorite cola. Stiff crimson blotches covered the front of her crumpled fatigues.

My foggy brain couldn't register the name. "Dan?" I asked in what had become my normal tone of voice—loud enough to be heard above the continuous clatter of choppers landing and taking off, above the squeals of protesting gurney wheels, above the relentless moans and screams I tried to block out.

"Shh!" Mickie glanced toward the ER. "Sarah's Dan—the pilot she's engaged to."

"Oh, that Dan." I didn't want to ask.

Mickie leaned against me, her lips to my ear. "His chopper hasn't come back yet."

My blood turned to ice. "Maybe he landed at another hospital."

Mickie clicked her fingernails against her half-empty soda can. She shook her head. "It's missing, Vange."

"How long . . .?" I shivered in the humid hall.

"Since—oh, lordy, I don't even know what day it is. When were we called out of the Officers' Club? Three, four days ago? Since then."

"Three days. Maybe—"

"It was hell out there, Vange. Someone reported hearing an explosion where he last reported his location."

"Maybe it wasn't him." *Seth.* He'd been out there, too. My stomach lurched.

"There's been no radio contact. It doesn't sound good. Captain Martin went looking for him, but all he found was a smoldering wreck. His chopper took a few rounds when he tried to get closer, but he made it back."

"Maybe Dan got out. Maybe he's wandering in the jungle. Maybe . . ."

I ran out of maybes.

Mickie swigged the last of her soda then tossed the empty can in the trash bin nearby.

"One thing I've learned in the short time I've been here," she said, looking me square in the eyes. "It's better to look on the bad side and be pleasantly surprised if you're wrong than to hope for something that will never be." She stood. "I gotta go clean up the ER."

I shoved the unopened soda into my pants pocket, expecting to force the bulky can in, but it slipped in easily.

"Where's Sarah?" I asked, pushing my protesting body from the bench.

"Cleaning up the ER, still looking out every time a chopper lands."

"Vange, someone here to see you."

I peered at my alarm clock: 1400 hours. Night shift wasn't so bad. Sleep in the day, though, was impossible. Pulling a sheet or pillow over my head didn't help. The daylight filtered through the damp sheet, and the pillow reeked of mildew. At best I snoozed, but at least I didn't have to huddle under the bed. Most of the rocket attacks came at night.

"Get up, Vange. Here—" Beth thrust something in my face. "Put this on."

Groaning, I flipped the top sheet aside and threw my legs over the side of the bed.

"All right, all right," I grumbled, slipping into my worn chenille robe and pushing my glasses on. "Does anything ever dry around here? I can't go out there in this wet rag. Who is it anyway?"

She giggled, mischief gleaming from her eyes. "You'll see." With that, she shoved me into the hall.

Captain Seth Martin stood just inside the door, a sheepish, lopsided grin spreading across his tanned face, arms wrapped around a neatly folded, fuzzy blue blanket. A mechanic's light rested on top. I pushed my hair, still mussed from sleep and always damp, behind my ears, trying to appear calm. My insides, though, felt like overcooked rice—

mushy and steamy. I clutched the lapels of my robe together and wished I'd put on my new one. What was it about this man that turned me into a lovesick schoolgirl?

"Captain Martin," I said, doing my best to act irritated, "what are you doing here in the middle of the day? I'm on night shift, you know."

A blush crept across his cheeks and spread to his ears. He handed me the blanket and light. "The electric blanket's an extra my mom sent me."

I frowned. Why would he give me an electric blanket when it was always so blasted hot?

"Put it on your bed," he explained. "It'll take care of the dampness."

"How am I supposed to sleep under an electric blanket? Isn't it hot enough already?"

A faint smile tugged at his lips. "I apologize, Lieutenant Blanchard. I didn't make myself clear. Let me rephrase that. Put it on your bed *when you're not in it* and turn it on while you're working your shift. The heat will keep your sheets dry."

"I see." I raised the lamp. "And this mechanic's light?"

His eyebrows shot up. "You know what it is. I'm impressed."

"My dad was a mechanic. I spent a lot of time in his garage."

"I see. Hang it in your locker to keep your clothes dry."

I sniffed discreetly then took a step back.

"Are you insinuating, Captain, that I smell like a walking mold garden?" I tried to sound insulted, but a flirtatious lilt had crept into my voice. "Since you've obviously learned how to deal with this infernal humidity, tell me—how can I get my hair to stay dry? Maybe I'll just have it lopped off."

His long fingers ran through my thick, uncombed hair. My knees turned to mush. It was all I could do not to lean towards him.

"Too beautiful to cut. Live with it, kemosabe. When's your next day off?"

"Why?"

"I don't believe you've had a proper tour of the Seventy-First yet."

"I'd love—"

Sarah's worry-creased face flashed before me. With each passing day, the chances of Dan returning grew slimmer. Her muffled sobs invaded what sleep I managed to get. I swallowed.

"I have plans for that day," I said, turning to go. "Thanks anyway."

Grabbing my arm, he pulled me back. His eyes probed mine. I glanced away.

"What about dinner?" His soft voice drew my eyes back to his. "At the Officers' Club."

My heart urged me to go. My head, though, screamed no.

"I don't think so." I put the blanket and light on the floor. "I don't need these."

He folded his arms across his chest. A look of amusement flashed across his face. "Woman, what is your problem?"

My cheeks burned. I took a deep breath. "Captain Martin, you're a nice guy, but I . . . already have a boyfriend. Back home."

His eyebrows arched. "Oh?"

"His name's Bill. My high school sweetheart. We're getting married after my tour."

Ouch! I never lie. And that was a whopper and a half. *Forgive me, Father, for I have sinned . . .*

"Is that so?" he said, tilting that handsome head to one side.

My heart somersaulted. "Yes."

*He knows I'm lying.*

"No, I . . . I take that back," I stammered. "I broke up with Bill before I left for basic. I'm sorry. I never lie. I'm not very good at it."

"Evangeline, if you want me to leave you alone, I will. I'm not 'The Rapper.'"

"The what?"

"The Rapper—you've heard the song by the Jaggerz?"

I shook my head.

"It just came out this year."

"I haven't heard it. I've been too busy with nursing school, military training, and trying to keep my sanity here."

He nodded.

"I . . . I just don't want to get involved with anyone."

"I understand."

Somewhere an alarm clock went off.

"Evangeline."

He pulled me to him, gently kissed my surprised lips, and released me. Then he left. I stood there, stunned, confusion swirling in my mind and heart, until someone yelled, using a few choice phrases, to shut the cursed alarm off. I gathered the blanket and light from the floor and headed back to my cubby. After I turned off the alarm, I spread the blanket on my bed and hung the light in my locker. Then I stood at the window, staring at the rain. My head told me I'd done the right thing, the smart thing. But my heart—oh, my heart screamed to run after him.

In the distance a shell exploded. The hooch shuddered.

What was I thinking? I had a job to do. I grabbed my towel and headed for the shower.


"Mail call!"

Mickie tromped into my bedroom, lugging a brown package the size of a milk crate and dropped it on the bed, which promptly protested the load.

"Hey, easy on the springs," I said. "You know how hard it is to get stuff around here. I'll be sleeping on the floor until the end of my tour."

She raised her eyebrows in mock surprise. "What? You mean you don't sleep on the floor now?"

I grinned, glad to see her. Working opposite shifts, we hadn't had much time together over the past month. Today was the first simultaneous day off we'd had since we arrived in-country, and we planned to spend it getting caught up.

"Take off your boots and stay a while," I said, placing my can of caffeine, dripping with condensation, on the nightstand and easing onto the bed.

"Don't mind if I do," she said. Bending over, she unlaced her boots and kicked them across the room, then plopped beside the package. Then she noticed the blanket.

"What's this?" she said, smoothing her hand over the soft nap.

"What does it look like? A blanket."

She gave me a wry smile. "Where'd you get it?"

"Seth. Captain Martin. It keeps the sheets dry."

"I know." She looked like the cat that swallowed the canary.

Irritation shot through me. "If you knew, why'd you ask?"

"Because it was a way to bring up the subject."

"What subject?"

"You and Seth."

"That's not a subject," I said, pulling out a pair of scissors from my nightstand drawer. "Let's open the package."

She snatched the scissors from my hand. "Not yet."

I crossed my arms. "There's nothing to talk about."

She stared at me with her I-know-better-than-that look. I glared back.

I raised my arms in mock surrender. "He came to see me a week ago."

"I know."

"If you know so much, then why are you asking so many nosy questions?"

"Why didn't you want to take the blanket and the light?"

"Who told you that?"

She traced the edge of the address label with her finger. "Beth. She heard everything."

"She had no business listening in on a private conversation, let alone telling someone else about it."

"Vange, you two were standing in the hall—anyone in the hooch could hear you talking." She gave me a knowing look. "What are you afraid of?"

*Falling in love. Or is it too late for that?* I hadn't seen him since that day. He seemed to be avoiding me. Or not making the effort to see me. I should have felt relieved, yet I found myself glancing out to the helipad every time I heard a chopper and feeling a tinge of disappointment when it wasn't his. I thought of him every time I slipped into dry clothes and relived that kiss every time I closed my eyes. I plucked a fuzz ball from the blanket and rolled it between my fingers. Had he used this blanket?

"Accepting his gift would give him the wrong message," I said finally.

"And what message would that be?"

"That I want a relationship with him," I said. "I'm not dumb, Mick. I know he has feelings for me. I don't want to encourage them."

"And you don't have feelings for him?"

"I don't want a relationship at this point in my life. That's why I broke up with Bill. It's all I can do to keep up with my responsibilities here—and keep my sanity in the process. I have to be a nurse first. I can't afford to be distracted."

"Vange, the guy's nuts about you. Everyone can see that," she said, snatching the scissors from the bed and attacking the over-taped package. "There's a difference, you know, between stubborn and stupid. And this time, my friend, you're being stupid."

The package, addressed to both of us, was from Mickie's mother, Mama Rose. Mama had taken me, an only child with no other close relatives, under her wing when my mother died eighteen months after my father. "No one should be alone in the world," she'd said.

After fighting the overabundance of packing tape, we ripped off the paper grocery bags and groaned.

"She must have used a whole roll," Mickie said, twisting the scissors under the tape at the top edge of the box.

"Here," I said, tossing her my utility knife. "Use this before you break my best pair of scissors."

Moments later we were squealing in delight as we unpacked cream rinse, hair spray, contact lens solution, Tampax—things we couldn't get here. Mama had even sent two bottles of perfume—Charisma for Mickie and Bird of Paradise for me—each wrapped in a soft terry washcloth and stuffed in a plastic bread bag. There were edible goodies, too—Twinkies, homemade fudge, and pumpkin bread, all lovingly and carefully packed. At the bottom were two shirt boxes wrapped in white tissue paper and tied with red and blue yarn.

"This one's yours," Mickie said, tossing one to me.

I gasped when I lifted the lid. Inside were two pair of bikini underwear, one red silk, the other black lace, with matching bras. Mickie squealed. I blushed.

Underneath the underwear was a note: "Never forget, Cara Mia, that you are a woman first. Love, Mama Rose."

CHAPTER SIX

# NO SECOND CHANCES

"What's this?" I asked Beth on a slow day the following week. We were restocking supplies in the ER when I noticed a clipboard hanging on the wall with my name on it.

"That's the 'NB' list," she said.

"NB? What's that?"

"New Blood."

I leaned closer. Beside both mine and Mickie's names, which were at the bottom of the list, were our blood types—A-positive, mine, and AB-positive for Mickie.

Dropping the rolls of gauze she had stuffed in her arms on a gurney, Beth opened a wall cupboard. "Everyone who works at the Seventy-First is listed, along with their blood types."

"In case we get wounded?" Visions of lying bleeding after a rocket attack flashed through my mind. I shuddered.

Her chestnut ponytail swung as she shook her head and began placing the gauze on the shelf. "When we run out of a particular blood type—which is easy to do during a push—we check the list to see who has that type and, um, recruit a donor on the spot."

"Ah, so that's why everyone said 'new blood' when they met us that first night. They meant it literally."

Beth grinned, her dimples punctuating the sparkle in her brown eyes. "You got that right."

She shut the cupboard door then pulled a pencil from her ponytail and checked off a box on our job sheet. I scanned the list. There it was: "Martin, Capt. Seth Gabriel, AB-negative."

"Blanchard!"

Startled, I swung to the doorway, where Major Lennon stood. How long had the nursing supervisor been standing there?

"I need to see you in my office. Now."

"You've heard of Medcaps, haven't you, Lieutenant?" she asked me as I sat on the wooden captain's chair in front of her desk.

"Yes, ma'am. Medical Civil Action Patrols."

Lifting a sheet of paper from one of several neatly stacked piles in front of her, she reached to the top of her head and pulled her glasses from her graying russet hair and slid them on. Her lips twitched as she studied the paper.

"Fortunately, we're in a slow period—the only time we can afford to send medical teams to the outlying villages in II Corps."

She placed the paper on the blotter in front of her, folded her arms on the desk, and leaned forward, hazel eyes peering at me over her glasses. I shifted my weight on the hard wood.

"You've done good work in the two months you've been here," she said with the customary nod that was as close to a smile as she ever gave. "Dr. Greene's requested you accompany him on a Medcap that's leaving tomorrow morning for Plei Le Lahu. You'll assist him treating the locals for everything from headaches to toothaches to sprains to fractures to infestations."

She leaned back and studied me for several seconds, her hands in a prayer position against her lips. Then her gaze shifted to a gold-framed photo on top of the stack of papers closest to me. Her face softened—just for an instant. If I hadn't been watching her, I would've missed it. Dropping her hands, she lifted her pen and scribbled on the paper.

"The chopper leaves tomorrow at 0700 hours. Be at the helipad outside the ER—"

"Chopper?" I interrupted. "I thought we'd be traveling by Jeep."

She shook her head. "The terrain is rough, the roads are mud, and we have reports that the VC have blown up several bridges. Going by chopper reduces the chance of an ambush."

"I see."

"All right then." She flipped open a file, pulled out a paper, and handed it to me. "Here's a list of the medical supplies you'll assemble. Today. Lieutenant Phillips, who'll also be going, will help you. Meet Dr. Greene and Captain Martin at the helipad at 0600 hours to help them load the chopper."

"Captain Martin?" So much for my plan to avoid him. I didn't know if I was mad or glad.

"He's an excellent medic, as well as our finest pilot." Her eyebrows arched as she peered at me over her glasses. "Is that a problem?"

*Yes.* "No, ma'am."

"Good. That will be all, Lieutenant." She turned her attention back to the file on her desk. "Dismissed."

As I rose and turned to leave, my hip brushed against the stack at the edge of the desk. Papers and files scattered to the floor, the framed photo toppling over and landing on top.

"Oh, I'm sorry," I gasped, bending to retrieve the documents. I lifted the frame gingerly, inspecting it to make sure the glass hadn't broken. A beaming couple in Army uniform—in their mid-twenties, I guessed—stood in front of a MASH-type tent. He stood behind her, his arms wrapped around her waist, pride and joy in every line of his handsome features. Her face glowed as she leaned back against him. I brought the black-and-white snapshot closer, staring at a much younger Major Lennon. My cheeks grew warm as I carefully placed the frame on her desk. I glanced at her left hand. No wedding ring. I stacked the papers on her desk and straightened the pile.

"His name was Captain Peter Hansen," she said, gazing at the photo. "I met him during the Korean War. I was an Army nurse assigned to a field hospital. He was a medical evacuation pilot.

"We fell in love. He wanted to get married right then and there. He even had the chaplain lined up. But I wanted to wait until we got home." She stared out the window next to her desk. "He was shot down on his last mission."

Major Lennon's words echoed in my mind that night as I listened to the dull thud of outgoing artillery and the whistles of incoming mortars, and huddled under the electric blanket. October in the Central Highlands meant a change in seasons: the monsoons were winding down and the cool season, which ran from November through January, was coming on. The mornings and evenings were damp and chilly, and the nights could be downright cold. Seth's blanket did more than keep my bed dry; it kept me warm. I hadn't even thanked him.

*We fell in love.* Sleep eluded me as I relived each moment I'd spent with Seth. The way he said my name. The way he called me "kemosabe." The way he held me during the rocket attack that first day. The gentle kiss that stirred a tempest of passion.

*He was shot down on his last mission.* Sometimes life doesn't give second chances. Sometimes not even first chances. I didn't want to end up like Sarah. It was Seth who'd found the burned chopper a week after it went down and brought Dan's body back. At least she didn't have to wonder anymore. I didn't want to end up like Major Lennon, either. If only I could peek into the future.

*God, if you're real, help me. Please. I don't know what to do.*

I was still miserably undecided when the Jeep came for Beth and me the next morning.

"Did you pack extra fatigues?" she asked when we met at the front door of the hooch.

"No, was I supposed to?"

"In case you haven't noticed, it's raining." She dropped her duffel bag on the wooden floor. "Better to have an extra set of dry clothes than go around miserable and wet all day."

Tires screeched outside.

"Doesn't Soup ever drive slow?" I asked.

Beth grabbed her duffel bag and opened the door. "Run back and grab some extra clothes," she said over her shoulder. "And don't forget extra boots. And your field jacket."

I crammed two extra sets of fatigues and socks, as well as a pair of boots and my rain poncho, into my duffel bag, zipped it shut, then headed for the door. On an impulse, I scooted back and grabbed the red silk bra and panties Mama Rose had sent me.

*I must be crazy*, I thought as I rushed out the door.

We arrived at Plei Le Lahu around eight. While Seth and Walt met with the chief to let him know we'd arrived and get his permission to set up, Beth and I waited by the chopper with Buzz Kelsey, Seth's copilot. The rain had stopped.

Nestled in a glen full of lush vegetation, the village was neatly arranged along the banks of a stream, where a handful of scantily clad children splashed playfully in the morning sun. Bamboo hooches stood seven feet above the ground on stilts, around which an assortment of animals—dogs, cats, chickens, and pigs—barked, sniffed, squawked, and snorted their way around, scrounging for breakfast.

A young girl—about sixteen or seventeen—her coarse ebony hair tied at the nape of her neck, a crying baby swaddled to her bare bosom, approached us hesitantly.

"Sick call?" she asked, her dark eyes filled with hope.

Beth nodded. "Sick call. Yes."

With a glimmer of a smile, the girl turned and hurried to one of the hooches at the edge of the village.

"They know English?" I asked, watching as she climbed a bamboo ladder to the open front porch.

"They know a little bit of everything," Buzz said. "English, French, Vietnamese—"

"Wait," I said. "Vietnamese?"

"These are Montagnards, mountain people. They're the most primitive people in the country, but they're not Vietnamese," Beth said. "Didn't you notice how different she looks from our hooch maid?"

Luu Thi Bian's slanted eyes and Oriental features came to mind. The girl we just met looked more like she was from the Philippines than Vietnam.

"I see what you mean," I said.

"There's no love lost between them, either," Buzz said.

"Why's that?"

Beth shrugged. "Why don't you ask Seth? He's made quite a few trips to the Montagnard villages."

"Time to stop jawing and get to work," Buzz said, nodding in the direction of the village. "Here come Walt and Seth."

We lugged the medical supplies to an open-sided bamboo hut next to the chief's hooch, where we'd hold the clinic, while Buzz set up a speaker system and played a tape for the villagers that explained in their language what we were doing and how to proceed. The tape wasn't needed, as Medcap had visited Plei Le Lahu several times in the past, but protocol dictated it be played.

"Thank God we didn't have to hoist these boxes up a ladder," I said, pulling open the top flaps. Unlike the rest of the structures, the hut where we'd hold the clinic rested only two feet above the ground and appeared to be the gathering place for the villagers.

"Thank heaven we didn't have to do the ritual thing," Beth said while we unloaded medicines and bandages on two makeshift bamboo tables under the A-shaped, broad-leafed thatched roof.

"What ritual thing?" I asked.

"In most of these villages, they won't let us start medical treatment unless we participate in their welcoming ceremony," she said.

"That's understandable," I said. "The ritual establishes trust."

"And makes the medical team less than efficient."

"How so?"

"The ritual involves smoking a peace pipe, which is usually packed with dope, and drinking homemade rice wine from a communal cup."

I shuddered. "Oh, I'd never even think of drinking out of a cup someone else drank from, let alone . . ."

"I don't know how, but your Seth pulled it off—again."

"He's not 'my Seth.' I haven't seen him since—"

"Since you stupidly sent him packing."

"I'll ignore that comment. But how could he convince the chief to forgo the welcoming ritual if it's so important?"

Beth shrugged. "I think it has to do with his religion."

"Whose religion?"

"Seth's. He usually brings his Bible when he comes on these Medcaps." She leaned close, her lips to my ear, and spoke low. "I've seen him reading it to them—he knows their language—and praying with them. Word spreads."

"What word?"

"That Captain Martin's God is stronger than their gods."

As I assisted Walt, Beth worked with Seth, who'd pretty much ignored me since giving me a curt nod and a mumbled "Good morning, Lieutenant," when I arrived at the helipad. I watched him slip candy bars and lollipops to the children, who squealed in delight. By lunchtime we'd seen about half the villagers, mostly babies, toddlers, children, and pregnant women. My heart went out to them, especially the children. Poor as they were, these Montagnard mothers kept their children clean.

Our last case of the morning was pulling a nasty tooth from the diseased gums of a ten-year-old boy and giving him a shot of penicillin.

"Walt," I said when we finished cleaning up our station and setting up for the afternoon. "How come there are men in this village? I thought all those capable of fighting were conscripted into the NVA."

Walt shook his head. "The Montagnards would rather die than fight for the VC," he said. "They hate communism. They hate Ho Chi Minh."

I met Beth and Buzz for lunch. The three of us sat on a blanket beside the stream at the edge of the village. Walt had begged off, claiming he needed a little shut-eye. Seth disappeared as soon as he and Beth had cleaned up their station and set up for the afternoon.

"Beans and wieners again!" Beth groaned. "Every time we go on one of these missions, you bring the same old thing. Couldn't you have picked something else?"

"I'm insulted," Buzz said, his freckled face contorting into a fake hurt expression. "I bring lunch, and you complain."

"What do you have?" she asked, snatching his C-ration. "Oh, yummy. Ham and lima beans. Not any better. Vangie, what do you have?"

I glanced at my unopened field meal. "Same as you. Hot dogs and beans. Where's Captain Martin?" I asked, hoping to sound casual.

Buzz shrugged. "Sometimes he likes to eat alone."

I watched the water frolic over the stream bed. Should I or shouldn't I? *If I had to do it over . . .*

"I'm not hungry," I said, slipping a can of cola into the side pocket of my fatigue pants. "I think I'll take a walk."

Beth's face registered surprise, then understanding.

"Here," Buzz said, snatching the field meal out my hand. "Let me relieve you of this."

I glanced around. Which direction . . . ?

"He went back to the chopper," Buzz offered. "That way."

I smiled. "Thanks."

As I headed to the field where the Huey was parked, I had no idea what I'd say when I came face-to-face with Seth Martin. All I knew was that I had to get a second chance. I just had to.

CHAPTER SEVEN

## SEMPER FI

I found Seth in the clearing with the chopper, but he wasn't alone. Surrounding him were most, if not all, of the children in the village, hopping up and down, shouting and waving their arms to get his attention. *What on earth?* I stopped. Maybe this wasn't such a good idea after all. Then he turned and spied me. A mélange of emotions crossed his face in an instant: surprise, hope, then alarm.

"It's okay," I mouthed, giving him a weak wave and an even weaker smile. He nodded, relief washing over his features. After the cool treatment he'd given me all morning, the last thing I expected was the grin that broke out on his face.

"Just what we need," he shouted, beckoning me to join the group, "a catcher. You *do* know how to catch a baseball, don't you, Evangeline?"

Hope poured from the children's dark eyes. I wasn't the most gifted female athlete in the world, but how could I say no? Tossing my unopened can of soda towards the chopper door, I made my way through the crowd of bouncing kids and snatched the baseball from his hands.

"You bet I do," I said, smiling and nodding so the children understood.

A teenage boy, his face badly scarred, hung back, watching Seth as he assigned the children their positions. Pointing to the older boy, then to left field, Seth spoke to him in his language. The boy's face lit up. As he scooted to left field, I noticed his left arm ended at the wrist.

It was obvious that this wasn't the first time they'd played baseball with "Cappin Martin." The children did better than I'd expected, but the teenage boy with one hand surprised me the most. He fielded the ball with speed and accuracy the few times it was hit to him. And when it was his turn to bat, he approached the plate with confidence, grasping the wooden bat with a firm, one-handed grip. Missing on the first swing, he connected on the second, sending the red-smudged ball soaring into the outfield and all the children scrambling after it. As the boy sprinted around the bases, Seth shouted to the infielders to "stay on your bases." They didn't, of course. It was more fun chasing after the ball.

"Hey, you two!" Buzz yelled over the pandemonium just as the base runner crossed the makeshift home plate. As I turned toward Buzz's voice, the ball came flying from third base, smacking the outer edge of my right eye, near my temple. Stars of light flashed through my brain. I crumpled to the ground. The children huddled around me, suddenly silent.

"Evangeline!" Seth knelt beside me, pulling me to a sitting position and cupping my face in his hands. "Are you all right? Buzz! Ice! In the cooler."

"I'm . . . I'm fine." I smiled at the children, who looked like they were spinning where they stood. "Really."

They looked to Seth, who said something in their language. I heard my name, Evangeline.

"What's he saying?" I whispered to Buzz, who knelt beside me with the ice pack.

"That Nurse Evangeline is all right, and they're to go back home."

Reluctantly the children headed back to the village, peeking over their shoulders as they trudged away.

"Can you get up?" Seth asked.

"I think so." The wooziness seemed to be subsiding. But my heart throbbed in my throat with Seth so close.

He grasped my hands. "Let me help you."

I stepped to the Huey on wobbly legs, Seth's arm around my waist. He led me to the open chopper door, where he gently guided me to a sitting position.

"Here you go," he said, taking the ice pack from Buzz. "This'll keep the swelling down."

Buzz whistled. "You're gonna have one heckuva shiner, Vange. I can even see the stitches."

"Stitches?" I mumbled, running my fingers over the pulsating bump.

Pushing my hand aside, Seth put the ice pack against my throbbing eye.

"You know," Buzz said. "The stitches on the seams."

"Seams?"

"On the baseball."

"Oh, those seams."

Seth grabbed my shoulders and turned me to him. "What day is it?"

I shrugged. "Wednesday?"

He frowned. "When were you born?"

"That's easy. November 5, 1949."

"Oh, so you'll be turning twenty-one in a couple of weeks."

With all the busyness, I hadn't realized my birthday was coming up.

"Are you satisfied, Captain Martin?" I said. "I don't have a concussion. Just a little bump on the head." I groped the floor behind me.

"What do you need?" Seth asked.

"My purse. It's in my duffel bag."

Buzz snorted. "Typical woman. Gotta whip out her compact so she can see what she looks like with a black eye. Vanity, vanity, all is vanity."

"That's not it," I said, putting the ice pack on my lap and twisting around. "I need to take my contacts out. I can feel my eye swelling like a pregnant watermelon."

"Hold still, Evangeline," Seth said, putting the ice pack back on my eye and pressing my hand against it. "Keep this on. I'll get it."

While I held the compress to my eye, Seth rummaged through the bags in the chopper until he found mine. Unzipping it, he pulled my purse out. The red silk bra and panties that I'd shoved in at the last minute tumbled out onto the ground.

"Oo-oo—whee! Oo la la! Lookee what we got here!" Buzz said, brandishing my lingerie between his thumb and index finger.

My face flamed. *Oh, no!* What would the honorable Captain Martin think of me now? *Stupid. Stupid. Stupid. What were you thinking?*

Seth snatched the underwear from Buzz's grasp.

"What's your problem, Kelsey? You act like you've never seen women's underwear before," he said, stuffing them in my bag. "Why don't you go back to the village and tell Beth and Walt we'll be a bit late. Need to keep the ice pack on her eye for a spell."

Buzz gave Seth a sure-you-do grin and winked. "Gotcha, Cap."

"One more thing, Lieutenant Kelsey."

"Yes, Cap?"

"I won't hear about this from anyone."

The grin vanished from Buzz's face. "No, sir," he said, turning to go. "You certainly won't."

"How's the eye?" he asked me as Buzz strode off.

"Hurts like the dickens. I hope I'm not going to end up with a dimple like yours."

He smoothed his fingers over the indentation on his cheekbone below his left eye and chuckled. "We'll have matching dimples then."

I groaned, imagining what I'd look like. Sitting beside me, he lifted the ice pack from my eye and leaned close—so close I could smell his sweat. A thrill shot through me.

"Looks like it'll be okay," he said, caressing my cheekbone with his thumb. "The ball didn't hit you as hard as the one that hit me. A couple of days, kemosabe, and you'll be fine. But just in case . . ."

His lips brushed my cheek, just below my eye. *Don't stop. Please don't stop.* I leaned into him and closed my eyes. My head throbbed.

"My contacts," I said, pulling away from him. "I need to get them out. Now."

He dropped my handbag in my lap. "Here. I know better than to rummage through a woman's purse."

After both contacts were safe in the case, I tilted my head back and tried to squeeze eye drops into my eyes. But my shaking hands wouldn't cooperate.

"I'm getting more on my cheeks than in my eye," I muttered.

"Allow me," Seth said, taking the eye drops. "The best way to do this is if you put your head in my lap."

I complied. Gladly.

"You've got the most beautiful eyes I've ever seen, Evangeline," he said, twisting the cap back on the bottle when he was done. "I've never seen irises that color."

I sat up and reached for my purse. "Thanks," I mumbled, rooting for my glasses case. "Ah, here it is."

"Why do you wear contacts that make your eyes a common blue?"

"Because," I said, putting on my glasses and blinking. "I got tired of being called 'Vangie with the violet eyes.' I felt like a freak."

"You're not a freak, Evangeline," he said, pulling out a flashlight from a bag behind the pilot's seat. Switching it on, he removed my glasses, then flashed its beam in my right eye, then my left. "Pupils reacting normally. Vision blurred?"

I shook my head. "Not too much. Probably from switching to glasses."

He slipped my glasses over my eyes. "Headache?"

"A little."

He reached into the bag and pulled out a bottle of aspirin, then leaned down and scooped up the can of soda I'd tossed on the ground earlier.

"Here. This'll help," he said, dropping two tablets in my hand.

He opened the can and handed it to me. I slipped the pills in my mouth and washed them down with the cola. We sat in the open chopper door for a few minutes, watching a soft breeze whisper through the amber rice field across the clearing.

"Feel like taking a little walk?" he asked.

"Shouldn't we go back to the village?"

"Walt and Beth can handle the clinic for a while. We saw most of those who'll let us treat them this morning. All that's left are the older men and women, and they're pretty superstitious. They prefer their own village doctor to us."

Snatching a folded shirt and a hand towel from behind the pilot's seat, he grabbed my hand and headed towards the stream. "Come on. I want to show you something that's almost as beautiful as your eyes."

We followed a jungle trail for about a quarter of a mile until we came to a thundering, ten-foot waterfall. I gasped. Pine trees arched over the edge of the pool at the base of the falls. Mounds of glossy, dark green shrubs with large, delicate-looking white flowers sprouted from the spongy humus beneath our feet.

"Paradise must have been like this," I said, inhaling a heady, sweet fragrance that reminded me of the flowering bush in our front yard back home in Pennsylvania. "Are those bushes jasmine?"

He shook his head. "Gardenias. They bloom all year round in this spot—the steady hot, humid conditions are just right."

"Amazing." I gazed at the lush emerald foliage that formed a tropical canopy above us. "It's another world in here. Hard to imagine there's a war raging just a few miles away."

"I sure hope it survives the war." He sounded angry.

"What do you mean?"

"The military's defoliation program."

"What's that?"

"You haven't heard about it?"

I shook my head.

"They're spraying the jungles with a defoliating agent—a chemical that kills the vegetation. It's supposed to help us win the war by taking away the VC's hiding places. Cuts down on sniping."

"Oh." A profound sadness welled up in me.

"It's also destroying a way of life—and the innocent people who are content with their primitive lifestyle. So far, though, they haven't sprayed here in the mountains."

"Why not?"

"Charlie would rather avoid the 'yards. No sense in wasting precious chemicals."

"'Yards?"

"Short for Montagnards, the tribe that inhabits these mountains." Anger flashed in his blue eyes. "War is hell."

I surveyed the tropical paradise that enfolded us. *Oh, God, protect these people and these beautiful flowers.*

"I apologize for waxing political on you, kemosabe. I brought you here to show you something beautiful, not make you sad." He slipped off his shirt and pulled his T-shirt over his head. "And for another reason . . ."

Sprouts of sandy hair curled on his lean, muscular chest. My face grew warm.

"Cool down, kemosabe, it's not what you think," he said, dipping his towel into the pool, then swabbing it, still dripping, over his torso. "It gets pretty hot playing ball in the tropical sun. I don't like to go back to the clinic all sweaty and smelling like a jock."

I grinned, relieved, yet disappointed. "Well, aren't you?"

"Aren't I what?"

"A jock. I saw the way you threw that baseball—just before it hit me. You played in high school?"

He swabbed under his arms. "And college."

"Really? Where?"

"Penn State."

"Good college. What position?"

"Pitcher."

"Starter or reliever?"

"Starter."

"You must have been pretty good to be a starting pitcher for Penn State."

He shrugged.

Bending over, he dipped the towel in the pool again, then wrung it out and handed it to me. It felt refreshingly cool. I needed something to cool me down.

"Would you mind getting my back?" he asked.

"Not at all." This certainly wouldn't cool me down.

He turned, his broad shoulders tapering to a lean waist—a waist I wanted to throw my arms around. Then I noticed the tattoo—the words *Semper Fi* centered on a shield on his back left shoulder. At the bottom of the shield two swords formed an "X."

"What's this?" I asked, tapping the tattoo with the towel.

"It's a tattoo."

"I can see that. But '*Semper Fi*'? Isn't that the motto of the Marine Corps?"

He turned, pulling the towel out of my hand. "Yes, and also the Eleventh Infantry of the U.S. Army."

"I didn't know that."

He unfolded the clean shirt and slipped it on. "You do now."

I stepped up to him and pulled the buttons through the buttonholes. "You surprise me, Captain Martin. I didn't take you for a man who'd get a tattoo. You don't seem . . . you *aren't* . . . the type."

A blush—not from the tropical heat, I was sure—crept across his face.

"Had it done back in my stupid days."

I leaned back. "When was that?"

"Right before shipping over here the first time. I hung out with the guys from the Wandering Eleventh. One night we were all drinking and someone came up with the idea for all of us to get tattoos. Like I said, those were my stupid days."

I smiled up at him, drinking in those blue eyes that had apology written in them. "At least you didn't get a naked woman. Or a snake. *Semper Fi* sounds patriotic."

"Do you know what it means?"

I shook my head. "It's Latin, right? I took Latin in high school, then again in nursing school."

"*Semper Fi* is short for *Semper Fidelis*—it means 'always faithful.'"

I gazed up at him.

"Faithful—that's an important word for you, isn't it?" I said. "I mean, you have *Semper Fi* tattooed on your body, and you call me kemosabe."

He grinned. "Guess we make a good pair, then—I'm always faithful, and you're a faithful friend."

Pulling his Army knife from his back pocket, he stepped to the nearest gardenia bush and sliced through the stem of one of the flowers.

"For the nurse," he said, placing a creamy white blossom in my palm. "The Chinese call it *zhi zi*. One of the most versatile herbs there is. When prepared, it can be used for a variety of ailments and injuries." He paused, grinning. "Even reduce the swelling of a black eye."

"How do you know so much about it?"

"Studied Chinese herbal medicine. In these tropical jungles in wartime, you never know when it'll come in handy."

I held the soft white petals to my nose. "And here I thought you were being romantic."

He grinned, a mischievous twinkle in his blue eyes. "In Eastern culture, the gardenia symbolizes love, unity, grace, and strength. According to legend, the nightingale chooses its mate only when the gardenia first blossoms."

I stifled a giggle. "In the story I heard, it was the lily of the valley, not the gardenia."

A sheepish grin spread across his reddening cheeks. "Caught me. See? I try to romance a gal, but it backfires. I'm just not the romantic type, I guess."

"I wouldn't say that."

"What would you say then?"

I thought for a moment. "*Semper Fi.*"

He gave me a quizzical look.

"A faithful person always tells the truth. He can't be deceitful."

Voices sounded down the path.

"Group of women from the village coming for their daily bath," he said, wrapping his towel in his sweat-stained shirt and tucking the wad under his arm. "Time to go. They're going to think we got lost."

"Tell me about the boy," I said as we strolled across the clearing to the village, our fingers intertwined. "The one you put in left field—who nearly knocked me over before the baseball did."

"I call him JimBoy. He's the chief's son."

"What happened to him?"

"He was only ten when it happened. He was walking with his mother to Pleiku, where they sell the fruits and vegetables they raise, and he found a grenade. Not knowing what it was, he picked it up and pulled the pin."

"He's lucky to be alive," I said.

"He's smart and quite resourceful. A big help to his father. He'll make a good chief someday—if they survive the war."

We were almost back to the village when Buzz came bounding across the field from the chopper.

"We gotta pack up and get back to base. Pronto. Charlie ambushed some of our guys coming back over the fence. Looks like another Mas-Cal."

# CHAPTER EIGHT

# TISSUES, TEAPOTS, AND GARDENIAS

"Sarah's leaving," Mickie announced. Wearing silky PJs, her brown hair pulled into a frizzy ponytail on top of her head, she plopped down on my bed amid the piles of laundry. I'd slept in—something I'd started doing on my day off—and was trying to get the sorting finished before Luu Thi Bian came.

"Hold on a sec. I'm almost done." I shoved the piles in a laundry bag, fatigues on the bottom, underwear on the top, then placed the bag outside my door for the hooch maid.

"I know," I said, closing the door. "Beth told me."

"You going for breakfast?" She yawned. "I need some coffee."

I eyed the can of beer in her hand. *Coffee would be better than that,* I was about to say, but decided against it. I didn't feel like arguing this morning.

"Don't have time," I said, positioning myself on the bed for a girl-talk. "I'm meeting Seth in an hour. He's flying down to Tan Son Nhut to get a shipment of med supplies that came in. I'm going along."

A mischievous grin spilled across her pale face. "Spending a lot of time with him lately, huh? Glad to see you've gotten past your stubbornness."

"Sarah's transferring to Cu Chi," I said, taking a sip of my lukewarm cola. "We're taking her with us today."

Mickie gulped the last of what had become her favorite morning beverage. "After what she's been through, you'd think they'd send her to Cam Ranh Bay and the beaches, not a burn unit next to a petroleum dump," she said, wiping her lips with her sleeve. "And with that artillery battery nearby, she'll never get any sleep."

I plucked the box of tissues from my nightstand and dropped it on the blanket between us.

"She requested it," I said. "She wants someplace noisy—and busy. Says it helps to keep her mind off Dan."

Sniffling, she yanked a few tissues out—I counted four—and crumpled them in her hand.

"Easy," I said, "That's my last box of soft stuff until the next care package."

"She won't be at the Twelfth very long. Her DEROS is sometime in December. Six weeks, I think she said."

Seth's DEROS—Date of Expected Return from Overseas—was seven months away, at the beginning of June. Mine was two months later. I didn't want to think about it.

"I heard the Twelfth's getting deactivated in December," Mickie said. "Part of Tricky Dicky's Vietnamization plan."

Something else I didn't want to think about.

"Wonder when they'll send Sarah's replacement," she said. "Soon, I hope." She pulled a tissue from the wad in her hand and began shredding it, dropping the ragged pieces on the blanket. I decided, with what I was about to tell her, to ignore her nervous habit this time.

"They're not sending a replacement," I said.

Mickie's eyebrows shot up. "Why not, for heaven's sake? It's just gonna make it harder on the rest of us, having to take up the slack."

I took a breath. "Because the Seventy-First is getting deactivated at the same time. Seth told me."

She stared at me, her expression blank.

"We need to decide where we'll request to go," I said.

Mickie blinked, then tossed the wadded tissues on the bed. "Just when I was getting used to Rocket City. I need to think about it. Along the coast, for sure. Maybe Cam Ranh Bay. Hey, wait—what about the 283rd—Seth's unit?"

I sighed. "Staying here."

"Oh." Cursing the war, the government, and the Army, she yanked more tissues from the box—five this time.

"They're not shutting down the base," I said, putting the box of tissues back on the nightstand. "Just deactivating the hospital."

"I know you, Vange. You've already picked the next hospital. Where?"

"Qui Nhon. It looks to be the closest to Pleiku—and Seth says he could make the trip on his off day. And since Qui Nhon's in II Corps, he'll bring the casualties he picks up to the hospital there."

"But you won't be together, Vange. Not like here."

I reached across the bed and grasped her hand. "I know." Hot tears welled in my eyes. "I know."

After Mickie left, I packed my shower things, makeup, perfume, and the black lace lingerie Mama Rose sent me in my overnight bag. Seth was taking me out to dinner—someplace special, he said, but wouldn't say where. I argued he had to tell me so I knew what to wear, but all he said was "Bring a nice dress." I'd brought a few civilian clothes with me in-country, but nothing appropriate for a dinner date. But what did I find when Mickie and I opened our latest care package? My black cocktail dress, neatly folded inside a plastic cleaner's bag with a scented sachet hanger and note resting on top. "When you're feeling down, Cara Mia, put this on. A pretty dress always makes a woman feel better. Love, Mama Rose."

"Mama Rose," I murmured now, draping the dress over the sachet hanger, "you always know what I need." I zipped it in a black garment bag, then, on a whim, tucked my robe in the overnight bag. Neither

Seth nor I had to be back on duty until tomorrow evening. Tonight I'd be all woman.

Sarah was attempting to fit a thick book in her oversized handbag when I stopped by her room to help her with her bags.

"I'll do that," I said, draping the garment bag across the bed and dropping my purse and overnight bag on the floor. "Finish packing."

Somehow I didn't feel it was right for me to pack the framed photos of her and Dan, which looked to be the only things left, with the exception of a tea set on her nightstand.

Smiling softly, she handed me the book. It was a Bible. "Thanks, Vange."

While Sarah wrapped a hand towel around each photo, I rearranged her handbag, putting the Bible, which was the largest and heaviest item, on the bottom. When I was done, I glanced around to see if there was anything else to pack. Sarah, her wispy blonde hair arranged in a French twist, stood at the window, staring outside. The seams of her crisp uniform shirt drooped over her shoulders. I glanced at my watch. We had another fifteen minutes before her ride came.

"I'll start taking your stuff outside," I said, grabbing her duffel bag.

"Not yet," she said, turning from the window and stepping to the bed. "We still have time. Let's have tea."

"There's tea in that teapot?" I said, aghast. How could she think of tea at a time like this?

With a soft smile, she lifted the blue-and-white flowered teapot and poured the steaming liquid into two matching cups. "I brought a thermos of hot water from the mess after breakfast," she said, handing me a cup. "I always have tea on hand. You know that."

I nodded. Sarah was the tea lady of the hooch. Of the hospital, for that matter. No matter what time she got off duty, she had to have a "cuppa." You'd think she was British.

"You going to drink that standing up?" she asked, patting the bare mattress beside her.

"You amaze me," I said as I complied. "I've known Seth only for a couple of months—been seeing him only a few weeks, but I'd be a basket case if anything happened to him. You've been so calm since . . . since . . . "

She sipped her tea. "Oh, I'm tearing up inside, Vangie. I feel like crying every time I think of him, which is every minute. But it's getting better. I've learned that peace and grief can exist side by side."

"Aren't you angry?"

"About what?"

"That God didn't answer your prayers?"

Folding her hands around her teacup, she shook her head. "No, I'm not mad at God."

"Why bother praying, if he doesn't answer? How do you know he even hears?"

She turned to me, a strange mixture of love and sorrow in her gray eyes. "Is that what happened? You prayed for something, and when you didn't get what you prayed for, you lost your faith."

*How did she know?*

"It happens a lot, Vangie. People give up on God when they need him most."

I shook my head. "How can you have faith when it's let you down?"

Putting her cup on the nightstand, she slid next to me and wrapped an arm around my shoulders.

"Dear, dear Vangie, I've learned that there are two kinds of faith: faith in what God *does* or what you think he'll do for you, and faith in who God *is*. The first kind will let you down because we humans can never understand the mind of God. It's too easy to blame him when things don't go the way we want. The second kind is like bedrock. Because God never changes. You can build on it, and when the storms come, your faith won't crumble like a sand castle."

"You have a strong faith."

She squeezed my shoulder. "I have a faithful God."

Tires screeched on the pavement outside.

"Soup's here," I said, placing my empty teacup on the nightstand. "I'll take your stuff to the Jeep while you pack the tea set."

I grabbed her bags and headed for the Jeep. When I returned to the room, she handed me the box with the tea set.

"For you," she said. "Happy birthday."

When we arrived at Tan Son Nhut Air Base, Seth borrowed a Jeep and took Sarah to headquarters, then dropped me off at the women's quarters while he and Buzz loaded the supplies on the chopper. After two and a half months in the highlands, I'd forgotten how suffocating the tropical heat could be at the lower altitudes. The first thing I wanted was a shower, but by the time Seth picked me up, I'd be a walking bead of sweat. So I'd put the three hours to good use. First, a nap. Seth had made arrangements for me to use an unoccupied room in one of the hooches for the afternoon. Apparently his reputation as a crack Dust Off pilot opened doors.

LuAnn Something-or-other, a black WAC with a moderate Afro, was waiting for me in front of the hooch.

"You must be someone really special," she said as she led me to my room.

*Why would she say that?* I wondered, dabbing my sweaty forehead with my sleeve.

I knew why when she opened the door. A vase of white gardenias sat on the nightstand, filling the room with their exotic fragrance. A flowered bedspread draped over the single bed, which was pushed lengthwise against a wall. Two pillows in matching pillow shams leaned against the wall, giving the setting a daybed look. And wedged between the curtained window panes was—oh, heaven!—an air conditioner, running full blast.

Clutching my purse, overnight bag, and dress, I stepped to the nightstand. A small white envelope with "Evangeline" neatly written in blue ink nestled among the shiny dark green leaves. How did he manage all this? I turned to LuAnn, who stood just inside the doorway.

"How? Who?" I stammered.

Her brown eyes twinkled. "Let's just say Captain Martin called in a few favors."

"Oh." I dropped my purse and overnight bag on the bed, then hung my dress on the locker door.

"The shower's two hooches down, to the left as you go out the back door," LuAnn said. "If there's anything you need, I'm next door. First room on the right."

"Thanks," I said as she turned to go. "Wait! You wouldn't happen to have a hair dryer, would you?"

"As a matter of fact," she said, a grin spreading across her high cheekbones, "I do."

After giving me instructions for using the hair dryer—"If it shuts off while you're using it, just give the motor a few hard taps"—LuAnn left. Now I could read the card. I lifted the white envelope from its bed of green leaves and studied the handwriting. I didn't even know if it was his.

*You're a fool, Blanchard. You think you're in love with the guy, and you can't even recognize his handwriting.*

I slid the florist's card from the envelope. There was no name on the "Happy Birthday" card—only three words: "Remember the nightingale."

CHAPTER NINE

# DINNER DATE

When LuAnn rapped on the door and announced Seth had arrived, I was still fighting with my hair.

"Aw, nuts!" I said, tossing my hairbrush on the bed.

"Calm down, sweetie pie," LuAnn drawled. "What time'd he say he'd be here . . . 1700 hours?" She glanced at her wristwatch. "You're all right. He's fifteen minutes early."

I'd never had a date show up on time, let alone early. "Cool your tool, sweetheart," Bill would say in that laidback way of his. "I'm here, aren't I?" The guys I dated after Bill seemed to run half an hour behind and couldn't understand my ire when they finally showed their faces.

Falling asleep while drying my hair hadn't helped either. LuAnn's contraption had lived up to her warning. By the time I woke up and realized the dryer had shut off, I'd lost half an hour.

Stomping my foot on the wooden floor, I yanked out the bobby pins that refused to hold my tresses in a French twist.

"Look at me!" I choked. "I'm still in my slip, I just snagged my only pair of pantyhose on the floor, and—"

"You'll be fine," LuAnn said, with a dismissive wave of her hand. "Why don't you put on your dress while I tell Romeo you'll be a few minutes?"

Good idea. Dress first, then the hair. Maybe LuAnn could help me get it to stay up. I slipped the black satin over my head and pulled the sequined straps over my shoulders, hooking them together at the nape of my neck. I tugged at the back zipper then adjusted the sequined bow just above my waist. I eyed myself in the full-length mirror. The dress wasn't as snug as the last time I'd worn it, when Bill proposed—and I turned him down—but at least it didn't hang off me. The V-neckline revealed just enough to hopefully whet Seth's appetite.

"Do you think this is too short?" I asked LuAnn when she returned.

Her Afro bounced as she shook her head. "Just a couple of inches above your knees. You got great legs, honey. Show 'em off." She folded her arms across her chest and frowned. "But a couple minor details."

I smoothed the slim-line pencil skirt over my hips. "Panty lines showing?"

"That, too."

"What should I do?"

"Take 'em off. That's what pantyhose are for."

Off came the black lace bikini undies. Too scratchy anyway.

"What else?" I asked, shifting my weight from one hip to the other while I pulled the hose over my thighs.

"Does that dress have a lining?"

"Yes, why?"

"You don't need the slip."

"Good point." I tugged the half-slip from under the dress and tossed it on the bed.

"The bra's gotta go, too," she said.

I bristled. "I'm not one of those braless hippies. I'm wearing the bra."

"Suit yourself. But with that open back, you need one of those backless numbers."

I twisted around, surveying my reflection. Sure enough, the top of the bra stretched across my back, the base line of a triangle of black lace and sequined satin.

"What'll I do?"

"How tight's the bodice? Tight enough so the girls don't bounce?"

I tugged at the seams under my arms, slipping my thumbs between the dress and my skin to see how snug the top fit.

"I just won't fast dance," I said, dropping the bra on the bed.

"Now for your hair," she said, snatching the hairbrush from the bed. "Sit down. I was the best beautician south of the Mason-Dixon Line before I became the best supply clerk in Southeast Asia."

"It won't stay up," I said, lowering myself to the bed. "It's too long and thick. I should have trimmed it a month ago."

"I don't know what you're worried about," she said, sweeping the bristles expertly through my mane. "Most gals would kill to have silky hair like this."

"But it won't hold a curl. Never did. Not even before the humidity made it impossible to dry, let alone style. I've been thinking about cutting it short, like the Beatles."

"Suit yourself," she said, fastening a side section behind my ear with a bobby pin. "But tonight, Juliet, you're wearing it down. Shut your eyes."

A cool mist drifted on my cheeks as she waved a can of unscented hair spray over my head. Then she plucked a gardenia from the vase and secured it behind my ear on the swept-back side with a couple of bobby pins.

"Earrings?" she asked.

"Just what I'm wearing."

"Back in a minute," she said, scooting out the door.

"Here," she said, handing me a pair of diamond-studded danglies when she came back. "These'll go with your dress a lot better than those gold hoops."

I waved my hands in refusal. "I can't. What if I lose them?"

"You won't," she said. "Besides, they're not real."

I slipped the silver wire loops through the pierced holes in my lobes. "They're perfect."

"This too," she said, handing me a matching bracelet.

"Thank you, LuAnn." I fastened the silver clasp on my left wrist. "I'll get these back to you tonight."

"Keep 'em," she said, plucking a loose thread from the front of my dress. "I never wear 'em. They were a gift from someone I'd rather forget."

"You sure?"

"As sure as I am that if Captain Martin isn't already in love with you, he will be by the time the night's over."

I glanced at the vase of gardenias. "You keep the gardenias."

Her eyebrows arched. "You sure?"

I nodded.

"Thanks, Lieutenant." She cocked her head. "Sounds like a Jeep just pulled up. Get your shoes on. I'll pack up your stuff."

While LuAnn gathered my things and stuffed them into my overnight bag, I slipped on my black patent leather heels and buckled the ankle straps. Then I surveyed my reflection in the mirror.

LuAnn whistled. "You're gonna vamp him tonight, for sure."

"How can I ever thank you enough?"

"Just don't break his heart," she said, handing me my bag. "He's a real special guy around here."

I gave her a hug. "I won't."

Seth was pacing the broken sidewalk, hands shoved in his pressed trouser pockets, his back to me, when I stepped out of the hooch. I stood on the top step, enjoying the way I felt when I looked at him. If I thought him handsome in his loose, wrinkled, sweaty jungle fatigues, the sight of him in his crisp short-sleeved shirt, pressed uniform trousers, and black leather dress oxfords sent my heart to my throat.

Wolf whistles and cat calls sounded from across the street. "Hey, babe, I'm available." Seth turned to face me. His jaw dropped. What I saw in his eyes that moment told me everything I needed to know.

"Let's get going," I said, tossing him my overnight bag. "I'm hungry. I haven't eaten all day."

Heads turned as Seth escorted me across the Tan Son Nhut general's mess hall. Although "mess" hardly described the place. Crisp white linen tablecloths draped the tables. Wall sconces decorated the wood-paneled walls, which reflected a soft sheen in the low light. Music played softly in the background while diners mingled, chatting over hors d'oeuvres and shrimp cocktail. It was more like a classy restaurant in the middle of Manhattan than a military mess in the middle of a war zone. We followed the waiter to a corner table with a vase of gardenias. I glanced around. No other table had flowers.

"What'll you have to drink?" Seth asked me when we were seated in the molded captain's chairs.

"Water. If it doesn't taste like sulfur."

"They bring in bottled water."

"Water, then. Lots of ice."

"Water for the lady—lots of ice, please—and a lemonade for me," he told the uniformed waiter.

"You're not drinking?" I asked him after the waiter left.

"Don't drink. Even if I did, I couldn't. I'm flying tonight. Remember?"

I frowned. "I thought you were off until tomorrow night."

"I am. But we're flying back to Pleiku tonight after dinner."

My cheeks grew warm. "I knew that. It's just that for a moment I forgot where we were."

He reached across the table and grasped my hand. His palm felt like sandpaper—rough and dry. He leaned toward me, his eyes peering into mine.

"Your eyes. They're violet tonight. Don't you have your contacts in?"

I glanced away. "I'm wearing a spare pair. They're clear."

A tender smile tugged at his lips. He knew why I chose the clear contacts. "Let's order," he said, releasing my hand. "I'm hungry."

We ordered filet mignon—medium for me and rare for Seth—and baked potatoes with sour cream. Oh, heaven, I hadn't had real food like this since I'd left the States. I felt like a country bumpkin visiting the big city for the first time. I was ready to plunge my fork into my salad when Seth reached across the table and grabbed my hand, bowed his head, and said a blessing. Somehow I wasn't surprised.

"How did you come to be so religious?" I asked him as I poured house dressing on my salad.

"I'm not religious," he said.

I lifted my water glass and took a sip. "What do you call it when you bow your head and say grace in a restaurant?"

"Obedient."

I didn't feel like getting into another discussion about religion—I was still trying to make sense of everything Sarah told me. So I asked him about his family, a safe topic.

"Dad's a college professor at Penn State. Mom teaches elementary school in State College. No brothers and sisters. No aunts and uncles."

"Being an only child is lonely," I said, dabbing sour cream on my potato.

"Your parents still in Johnstown, where you grew up?"

I swallowed. Maybe this wasn't such a safe subject after all. "You could say that."

He watched me as I cut my steak. "Is it too tough?"

"Being an orphan? Sometimes."

"I meant the steak. You're not slicing, you're sawing. So hard the table's shaking."

This wasn't the table conversation I had planned. "The steak's fine," I said, blinking back the tears and trying to swallow the lump in my throat that choked me every time I thought of my parents. Seth reached across the table and pushed a stray strand of hair behind my ear.

"Tell me about it."

I took a breath. "I'd always wanted to be a nurse. Ever since I was a little girl. I'd go around the house saying, 'I'm going to be a nois with a pois.' I couldn't say my r's. Then my father died from cancer in my senior year in high school. He'd been laid off from the steel mill for several years before that, so whatever money they'd saved for nursing school was gone by then. His life insurance paid just enough to bury him."

He nodded, encouraging me to continue.

"It was Mickie's idea—to enlist in the Army and let Uncle Sam pay for nursing school. But my mother refused to sign for me. I was furious. She wanted me to work as a nurse's aide in the local hospital. 'Just think of the money you'll save if you live at home,' she said. She'd cook for me and do my laundry."

"But that would have smothered your independent spirit."

I nodded. "We were too much alike. I accused her of manipulating me, of controlling me, of destroying my dreams, my life. I gave her so much grief that she gave in. 'You'll end up in Vietnam,' she said. I told her they only send the ones who volunteer. I was safe. Three years later she was dead, and I was on a plane to Vietnam."

"Regret is a terrible thing to live with."

"I don't regret that I was sent here. I've learned a lot. I'm tougher than I thought I was. Whatever they throw at me, I can handle."

He nodded. "War will either make you or break you."

"What I regret is how I treated her. I never had a chance to tell her I was sorry, to make it up to her."

He rubbed my cheek with the back of his hand. "I'm sure she understood, kemosabe. She was young once, too."

"I hope . . ." I stopped myself just in time.

"Hope what, Evangeline?"

"Nothing. What's for dessert?"

He blinked then picked up the dessert menu. "Chocolate, strawberry, or pineapple sundae."

"What's there to choose? Chocolate, of course."

After we finished our sundaes—served in real parfait glasses—he took me to the Officers' Club, which was just as classy as the officers' mess. But noisier. Way noisier, with rock and roll blaring from the speakers instead of soft dinner music.

"What'll you have?" he asked me after escorting me to a table. My skin tingled where his hand rested against my bare back, where his lips brushed against my ear.

"Cola. Lots of ice."

My soul thrilled as I watched him shoulder his way through the crowd to the bar to order our sodas.

"Well, lookee who's here!" A mean voice punctured the moment. I looked up into Bubba's sneering face.

"Come on, sweetie. Let's dance."

"No thanks."

He grabbed my arm. "Come on, honey. The good captain won't mind."

I pulled my arm away. He bent over, his beer breath reeking in my face.

"Hot temper? I like a woman with spunk. Bet you're hot in bed, too."

I slapped him. Hard. He raised his hand as if to strike me back, then stopped. He glanced at the bar, then spat on the floor beside my shoe.

I glared at him. "Did you get a promotion, Sergeant? Or did you beg, borrow, or steal that lieutenant's shirt?"

Hatred glowed from his narrowed eyes.

"Just as I thought," I said. "Get out of here, Wilcott. Don't even bother to wipe your slime off the floor."

CHAPTER TEN

# BULLIES AND HEROES

"Enough ice?" Seth placed a filled tumbler on the wooden tabletop in front of me and sat down. I shivered.

"Cold?" he asked, sliding his chair closer to mine.

"A little. I'm not used to AC anymore." Which was only part of the truth. Bubba's sudden appearance had rocked me to the core. I'd thought I'd seen the last of him when we deplaned at Long Binh. He scared me—even more than the nightly rocket attacks. But I wasn't about to show it.

Putting his arm around me, Seth rubbed my bare arm. "Dancing will warm you up."

I glanced at the bobbing crowd on the dance floor. And thought of "the girls."

"Maybe the next slow set?" I said, my lips to his ear, loving the feel of his fingers caressing my arm.

"What are these red marks?"

I looked at my upper arm where Bubba had gripped me.

"What happened?"

What was I to say? I told him.

"Good for you, Evangeline. Standing up to a bully is the only way to let him know he can't control you."

"That's what my dad would say when Spike harassed me."

"Spike?"

"The neighborhood bully. He always managed to know when I went to the drugstore for an ice cream cone. He'd wait until I was halfway home, then jump out, grab my cone, and threaten to smear it in my face. Then one day I realized he never did it—only threatened. So I called his bluff. 'Go ahead,' I said. I'll never forget the look on his face."

Seth chuckled. "Bet he left you alone after that."

I shook my head. "The next time he grabbed my ice cream cone, he licked the whole thing and handed it back. I took one look at my ruined ice cream cone—it was chocolate—then smeared it in his face."

*Take that, you big bully. Don't you ever bother me again.*

Seth chuckled. "Good for you, Evangeline."

"After that he left me alone—for a while." I sipped my cola and shivered again, remembering. "When I was a freshman in high school, he started being nice to me, even asked me out."

"I hope you turned him down."

I shook my head. "I thought he'd changed. He carried my books, left Hershey's kisses in my locker. I wasn't allowed to date until I was sixteen, but my parents allowed me to go with him to his class picnic at the end of the school year."

Even after all these years, the memory still made me sick. I swallowed. "He persuaded me to go for a walk along a trail in the woods—just him and me. Then, when he got me alone in a secluded meadow, he tried to rape me."

"Tried?"

"I'd been taking judo."

"Ouch. I almost feel sorry for the jerk."

"Don't. He started spewing his poison. He called me 'Vangie the Virgin.' It stuck. Everyone was scared of him, so they joined in the name calling and ridicule. Until I graduated, Mickie was the only one who stuck by me. And Bill."

Seth pulled me to him. Resting my head on his shoulder, I nuzzled in the crook of his neck, inhaling the pungent scent of his cologne.

His lips brushed my forehead. "Then Spike was finally out of your life."

"I wish." Tears slipped out of my eyes. "He was the drunk driver that killed my mother."

"Hey, you two, cuddling time ain't till later."

Buzz pulled out a chair across the table and plunked his drink down in front of him. Reluctantly I pulled away from Seth, who handed me his handkerchief.

"Wow, Vange," Buzz said, leaning toward me. "You look fantastic! Never saw you with your hair down and all dressed up." He winked at Seth. "Big plans for tonight, huh?"

My face warmed. I glanced at Seth. A blush spread from his cheeks to his ears.

"There'd better not be any alcohol in that glass," he said, pointing to Buzz's drink. "We're flying out in an hour."

Buzz grinned. "No, we're not. That's what I came to tell you. Charlie's launched a nastier than usual rocket attack on the air base."

"We've dodged rockets before."

"It's crazy. Everyone knows all they do is set it up, point the thing in the general direction, and light the fuse. Any hit they get is pure luck."

"Unless some hooch maid smuggled a map of the base and gave it to them." Seth stood. "Keep Evangeline company, Buzz, while I find overnight accommodations for her."

"Sit down, Cap. It's already taken care of. I took the liberty of finding—and securing—an unoccupied trailer in the officers' living section."

I could tell Buzz was trying to keep a straight face.

"For who?" Seth asked.

It was Buzz's turn to blush. "For . . . uh . . . for Vangie, of course."

"That won't do."

"Why not?"

"Because she'll be all alone in that trailer."

*Not if you stay with me.*

"If you're so afraid of leaving her alone, then stay with her. For cryin' out loud, Cap, it's only one night."

Seth snorted. "And her honor. No, Buzz. I won't have the gossip mongers eating this up. I'm going to make a few calls. Maybe she could stay in LuAnn's hooch."

He planted a soft kiss on my cheek. "I'll be right back."

He turned to Buzz. "Stay with her, Buzz. Stick to her like glue, if you have to. And if some tall, meaty clown with black curly hair and a sneer on his ugly face drops by, tell him I want to talk to him."

The tumbler slipped out of my hand and landed on the table so hard, ice cubes jumped out and into the floor. "No. I can take—"

But he'd already left.

"Does that tall, meaty clown with an ugly face happen to be a bully by the name of Bubba?"

I nodded. "He asked me to dance a few minutes ago. I said no."

"I passed him outside when I was coming in. He was shooting his revolver in the air and shouting obscenities. Drunk as a skunk. A couple of MPs came and got him, but because his daddy's some big shot in Washington, all he'll get is a slap on the wrist."

I grabbed my handbag and stood. "I'm going to the ladies' room. This smoke is making my eyes burn."

I was halfway across the room when I realized someone was following me. I spun around. "Buzz! What are you doing?"

He grinned. "Following orders."

"Well, you can't come into the ladies' room with me."

He shrugged. "I'll wait outside the door."

"Suit yourself." I turned and bumped my way through the crowd with Buzz at my elbow. In the restroom, I freshened my makeup. An officer's trailer! I peered at my reflection in the mirror. Vangie the

Virgin had no clue how to seduce a man. I used my last tissue to dab my burning eyes, then stuffed it back in my handbag.

True to his word, Buzz was right outside the door. On the way back to the table, he ordered refills—a cola for me, lots of ice, and a 7 and 7 for himself.

"Seth's lucky to have a friend like you," I told Buzz when we'd settled in our seats at the table. I was hoping Seth would be there, but he wasn't. "How long have you known him?" I asked.

"Two years. I've lost count of the missions we've flown. Do you know he's been nominated for the Medal of Honor?"

"He's never said anything."

"He won't."

"Were you with him?"

He nodded.

"Tell me about it."

He glanced around the smoky room then nodded. "Let me know when you see him coming. He gets upset when it's brought up."

I positioned my chair so I could see the door. Buzz scooted his chair closer to mine so I could hear him above the music.

"It was about a year ago. Early October. A Vietnamese unit on the border had come upon a VC training camp. Fortified bunkers, the whole nine yards. They were trapped in the high grass. Charlie wanted to make sure they wouldn't get out.

"We'd already flown seven hours. We were still in the air when the call came in. Took us forty minutes to get there. We flew through some horrendous rain and thunderstorms—it was towards the end of the monsoon season here in the highlands. We had no communication with the ground troops, so we had no idea how many injured or dead were scattered down there. And we had no protection."

"What about the gunships?" I asked.

"Left to refuel and rearm. Cap went in twice, but they were keeping low in the tall grass. Any movement would've meant death. Cap circled again, higher, out of range, figuring they'd see us. Finally we saw someone waving a shirt. Cap didn't want to use the hoist. When we use the hoist, see, we have to hover two hundred feet above the jungle and hold that position. We make an easy target. So Cap dropped down beside him, and we pulled him on board. They started popping up and waving. We picked them all up—right in front of Charlie's gunners. They got one guy. But that's all."

"Just one? Amazing."

"We took them to Moc Hoa, a Special Forces camp, refueled, and headed back. We flew low, just above the grass. I was at the controls, and Cap was with Eddie, hanging out the door on the skids and pulling the wounded on board. All this, of course, while under fire."

"That must have been terrifying," I said. "It's a miracle you all weren't killed."

"By this time, I was past being scared. We lost the radio and most of the instruments, and the transmission took some hits. When we got back to camp with the second load, we found out they got the main rotor. Hydraulic fluid was leaking all over the place. There were still wounded out there, so out we went again, Cap at the controls.

"We had nine men aboard when we saw someone lying near one of the VC bunkers. So what does Cap do? He hovers backward so he could shield us from the fire that was sure to come from the bunker. Eddy grabbed the guy and started pulling him aboard. Just then a VC popped up in the grass in front of us and opened fire with his AK-47 at point-blank range.

"The windshield blew apart. Shattered Plexiglass flew everywhere, tore into Cap's leg and left hand, my left thigh and arm. Eddie yanked the guy into the chopper, and we got that baby out of there."

I was speechless. *Not without your wounded.* This must be the story I'd heard about him when I first came in-country while we were waiting at Long Binh.

"He always prays before we take off," Buzz continued. "I'm beginning to think that's why we aren't dead."

"Has he been telling stories again?"

I jumped. I hadn't seen Seth come in. How long had he been standing behind us? Just then Elvis's new hit, "The Wonder of You," began to play. I rose from my seat and grabbed his arm.

"I believe, Captain Martin, I promised you a slow dance."

CHAPTER ELEVEN

# A DIAMOND AND A CROSS

"How much did you hear?" I asked Seth during the second stanza, snuggling close to him.

"Enough."

His fingers caressed the skin on my back just above my dress. Goose bumps popped up on my arms.

"Buzz told me you get upset when it's brought up. Why?"

"I'm not a hero, Evangeline. I did what any other pilot would have done."

"That's debatable." I arched my neck back to look at him. "Don't be angry with Buzz. I asked him to tell me."

The muscle in his cheek twitched, then he smiled. "Okay, he's off the hook." He pulled me closer, his freshly shaven face against mine.

"So where am I staying tonight?" I asked. "Did you get hold of LuAnn?"

"No. I'm sorry. I called around, but nothing's available." He sighed. "Looks like it's the trailer. Buzz and I will be staying, too. In another room, of course. I struck out trying to find another female to stay with you. I'm sorry."

*I'm not.* "Why do you keep apologizing? You tried."

"Because I know what it'll look like, how the gossip flies. The last thing I want is to ruin your reputation."

"You *are* old-fashioned, aren't you? I mean, look at what goes on here. Who would care?"

"I would."

"Why?"

"Because I . . ." He took a breath. "You're not like the other nurses, Evangeline. Or any woman I've ever known. You've got a freshness, an innocence about you that's rare these days."

A mix of emotions churned in me. Guilt for what I'd planned—I mean, I had no underwear on. Thankful that I'd said no to Bill. Glad, for once, to be Vangie the Virgin.

His fingers traced my lips. "You're tough yet tender. You fight for the underdog. You stand up to bullies."

I giggled. "Wait. Let me get my cape."

The music stopped, but we kept dancing. Then "Bridge over Troubled Water" began to play.

"I love this song," I said, putting both arms around his neck and clasping my fingers.

He put his lips against my ear and sang softly. His gesture was awfully sweet—and sweetly awful. He might be a crack pilot, but he was tone deaf. I stifled a giggle.

"I hope you don't aspire to become a singer," I said.

He grinned. "That's another thing I love about you—your total, or should I say brutal, honesty." An intense look replaced his grin. "Marry me."

My heart jumped to my throat. I stopped dancing. Did I hear him right? He took my face in his hands, his thumbs caressing my cheeks, those blue eyes pouring into mine. "I love you, Evangeline. I've loved you from the moment I set eyes on you."

A joy I'd never known flooded me. *This is what love is supposed to feel like.*

"On the plane," I murmured, snuggling closer, loving the sound of his heartbeat, the musky scent of his cologne.

"Sooner. At Travis. There you were, cuddled up on your gear, trying to get some sleep, that long, black mane pulled up off your neck . . ." He ran his fingers through my hair in a soft caress that tingled every nerve ending in my body. "Don't ever cut it."

Someone bumped into us. "Hey! You gonna dance or hog up the middle of the floor?"

"Sorry," Seth said. We started a slow side-to-side step again. I shifted in his arms, arching back to gaze at his face.

"I'm sorry for the way I behaved after you brought me the lamp and blanket," I said.

He planted a soft kiss at the end of my nose. "Forgiven."

"I was afraid. . . . Sarah and Dan. So I pushed you away."

His lips brushed my forehead. "I understood. War's not exactly the setting for romance."

"Did I ever thank you? I don't remember. Thank you."

He sighed, his arms tightening around me. "Do you always talk a romantic moment to death? Or is that your way of turning me down?"

I stopped dancing. Placing my hands on either side of his face, I gazed into his eyes.

"No," I whispered.

The muscle in his cheek twitched.

"I mean, no, it's not my way of turning you down," I said.

"Do you want to think about it?" His voice sounded husky, strangled.

"I don't have to."

Disappointment clouded his eyes as he loosened his embrace.

"My answer is yes. I'll marry you."


We stayed up until midnight making plans. In the living room, of course. With Buzz snoring away in one of the two bedrooms. Both our tours were less than half over. His was up in June, mine in August. A wedding back home would be nine, ten months away. Major Lennon's words haunted me: *He was shot down on his last mission.*

"Can't we get married here?" I asked over a second cup of coffee. The Moody Blues sang softly in the background. The trailer came fully furnished, including a top notch stereo system with a stack of albums, most of them recent. I'd changed into a pair of cutoffs and a tie-dyed T-shirt. Seth still wore his uniform pants, but had shed the dress shirt and tie.

"If that's what you want."

"I do." I curled my bare feet under me on the soft leather sofa and turned to face him. Wisps of sandy hair coiled in the V-neck of this white T-shirt. "What about you? Is that what you want?"

"Yes. And no."

"Does that mean it's not what you want, but you'll go along with it because it's what I want?"

"You're putting words in my mouth, kemosabe."

Fear ran like ice through my veins. "You asked me to marry you on an impulse. You didn't expect me to say yes. Now you're trying to get out of it."

"Wait here," he said, getting up from the sofa. His size-twelve feet, still in his black dress socks, left imprints in the shag carpet as he stepped to the breakfast bar, where his shirt and tie hung over the back of a chair. I closed my eyes and leaned my head back against the sofa. *You really blew it this time, Vangie.* The leather on the cushion beside me squeaked as he sat down. I opened my eyes.

"Here," he said, handing me a white, rectangular jewelry box. "Happy twenty-first birthday."

"But I thought the flowers and the dinner were my birthday gifts."

His eyes twinkled. "Aren't you going to open it?"

My fingers shook as I pushed up on the lid of the hinged box. When I saw what it contained, I caught my breath. Resting on a bed of white velvet was a small gold cross on a gold chain. A tiny diamond embedded in its center sparkled in the lamplight as I lifted it from the case.

"Oh, Seth," I whispered. "It's beautiful." He took the necklace from my trembling fingers, undid the clasp, and slipped it around my neck.

"I had it made just for you," he said. "Gold, you see, is the most precious metal there is, and a diamond is the most valuable gem." Grasping my shoulders, he turned me to face him. "Always wear this, Evangeline, to remind you of how precious and valuable you are to me."

If I had any doubts, this gift—and his words—washed them away. Taking my chin in his rough hand, he kissed me, a soft kiss that stirred a tempest of longing.

"I will," I whispered, kissing the dimple on his cheekbone. "And in case I haven't told you, Captain Martin, I love you."

"Time to get up." Buzz's voice cut into my dream. I'd been shopping for a wedding gown, but all I could find were black cocktail dresses. I snuggled closer to Seth, but it was the back of the sofa I snuggled up against. I blinked. Buzz stood over me, two mugs of steaming coffee in hand.

"Where's Seth?" I asked, pulling myself to a sitting position.

He handed me one of the mugs. "In the shower."

"What time is it?"

"It's 0600. He wants to be airborne in an hour."

Last night. The proposal. Or did I dream it? My hands flew to my throat—and felt the dainty chain of the necklace. It was real. By the end of 1970—in seven weeks—I would be Evangeline Martin. I sipped my coffee then sputtered, choking down the bitter liquid.

"Too hot?"

"No. Too black." I shoved the scratchy military blanket aside—Seth must have covered me—and headed for the kitchen. "Sugar. I need sugar. And milk. There *is* milk around here, isn't there?"

I was rummaging through my overnight bag at the kitchen table, looking for the fatigues I'd worn on the trip down yesterday, when Seth walked in. The sight of him just out of the shower, freshly shaven and sandy crew cut still damp, filled my soul with longing.

"Good morning, love," he said, kissing me full on the lips and stirring up the desire even more. "Leave any coffee for me?"

"Plenty," I said, pulling a folded set of fatigues from my bag. "When are we leaving?"

He poured himself a mug of coffee then sat across from me. "I'd like to leave here in fifteen minutes—you *can* be out of the shower by then, can't you?"

"I'll shower when we get back to Pleiku," I said. "I can be ready in five."

He took a taste of his coffee, grimaced, then put the mug back on the table. "You have hot water here."

I shivered, thinking of the cold showers at Pleiku. "Good point," I said, getting up and pouring the rest of my coffee down the drain. "I'll be out in ten."

As I headed down the hall, I heard Seth's laugh. "Buzz, that's the worst stuff you've ever made! What did you do, fall asleep dumping the grains in?"

We landed at the Seventy-First midmorning, and, after we unloaded the medical supplies, Seth drove me to my hooch. As we turned the corner, my blood turned to ice. An ambulance, lights flashing, was parked in front. I scrambled out as soon as the Jeep came to a stop and sprinted up the sidewalk to the front door.

Inside, the sounds of muffled crying mingled with the voices of the medics. "Too late . . . bled out before we got here."

A group huddled together outside the door to Beth's room. I spotted Mickie's brown fuzz and headed for her. Before I got there, though, the crowd parted and a gurney with a body bag edged through. I scanned the group to see who was missing. Who was on duty? We watched wordlessly as the medics shoved the gurney in the back of the wagon. After they'd driven off, I turned to Mickie. Her face was ashen, her brown eyes wide with shock.

"Who . . ." I took a deep breath. "Who was in the body bag?"

Her bottom lip quivered. "Beth," she whispered. I could barely hear her.

"What happened?" I asked.

"Hooch maid stabbed her," DeeDee answered.

"Luu Thi Bian? Why?"

"I'll tell you why." Seth's angry voice sounded behind me. "Beth probably caught her with a map of the base."

"I heard shouting," DeeDee said. "Vietnamese and English. Then the sounds of a scuffle and something breaking."

"I rushed out of my room when I heard the yelling," Mickie said. "I saw her—Luu Thi Bian—rush out of Beth's room and run out the door. I found Beth on the floor beside the bed, her .45 in her hand."

Seth stepped into Beth's room, where Army personnel had begun their investigation. He returned in less than a minute, carrying the pistol in one hand, the magazine in the other.

"It wouldn't have done her any good," he said, holding up the empty magazine. "It wasn't even loaded."

DeeDee snorted. "Even if it was, she couldn't shoot it. She didn't know how. None of us do."

I draped my arm around Mickie's shoulders and guided her to my room. We sat on the bed. I fingered the necklace. How could I tell her my news now? I didn't want to wait too long. We wanted to be married in the Pleiku chapel before December 15—that's when the Seventy-First was being deactivated. Hopefully a two-week leave for the two of us would be approved so we could honeymoon in either Japan or Hawaii, before I had to report for duty at Qui Nhon.

I pulled a shivering Mickie to me and rubbed her back.

"I need a beer," she said.

"Good heavens, Mick, it's not even noon."

She shrugged. "Get me one. Please. My knees are mush. In my little fridge."

"No."

She pushed me away. "Then I'll get it."

I gripped her shoulders and lifted her chin, but she turned away, avoiding my eyes.

"What's happening to you?" I said softly.

She stared out the window, her body limp under my grasp. "Vietnam is what's happening to me." Her words were flat, her voice hoarse.

"Look at me."

She turned her face to me. Her lifeless eyes scared me.

"Don't do this to yourself. It's not worth it," I said. "Go home if you have to."

She snickered. "Like they'll let me. The only way you go home before your tour is up is in a body bag. You know what happens to those poor boys. We patch them up, and they send them back out. We patch them up again, and they send them back out again. Until we can't patch them up anymore." She started sobbing. "Will it ever end?"

I wrapped my arms around her and felt the hot tears running down my cheeks, too. I don't know how long we sat there, holding on to each other, sobbing—for Beth, for all the boys we couldn't fix, for all the ones we did, for what this war was doing to us—until the anger was spent.

"Promise me something," I said, plunking down a box of tissues on her lap.

"What?" She yanked out a couple of tissues.

"That you'll ease off the beer. And any alcohol, for that matter. You don't need it."

She blew her nose and dabbed her eyes then sat on the bed, once again staring out the window. I glanced around my room. My overnight bag and purse were on the floor just inside the door, and my garment bag hung on the door of my wall locker. *Seth.* I hadn't even heard him come in.

Mickie sniffled then turned to me, her glistening brown eyes filled with panic.

"What will I do? How will I cope?"

Sarah's words came back to me. *People give up on God when they need him most.*

I reached under my bed and pulled out the box she gave me.

"I'll tell you how," I said, opening it. "But first we're going to have tea."

CHAPTER TWELVE

# BEAUTY FROM ASHES

"It's no use." Mickie stomped her boot in the red dust, clearly disgusted. "This is my fourth time out, and I can't even hit the target, let alone the bull's-eye!"

Seth stepped beside her. "Are you holding your breath when you squeeze the trigger?"

"For the hundredth time—yes."

"Do it again. This time I'll watch."

She tossed her head, glared at him, then spread her legs in a shooting stance, feet shoulder-width apart. Gripping her .45 with both hands, she stretched her arms in front of her, aimed at the target fifty feet away, then pulled the trigger. BOOM! Fire flashed from the muzzle; her arms jerked upward with the recoil as the empty shell popped out and onto the ground. I held my breath against the acrid smell. After half an hour of this, I was sure lunch was going to taste like gunpowder.

"It would help, Lieutenant Molinetti, if you could keep at least one eye open when you shoot," Seth said. "And relax."

"You said to grip the handle firmly," Mickie said, giving him her best pout.

"Grip firmly, yes. Wring it to death, no. One more time. And keep those eyes open. Hold still until you see the round hit the target."

She snorted. "Like that's gonna happen. Why can't I rest my wrists on something solid? It'll help my aim—keep me from shaking so much."

"Because you have to be able to react quickly. In an emergency situation, hesitating for even a fraction of a second—"

"Okay, okay, I get it."

She nudged the red dirt with her boot, took her stance, inhaled sharply, then fired. This time her bullet pierced the outer ring.

"I hit it! I hit it!" She pumped her fist in the air, shooting me a triumphant look. "My one to your ten, Vange. But a hit nevertheless."

Seth grinned and nodded his approval. "See? I told you, you could do it." He glanced around the shooting range then checked his watch. "That's it for today, ladies. Be back here at 0900 hours tomorrow."

Mickie groaned. "That's my day off."

"I'll see you tomorrow, Lieutenant. And don't forget to pick up your empty shells."

After she left, Seth and I headed for the officers' mess for an early lunch.

"It's been approved, then?" I asked as we settled into our chairs.

"Ten days, from December sixteenth through the twenty-sixth," he said. "I booked the chapel for the sixteenth."

"Hawaii or Japan?" I asked.

He reached across the table and squeezed my hand. "Japan. I'll take you to Hawaii for our first anniversary. Unless, of course, Seth Junior is on the way."

My thumb caressed his hand. "What if it's a girl?"

He chuckled. "With women's lib, I'm sure by the time she's old enough, they'll have to allow girls in Little League."

"You and your baseball." I stirred sugar into my tea. "How's Buzz?"

Seth's copilot had requested compassionate leave to accompany Beth's body to her hometown in Ohio for burial. I'd been surprised when Seth told me they were cousins.

"Subdued. They denied his request. She wasn't a close enough relative. He was furious."

"I would be too," I said, squirting ketchup beside my fries. "They grew up together."

"Good thing it's been slow. He's too distracted to be of much use."

"Give him time, Seth. It's only been a week."

The pain from Beth's death hit afresh. And the fear. Even though we were rocketed nightly, I'd felt safe. The bunkers, though filthy and crawling with rats and snakes, protected us from the explosions. The rockets rarely, if ever, scored a direct hit. But the enemy had been closer than I'd imagined. She'd cleaned our rooms and sang while she hung our clothes on the line. She'd laughed at our jokes, even when she couldn't understand the punch line. All the while waiting for the opportunity to betray us. I shuddered.

"By the way, Annie Oakley, where'd you learn to shoot like that?"

Seth's voice jolted me out of my reverie. I blinked, refocusing my attention on the man across the table. Ketchup and mustard oozed out of the bun and dripped on his plate as he bit into his hamburger. "Is that a demotion? From kemosabe to Annie Oakley?" I asked, wiping a blob of mustard from his chin with my napkin.

He chuckled, his blue eyes twinkling. "Demoted? You? Never." He dipped one of his fries in my ketchup. "Seriously, Evangeline, you didn't acquire skill like that in basic."

"My dad taught me. He was an avid hunter. And since he had no sons . . ." The sadness welled up with the memory. "But I was a disappointment to him."

"I can't imagine you being a disappointment to anyone."

"I was ten when he started teaching me to shoot with a .22 caliber rifle he made himself. We'd go to the local rod and gun club every month. I wanted to make him proud, so I set up a target in our backyard. I'd gotten off only one shot when my mother came running out, screaming that I was going to kill someone. I think it was then I started wishing we lived in the country instead of a steel mill town with houses ten feet apart and a postage-stamp backyard."

I sipped my tea. "I was almost thirteen when he took me small game hunting for the first time. By then I had my own shotgun. Our gundog flushed out a ringneck. I froze. I couldn't shoot an innocent pheasant. I . . . I don't know how I'd ever kill a human being."

"When you're faced with life or death, you choose life. Every time. It's instinctive."

I shook my head. "I don't think—"

"*Don't* think, Evangeline. React. If you take time to think, you're dead."

The next two weeks were the busiest of my life. We were short by two nurses—Sarah and Beth hadn't been replaced, but it helped that some of the casualties that normally would have come to the Seventy-First were taken to the Sixty-Seventh Evacuation Hospital at Qui Nhon. I was relieved when Mickie informed me that she'd requested Qui Nhon. I couldn't imagine life without my best friend. Packing up all the medical supplies and equipment, preparing to deactivate the hospital, and planning a wedding left no time to process all that had happened. No time to grieve. No time to rejoice.

Since there wasn't time to shop for a wedding dress, I'd be married in my dress greens with Mickie as my maid of honor. Buzz would stand up for Seth as his best man. Seth took my high school class ring for size and picked up our wedding rings on a trip to Saigon for the Army. He had our gold bands engraved with our initials, SGM and EJB, and our wedding date, 12/16/1970.

The day before the wedding I received a package from Mama Rose. Inside I found a card addressed to "Captain and Mrs. Seth Martin," a small book wrapped in white tissue paper, a bottle of bubble bath secured in two bread bags, and a letter on her usual rose stationery.

"Dear Vangie, I am beside myself with happiness for you. Thank you for the picture of you and your soon-to-be husband. My, he's handsome! And from what you wrote in your letter, deserving of you. At last! I didn't want to say anything before, Cara Mia, but Bill wasn't for you. He can be a schlemiel at times.

"I wasn't sure of the proper way to address the wedding card. So I went with my gut feeling—'Captain' instead of 'Mr.' and 'Mrs.' instead of 'Lieutenant.' Speaking of which—Congratulations on your promotion to First Lieutenant. Michaelena wrote me with the news. I know you watch out for her, just like you always have. No easy task, I know. She can be a handful at times.

"I hope you get this before your wedding day. It will be the 'something old' that you carry down the aisle. May God keep you all safe, and may you have a long and happy life with the man of your heart. Love, Mama Rose."

I pulled away the tissue paper from the book and smiled softly. My mother's white prayer book, a gift from my father on their wedding day. I'd had it packed with my things that I stored in the Molinettis' attic. I opened the front cover. The blue ink, blurred with age, splotched in a couple of places, was still readable. "My dearest Elizabeth, May each word of this gift be a measure of my love for you—forever and always. Your devoted husband, Ray. May 19, 1945." Beneath the date, Mom had written, "I love you, Ray. Forever and always, Elizabeth. November 5, 1966." The day Dad died. My seventeenth birthday.

On December 16, 1970, in a brief morning ceremony with only five people in attendance, Seth and I promised to forsake all others and take each other for better or worse, richer or poorer, in sickness and health, "as long as we both shall live." I didn't want to use the phrase "till death do us part."

Seth easily slipped the ring on my finger, but I had trouble getting his over his knuckle. He winced as I pulled his finger toward me and shoved it in place—just as I remembered this was the hand that was injured when the windshield of the chopper shattered a year ago. *Sorry,* I mouthed. He took my face in his hands and kissed me. *Mrs.*

*Seth Gabriel Martin*, I thought, wrapping my arms around his neck. *Forever and always.*

We spent our first night as husband and wife in a plush hotel in downtown Saigon. Buzz flew us to the Tan Son Nhut Air Base from Pleiku in the chopper, which would get some much-needed repairs while we were gone. It was early evening by the time we arrived at the hotel, exhausted from the emotion and the travel.

When I saw the room, it was all I could do not to squeal like a schoolgirl. I didn't know which excited me most, the queen-size bed with a mattress more than an inch and a half thick or the deep, claw-foot bathtub.

"Why don't you take a nice, long soak?" my new husband suggested, kissing the back of my neck. Goose bumps sprouted on my arms.

"Married not even twelve hours, and you can read my mind already," I said, leaning back against his solid body.

"I'll go down to the restaurant and bring back supper. What'll you have?"

"Surprise me."

"That," he said, planting soft kisses on my bare shoulders, "is what I plan to spend the rest of my life doing, Mrs. Martin."

By the time I emerged from the bathroom an hour later, he'd had the small table by the picture window set with a white linen tablecloth, candles, china, and silverware. He sat in the overstuffed chair near the window, his chin on his chest, softly snoring. Tightening the sash of the silk kimono he'd given me as a wedding present, I stepped to him and curled up in his lap. His arms wrapped around me, and he buried his face in my hair.

"I thought you were sleeping," I said, snuggling closer. "Why is your hair wet, and why do you smell like chlorine?"

A crimson blush flooded his cheeks and ears. "I took a quick swim in the pool while I waited for our order."

"Didn't want to waste any time, did you?" I undid the top button of his shirt. "In that case, Captain Martin, we'd better get busy."

The next week and a half were heaven on earth. Okinawa surprised me with its breathtaking beaches and rich history. We spent our days sightseeing or just lounging on the beach. Wherever we went, Seth took along his artist's pad. His pencil sketches amazed me. He'd captured the beauty of the Vietnam countryside, the simplicity of the people, the hopeful faces of the wounded as they lay on the battlefield, looking up at approaching Dust Offs. Black-and-white portraits of Buzz, Beth, and Sarah and Dan. He'd managed to capture not just what they looked like, but their very essence. Their souls shone from their eyes.

"These are beautiful!" I said, flipping through the pages. "Did you study art?"

"Minored in it."

I closed the sketch pad and handed it back to him. "When we get back to the world, you can open a studio."

He grinned sheepishly. "I'm afraid I'll have to find a real job. I have a wife to support now."

We visited the Southeast Botanical Gardens, the Shuri Castle ruins in Naha, and the Gyokusendo, an extensive limestone cave on the southern part of the island.

"The Shuri Castle, the palace of the Ryūkyū Dynasty, was almost completely destroyed in 1945 during the Battle of Okinawa," Seth told me as we toured the ruins.

Sadness welled in me as I envisioned what it must have looked like. "War is hell," I said. "It destroys history, beauty, and lives."

"'I am sick and tired of war. Its glory is all moonshine. It is only those who have neither fired a shot nor heard the shrieks and groans of the wounded who cry aloud for blood, for vengeance, for desolation. War is hell.' Do you know who said that, Evangeline?"

I shook my head.

"General William Tecumseh Sherman."

"Oh."

"He also said, 'I hate newspapermen. They come into camp and pick up their camp rumors and print them as facts. I regard them as spies, which, in truth, they are. If I had my choice I would kill every reporter in the world, but I am sure we would be getting reports from Hell before breakfast.'"

I thought of how the newspapers back home skewed the facts to further their own agendas.

"He must have said that after Kent State."

He chuckled. "No, love. General Sherman served in the Civil War."

"Oh." I bit my lip. "I never was good in history. Or geography. I couldn't remember all those facts, no matter how hard I studied. Besides, I never understood how it would help me be a better nurse. How come you know so much?"

He grinned. "When your father's a history professor at Penn State, you don't dare bring home anything less than an A in the subject."

I batted my eyelashes. "And here I thought you'd studied up on it so you could impress your new wife."

A faint blush spread across his cheeks. "That too."

Our last day in heaven came all too soon.

When I awoke, I reached to his side of the bed. It was empty. I rolled on my side and opened my eyes. Seth sat by the window, his open Bible in his lap, head bowed, eyes closed. I lay watching him, imprinting to memory every line in his face, every hair on his head. His after-five shadow. His long, calloused fingers resting on the page. Once we got back to 'Nam, he'd drop me off at Qui Nhon, then fly the chopper back to Pleiku. My insides felt hollow. I missed him already. A lump rose in my throat. I squeezed my eyes shut to control the tears that threatened to spill out. *War is hell.* In the midst of hell, I'd found my heaven. Beauty from ashes.

What I didn't want to think about that last morning was how quickly beauty could turn back to ashes.

CHAPTER THIRTEEN

# QUI NHON

"Something big's coming down," Seth told me in the middle of January.

We were lying on the beach outside my villa at Qui Nhon, enjoying the view of the South China Sea and a rare two days together. I handed him a bottle of baby oil and rolled onto my stomach. Unscrewing the cap, he poured a small amount in his hand then smeared it over my back. Usually he said something like, "You're gonna fry, woman." But no wise cracks escaped his lips today. I waited until he settled down beside me.

"How big?" I asked.

He twirled a loose strand of my upswept hair around his index finger. The muscle in his cheek twitched.

"As big as, if not bigger, than the operation in May."

In May—a lifetime ago—I was finishing up nursing school, getting ready to go to Fort Sam for officers' basic training. I'd been too caught up with what was going on in my life at the time to pay much attention to what was happening on the other side of the world.

"What happened in May?" I asked.

"We launched an offensive in Cambodia, where Charlie had set up base camps, supply depots, and ammo stockpiles, thinking they were safe. U.S. troops, up to that time, weren't allowed in Cambodia, remember? The fighting lasted two months. We evacuated thousands of wounded under some of the worst conditions I've ever flown in. Because of the jungle canopy, we had to use the hoist for half the evacs."

Buzz's words came back to me: *When we use the hoist, we have to hover two hundred feet above the jungle and hold that position. We make an easy target.* A shiver shot up my spine.

"What's coming down?" I asked, twisting my wedding ring around my finger. The gold sparkled in the morning sun.

"Another major offensive. The success of the Cambodian strikes gives Washington the idea that we could do it again. In Laos."

More forbidden territory. I swallowed. "When?"

He stared at the incoming waves crashing on the shore. "Early next month."

Fear, like icy fingers, clutched at my insides.

He rolled over to face me, propping himself on his elbow. "I don't know when I'll see you again. I've been told this is my last leave until this Laos thing is over."

"But you'll still bring casualties to the Sixty-Seventh, won't you?" I asked.

"Yes, but I'll have to get back to Pleiku pronto."

My fingers traced the outline of his face. "We'll get through this, sweetheart. And someday we'll tell our children and grandchildren war stories while they roll their eyes."

He pulled me to him, his blue eyes intense. "If anything happens, Evangeline, you'll be all right. God will take care of you." Then he leaned over and kissed me.

The hospital at Qui Nhon inhabited a large, airy, permanent building right on the airstrip, not a handful of ramshackle Quonset huts bunched together. And, unlike Pleiku, it was well equipped. But the pace at the Sixty-Seventh was slow compared to the Seventy-First. When I reported for duty at the end of December, I'd bristled when

Major Lennon, who'd also transferred to Qui Nhon, told me she'd assigned me to the medical unit.

"This isn't a demotion, Lieutenant Martin. Your work in the OR at the Seventy-First was superb," she assured me. "However, I like to assign my nurses to a relatively non-busy area after they've worked in ER or OR—assignments that push you to the limit. Not that the medical unit isn't busy—it is. It's just not as intense and demanding."

She was right. Although the wards were full, the pace of the work wasn't as hectic. I didn't need to crash on my cot as soon as I returned to the third-floor room I shared with Mickie at the end of my twelve-hour shift. And my patients, unlike those at Pleiku, were conscious and able to talk, which helped to pass the time. And only a few of them left in a body bag.

"Guess who I saw today?" Mickie asked me one day after we got off work. I hadn't seen Seth for two weeks and was thankful she and I worked the same shifts.

"Who?" I said, nudging aside the fatigues I'd just shed and stepping into a pair of cutoffs.

"Come on, Vange, guess."

I slipped on an oversized T-shirt and sat on my bed. "I'm bushed after tending another FUO today. I can't even think right now."

"Those fever-of-unknown-origins can be buggers. All right, I'll give you a hint: he's tall, dark, and ugly—and wears a constant sneer on his face."

I pulled my hair tie out and shook my ponytail loose. "I don't know, Mick. Who?"

"Sergeant Robert William Wilcott. Otherwise known as Bubba the Bully."

My jaw dropped. "Did he come into ER?"

"Nope. Saw him walking to the mess."

"I thought he was at Tan Son Nhut."

"He's stationed here, Vange. Just got transferred."

I stared at her.

"I was on my way to the officers' mess for an early lunch—things were slow today—and I saw him walking with a couple of other grunts. So I followed him."

"Mick!"

"Relax, Vange. He didn't see me. And even if he did, he wouldn't know me from Eve."

"Not if he spied that fuzzy mop of yours."

"I don't think he ever really saw me on the plane back in August, Vange. He only had eyes for you."

I snorted. "Yeah, right."

She bent down and yanked open the door of the small refrigerator she brought from Pleiku and pulled out a can of cola. Our talk after Beth got killed did some good. She hadn't had a drop of alcohol since. And she attended Sunday services with me in the base chapel.

"Do you happen to have another cola in there?" I asked.

"Last one." She tossed me the can.

"Thanks." I caught it, then put the frosty can on the nightstand between our beds.

"Aren't you going to open it?"

"When I can do so without pop spurting all over the place. It feels awfully cold. How high do you have that thing set?"

"As high as it can go." She shoved a pile of clothes aside and plopped on her mattress.

"Are you sure it's safe? I get shocked whenever I open it. Maybe you should replace it."

She rolled her brown eyes. "Relax. It's only a little short in the wiring or something. Besides, I haven't found another used one, and a new one costs way more than my meager budget can handle."

"Sometimes, my friend, you're too practical. You hang on to things too long."

"It comes with being the oldest of six in a poor Italian family."

"You weren't poor, Mick. Just a little hard up at times. Nevertheless, there's a time to keep and a time to cast away. If you want my opinion—and I'm sure you don't—it's time to cast away that piece of junk. It's a fire hazard."

"A time to cast away—isn't that from that song we liked in high school? 'Turn, Turn, Turn' by The Byrds. To everything . . ."

*That phrase wasn't in the song,* I was about to say, but I didn't feel like explaining that I'd found it in Seth's Bible. I'd picked it up one morning when he was in the shower and opened to the page he had bookmarked. *To everything there is a season, a time to every purpose under heaven.* I copied the verse, and the next seven, in my journal. I'd read Ecclesiastes in high school religion class but never had those words impacted me like they did that morning on our honeymoon. It was as though they jumped out at me.

"You have a good memory," I said to Mickie. "Now tell me about my nemesis."

"I was shocked, Vange. Next to the VC—and a traitorous hooch maid—Bubba's the last person I care to meet up with. Especially here. It's heaven compared to Rocket City. We haven't been shelled since we got here."

"Can you ever stay on topic?"

She shrugged and sipped her cola. "He and his buddies sat at a table next to the wall, which made it easy to eavesdrop. They didn't even notice when we put our trays on the table next to theirs."

"You ate in the grunts' mess?"

"What I wouldn't do for a friend. Anyway, he was pretty PO'd about something. Didn't even bother to lower his voice. So I found out some pretty interesting stuff."

"Like what?"

"Like he got in big trouble for impersonating an officer when you saw him in Tan Son Nhut."

"I thought his father got him off the hook."

She smirked. "Not this time. He said his old man flew over after the lieutenant T-shirt affair and threatened to have him dishonorably discharged if he didn't clean up his act."

"I wonder why he'd go to such lengths. Why not just pull some more strings?"

"His congressional aide job was on the line. Guess they're getting tired of helping Daddy-O get his naughty little boy out of trouble. Did you know Seth wrote him up for disrespectful conduct toward an officer after the plane fiasco? And get this—his dad warned him not to mess with a Medal of Honor recipient—and that includes his wife. Is Seth getting the Medal of Honor?"

I shrugged. "He hasn't said anything."

"He wouldn't. He's the humblest hero I've ever met."

"Did Wilcott say anything else?"

Mickie squirmed on her mattress. "Just that he asked to be transferred here."

"Did he say why?"

She looked away. "He said he had a score to settle."

The first week in February Mickie and I accompanied Dr. Harvey Bell, an eye surgeon from the Sixty-Seventh, on a Medcap to the Qui Hoa Leper Hospital nearby. Since we'd be traveling on unsecured roads, more than the usual guards accompanied us. I was helping Harvey and Mickie pack supplies in the Jeep when I heard Bubba's voice. I almost didn't recognize it without his sneering tone.

"Need some help, ma'am?"

"No, thank you, Sergeant. This is the last box."

I didn't sense his usual hostility. The talking-to his father gave him might have done some good. Then again, maybe he had some devious plan up his sleeve and was biding his time.

"What's *he's* doing here?" Mickie whispered, settling in the back seat next to me.

I shrugged. "I'd rather pretend he's not, if you don't mind."

She glanced at the Jeep behind us. "Good luck."

"I think I died and went to heaven!" Mickie said as we pulled up to a well-maintained, white facility. "It's so beautiful—and so quiet. Like there's no war going on outside of this little valley. No wonder the guys fight over who gets guard duty for these Medcaps."

"The Vietnamese are afraid of lepers," Dr. Bell said. "So they leave them alone. Even the VC don't bother them."

While the guards unpacked our supplies, Mickie and I found a restroom, where I lost my breakfast.

"Bumpy roads," I explained when Mickie raised her eyebrows at me. "My stomach's been a little unsettled ever since I saw Seth last. I don't know when I'll see him again."

While Mickie and one of the medics made rounds, I assisted Dr. Bell in the OR. I enjoyed working in a well-organized, sanitary hospital for a change. Qui Nhon was a big improvement over Pleiku, but it was still a far cry from this place. The tile floors shone, the louvered windows glistened in the morning sun, and the wards weren't overcrowded. And each patient had a clean bed. Just thinking about the conditions at Pleiku brought shame, embarrassment, and pity for the boys who deserved more.

My stomach still hadn't settled down, so, to keep my mind off the queasiness, I chatted with Dr. Bell while we worked.

"Leprosy isn't the horrible disease most people imagine," he told me. "The biggest problem is misinformation. If it's treated properly in its early stages, the patient has a good prognosis. It's not always fatal. Unfortunately, they let it go until it's too late."

"I noticed quite a number of people here who don't appear to have leprosy. Are they aides?" I asked.

"Most of them are families of the lepers," he said. "Once they move into the colony, they're not allowed back home. So they bring their families with them. The disease isn't as contagious as most people think. It's actually caused by a virus that nine out of ten people have a natural immunity to. So the isolation isn't really necessary."

"So we can't get it by touching someone with the disease?"

He shook his head. "Only continuous close contact over a long period of time puts one at risk."

We finished our work by early afternoon then went to lunch, which the French nuns who ran the facility had prepared. I ate light. The nausea had passed, but I didn't want to take any chances. The trip back would be just as bumpy, and I didn't want my lunch all over my traveling companions.

"The architecture of the building—is it French?" I asked Dr. Bell as I dipped a tea bag in a cup of hot water.

"Yes, it is," he said, smearing butter on his croissant. "I'm impressed you recognized it."

"I took French in high school and, along with the language, learned about the country, including the architecture."

"Then you know that Vietnam was once a French colony?" he said.

I nodded.

"Hence the French architecture you encounter in this strange, war-torn country," he said. "But that's about the only influence the French had—on the buildings. The Vietnamese hated them."

"Do you know Vangie's French?" Mickie blurted.

He raised his eyebrows. "With a name like Martin, I never would've suspected it."

"My maiden name is Blanchard," I said. "My paternal grandparents emigrated from France after the First World War."

"Your *maiden* name? You're married?"

"She got hitched in December," Mickie said.

He frowned. "I don't encounter many married nurses in-country. In fact, I don't think I ever have."

"She met him here," Mickie said, her voice dripping with pride. "He's a Dust Off pilot."

Understanding dawned in his hazel eyes. "Seth Martin! Of course! *You're* the nurse he married! I didn't realize that's who you were." For an instant a guarded expression shadowed his face then vanished with his kind smile. "Well, Lieutenant Martin, a belated congratulations. He's one of the finest Dust Off pilots we have."

After lunch, Mickie and I went to the beach for an hour before heading back to Qui Nhon. Mountains surrounded the leprosarium on three sides; the South China Sea was the fourth boundary.

"So this is where the guards disappeared to," I said, spreading my towel on the sand.

Bubba's head jerked around, and his eyes met mine. For just an instant, if even that, I thought I saw the old hatred there. But he smiled, pushed himself to his feet, and trudged through the sand toward us.

"Afternoon, Lieutenants," he said, lowering himself beside me. "Mind if I sit here?"

*Yes, I mind.* I shrugged.

"Congratulations, ma'am. You must be mighty proud. Your husband getting the Medal of Honor and all."

"He hasn't gotten it yet, Sergeant."

"You must be mighty worried, too. With Lam Son and all."

"What's Lam Son?" Mickie asked.

"You don't know about the major offensive we're launching in Laos next week?"

Mickie tossed her head. "No, I don't, Sergeant, but I bet you're gonna tell us."

He stretched his long legs out on the sand.

"Lam Son means 'sure win.' It'll take away Charlie's refuge in Laos. Like we did in Cambodia last spring. Only this time U.S. troops won't be allowed across the border. Only the slants."

I glared at him.

"Excuse me, ma'am," he said, appearing contrite. "I meant the South Vietnamese troops."

Mickie clicked her tongue. "Then what's there to worry about, Sergeant, if U.S. troops aren't going to be in on the action?"

"The ban on U.S. units in Laos doesn't include Dust Offs. They're considered non-combatants. They'll still evacuate the casualties. You know what that means, don't you?"

Mickie's fuzzy ponytail bounced as she shook her head.

"It means the only friends they'll have on the ground will be the slants—I mean, South Vietnamese. That could be a big problem when it comes to communication. Laos is rugged, mountainous, and our flyboys aren't familiar with the territory. It could get real ugly fast."

My stomach tightened. I knew how important the information the ground troops provided was to the Dust Offs. Would the reports the South Vietnamese gave be as reliable?

"Yep, it's gonna be a lot worse than Cambodia. Did you know in May alone, four Dust Offs were shot down? Ten crew members were wounded. One killed."

Mickie snorted. "Why are you telling us this, Sergeant? Besides wanting to scare Lieutenant Martin."

He raised his eyebrows. "I'm sorry, ma'am. I didn't mean to scare you. Honest." He pushed himself to his feet and brushed himself off, scattering sand over us.

"I just wanted to warn you," he said as he turned to go, the sneer back in his voice. "Come this time next week, Lieutenant *Martin*, you just might be a widow."

"You son of a—" was all I heard Mickie say before I lost what little lunch I'd eaten.

## CHAPTER FOURTEEN

# LAM SON

*67<sup>st</sup> Evac Hospital, Qui Nhon*
*Feb. 9, 1971*
*12:30 a.m.*
*Dearest S,*

I miss you so much! It's hard to believe in eight days we'll have been married for two months. I wanted to make a special dinner for Valentine's Day. And to prove to you that I <u>can</u> make more than macaroni and cheese.

I've been put on call in case they need me in the OR. How I wish I worked ER! Then I would know right away when your chopper landed. Then I could hope for a few moments with you. Just to touch you. It's been so long . . .

Sometimes it feels as though it was all a dream. Then I look at my wedding ring and the necklace, and I know it was no dream.

I have some wonderful news, but I'll wait until we're together. I want to see the look on your face when I tell you.

Soon this will be over, and we'll be together again. Until then, my love, Vaya Con Dios.

I love you.
*Always,*
*Your "E"*

I folded the letter, slipped it into the envelope, and addressed it to "Captain Seth Martin, 283rd MHDA, Pleiku." I'd leave it in the ER for Seth or one of the other Dust Off crews from Pleiku, who would give it to him. I snapped off my reading light and slid down under the sheet. Putting my hands on my belly, I smiled into the darkness. I couldn't wait to tell him. *God, let it be soon. Please.*

A week later Major Lennon interrupted my rounds.

"Lieutenant Martin."

I looked up from taking my patient's vitals. She stood at the foot of the bed. She made it a practice to touch base with all her nurses at least once a week, so I didn't think anything of her appearance.

"I'd like to speak to you in my office," she said. "Now, please."

My heart jumped to my throat. *Seth! Oh, dear God, please don't let it be Seth.* I scanned her face, her eyes, but they told me nothing. I followed her through the ward and to her office with shaky knees.

"Have a seat, Lieutenant," she said, closing the door behind her. She stepped across the small room and sat behind her desk. Several piles of files and papers were neatly stacked on top. The framed snapshot rested in the middle, towards the top of her blotter. I wondered if she'd regretted revealing so much of her personal life that day when she told me about Pete. She'd never alluded to it since and had been her usual warmly professional self. I lowered myself onto one of the wooden captain's chairs, my clipboard on my lap.

"I'm afraid I have some bad news. Captain Martin's chopper was shot down this morning."

My world stopped.

"Your husband's alive, Lieutenant, but injured. Shrapnel wounds in his back and shoulder. Another Dust Off evacuated Lieutenants Kelsey and Halburn—both were wounded—but Captain Martin was pinned down near a bunker by heavy mortar. They were unable to get to him."

My blood turned to ice. The sudden buzzing in my ears made it hard to hear her words.

". . . tried a second time . . . waved them off."

*Oh, dear God, keep him safe! Surround him with your angels.*

Beyond the office door, hurried footsteps, muffled voices, creaky wheelchair wheels performed a cacophony of purpose. Fifty feet away on the helipad, choppers took off and landed. Soldiers and officers hurried to the mess for an early supper or a late lunch. In the villa, the day shift kicked off their boots and plopped. Outside this little room, life went on. Mine hung suspended.

"Evangeline, look at me."

Major Lennon's face blurred in the light filtering through the grimy window behind her. I blinked, trying to focus, but it was no use. The next thing I knew, she was in the chair next to me, pushing tissues into my hand. Questions swirled around in my brain but couldn't find their way to my mouth.

"I . . . I'm so cold," I whispered.

Footsteps. Something draped across my shoulders. I blinked. A field jacket.

"Where is he now?" I asked, my voice cracking.

"Still out there. Radioing vital information from the ground."

"Are they going to try again?"

Compassion poured from her brown eyes. "Not at this time."

*Oh, God, please.* I searched her eyes.

"He doesn't want any more rescue attempts," she said. "The landing zone's too hot."

"I see," I said. But I didn't. After all he did for others, surely they'd keep trying.

"You can wait here, if you like," she said.

"My rounds . . ."

"Covered."

I wanted to go back to my patients—work would keep my mind occupied and the fear at bay. But I couldn't move. All I could do was shiver and wipe the silent tears that flowed from eyes that couldn't see the future anymore. And hold back the sobs that threatened to rip out of my soul.

How long I sat there, I don't know. A cup of tea appeared on the desk in front of me. My hands trembled as I reached to pick it up, so I left it there. Major Lennon had disappeared. I was alone. Alone. *Please, God, bring him home to me. If you do, I won't be angry anymore that you took my father. And then my mother. Bring Seth back—I don't care how badly he's hurt. I'll take him in any condition. For better or for worse. In sickness and in health. I meant that. Bring him home, God, and I'll never doubt you again. I promise.* The door hinges squeaked.

"Vangie." Mickie's voice floated through the haze. "Do you want to go back to the villa?"

I nodded.

"Here." She wrapped my icy fingers around the warm cup. "Drink this."

Paper rustled. Something touched my lips.

"Eat this. It'll settle your stomach."

I pushed her hand away.

"Come on, Vange. I can't carry you. So either you get something in your stomach or I get a wheelchair and push you the half mile to the villa."

After I nibbled on the crackers and sipped the tea, I turned to Mickie, who sat in the chair next to me. Major Lennon was back behind her desk, watching us.

I took a deep breath. "I'm ready."

"Until this crisis is resolved, Lieutenant Martin, you're excused from duty. Lieutenant Molinetti, you have the night off to stay with Lieutenant Martin. But I expect you back on duty tomorrow."

I stood. The crackers and tea had done their job. Although my knees still felt like water and my brain was stuck in neutral, I didn't feel like a gob of jelly.

"Thank you, Major," I said in a voice that was too high pitched to be mine.

*I'll report to duty tomorrow, too,* I tried to say, but the words wouldn't come. I wanted life back to normal—as normal as it is in a busy evacuation hospital in Vietnam. I wanted to be working, taking my patients' vitals, joking with them, writing up reports. I wanted to listen for the choppers, wondering if one of them was Seth's. I wanted to snuggle under the sheets and fall asleep in his arms. Now I'd be lucky to get to sleep. Like Sarah, I'd muffle my heartbreak in the pillow, hoping no one heard. But everyone would. And they'd smile kindly and treat me like a piece of cracked porcelain.

But I wasn't porcelain. I threw back my shoulders.

"Let me know, Major, when my husband's been evacuated," I said.

"Of course."

"They'll bring him to the Sixty-Seventh?"

"I'll make sure they do. If that's all, Lieutenants, you're both dismissed."

All that night we waited, listening for a knock on the door or the ring of the hall phone that would summon me to the ER. When the sun rose golden over the South China Sea, we still huddled together on my bed. Shortly after sunrise the phone jingled. Mickie scrambled to answer it. *A phone call is good news. If he were dead, they'd tell me in person.*

I stared out the window, seeing only Seth's face in my mind's eye. The door closed quietly behind me. Mickie stepped to my side and draped her arm around my shoulders.

"Lennon's on her way."

*Oh, God, no. Please.*

Half an hour later three sharp raps on the door announced her arrival. Mickie let her in. I stood to salute her.

"I wanted to update you in person," she began. "Sit down, Lieutenant. It's quite a story."

I lowered myself to the bed. Mickie sat next to me, her arm around my shoulders.

Major Lennon removed her garrison cap and smoothed her graying russet hair. "Your husband is still alive. He's been radioing enemy positions to overhead aircraft. Thanks to his keen observations, several airstrikes have been successful."

*Oh, thank you, God.*

"When are they going to get him out?" I asked.

"They're doing all they can, Lieutenant. The LZ is still hot, and Captain Martin has insisted they evacuate the wounded first." She smiled. "He's been putting his medic training to good use."

I breathed a sigh of relief. "Then he's not lying there, injured and unable to move."

She shook her head. "To the contrary."

I glanced at my alarm clock: 0900 hours. "What day is it?"

"Wednesday, February 17," Mickie said.

Major Lennon stood and positioned her cap on her head. "They're doing all they can to get him out of there, Lieutenant. I'll keep you posted."

"Is that good news or what?" Mickie said after she left.

"What if they can't?"

"Don't even think like that, Vange. You heard Lennon. Come hell or high water, they'll get him out. And they won't listen to his BS about getting the wounded first. He is, after all, a hero."

"Maybe you're right."

She grinned. "Aren't I always?"

"But that's not the reason they'll spare no effort to rescue him—and soon."

Her neatly plucked eyebrows furrowed. "What do you mean?"

"It wouldn't do for him to get captured in a country where American troops aren't supposed to be."

She snorted. "Politics."

"Sometimes politics comes in handy," I said, opening my locker. "I'm going to take a shower then head for the mess."

"Good idea," she said, tugging at the front of her shirt. "Time to get out of these stinkin' fatigues."

The day dragged. I tried reading but found myself stuck on one sentence, my eyes scanning the words over and over, my brain in Laos. I did both mine and Mickie's laundry then reorganized the clothes in my wall locker. I mopped the floor and washed the inside of our window. After I took another shower, Mickie and I headed to the mess for supper. This time it was busier than it had been at midmorning. I scanned the room for an empty table.

"Let's sit with Sharon and Nancy," Mickie said, heading for their table.

"Sorry to hear about your husband, Vangie," Nancy said as she pulled put a chair.

Sharon nodded.

*What do I say—thanks?* I settled in my seat. "Pass the salt, please."

They took the hint, but the atmosphere at the table was stiff, the conversation stilted. I drank my tea and nibbled on a slice of bread, listening but not listening as the three nurses discussed the weather, their patients, and the latest news from the world of entertainment—all safe subjects.

"I think *Patton*'s gonna win the Academy Award for Best Picture."

"Oh, wasn't George C. Scott just terrific in that movie?"

"I didn't really care for it. Who d'you think'll get the Grammy for Record of the Year?"

"The Carpenters. Definitely."

"You like them? I think they're too mushy. Led Zeppelin, on the other hand—"

"Ugh! I hate that metal stuff. How many songs did they have in the top one hundred last year anyway? The Carpenters had three—'We've Only Just Begun,' 'Close to You,' and 'Ticket to Ride.'"

"You're all wrong," someone said. "'Bridge over Troubled Water' is a shoe-in for a Grammy."

A lump rose in my throat. My plate blurred. The chair legs scraped the wooden floor as I stood suddenly.

"I . . . I have to . . . do something before work," I said, avoiding their eyes. Heads bobbed in polite nods.

"Catch you later, then."

"Leave your plate. I'll take care of it."

No one said, "You haven't even finished eating." No one said, "What's more important than this grub?"

"Wait, I'll go with you," Mickie said, tossing her napkin on the table.

I shook my head. "Finish your dinner."

"I'm not hungry," she said, rising. "Besides, I just remembered. I have to mail my mother a birthday card. Today."

"Your mother's birthday was in August," I said as we strolled back to the villa.

"So I'm busted," she said. "What are you gonna do about it?"

"Nothing," I said, "but sometimes, Mick, I just need to be alone."

"Yeah, friend, but not today," she said. "Not today."

"How can I eat—how can I go about my normal routine—when Seth's out there somewhere?" I said when we got back to our room. "I have no idea if he's been captured, how badly he's hurt . . ." The sobs tore out of me. Mickie wrapped her arms around me.

"He's alive. They'll get him out," she murmured, rocking me back and forth, running her hand over my back. "God will take care of him. Hold on to that, Vange."

I didn't know if I could. God had let me down before. But maybe this time it would be different.

Surprise registered on faces as I reported for my shift on Friday. Major Lennon's eyebrows rose, but she said nothing. As I made my rounds, I tried to ignore the knowing looks, the too-polite conversations, the kindly, feel-sorry-for-her tone of voice.

I shoved thermometers in mouths, wrapped blood pressure cuffs around arms, scribbled pulse rates on charts. I listened for the whomp-whomp-whomp of chopper blades. There were plenty, but nobody came for me. I felt Major Lennon's eyes on me even when I didn't see her. Towards the end of my shift, she called me into her office.

"There's been some news," she said when I sat down. I searched her eyes. A faint smile tugged at her lips. "Captain Martin's been picked up, along with several of the South Vietnamese casualties who were with him. He's on his way here."

Tears filled my eyes. "When—"

"The chopper should get here in about an hour. I'll let you know as soon as it lands."

*Thank you, God! Oh, thank you, thank you, thank you! I'll never doubt you again.*

An hour came and went. Then an hour and a half. Where were they? My shift ended, and I parked myself in the hallway outside the ER. Mickie plopped down beside me.

"I told you they'd get him out," she said, handing me a can of cola.

"Thanks." I pulled the tab and lifted the can to my lips.

"Lieutenant Martin?"

I looked up. I hadn't heard Major Lennon approach. My heart pounded. Behind her stood Chaplain Barger. The can slipped out of my hand and bounced on the tile floor, soda splattering everywhere.

"What happened?" My voice choked in my throat.

"The Dust Off took several hits while rescuing Captain Martin. They made it out of Laos but crashed five kilometers southwest of the border. Another chopper landed some time later. The Dust Off carrying your husband was burning. It looked like it had exploded."

*I almost trusted you, God.* "He's dead then."

She shook her head. "We don't know. They found the bodies of the crew and the seven wounded South Vietnamese they'd picked up.

Someone must have dragged them out of the chopper. But your husband's body wasn't there."

I held my breath.

"They searched the area—as quickly as they could—a VC unit was only minutes away—but this was all they found."

She pressed something clinky and metallic in my hands. My tears splashed on the object I held—Seth's dog tags.

"Your husband, Captain Seth Martin, is missing in action."

CHAPTER FIFTEEN

# UNTIL TOMORROW

"How far along are you?" Mickie asked me a week later while we sunbathed on the beach outside the villa.

"What are you talking about?"

"You can fool Major Lennon. You can fool all the rest of the nurses and the doctors, but you can't fool me."

I swallowed the lump that rose in my throat. "As close as I can guess, nine weeks."

"You must have gotten pregnant on your honeymoon. When are you gonna tell Lennon? Our tour ain't over until August. That's five months away. You'll be—what?" She counted on her fingers. "Seven months."

"I wanted Seth to be the first to know," I said, staring at the blurred waves lapping the sand.

"You gotta tell her."

I shook my head. "Not yet. He still might . . . I'll wait until May. I don't think I'll show until then. My fatigues are baggy anyway. No one'll know."

"Think of the baby, Vange. You're working the sick ward—all kinds of stuff you don't want to be exposed to in your condition."

"I've gotten all my shots. I'll be fine. So will the baby."

She sighed. "You aren't thinking right, friend. What about the FUOs? You don't know if those fevers are from something contagious. I ought to tell Lennon myself."

Alarm shot through me. "Don't. Please. If Seth shows up before then, we'll go home together. If not, I'll tell Major Lennon. I promise."

Mickie shook her head. Her fuzzy brown ponytail bobbed on top of her head. "I don't like it. I don't have a good feeling."

I grabbed her arm and squeezed. "Please? Two months. I'll tell her at the beginning of May."

Her brown eyes, brimming with worry, searched mine. "Promise?"

"I promise."

In the middle of March, I was summoned to Major Lennon's office. My heart pounded against my rib cage as I closed the door behind me and stepped across the floor.

"Sit down, Lieutenant," she said, scribbling on a paper on the desk in front of her. "I'll just be a minute."

I lowered myself to the chair and clasped my hands in my lap. Thoughts swirled in my head; hope mushroomed in my heart. Did they find Seth? Was he alive? In a POW camp? *Seth, Seth, Seth, Seth,* the wall clock ticked the seconds by. Or maybe Mickie went back on her word and told her about my pregnancy. I'd slipped on the wet floor last week after the hooch maid swabbed it down. I would have fallen if Mickie hadn't grabbed me.

"You're worse than a mother hen," I complained after she told me I'd be safer back home.

Major Lennon's sigh jerked me out of my reverie. Pushing her reading glasses on top of her head, she leaned back and placed her hands together in a prayer position in front of her mouth, her thumbs under her chin.

"The order has come down to pack up your husband's possessions," she said after studying me for a moment. "The men of the 283rd have offered to do it."

*So they're giving up on him.* "I see."

"Unless, of course, you'd prefer to do it yourself."

I shook my head. I wanted to remember his room as I saw it last—bed smartly made, blanket so tight around the mattress a dime would bounce on it, his Bible on the nightstand beside a snapshot of us on our wedding day. A room waiting for its occupant to return any time.

"I understand. I was the one who packed up Pete's belongings," she said, tapping her fingers together. "Where do you want them shipped?"

"I . . . I don't know. Maybe to his parents, in State College, Pennsylvania."

"Is there anything you'd like to keep with you for the rest of your tour?"

I stared out the streaked window behind her. *Him.* "I don't know. Would it be possible for me to go through his . . . to go through them?"

Pulling her eyeglasses from the top of her head and shoving them on, she picked up a clipboard and studied it.

"Fortunately, they haven't even started. But you'll have to go to Pleiku ASAP. How about tomorrow?"

The next day, I hitched a ride to Pleiku in one of the 283rd's Hueys after they'd brought their wounded to Qui Nhon. Soup, wearing his ever-present boonie hat, dropped me off in front of Seth's hooch.

"The crew is out on another mission. Won't be back until late this evening, so you'll have the place to yourself," he said, shoving the gearshift in neutral and letting the engine idle. "Buzz and Eddie, you know, were sent home. Last I heard, they were at Walter Wonderful."

Maybe I'd ask to work at Walter Reed Army Hospital after I had the baby—unless Seth was found before then. Maybe he'd turn up there.

"I'm glad to hear they're recovering," I said, reaching behind the seat for my tote bag. "Thanks for the lift."

He smiled awkwardly. "Sure you don't want me to help?"

I shook my head. "Thanks anyway."

He leaned over and pecked me on the cheek. "Be back in a couple of hours then."

A sense of betrayal swept over me as I watched him drive away. Packing up Seth's stuff was like saying we'd given up on finding him. *Never!* I vowed as I inserted Seth's key into the lock. *I'll never give up on him. If it takes as long as I live.* Just like Evangeline in Longfellow's poem, I'd search for him until I found him or died. *Till death do us part.* I took a breath and pushed the door open.

Neatly packed boxes lined the inside wall. His Bible, along with his shaving bag and wallet, lay on the bare mattress. I swallowed, but the lump in my throat wouldn't go away. *They must have worked half the night.* I stepped across the room, my boots treading softly across the wooden floor. Sitting on the bed, I picked up his Bible reverently and opened it. Our wedding day picture was tucked in the book of Job. The guys must have shoved it in randomly, yet I knew it wasn't chance that it had been placed between the pages of chapter thirteen. Someone—Seth or JD, who gave him the Bible the night before he was shot down—had underlined verse fifteen: "Though he slay me, yet will I trust in him." In the margin, in Seth's neat hand, was printed, "No bargains, just trust."

I leafed through the pages, looking for more verses he'd underlined. It was like he was in the room with me, whispering in my ear. A warmth coursed through me. I stopped in the book of Daniel.

"Our God whom we serve is able to deliver us from the burning fiery furnace, and he will deliver us," he'd underlined. "But if not . . . we will not serve thy gods nor worship the golden image which thou hast set up." He'd underlined "But if not" twice.

I closed my eyes, trying to understand the kind of faith that would underline "but if not" twice. *But if not* described a faith that didn't depend on what God did or didn't do, a faith that stood firm whether or not he answered prayers the way we wanted them answered. Sarah's words came back to me: *There are two kinds of faith: faith in* what God does and faith in who God is. *The first kind will let you down because we can never understand the mind of God. It's too easy to blame Him when things don't go the way we want. The second kind is like bedrock. You can build on it, and when the storms come, your faith won't crumble like a sand castle.*

Seth had the second kind of faith. And now I wanted that kind of faith, too. I needed that kind of faith. But how to get it? I couldn't snap my fingers and voila! I would instantly have it. Maybe it was the kind of faith that was earned. Or learned. The anger I'd felt when Seth first went missing had dissipated. I found myself talking to God through the long nights, pleading with him to send my husband back safe and sound, promising him if he did, I'd believe in him, trust him. *No bargains.*

I leafed the pages some more and stopped in the book of Habakkuk: "Although the fig tree shall not blossom, neither shall the fruit be in the vines; the labour of the olive shall fail, and the fields shall yield no meat; the flock shall be cut off from the fold, and there shall be no herd in the stalls: *Yet I will rejoice in the LORD, I will joy in the God of my salvation. The LORD God is my strength . . .*"

The words blurred, and tears splashed on the open pages in my lap. I pressed the book against my chest, close to my heart, as I sobbed until I couldn't anymore. Until I fell across the mattress, spent. I slid off the bed, onto my knees on the bare wooden floor.

"Oh, God," I whispered, clasping my hands together. "I don't know if I could ever have the kind of faith my Seth had. But I want to. I need to, if I'm to survive without him. No bargains. I'm still shaky in the trust department, but I'm willing to take this one step at a time. Help me. Please."

How long I knelt there, totally spent, I don't know. I had no words left. But I felt as though my heart was lifted up to heaven. A calm, a peace settled over me, then in me. I sensed a presence in the room. A velvet-like presence that permeated every molecule in the air around me, every cell in my body, every fiber of my being. Joy flooded my soul. I couldn't understand it, but I didn't have to. I pushed myself up from the floor and scanned the room. I had little work to do, thanks to the wonderful men of the 283rd. I picked up Seth's Bible and his wallet and slipped them in my tote bag.

Three weeks later, on April 9, Operation Lam Son 719 concluded. It turned out to be the last operation of the Vietnam War that America supported. Later we learned that during those two months, Dust Offs evacuated 6,632 wounded. Ten choppers went down, with fourteen Dust Off crewmen injured and six killed. One MIA/BNR—missing in action/body not recovered. But I knew someday, somehow, the missing pilot would be found.

"You have a new patient," Major Lennon told me two weeks later. "He's NVA. A Dust Off brought him in. He wandered into a pickup site, delirious. FUO."

"Not another fever of unknown origin!"

"I don't trust this guy. Make sure you have your weapon handy," she said. "Even if you can't shoot it. It'll make him think twice."

"Oh, I can shoot," I said, "but only targets. I've never . . . I don't think I could ever shoot a human being."

"If he tries anything, Lieutenant, don't hesitate."

"If he's dangerous, won't he have a guard?"

She shrugged. "He's not anybody important. A mere peon who got left behind because he was too sick to go on. But that doesn't mean he won't do anything in his power to inflict damage on the enemy, which is us."

Our POW stayed feverish for a week. Then his fever broke. As he got stronger, he ambled through the ward, looking around. I had the impression he was checking things out, like where the exits were, how many nurses were on duty. I didn't trust him either. He had shifty eyes. He avoided everyone, even the other Vietnamese patients in his ward, and would never look me straight in the eyes. I took Major

Lennon's advice to heart and strapped my .45 beneath my green shirt, which I wore over my Army tee. My fatigues were now snug, but I had just enough room to hide my pistol under the shirt. After some officers from intelligence came to interrogate him and he clammed up, I started loading it.

I was on night shift when he tried to escape. Around three a.m. I was alone, getting caught up on paperwork at the nurses' station, when I heard a soft footstep, then what sounded like the squeak of the hinges of the cupboard where we kept the surgical instruments for the medical unit. I knew it wasn't the other nurses—they were in the break room and wouldn't be back for another fifteen minutes. Since the lock on the cupboard door was broken and hadn't been fixed, I got up to investigate. Nothing appeared to be out of place, but an uneasy feeling gripped me. I hurried up the hall to our POWs ward. Snapping on my flashlight, I checked the beds. All were occupied, except one. Alarm coursed through me as I spun around and hurried to the phone at the nurses' station.

As I reached for the handset, he grabbed me from behind. The sharp blade of a scalpel flashed before my eyes as I wrestled to break free. Elbowing him in the stomach, I pushed away and spun around. Hatred burned in his slanted eyes. I yanked the .45 out of the holster and aimed.

"Die, whore," he hissed, lunging at me.

The last thing I saw before I squeezed the trigger was the point of the blade inches from my belly.

"You know you can stay with Mama."

Mickie sat on her bed watching me pack. After the attack, I told Major Lennon about my pregnancy and requested to return stateside. I couldn't take any more chances with my—our—baby's life.

"I know, but Johnstown's too far from State College."

"Are you sure you want to live with Seth's parents? You've never even met them! How do you know you'll get along?" She shifted her weight. "Mama'll be hurt."

"With your five brothers still living at home, she has a full house. Besides, should Seth show up, the first place he'd go is home—the home he remembers."

"I don't know, Vange. . . . how long you plan to stay there?"

I shrugged. "I'm not sure. The VA hospital in Altoona is only forty miles away. I was thinking of getting a job there and moving to Tyrone when the baby's old enough. It's about halfway between State College and Altoona."

"Haven't you had enough of the military? Why on earth would you want to work in a VA hospital?"

"I could watch for Seth."

She opened the door of her little refrigerator. "Ouch, that shocked me! Is it my imagination, or is this thing getting worse?"

"It's getting worse."

"One last can of cola. You want it?"

I nodded. "I'll save it for when I board the Freedom Bird."

"Ah, the plane that'll take you out of this place. Lucky you. I've got another three months before mine. When did you say the baby's due?"

"Early October."

"Good. I'll be home then."

I stuffed the last of my clothes in my duffel bag then scanned the room.

"I think I got everything," I said, zipping the bag.

"Good thing Uncle Sam shipped the rest of your stuff. Not that you have a lot, but one bag's enough in your condition. I wish I were going with you—to carry your duffel."

I smiled. "Don't worry about me. I'll be fine."

I slipped the wedding picture in Seth's Bible—I'd look for a nice frame back home—and tucked the Bible in my tote bag.

"Well, Mick, this is it." I pulled the straps of my purse over my left shoulder and the handles of my tote bag over the other. I reached for my duffel bag, but Mickie had beat me to it.

"I'll carry it," she said. "I'm coming with you to the helipad."

Ten minutes later we stood on the tarmac, holding back tears and watching as the crew loaded the chopper that would take me to Tan Son Nhut, where I'd catch my Freedom Bird. My stomach tightened—then I felt a soft fluttering in my abdomen.

"Mickie," I exclaimed, placing my hand on the spot, "I think I felt the baby move!"

Her face broke into a grin. "Get outta here," she said, putting her hand reverently where I pointed. "Isn't it too soon? But, hey, what do I know?"

The urgent wailing of a siren cut into the humid air. Fire. I hadn't heard any rockets. I scanned the horizon. Black smoke roiled in the sky above the villa. Mickie's alarmed eyes met mine. A voice from the chopper's radio confirmed our suspicions: The villa was on fire. Mickie gave me a quick hug.

"Gotta go, Vange. See you in three months."

I watched her race across the tarmac toward the billowing, angry tower of black smoke in the distance and breathed a prayer. Hours later as I settled in my seat on the plane, I overheard two soldiers in the seats behind me.

"That was a nice villa, too. Good thing everyone got out in time. Do they know what caused it?"

"Some nurse had a little refrigerator in her room . . ."

*Oh, Mickie.*

As I watched the emerald jungle pass beneath me, my heart broke in two. Seth was down there somewhere, I was sure of it. I pulled my journal from my tote bag and opened it to a blank page.

*May 4, 1971*
*Somewhere over Saigon*

*Dearest S,*

*I'm leaving the place where we met, fell in love, and married. Where our child was conceived. I'm leaving a piece of my heart—the biggest portion of it—here, for I'm leaving without you. But I know, beyond a shadow of a doubt, that someday we'll find each other again.*

*Take care, my love. Vaya Con Dios. I love you. Always.*

*Until tomorrow,*
*Your "E"*

# Part Two

# Pennsylvania USA

# 2007

*"Forgetting the past and looking forward to what lies ahead..."*
— ST. PAUL, FIRST CENTURY A.D.
(Philippians 3:13 NLT)

*June 25, 2007*

*Dearest S,*

    *This will be the last time I write you.*

    *Exactly thirty-six years, four months, and nine days ago, you were shot down. MIA/BNR—missing in action, body not recovered. Every year when your case came up for review I resisted changing your official status. After all, there was—and still is—no conclusive evidence either way.*

    *I'm fifty-seven years old now. Our son is raised. Your parents are gone. I'm retired.*

    *Last month the transmission went out in my SUV. I spent days calling around, trying to find an honest, reputable mechanic who wouldn't take advantage of a woman alone. I ended up buying a new car.*

    *Then the washer and dryer went on the same day. The next week the hot water heater quit. Maybe I should have stayed in the townhouse instead of buying the country cottage, but I wanted peace and quiet after a lifetime of noise and busyness. I look into the future, and those years look long and empty.*

    *I can't remember what you looked like or how your voice sounded, except the sensual way you said my name. The image is fading, like the framed snapshot of us on our wedding day that I kept on my nightstand.*

    *So, darling, this year when your case came up for review, I—how can I even think it, let alone write it?*

    *Bill called. You remember him? My high school sweetheart. The one I lied to you about so you'd leave me alone. He wanted to remind me of our fortieth high school class reunion next weekend at his log cabin resort. Mickie and I are going. Bill's a widower now.*

    *I've removed my wedding ring and tucked it away in an envelope with the wedding picture—and put them with the one hundred composition books I've filled with stories of my life and Gabe's since* the day you disappeared. I didn't want you to miss a thing—his first tooth, his first day of school, his first homerun, our first grandchild. Whether these journals will go to the attic, the basement, the shed, or the burn pile, I haven't decided.

I've loved you since you pulled rank on the plane going to 'Nam and made Bubba the Bully get up out of his seat and salute me. I love you still.

But if I'm to find companionship for my golden years, I must forget—force myself not to remember. I know you'll understand.

Goodbye, my heart.

Your "E"

CHAPTER ONE

# ROAD TO THE FUTURE

"I can't find my cell phone."

I rummaged through my new purse—a blue paisley quilted number bulging like an overstuffed turkey. "It's not in this silly purse you talked me into buying."

"You liked it yesterday."

"That was before I tried to fit all my stuff in. It's way too small. I like lots of compartments and pockets."

Mickie laughed, pulling down the sun visor against the morning sun and easing into the passing lane. "Vange, you need a purse, not a portable file cabinet. When did you see it last?"

I'd changed purses the night before when we returned to the motel after an all-day shopping trip—trip for me, spree for Mickie—at the humongous Grove City Outlet Mall. Did I say "mall"? Wrong word. The place was a village—a paradise for shoppers like Mickie. Not for me, though. I follow the three-get rule: Get in, get what I need, and get out. I'd thought the day would be a long one until I found Borders.

"Wait a minute!" I said. "I called Gabe when I was in the sports section at Borders to ask him about a book Sammy wanted. Maybe I left the phone in the bookstore."

Mickie shook her dyed brown curls out of her eyes. "You couldn't have left it there."

"Why not?"

"Because I saw it at Coldwater Creek when you paid for the dress. Speaking of which—that shade of purple is perfect for you. With those violet eyes and snow white hair, you'll be a knockout at the dinner! Look out, men of the class of '67!"

"Yeah, right," I muttered, pulling out the contents of the purse one by one and dropping them in my lap: two purse-size packages of tissues, hand cream, pick comb, hairspray, three pens, a yellow highlighter, a small magnifying glass. Then my fingers felt wire.

"I found the charger," I said, fishing it out by the jack. "But no phone."

"Don't freak out, Vange. Here." Mickie plucked her cell phone off the console between the seats and tossed it to me. "Call yourself."

Grinning, I reached over and snapped off the radio. "Why didn't I think of that?"

"Because, my dear friend, you have anxiety issues."

"I do not," I muttered, punching in the numbers. The electronic notes of "You Are My Sunshine" filled the car. Relief filled me.

"I can't tell where it's coming from," I said, twisting around to the backseat, where overflowing shopping bags—mostly Mickie's—were stacked. The ringing stopped. I heard my own voice. "Hi, this is Vangie. Leave a message . . ." I disconnected and redialed. Somewhere in that towering mass of capitalism at its best was my cell phone.

Mickie twisted around and waved at the crammed backseat. "I'd say we've had a productive trip, wouldn't you?"

"You make me nervous when you do that!" I scolded her.

"Do what?"

"Take your eyes off the road and your hands off the wheel! I don't know how you stay on the road." I tossed her phone on the console. "Pull over. I'm taking over."

"Geez, Vange. Why are you so uptight this morning? Your cell is here somewhere. We'll stop at the next rest area."

I repacked my purse. "And where, exactly, is that?"

She shrugged. "You're the navigator. Check the map."

I reached into the seat pocket behind me and pulled out the atlas, marked with paper clips, stuffed with Mapquest directions, and stained with coffee, and opened it to the map of the western half of Pennsylvania.

"Where are we?" I peered into the sun for a road sign.

"On I-80 East. In Pennsylvania."

"I know that. What mile marker? Oh, here's one coming up. Mile . . . forty-seven." I held the magnifying glass over the page. "The next rest area is just after mile eighty-six. That's eight miles past our exit. I can't wait that long!"

"Too much coffee?"

"No. Anxiety issues."

"Lighten up!" she said, grinning. "We're footloose and fancy-free. And about to spend a glorious week having loads of fun at Bill's swanky resort."

"What's fun for you isn't always fun for me," I said, slipping the atlas between my seat and the center console. "You'll hit every shopping mall and art store within fifty miles—and try to drag me along with you. While all I want to do is relax in a log cabin or sit by the Clarion River and catch up on some reading."

"Come on, Vange. We're finally free—no jobs, no kids, nothing to tie us down. Hey, remember that Andy Williams song we liked in nurses' school? You typed the words on a sheet of blue construction paper then glued a picture of a seagull on a beach at the top. What was the name of it?" She hummed softly. "Like the bluebird something." She snapped her fingers. "That's it! 'I Wanna Be Free!'" She belted out the words to the song I'd long forgotten.

I giggled. "Oh, Mick, we're not barefoot teenagers in bikinis anymore."

"We're as young as our hearts want to be. How did you say it the other day? 'The spirit is willing but the flesh is weak.' . . . No, that's not it . . . something about the spirit inside us."

"Treasures in jars of clay. But it's not what's inside this jar of clay that I'm worried about. It's the jar itself." I pulled up the flap over the mirror on my sun visor and adjusted my eyeglasses. "This old jar's chipped and cracked."

"Why are you obsessing about the way you look? This isn't like you."

I pushed the sun visor up—and squinted against the road glare. "I'm not obsessing about the way I look."

"For a person who's not obsessed about the way you look, you sure took a long time getting ready this morning. How many pairs of capris did you try on? And polo shirts? And that was after you spent fifteen minutes ironing what you laid out last night. And don't think I didn't see you checking for wrinkles around your eyes."

I sighed. "Suzie will look like Twiggy—she always does. DeeDee will act as though she's better than the rest of us. Tommy will spout off the f-word every other sentence, and Joe will probably tell an off-color joke that will embarrass every woman there like he did the last time. And—"

"Vange, that was twenty years ago. Those perverts have either grown up or died by now."

I peered out over the concrete sides of the bridge we were crossing to catch a glimpse of the Allegheny River flowing below. "I'm fat."

"Says who?"

"All the charts—"

"Don't pay attention to those stupid things. They aren't healthy. Look at those women in our exercise group who lost all that weight. They look like a bunch of dried-up prunes. I tell you, Vange, fat fills the wrinkles." She gave me a knowing look. "What are you *really* stressed about?"

"You know me too well." I took a deep breath. "I'm . . . I'm . . . What I'm really anxious about is . . . seeing Bill again."

"Ah, your old high school sweetheart. I think he wants to sell us all shares in his resort or something."

"Bill would never—"

"Why else would he host a weekend-long class reunion and invite everyone to stay at his resort rent-free? I'm telling you, Vange, he's up to something."

"Bill isn't like that."

"How do you know?"

"I know Bill. There isn't a devious bone in his body."

She snorted. "*Knew* him, you mean. When did you see him last? At our twenty-year reunion. I don't recall you spending very much time with him. Roz made sure of that. People change, you know."

I watched as the purple blossoms of the crown vetch that covered the passing embankments gave way to a yellow-flowered meadow.

"Roz died last year. Breast cancer," I said, glancing at the speedometer. "Don't you think you better slow down?"

She zipped by two tractor trailers that were clipping along pretty good. Then she wrenched the wheel, and the car jerked back into the right lane, inches from the front of the monster truck. I jumped as the horn blared.

"Sorry," she said, glancing into the rearview mirror. "I wanted to get around those two clowns playing leapfrog in their rigs." She punched a few buttons on the steering wheel with her thumbs. "There. We're on cruise control. Nine miles over the speed limit. Happy?"

"Why nine?"

She shot me a mischievous look. "Because anything ten miles over the speed limit can get you pulled over. And I can't cry my way out of a ticket anymore."

With one hand on the wheel, she pulled a CD from the sun visor and fed it into the player. "How about some oldies but goodies?" she said with a wicked grin.

"Save the Last Dance for Me" blasted through the car. Back in the day, it was one of Bill's and my favorite songs. I remembered how he'd sing the words to me in his rich tenor while we danced.

"What's our exit number again?" Mickie's voice broke into my thoughts.

I pulled the map onto my lap and held the magnifying glass over the page. "Seventy-eight. And don't forget my anxious bladder."

"We just passed mile marker fifty-seven. Can you hang tight for another twenty minutes?"

I grimaced. "Just don't hit any potholes or bumps."

"Hey," she said, her brown eyes twinkling, "Do you know when you're going sixty miles per hour, your tires aren't even hitting the road?"

"Mick—"

"All right, all right," she said, cranking up the radio. "Maybe a trip down memory lane will take your mind off my driving."

The miles passed without conversation, the music penetrating and lifting the fog of decades, until I noticed the sign for our exit.

"Exit seventy-eight," I said, pointing. "Right up there."

She thumbed some buttons on the steering wheel, and the car jolted softly as the cruise control shifted off. We exited the interstate, then turned north on Route 36. A small country-style restaurant with log siding, forest green metal roofing, and red gingham curtains sat back from the road on our left. I checked the time on the dashboard. Eleven-thirty.

"Restroom," I said, pointing to the restaurant.

"Lunch," Mickie said, flicking on the blinker and easing into the suicide lane.

Ten minutes later, we were ensconced in a rustic booth, sipping hot tea. My cell phone, which we found under an American Eagle shopping bag, lay on the table next to my saucer.

Mickie nodded at my hand. "You took off your wedding ring."

I placed my cup in the saucer and stared at my bare ring finger. Seth's face flashed before me. An invisible fist squeezed my chest.

"I . . ." How could I even say it? I gazed into Mickie's questioning eyes. "I filed a request to have Seth's status changed. From MIA to Killed in Action."

"What?" she sputtered, choking on her tea. "When?"

"After last month's National League of Families meeting in Washington, I met with the review panel and . . . I told them . . ." The too-familiar pain jabbed my heart. I glanced out the front window beside me. A dusty black rig rumbled by.

"You didn't tell me," she said in a strangled voice.

I swallowed. "Gabe and I talked about it. He never knew his father. Pictures—what few I have—and stories can only tell so much."

Eyes glistening, she reached across the table and squeezed my hand. "I'm sorry, Vange."

I sighed and shook my head. "I don't even remember how his voice sounded, except his off-key version of 'Bridge over Troubled Water' . . . and the husky way he said my name."

I stared out the window. A car pulled into the parking space next to ours and a well-dressed man got out.

"I'm tired of being alone," I said, turning to face my best friend. "I want someone to cook for. A man to mow the grass, fix the leaky spigots, and know what's wrong with my car. Someone else to make the decisions for a change. I want a man to hold me as I fall asleep and be there all night long. I've never had that, really. Seth and I were married only two months when he was shot down. And for most of those two months we were apart."

"What brought about this sudden change of heart?"

"It wasn't sudden. I've been thinking about it for two years—ever since I retired."

I poured the rest of the tea from the little stainless steel teapot into my cup, added two packets of sweetener, then stirred in creamer.

"You're still wearing the necklace," Mickie said.

I fingered the gold cross, running my thumb over the diamond in the center, that Seth had given me the night he proposed. *Gold is the most precious metal there is, and a diamond is the most valuable gem. Always wear this, Evangeline, to remind you of how precious and valuable you are to me.*

"So?" I said, blinking back tears.

"So, if you want a fresh start, you gotta let go and make a clean break from the past, my friend."

I sipped my tea. "This tastes funny."

"Don't change the subject, Evangeline Joy Blanchard Martin. You know what I mean. It's not easy. I know. I've had to make a break from my past two too many times. Two husbands. Two divorces." She shrugged. "I'm better off."

"Bill called me last week," I blurted. Her eyebrows shot up. "We talked a long time. He wants to take me to dinner this evening."

She gave me a wry smile. "And you were going to tell me this when?"

"Don't be difficult. I'm telling you now."

She snorted. "We've been together two days—three, counting the time I spent at your house—and you're only now revealing this juicy little secret? Some best friend."

The waitress brought our orders—a chef salad for me and a thick hamburger with curly fries for Mickie—and plunked down our plates on the polished pine table in front of us. I waited until she left.

"I didn't tell you," I said, my voice low, "because I still don't know how I feel about it."

"Don't you think talking about it with a trusted friend would help?" she said, loud enough for the couple across the room to hear. "It always did before."

"Keep your voice down," I said, draping my napkin on my lap. "He's supposed to call me this afternoon for my answer."

Understanding dawned in her eyes. "Hence the obsession with the lost cell phone."

A gray-haired couple followed the waitress past our booth, their brown leather cowboy boots scraping the wood floor. The man was tall—about six feet—and the woman was a foot shorter. Both wore jeans and denim shirts.

"You've got to stop that," Mickie hissed.

"Stop what?" I asked, pouring ranch dressing over my salad.

"Looking for Seth. Everywhere we go, it's like you're always searching for him."

I swallowed the lump that had formed in my throat when the tall man walked in the room. He *did* look like Seth—as I remembered him. As I envisioned him to be at sixty-two. I shook my head to clear the memory, the longing that still overwhelmed me at unexpected times.

"I've spent the past thirty-six years looking for him everywhere I went," I said, watching the couple slide into a booth. "The doctor's office, the grocery store, the beach, even at church. Any tall, lanky man with sandy brown hair got my heart racing and my insides quivering. I'd sidle up close and glimpse his eyes. I'd know my Seth by his blue eyes—the eyes, they say, are the windows to the soul."

I tore my gaze away from the cowboy couple and smiled. "But you're absolutely right," I said, folding my hands. "It's time to stop. I'll say the blessing."

CHAPTER TWO

# BILL

"Oh my gosh! Look at this place!" Mickie gushed, gunning the car up a small hill to a freshly blacktopped parking lot. Pulling into an empty parking spot between a black Cadillac Escalade and a green Ford Ranger, both with "Seneca Log Cabin Resort" decals on the door, she jerked the car to a stop. A tallish, bearded man wearing a ball cap on backward stood behind the truck, chatting with two younger fellows in faded blue jeans and white T-shirts, gesturing as he spoke. Wisps of gray hair poked out from beneath his ball cap. I looked away.

We were to register in the office, located in the main lodge before us. Thirty log cabins along the river were also a part of the resort, as was a spa and an indoor swimming pool. I pulled my compact out of my purse, brushed powder over my face as Mickie shut off the engine, and dropped the keys into one of the two cup holders on the console.

"I didn't think it would be so . . . so . . . *big!*" she gasped. "Just think—our own Dumpling did all this!"

"You *aren't* going to call him 'Dumpling,' I hope," I said, fishing the keys out of the cup holder and slipping them into my purse with my compact. I turned my attention to the view in front of us. Close up, the place was awesome.

Nestled in the wooded hillside, the lodge, built with real logs, boasted five sides—including two glass walls coming to a point in the front, which faced the river. Dark green Adirondack chairs, honey-and-black Amish rockers, and white wicker lounge chairs were arranged casually in cozy settings across a rustic deck with timber posts stretching across the all-glass front and perched out over the parking lot. The forest green shingled roof covered both deck and lodge and pointed loftily to cotton puff clouds drifting across a blue summer sky.

"Oh, wow!" I said. "The pictures on the brochure and the website don't do this place justice. Maybe I should have signed us up for the lodge. I hope the cabins are as nice."

The cabins were advertised as "modernly rustic," whatever that meant. The "modern" part I liked; it was the "rustic" I wasn't sure about. I'd taken Gabe to a "rustic" cabin resort when he was twelve. The place was a musty-smelling cubicle with neither electricity nor running water, which meant an outhouse by day and a bucket by night. Suddenly I wanted to turn around and go home—back to my bungalow in the country on five acres not too far from the aptly named village of Pleasant Gap. Where I didn't feel like a silly, lovesick schoolgirl. My domain, where I had things—like my emotions—under control.

"I'm sure the cabins will be fine," Mickie said, opening her car door. "Let's go check in."

I checked my hair in the mirror on the sun visor, pushed it up, then shoved my door open—right into the bearded man who had been behind the truck.

"Oh, I'm so sorry! I didn't see you!" I jumped out and rushed to him. He leaned against the driver's side door of the pickup truck, grimacing and holding his elbow.

"Are you hurt?" I said, reaching out to check his arm.

He stepped to the side, avoiding my touch.

"I'm a nurse," I said, giving him a meek smile. "I can help."

He shook his head and grinned, showing perfectly lined white teeth. Lines crinkled from his wire-rimmed, sun-darkened eyeglasses to his hairline.

"Are you, now? I'll have to keep that in mind," he said, rubbing his arm where the car door had slammed into it. His gravelly voice reminded me of something, but I couldn't put my finger on it. I noted his grease-stained T-shirt and scuffed leather work boots. *Probably a janitor or caretaker.* When he straightened up, he stood about three inches taller than me—about six feet, two inches tall. His salt-and-pepper gray hair was braided back in a queue—like the villagers in 'Nam.

"I'm sorry," I said again, feeling my face warm up. "I'm usually not so careless. Are you sure you're all right?"

"Vangie, the guy said he's okay, so let's go," Mickie called over the roof of the car.

A wave of shyness washed over me. "If you're sure . . ."

He grinned a lopsided grin and waved us off. "I'm fine. Honest. Enjoy your stay."

I followed Mickie up the stone pathway to the steps that led to the deck.

If I was impressed when I saw the outside of the lodge, I was doubly so when we stepped into the lobby. Blue and green braided rugs were scattered over the polished pine floor. A stone fireplace—its hearth big enough for a child of seven to walk in standing up—took up nearly an entire wall, floor to ceiling. Above the stone mantel hung a massive deer's head. I counted the points on its antlers. Twelve. I wondered where it came from. The Bill I knew was not an outdoorsman.

A green-and-beige checkered sofa, two matching overstuffed chairs on either side, and a round honey-colored pine coffee table faced the hearth, for a cozy, homey setting. A stack of logs waited in a circular black wrought iron log holder, gently releasing a damp, earthen, woodsy scent to the room. The view out the front glass wall was a breathtaking, panoramic view of the Clarion River. I stepped to the window. The river's lazy waters snaked through the emerald forest rising from its banks and arching over it. Pink and white mountain laurel blossoms crowned the hillsides. Stepping outside on the deck, I pulled my camera from my purse.

After snapping a dozen shots, I returned to the lobby. The log walls were the same warm, honey color as the furniture, a mishmash of old pieces that had been skillfully restored. On the wall to the right of the mantel hung a portrait of a man, woman, and two children, who looked to be preteen. I stepped closer. Bill, Roz, and their children. The ideal family. Roz, seated in the center, wore a royal blue silk dress, which accented her blonde hair and clear, gray eyes. Bill, in a dark blue suit, crisp white shirt, and tie, sat behind her, leaning protectively toward her. A boy of about twelve stood to Bill's right, wearing a light blue oxford shirt and a preteen smirk. He reminded me of the young Bill I remembered. To Bill's left stood a smiling girl of about seven, her hair a mass of blonde ringlets falling to her shoulders. She wore a dress the color of the sky on a perfect June day.

*They were happy together.* Why is it that we women think that our castaways pine for us the rest of their days? Where *was* Bill anyway? I scanned the room. Mickie was inspecting the old crocks scattered about. Pulling the straps of my purse higher on my shoulder, I stepped to the counter, where a young woman wearing her thick, wavy blonde hair in a French braid busied herself at a computer. I checked her name tag.

"Good afternoon, Colleen," I said when she looked up. "We're with the reunion."

She smiled and stood. "Welcome to Seneca Log Cabin Resort. Your name, please?"

"Evangeline Martin. I registered for a cabin with Mickie Molinetti."

Her smile faded. "Will you wait here, please? I'll be right back."

She stepped through a doorway to what looked like an office behind the lobby desk and shut the paneled pine door none too quietly. Several minutes went by. I was beginning to wonder what happened to her when a buxom, middle-aged woman with red hair stepped out of the room and closed the door firmly behind her. I heard a man's voice briefly before the door shut.

"We're sorry to keep you waiting," the redhead said with a smile. "You're with the reunion?"

I smiled as I read her name tag. "Yes, Marguerite. We registered for a cabin."

I gave her our names. She tapped the keyboard, and I heard a whirring sound. Plucking a paper from the printer tray, she placed it on the counter in front of me.

"You and Ms. Molinetti are in Cabin Four, Ms. Martin."

I bristled. "It's *Mrs.* Martin."

"Yes. Well. *Mrs.* Martin." She slid a clipboard toward me as Mickie stepped to the counter beside me. "If you and Mrs. Molinetti would sign in here, please." She pointed to a line and handed me a pen. We were the first ones to sign in for the reunion. I wrote my name then pushed the paper toward Mickie, who said, "It's *Ms.*, but you can call me Mickie." She scribbled her name then slid the clipboard back to Marguerite, who reached under the counter and brought out two gold folders with maroon lettering. Our school colors.

"Everything you need is in here," she said, opening one of the folders and pulling out a map. "Turn right at the bottom of the drive. Your cabin is the fourth one on the right."

The office door opened and out stepped Bill. He was as tall as I remembered—about six feet. His face lit up.

"Vangie!"

He stepped around the desk and opened his arms. "Come here. Let me give you a hug. You look great."

I stepped into his arms. My arms loosely draped around him. He was fit and trim. Clean-shaven. His cologne—English Leather, gosh, did they still make it?—wasn't overpowering. He wore his thick, white hair short. A forest green polo shirt with the resort's logo—a pine tree with "Seneca Log Cabin Resort" stitched in gold beneath—was tucked neatly into his khaki shorts, showing off his flat stomach. His black leather loafers, worn sockless, gave him a touch of casual class.

I stepped back and folded my arms in front of me, overwhelmed by a sudden shyness. "Do you greet all your customers like that?"

He threw his head back and laughed. "No. Only special ones." His hazel eyes gazed into mine. My cheeks grew warm. He turned toward the desk and tapped on my folder. "What cabin is she in, Marguerite?"

"She's in Cabin Four, Mr. Haluski, just like you told us."

She pronounced his name wrong. Bill's last name was pronounced *Ha-LUSH-key,* not *ha-LOO-ski.*

"Hey, Dumpling, how ya doin'?" Mickie stepped past me. I cringed, but Bill grinned.

"If it isn't Mickie Mole!" He opened his arms, and they hugged. He still towered over her. "Mole, you get shorter every time I see you."

"It's a good thing, then, that you see me every twenty years, huh?" she said, breaking out of the hug and giggling. "So, when are you going to take us on the Grand Tour? This place is just amazing. Hard to believe our own Dumpling did all this."

I winced. I wished she would stop calling him that. It wasn't funny. We weren't teenagers anymore.

"Bill," I said, touching his arm. "I'm just in awe. It's beautiful."

He glanced at the closed office door, a wistful look shadowing his features. "The resort was Roz's brainchild," he said. "Just about everything you see was her idea."

He stared at the door then took a breath. "You want the Grand Tour, eh? Let's see what we could do about that."

Pulling out his PDA, he tapped some keys.

"Today's Wednesday, July 2. Tonight I have a hot date—" He winked at me, and I blushed. "Friday is the Fourth—the day of the luau. Saturday's the dinner. Tomorrow morning I can give you the Grand Tour. Plus I have a surprise for you. Both of you."

Mickie clapped her hands in glee. "Oh, I love surprises! What is it?"

Bill shook his head. "If I told you, it wouldn't be a surprise. Just mark off the entire day tomorrow."

He glanced at his watch. "Well, ladies, I must run. Marguerite, get hold of Steve and have him show Mrs. Martin and Ms. Molinetti to their cabin and get the boys to carry their luggage."

"Yes, sir." Marguerite picked up her phone.

"Never mind, Marge," a husky voice behind me said. "I'm right here. I'll take care of it, Bill."

I turned. The man I'd hit with the car door stood by the fireplace, leaning against the stonework with his arms crossed casually and grinning at me. I stepped away from Bill.

"Ah, the man of the hour, as usual. Ladies, Steve will take good care of you. He's my right-hand man. And you," Bill said, putting his big hands on my shoulders and running them down my arms to my hands, "I'll see you tonight. Seven sharp. Dress classy."

Giving me a peck on the forehead, he released my hands and hurried back into the office. I turned to Steve. For some crazy reason I wanted to say, "It's not what you think." Instead I smiled and extended my hand. "I'm Vangie."

Mickie waved her fingers at him. "I'm Michaelena, but everyone calls me Mickie."

Steve took my hand—his touch was gentle, but his skin felt rough. A jolt of static electricity shot through my hand and up my arm.

"Vangie? I've never heard that name."

"It's short for Evangeline. You know the poem by Henry Wadsworth Longfellow?"

He shook his head, his forehead creased in a frown. His blue eyes—indoors, his glasses weren't tinted, so I could see his eyes—gazed into mine with a puzzled look.

"My mother loved it," I said, breaking eye contact. I'd promised Mickie I would stop looking for Seth in every man that crossed my path. Steve's eyes reminded me too much of Seth's.

"Evangeline," Steve repeated, a soft smile tugging at his lips. "That's too beautiful to shorten. May I call you Evangeline?"

A shiver went up my spine. I nodded dumbly, gently easing my hand out of his. *That's what Seth said when I told him my name.*

"We'd better get a move on," he said with a grin. "I've seen the back of your car."

We followed his truck to our cabin, perched on the forested hillside about thirty feet up the river bank. The two boys we'd seen earlier met us there. With the five of us, it didn't take long to get the car unpacked. After the boys left, Steve and I stood on the front porch.

"You're all set," he said, leaning into his upraised arm and wiping his sweaty brow with his shirt sleeve. "You got the nicest cabin in the resort. The only one with two air conditioners."

He stared at my necklace.

"She was Bill's high school sweetheart," Mickie called from the kitchen. As soon as the two boys left, she had plopped at the breakfast bar, opened a package of cookies and poured herself a glass of cold milk from the jug in the cooler.

"Bill's a great guy," Steve said. "He's had a rough year."

I smiled politely. Suddenly I didn't want to go out with Bill tonight.

"I just have one question, though," Steve said, rubbing his bearded chin with his thumb and forefinger.

"What's that?"

"Why on earth do you call him 'Dumpling'?"

I giggled. "I don't. Mickie does. You see, *haluski* is the Slovak word for dumpling. Bill's parents were Slovak. Mickie began calling him that in high school, so he started calling her 'Mole'—her last name is Molinetti. No one else is allowed to call him that. Not even me. And I never call her 'Mole.' It's a thing between just the two of them."

He laughed. I noticed his eyes did, too. A faded memory tried to surface. *Stop it!* I shook my head.

"I'll have to remember not to call my boss 'Dumpling' then." Steve reached into his back pocket, pulled out his wallet, and handed me a business card. "I'm the caretaker. If you need anything, just give me a call."

"Thanks," I said, tucking the card into my capris pocket. "I will."

As I watched him walk to his truck, I almost hoped something would go kerfluey so I'd have an excuse to call him.

CHAPTER THREE

# CATCHING UP

The cabin, to my great relief, had running water and electricity—and everything we needed: towels, bedding, dishes, pots and pans, baking utensils, a coffeemaker, a microwave, and a toaster oven. I even found a wire basket popcorn popper and a couple of mountain pie irons. The range, I discovered when I went to make a cup of tea, was fueled by propane. The white tank stood right beneath the kitchen window along the side of the building. Both front and back porches extended the length of the cabin and held a charming mix of wicker and old, refinished furniture. Carrying my tea to the back porch, I sat on an old-fashioned metal glider, covered with a patchwork quilt.

"I haven't seen a glider like this in ages," I said, pushing off with my foot. "I've been looking for one for my place."

Mickie lowered herself onto the cane seat of an antique gray rocking chair on the other side of the wicker end table.

"So," she said. "It's definite. You're going out with Bill tonight."

I nodded. "Guess so."

"I thought you hadn't made up your mind yet."

I stared at the rising forest of pine on the hill beyond the small yard. "I hadn't. I never gave him an answer. He just assumed—"

"Be careful, Vange. I don't want to see you hurt."

I gaped at her, startled. "Bill would never hurt me."

She shook her head and sighed. "Vange, when was the last time you were on a date? Thirty-seven years ago when Captain Seth Martin swept you off you feet. You're still so . . . innocent."

"With two ex-husbands, you know all about men, I suppose."

"Ouch. But, yes, I do know more than you. I'm just afraid Bill's using you to fill in the empty places."

"I know all about empty places, Mick. And I'm tired of them."

Her brown curls bounced around her face as she stood and leaned on the railing. "Just don't grab onto the first guy that comes along. Wait for love."

A sweet sadness welled up in me. "I had the love of a lifetime. I don't expect to find that ever again. But I can accept 'like.'"

"What about Larry and Linda? They were in their seventies when they met, fell in love, and got married. Look at them. They act like a couple of lovebirds everywhere they go."

"I don't think—"

"Don't sell yourself short, Vangie. Love comes when you least expect it."

At seven sharp Bill drove up in a glistening classic car. I stood on the front porch, cleaning my eyeglasses with a lens cloth, when the shiny green convertible pulled into the short driveway. Sporting a wide-brimmed beige hat with the front pulled down to his eyes, my former beau wore a tan double-breasted suit, white shirt, and red tie to match the band on his chapeau. A red silk handkerchief peeked out of the top of his front pocket. I wasn't sure if he paused to check the time on his gold lapel watch before he headed up the stone walkway or was posturing so I could appreciate his strange attire. I met him at the bottom of the steps.

"You look . . . sharp," I said, smiling and hoping my nerves weren't showing.

I'd brought only one "classy" dress—the one I'd bought for the dinner on Saturday. The off-the-shoulder violet polyester draped from a gold ring on my left shoulder to just below my knees and gathered at the waist to make me look slimmer than I actually was.

He pecked my cheek then frowned.

"What's wrong?" I asked. "Did you forget something?"

He pointed to my soft white, sculptured-knit cardigan. "Don't you have something that would go with your dress better than that?"

I almost said I could probably borrow Mickie's shawl, but a flash of anger stopped me

"It's the only thing I brought that would go with the dress," I said, draping the sweater over my shoulders. *If you don't like it, buster, too bad.*

"Yes . . . well . . . I'll make sure we don't sit near any air-conditioning vents," he said with weak smile. "Shall we go?"

He took my elbow and gently steered me to the passenger side of the convertible. The thing only had a front seat.

"Nice car," I said as he opened the door for me.

"It's a 1953 MG TD Roadster," he said, sounding like a father announcing "that's my son" after the boy hit a home run.

I was about to get in when I noticed something on my seat—a woman's red straw hat, a close match to his in style, with a beige band.

"Am I supposed to wear this?" I joked, twirling it around my hand. Other than sun visors, I don't like anything on my head. "I don't think it matches my dress. Unless we're going to a Red Hat Society dinner?"

He snatched the silly thing mid-twirl and positioned it on my carefully coiffed hair, angling it to the side and pulling the front brim down close my right eyebrow.

"There," he said, nodding. "Now you look the part."

"What part?"

"Didn't I tell you? Oh, I must have forgotten. When I drive any of my cars, I always dress in clothes the style of the year the car came out. Roz and I have over a dozen outfits."

"You mean you have a dozen of these old cars?" I asked as I squeezed my five-feet-ten-inch, twenty-pounds-overweight frame into the one-seater. My knees felt like they were nose level. "Does this seat move back?"

He shut the door without answering.

In the few minutes it took to get to the restaurant, I'd learned there were different kinds of "old cars." Depending on when they were built, there were antique cars, vintage cars, classic cars, and muscle cars. I probably would have learned even more than I wanted to know, but luckily for me, we pulled into the lodge parking lot just as Bill began to expound on engine size and transmission type.

A dozen tables were scattered about the spacious dining room of the restaurant, only two unoccupied. Bill led me to a cozy corner table near the stone fireplace. The décor matched that of the lobby with beamed cathedral ceiling, polished pine floor, and honey-colored log walls. Tall casement windows lined both exterior walls with red-and-green plaid cushioned window seats beneath.

"What will it be tonight, Mr. H.?" asked our waitress, a perky brunette with a sparkling smile.

"We'll have the prime rib and the bottle of the wine I set aside earlier," Bill said, removing his hat and putting it on the window seat. "And I'll have French dressing on my salad. Vangie?"

I put down my menu. *What if I don't like prime rib?* "Light Italian, please. And I'd like a glass of unsweetened iced tea. Oh, and no peppers on the salad."

"You don't like peppers?" Bill asked after she left.

I shook my head. I liked peppers, but it was easier than telling him that I'd heard on the news that the peppers were believed to be the cause of the current outbreak of salmonella.

"May I take this hat off now?" I asked.

"Whatever you want, my dear."

*I am not your dear*. I hung Roz's hat on the chair's back rung.

"How's your son?" he asked. "Weren't you having some trouble with him a few years back?"

"Gabe? He's fine. When was I supposed to be having trouble with him?"

"The last time I saw you."

"Bill, that was twenty years ago! Gabe was sixteen then and just wanted to play baseball. He was drafted, you know, by the Red Sox, after his senior year of high school, but in the second-to-last round. He wouldn't have gotten anything. Fortunately, we—his grandparents and I—convinced him he'd be better off spending four years in college and playing college ball."

Bill frowned. "I thought your parents were dead."

"Seth's parents, my mother- and father-in-law. Dad Martin was a professor at Penn State. That's where Gabe went—and pitched his team into the NCAA playoffs. Then he was drafted again and spent seven years in the minors before a shoulder injury ended his career. He's the pitching coach at Penn State now."

The waitress brought our salads and a basket of freshly baked rolls.

"That's nice." He offered me the basket. "Take a roll. They're made from scratch."

I plucked a fist-sized cloverleaf roll from the basket, tore it open, slathered some butter on it, and took a small bite. I usually ate only whole wheat.

"Mmmm, delicious," I cooed. "What about you? How are your kids? Any grandkids yet?"

"No grandchildren yet. Neither Will nor Collie is married. Like that makes a difference these days." He took a sip of his wine then put his goblet down. "Will oversees the spa and the exercise room here, and Collie is learning the ropes. Uh, that was her today at the desk."

"The pretty blonde? *That* was your daughter?"

"Yes, I'm afraid so. I apologize for her behavior. I told her we were going out tonight. Big mistake. She's still grieving." He sighed and stared out the window. "We all are."

I reached across the table and put my hand on his arm. He covered it with his own.

"I'm sorry, Bill," I said softly. "How long has it been?"

"Eighteen months. We caught it too late."

"I'm so sorry."

He absently caressed my hand then turned from the window to face me. "How long have you been retired?"

"Two years."

"Where did you work?"

"At the VA hospital in Altoona."

"All your career?"

I sipped my iced tea. "Thirty years. At first I worked the ER in the hospital in State College. Dad Martin knew some people there, so he put in a good word for me. I lasted five years only because I had a preschooler at home to take care of and didn't want to travel."

"You didn't like it?"

"When I came back from Vietnam, I was treated like a second-rate nurse, like I didn't even know how to start an IV. In 'Nam I did things only doctors do here. We had to."

"I see," he said absently.

He didn't. Most people didn't. The only ones who did were the ones who were there.

"Life, to quote John Lennon," I said, dipping my forkful of lettuce into the dressing, "is what happens while you're making other plans."

He snorted. "Tell me about it."

After a sumptuous dinner, during which we caught up and made small talk, we took a slow drive along the river road. The night was balmy, and the scent of pine heady. He reached across the brown leather seat and took my hand.

"You aren't wearing your wedding ring," he said, running his thumb along my ring finger. "Does that mean you've given up?"

*No. Yes. I don't know.*

"Seth's status is in the process of being changed from MIA to KIA," I said, watching the fireflies flit among the laurel bushes along the roadside.

"Ever consider getting married again?"

I'd been expecting the question. It was one I'd been asking myself for two years.

"If the right person came along, yes. I'm tired of being alone."

He lifted my hand to his lips and gently kissed it. He held my hand the rest of the way to the cabin.

When we got back, he walked me to the door.

"I'll pick you up tomorrow morning at ten."

"Oh, right, the Grand Tour."

He smiled and put his arms around me. "And the surprise." He kissed me gently on my lips. "See you in the morning."

As he drove off into the warm summer night, I stood on the porch, remembering another time I'd watched him leave. I'd just turned down his proposal. It was the first and only time I ever saw him cry. I wanted to see the world. He wanted to be my world.

*Full circle,* I thought as I stepped into the cabin.

CHAPTER FOUR

# THE GRAND TOUR

Bill showed up fifteen minutes late. I'd been on the front porch on a wicker rocking chair, watching the rippling water splash over the boulders in the river across the road, since ten—the time he said he'd pick us up. Mickie, who'd slept in, was applying her makeup in the tiny, room-to-turn-around-only bathroom.

"Aren't you ready yet?" I called through the screen door. "He'll be here any minute."

"Calm down, Vange," her voice carried on the lazy morning air. "I just have to decide what to wear."

Sighing, I stepped to the porch railing—made of rough hewn logs—and looked up and down the road. No Bill yet. Sitting back down, I found myself watching for the caretaker's little green truck on the macadam road between the cabin and the river. I wondered where he lived. Did he have one of the cabins? Or did he commute from a nearby town? Or maybe he was one of those mysterious mountain men who holed up in a hut in the middle of the forest on the opposite side of the mountain.

The sound of tires on gravel jerked me out of my wonderings. Bill's black Escalade skidded to a stop inches behind Mickie's new car. The driver's door flew open, and out stepped Bill, dressed in a fresh resort polo shirt and crisp black shorts. He headed up the stone walkway, a white plastic shopping bag with "Seneca Log Cabin Resort" in dark green letters dangling from his fingers.

"Oh, good—you're ready," he said when he spied me on the porch. He took the steps two at a time and thrust the shopping bag at me. "I thought you girls would like to wear these today."

"Hey, Dumpling." Mickie stood at the screen door, still in her robe, an inviting smile tugging at her lips.

"Hey, Mole," Bill countered, his eyes scanning her from head to foot. "Don't get dressed up on my account."

"I won't," she said, nodding at the bag. "Peace offering for being late?"

Avoiding Bill's reddening cheeks, I reached in the shopping bag and pulled out two forest green polo shirts with the resort's logo embroidered in gold. I raised my eyebrows at Bill.

He grinned. "Go ahead and change, Vangie. I'll wait. There's one there for Mole, too."

Mickie pushed open the screen door and stepped onto the porch. "Me? Aw, Dumplin', darlin', you shouldn't have." Snatching the shirts, she scanned the labels. "Medium. Just my size." She stood tiptoed and pecked him on the cheek. "Thanks, Bill."

"Roz designed the logo."

"Good for her," she said, handing the extra large one back to me.

"Do these come in any other color?" I asked.

Bill shook his head. "Forest green and gold are the resort colors. Roz—"

"We know—Roz picked them out," Mickie said, grabbing my arm. "Come on, Vange. Be out in a jiffy, Dump."

I gave Bill an anemic smile and followed Mickie into the cabin. The bottoms of my sandals squeaked on the polished pine floor as I strode briskly across the fireplace room. Stepping into my bedroom, I hurled the shirt on the high double bed.

"Green, in any shade, is not my color," I told Mickie, who stood in the open doorway. "We went together for two years. He should remember."

She shut the door quietly behind her. "Vangie." Her calm, low voice carried a note of warning.

I plucked the shirt from the bed, shook it out, and held it up against me.

"Ugh! Forest green doesn't go with my purple capris," I said, staring into the framed mirror on the old-fashioned dresser. "I'm not changing."

"Then don't."

"I don't want to be a walking advertisement."

"Then don't." She plopped on the bed and watched me.

"What's wrong with my lilac jersey?" I asked.

"Nothing."

I squirmed, uncomfortable under her gaze.

"What happened last night?" she asked softly.

I tossed the shirt on the bed and checked my watch. "Bill's waiting."

"Let him wait."

"But you're not ready."

"Just have to throw this ugly green polo shirt on," she said, patting the bed beside her. "What happened last night? You went straight to your room after a quick 'Good night, Mick.'"

I sat on the bed facing her. "It wasn't what I expected."

"What *did* you expect? Fireworks?"

I remembered how I'd felt when I first saw Seth. The fluttering stomach. The watery knees. The sudden loss of the ability to think and breathe.

"I *wanted* fireworks. Am I too old for that kind of stuff?"

"Vangie, give it time. You're both going through big changes in your lives."

I tugged at a snag in the white chenille bedspread. "It wasn't just the two of us last night. There were three—Bill, me, and Roz. He's not interested in me. He just wants someone to make into another Roz." I sighed.

"Men deal with things differently, Vangie. Were you ready to move on a year after Seth went MIA? Compared to you, Bill's had a short time to deal with Roz's death. Remember what the priest said at Pop's funeral last year? 'The grief is as deep as the love.'"

I pulled at the thread and made the snag in the bedspread longer. A sharp rap on the bedroom door startled me.

"Everything all right in there?" Bill's voice boomed through the door.

Mickie twisted towards the closed pine door. "Hold your horses, Dumplin'," she called. "We'll be right out."

She shrugged off her robe and dropped it on the braided rug. Then she slipped the polo shirt over her head and adjusted it around her hips over her white shorts. The green was perfect for her.

"We'll talk about this later," she said in a low voice.

"What will I tell Bill when he sees I'm not wearing his shirt?" I whispered.

"Nothing. Just be yourself, Vange. If he doesn't like you the way you are, he's not the one for you."

Something inside me gave way, and a strange giddy relief swept over me. I stepped around the four-poster and wrapped my arms around my best friend.

"What's that for?" she asked, hugging me back.

"For being you. Totally. Always. Unashamedly."

She grinned, her brown eyes twinkling. "Of course. Now, let's get going before Dumpling cooks too much."

Bill was leaning against the passenger door of his luxury SUV, hands in his pockets, face to the sky, whistling. My stomach tightened. Bill used to whistle when he was angry. "It calms me down," he explained when I'd asked him about it.

"Where's your shirt?" he asked me when we got to the SUV.

"Oh, she didn't want to mess up her hair," Mickie said, opening the back door and tossing in her purse.

Bill gave me a wary look, then a curt nod as he opened the passenger door for me. I detected the scent of car wax as I stepped over the gleaming chrome running board and slid onto the leather seat. Inside, the SUV had a "new car" smell.

On the way to the main lodge, Bill drove past the cabins along the river.

"We thought it'd be easier to build all the cabins the same," Bill said as we wound our way slowly up the river road. "Inside, though, we used different color schemes and furnished each with old pieces, all different. I think Roz hit every secondhand store and estate auction this side of the country looking for the right pieces for the right price."

"I like the way you incorporated the history of the place into the name," Mickie said from the backseat. "The Seneca Indians who lived in these parts were one of the six tribes of the Iroquois League of Nations. They called themselves 'people of the mountain.'"

Bill twisted around to give Mickie an appreciate grin. His hazel eyes gleamed with delight. "I'm impressed, Mole! Since when did you get so good in history?"

"Since I started creating Indian pottery."

"Bill," I said, tapping his arm. "Eyes on the road, please."

"Yes, dear," he said, winking at Mickie then turning to face the front. "I'd like to see some of your stuff. If it's good enough, we could sell it in the souvenir shop."

Mickie snorted. "It's good enough, Dump."

I suppressed a smile. Mickie's pottery had won state, regional, and national awards. But I wasn't going to say anything. Let Mr. High Hat find out in his own good time. Maybe it would take him down a peg or two.

"Yes, um, well." He cleared his throat. "As I was saying, Roz came up with the name. She thought it would be a good idea to tap into the historical aspect of the area."

"Is there anything *you* thought of?" Mickie said.

Bill tapped his thumbs on the steering wheel and pursed his lips. "Truthfully, not at first. Roz came up with the ideas, and I found ways to make them work—and people who could get the job done."

"Good ol' Saint Roz," I said. As soon as the words left my mouth, I knew I'd crossed the line. So I said the first thing that popped into my mind.

"I have to go to the bathroom."

The Grand Tour lasted an hour and a half. After a stop at the ladies' room, we toured the main lodge, which housed the restaurant, offices, and forty guest rooms, all tastefully decorated in a simple but elegant rustic theme. "Seneca Suites," perched on the hillside to the right of the main lodge, held ten suites for those who wanted the full pampering treatment.

"Ooohhh, a whirlpool tub!" Mickie said, running her hands over the fiberglass monstrosity.

"This was the suite I had reserved for you," Bill said with a shrug. "But you said you wanted a cabin."

Mickie glared at me. "*Who* said?"

Bill nodded toward me. I stared back at him. I didn't feel like explaining that a cabin was closer to nature. Simple. Quiet. Secluded.

"I'm not packing up and moving again," I said.

Mickie shook her head. "Me neither. Maybe next time, huh?"

After we visited the spa and the pool, we enjoyed a picnic lunch in a gazebo perched on the scenic overlook above the Seneca Suites. We had our choice of tuna, egg, or turkey sandwiches on wheat or white buns made that morning, pickled eggs, macaroni and potato salad, and a selection of soft drinks, bottled water, and iced tea. As we recalled old times and laughed, I began to relax. I sensed Bill did, too. Perhaps it was because the Grand Tour was over and he didn't have to prove his success to us anymore. Perhaps it was just spending time with two old friends. Perhaps it was Mickie's flippant jokes, pulling him out of the cavern of grief I knew so well myself. She always did have a way of easing him out of a funk.

"That was nice," Mickie said when we visited the ladies' room after lunch. "He only mentioned dear, departed Roz ten times."

"Eleven," I said, pushing the button on the hand dryer with my elbow and rubbing my wet hands beneath the warm air.

Mickie grinned. "You counted, too?"

I gave her a wry smile. "It would've been more, I'm sure, but I think he saw you roll your eyes at the spa."

"Oops." She giggled. "I never did like her. She always acted like she was better than us. Should've been voted 'Most Snooty' instead of 'Most Likely to Succeed.' Wasn't Bill voted 'Least Likely to Succeed'?"

"Yes," I said, remembering a gangly, shy boy whose thick, black-framed lenses distorted his timid hazel eyes. "I think he was."

She snorted. "What a joke *that* turned out to be!"

"Money was always important to him. The fine things in life. The expensive things his parents couldn't afford. I think that's why I broke it off with him. He wanted to be rich, and all I wanted was a simple life with the man I loved. *He* got what *he* wanted."

Mickie's eyes locked with mine in the mirror. "Bill's got a good heart, Vangie."

I shrugged. "The Bill I knew forty years ago did. This one I'm not sure about yet."

Mickie leaned toward the mirror and ran a finger over her eyebrow. "We'd better get going before he comes charging in. The new Bill is not as patient as the old Bill."

Bill still wouldn't tell us what surprise he had planned for the afternoon. All he said was that were we heading south.

"But first I have to stop at the house," he said. "It's just a couple miles down the road."

We headed back down the river road, passing our cabin along the way. I rolled down my window to enjoy the sweet scent of the giant pines that lined both sides of the road. Pinkish white blossoms of mountain laurel bushes, just beginning to open along the river banks, nodded as we passed.

"I thought the mountain laurel bloomed in early June, right after the lilacs," I said.

"Most do," Bill said, "but the ones along the river bank have always come into blossom late June, early July. Collie used to call them 'river laurel.'"

"Speaking of which," Mickie said from the backseat, "where *are* your kids today? I was hoping to meet them."

Bill slowed down and steered the SUV to the edge of the road, right wheels running on the berm, to let an oncoming car pass.

"Will's tending to some reunion details for me, and Collie has the day off." He glanced at the rearview mirror then eased the wheels back onto the road. "She's been working ten-, twelve-hour days helping me get this shindig off the ground. And she's taking her mother's death pretty hard."

"Is that part of your resort?" I asked, pointing to a red-shingled cottage in a copse of trees back off the road on the left. A garage, sided with the same red shingles, stood about ten feet behind the bungalow and off to the left. A white clapboard building—it looked like a shop of some sort—about the size of the garage sat along the back edge of the cut grass and to the right of the cottage.

"That's where Steve lives," Bill said. "You remember—the caretaker?"

I leaned forward to get a better look. Several wooden birdfeeders hung from the trees in the yard. Impatiens spread their riot of colors in beds along the edge of the front porch. Purple, white, and yellow blossoms peeked through the wire fence surrounding a vegetable garden in the backyard near the shop. Clusters of marigolds lined the fence on all sides. No green truck was parked in the gravel driveway. Like the rest of the resort, Steve's place was well maintained, and had a cozy, down-home look to it.

"Does his wife work for you, too?" I asked.

"Steve's not married."

A strange, sweet relief coursed through me. Why that would be good news, I had no idea. My heart had been treading new ground since I decided to change Seth's status. But there was something about that caretaker that made me want to find out more about him. *Silly woman!* I scolded myself. *You have the owner of the resort courting you, and you're more interested in the hired help.* The heart does strange things when it's hungry for love.

"How long has he been with you?" I asked.

"Hmmm . . . about ten—no, make that eleven years. It was in '96, right after the flood. He showed up one day and asked if I needed help cleaning up."

"He looks older than us," Mickie said. "A man that old shows up and you hire him on the spot?"

Bill shrugged. "Desperate times call for desperate measures. It turned out to be a win-win situation. He was looking for work, and I needed a fix-it man. Turns out the guy can fix anything. Don't know what I'd do without him."

"So where'd he come from? How do you know he isn't an escaped convict or something?"

Bill laughed. "Mole, I see you still have your suspicious mind. He came from an Amish community somewhere in Indiana County. Said he was tired of the old ways. Personally I think he lost his wife or something, and just wanted to get away. He doesn't talk about his past, and I don't ask."

An Amish background would explain the long hair and beard. But something didn't set right with me. Perhaps it was his eyes—or the way he said my name. It was like . . . *Stop it right now, Evangeline Martin! Let it go.* I gave my head a little shake to clear my thoughts then turned to watch the road ahead.

CHAPTER FIVE

# THE WOODCARVER

On the way to "the surprise," we stopped at a few restaurants along Route 36 so Bill could replenish their supply of Seneca Log Cabin Resort brochures—which, he explained, would make this a business trip and he could take the mileage off his income taxes.

Mickie complimented him on his sagacity. I couldn't bring myself to say anything. With her pottery business, she understood. But Mickie wasn't as successful as Bill. Couldn't he, just this once, put business aside and enjoy himself?

"Do you do much fishing in the river?" I asked when he returned from what he promised was the last brochure stop with three bottles of water, wet with condensation.

"Fishing?" He made it sound like a dirty word. "Don't have time for it." The crispness in his voice hurt. He placed the key in the ignition and turned it. The engine roared to life. I twisted the bottle cap, but it wouldn't budge.

"I don't believe that, Bill. It was you who taught me to fish," I said, lightly tapping the water bottle lid against the dash.

Bill pulled the bottle out of my hands, opened it, then handed it back to me.

"Sorry," I said, not sure if my face was warming up because of embarrassment or anger.

"Geez, Dump," Mickie said from the backseat, "it's just a car."

"Yes," he said, pulling out onto the highway without using a turn signal. "An expensive one. Or hadn't you noticed?"

"Oh, we noticed, all right," she said. "*Ad nauseum*."

He eased up behind a camping trailer stopped for the red light at the intersection. I took a sip of my water, glancing at him out of the corner of my eye. He blinked a couple of times. Were his eyes glistening? The light changed. The camper ahead moved, but we just sat there until the horn from the car behind us sounded. Bill started to say something, but shook his head, sighed, then made the left turn.

"Am I really that bad?" he asked, braking gently as we headed down a steep hill.

"Yes!" Mickie and I answered in unison.

He cleared his throat. "I'm sorry. I've been a pompous jerk."

"I wouldn't put it like that," I said, already sorry for being so quick with my "yes."

"I would," Mickie said.

He chuckled. "That's Mole—she always tells the truth, no matter how much it hurts."

"You bet," she said. "I live by my motto: 'Oh what a tangled web we weave when first we practice to deceive.' That's from one of Shakespeare's plays. *Hamlet*, I think."

I was about to comment that Sir Walter Scott, not the Bard of Avon, was the origin of the quote but sensed it would be better to keep my mouth shut. Some moments are too fragile, too precious, to ruin with blabber. We rode down the hill in silence—a comfortable silence, without a hint of the underlying tension that had been building since we'd gotten to the resort.

The town we were entering was charming. Well-maintained, two-story clapboard houses sat back behind giant oak trees on both sides of the road. A white clapboard house, with pristine pillars stretching to the second floor roof, hugged the sidewalk.

"What town is this?" I asked when we stopped at the red light at the bottom of the hill. "These old homes are beautiful, especially that white one with the pillars."

"Brookville," Bill said. "And that white house used to be the town library. If you like old homes, you'll love this."

He glanced in the rearview mirror, flicked off his right turn signal, then pulled in the center lane. His sheepish grin reminded me of the old Bill. The light changed and we crossed the intersection. As we drove slowly through downtown Brookville, I marveled at the quaint charm of the stores, mostly specialty and secondhand shops.

"I could spend a whole day browsing these shops," I said. "I'll have to talk Mickie into bringing me here sometime during our stay."

Mickie snorted. "Only if there's a mall close by."

"I'll bring you," Bill said.

I was about to say that he was too busy running the resort to take an entire day—I didn't want to feel hurried—but the ringing of my cell phone stopped me. I pulled it out of my purse and checked the caller ID. Gabe. I'd forgotten to call him when we got to the resort.

"I've got to take this," I said.

As Gabe chided me for neglecting to phone, Mickie and Bill chatted softly. I kept the call short, as in these mountains, the signal was spotty and could easily be lost.

"Anything important?" Mickie asked after I'd hung up.

"If you want to call getting chastised by your son for not phoning when you were supposed to important, yes," I said, placing the phone in its compartment in my purse. "That and he thinks he killed my gardenia."

"Oh, no!" Mickie said with a mock gasp.

I ignored her tone. "He took Sammy with him to check the house and water my plants, and Sammy used the water from the spring instead of the distilled water I bought especially for it." I sighed.

"Sammy?" Bill asked.

"My grandson."

"He probably did you a favor," Mickie said. "You have better things to do than coddle a finicky houseplant that belongs in a tropical climate."

Seth's words from long ago reverberated through time: *The gardenia symbolizes love, unity, grace, and strength. According to legend, the nightingale chooses its mate only when the gardenia first blossoms.* Seth had given me gardenias the night he proposed. I'd carried gardenias down the aisle. I closed my eyes and gave my head a little shake. *I'm sorry, Seth.*

"You may be right," I said.

The "surprise" turned out to be an afternoon and evening at the Groundhog Festival.

"That doesn't sound like a name that would draw in many visitors," I said.

Bill chuckled. "Surely you've heard of Punxsutawney Phil, the world famous groundhog that sees or doesn't see his shadow every February second?"

"Who hasn't?" I said.

"Well, you just might get to meet him. Now, ladies, help me to find a parking space."

The town square, where the festival was held, was jam-packed. Scores of people, young and old, mingled among the carnival-type rides, games, food vendors, and canopy-covered booths. The aromas of buttered popcorn, cotton candy, hot sausage, pizza, and french fries mixed with the laughter and shouts of children on the warm summer breeze. A magician awed a small crowd with his tricks on the bandstand, which was covered with a gigantic, oval canopy.

"There must be a hundred booths crammed in this tiny town square," I said as we strolled along the sidewalk. Vendors offering everything from T-shirts to jewelry to paintings to frames to decorated rocks lined both sides of the walkway. The town square was adjacent to the library. As we strolled past, I noticed a table laden with books just outside its glass doors. "Book sale" read the sign attached to the edge of the table. I'd been collecting the works of A.W. Tozer for years, hunting every secondhand bookshop I could find for my collection. I wanted originals, not reprints. As I headed to the table, Mickie grabbed my arm.

"Look!" she squealed, pointing to a large statue of the famous groundhog dressed in a tuxedo and top hat. "It's Punxsutawney Pete!" She rooted through her bag and pulled out her digital camera, then her cell phone and thrust them at Bill. "Take our picture, Dump, will you? Vange, you stand on one side and I'll stand on the other."

"I believe, Mole," Bill said with a chuckle, "his name is Phil."

She gave him a blank look. "What'd I say?"

"Pete."

While we were posing for Mickie's pictures, I noticed a woodcarver's booth. Gabe and Cammie loved woodcarvings, and festivals like these were perfect places to find unique gifts. After we'd taken at least a dozen pictures with the groundhog statue, which was one of two dozen "Phantastic Phils" scattered about town, we stepped to the plate glass window on the side of the library to get a close-up look of the real Phil.

"This is where he lives, except for Groundhog Day, of course, when he's at Gobbler's Knob for the forecast," Bill said.

"In an air-conditioned, man-made burrow?" I said. "I always thought they went out and got a new animal every year."

"Are you kidding?" Mickie said. "Pete here's over a hundred years old, right, Dump?"

Bill grinned. "That's right, Mole. In fact, *Phil* gets a shot of a special elixir every summer that extends his life seven years."

"Can I get some of that elixir?" she asked, giggling.

"I'll see what I can do," Bill said, winking at me. "What's next, ladies?"

"Funnel cakes!" Mickie said. "I make it a point to eat one at every fair or festival I go to."

"Funnel cakes it is," Bill said, then nodded toward me. "You want one?"

"Of course," I said, noticing the long line at the funnel cake trailer. "While we're waiting, I think I'll mosey along to that woodcarver's booth up ahead. Coming, Mick?"

"I'm kind of thirsty," she said. "I'll go with Bill and get a soft drink."

As they took their place in line, I headed for the woodcarver's booth. This artist—whose sign on the back wall of the booth read simply "The Woodcarver"—specialized in wildlife. Deer, elk, bear cubs, a raccoon, an owl, eagle, even a chickadee, all carved with a most skillful hand and observant eye, filled the tabletop. He'd captured a gundog on point with precision and emotion. I leaned over to get a better look. A Brittany! Gabe would love this. I lifted the carving to inspect it closer. What kind of wood? Oak? Pine? The carving was about six inches high, ten inches long, and three inches deep. My fingers caressed the soft sheen. Linseed oil? I scanned the back tent flap for award certificates. Surely work like this had won awards. But all I saw was a seller's license duct-taped to the back flap and a man's hand grasping the edge of the flap in the middle. I turned the piece over, looking for a price. It was on the bottom, scribbled on a small, rectangular label. I adjusted my glasses to see the numbers more clearly. Only a hundred dollars? Something like this, I knew from attending craft fairs with Mickie, was worth at least two.

Folding my hands around the carving, I looked over the other pieces on display. He not only did wildlife, but also exquisitely carved bird feeders. Cammie would love one of these! *I might just splurge and buy one for myself.*

I was examining the bird feeders when I noticed a rather large, unfinished woodcarving on a card table in the back corner of the booth. Wood shavings were scattered on the table and the ground beneath. A carving tool lay next to it, close to a metal folding chair. I stepped around to the side of the booth to get a better look. A departure from his wildlife theme, this carving was of a bridge with roiling waters beneath it. In the background, a woman's face, her features hazy, her long hair billowing back, watched over the scene before her like a sentinel. Something in my mind jiggled. Her high cheekbones and half-closed eyes reminded me of someone. In fact, the whole piece seemed vaguely familiar. I straightened up to see if the artist had returned. He was still behind the booth, talking to someone.

"I'll have it shipped when it's done," a hoarse voice said. "The final payment will be due then. I'll call you."

Oh, no! He's already sold it! Maybe he'd make another one? The artist backed into the booth, then turned around—and I gasped. Steve! He wore a soft light blue polo shirt—no logo—tucked loosely into blue jeans whose stiffness gave away their newness. Gray wisps of hair peeked out from under his ball cap, worn backward, like yesterday. His eyebrows—a bit of gray blending with sandy brown—arched in surprise. Then he smiled broadly—a warm, welcoming smile that lit up his blue eyes behind his eyeglasses. A funny little ping went off in my soul.

"Evangeline!"

A flood of shyness overwhelmed me, and I shivered in the hot afternoon. My stomach fluttered. Was I having a heart attack? I dismissed the thought.

"I was wondering about this piece," I said, pointing to the bridge. "It's sold, then?"

He frowned. "It's not even finished."

"But I just heard you say you'd send it when it was."

He shook his head. "I wasn't referring to that piece."

Relief coursed through me. "I'd like to buy it. When it's finished, of course."

His eyebrows furrowed as he studied it. "I don't know . . ."

"Please," I said. "There's something about it. . . . How much?"

He rubbed the beard on the chin with his thumb and forefinger. "Can't say. I've never done anything that big before, except the bird feeders, but those are a lot easier. I don't know how it'll turn out."

I waved my arm over the finished carvings on the tables. "If it turns out anything like these, it'll be fantastic. Your pieces are very emotional. Almost spiritual. You're quite talented."

He stared at the unfinished woodcarving.

"How much?" I persisted.

He shook his head. "I'm not sure I want to sell it. I don't know why. I'm sorry, Evangeline. Is there anything else you're interested in? I'll give it to you half price."

I laughed. "I've seen the prices on your pieces. And they're outrageously low. How do you expect to make a profit?"

He chuckled. "I'm happy if I break even. I look at any income I make from this as a way to support my habit."

I discreetly glanced at his forearms. No needle marks. I scanned his appearance with a nurses' trained eye—eyes, skin, posture, cleanliness. I sniffed lightly. No stale cigarette smoke emanated from him. I'd worked with addicts of all kinds, and this man was no addict.

"What habit is that?" I asked.

He waved his lanky forearm over the tables and grinned. "This."

A commotion approached us.

"Here." Mickie shoved my funnel cake, dusted lightly with powdered sugar and sliding off a paper plate, at me. I handed the dog carving to Steve.

"I'll take this," I said. "I also want two bird feeders, but I'm not sure which ones yet. And I'll take the bridge carving—when it's done."

Steve shook his head. "I already told you, Evangeline, the bridge carving's not for sale. Not now, anyway. But if I decide to sell it, you'll be the first person I contact."

I turned to Bill and pointed at the carving. "Tell your caretaker to sell me that bridge carving."

He looked from me to Steve, then at the carving, his hazel eyes alert, questioning. Then he shook his head at me, smiling sadly.

"I can't do that, Vangie. If Steve says it's not for sale, it's not for sale. He must have his reasons."

I turned to Steve to continue pleading my case. His eyes darted from my necklace to the bridge carving. He wore a strange, almost puzzled expression on his face.

"Steve?"

He gave his head a shake, as if to wake up from a daydream. "Pick out any two bird feeders you want, Evangeline. You can have two for the price of one."

I sighed, resigned. "I'm paying full price for the dog carving."

"If you insist."

Laying my funnel cake on the table, I reached into my purse for my checkbook. He grabbed my hand to stop me.

"You can pay me when I deliver your purchases to your cabin tomorrow. I'm sure you don't want to lug two bird feeders and a rather large woodcarving around all day."

I put my hand lightly over his. Why did this feel so right? Like I'd done it before?

I gazed into his twinkling blue eyes. "If you insist," I said.

CHAPTER SIX

# WHEN PAST AND PRESENT MEET

That night I dreamed of Seth. It was a strange dream. We were in a hangar, and he was working on his chopper. But he wasn't wearing his flight suit. Instead, he wore faded jeans, a grungy white T-shirt, and a baseball cap on backward. I sat in a metal folding chair behind him, next to his tool box, handing him whatever he asked for—just like we did in 'Nam.

"Chisel," he said in the dream, extending his hand behind him. His fingers were stained, not with grease or oil, but with what looked like wood stain.

As I put the tool in his outstretched hand, he turned around to give me a kiss. But it wasn't Seth's face that drew close to mine. It was Steve's. I woke up then, a cold sweat leaving me shivering in the humid July night. I threw back the quilt and sat on the edge of the bed, trembling. The glowing numbers on the old round alarm clock told me it was past two. Outside my screened window, a night owl hooted, startling me. *Tea. I need some tea.* Chamomile would settle my nerves. Slipping into my kimono and slippers, I headed for the kitchen.

As I waited for the water to boil, I sat at the small pine table. The dream unnerved me. While I frequently dreamed of Seth, I usually remembered only that I'd dreamed of him. This dream was intense, vivid. I could *feel* his presence. *Just when I've decided to move on with my life*, I thought, listening to the tick-tock-tick-tock of the old-fashioned wall clock. The kettle began to whistle, and I rose to pour the boiling water into my cup before the racket woke Mickie. Although Mickie could sleep through a tornado.

I set the ceramic lid of the teacup in place, turned off the kitchen light, and stepped out on the back porch. The scent of the pines rode sweet on the summer night air. Fireflies flirted in the moonlight. I settled on the quilt-covered glider and closed my eyes, letting the sound of the rippling river soothe my soul.

Maybe it was the bridge woodcarving that stirred up the memories I was struggling to forget. Or the oldies band that performed "Bridge over Troubled Water" so well it was as though Simon and Garfunkel were up on stage twenty feet away. Bill had brought canvas folding chairs and had set them right down front. Every chord reverberated in my soul. After the song, I'd excused myself, saying I needed to find a restroom. I strolled past Steve's booth. He'd already closed up for the night. The tables were bare. Other vendors had simply covered their wares with tablecloths or blue tarps or closed the tent flaps. Why did I purposely walk past his booth?

As I pushed the glider gently, listening to the night and sipping my tea, a noise—like creaky wagon wheels—jangled my nerves. I stopped the glider and held my breath. There it was again, on the stone walkway in front of our cabin. Did we lock the door when we came in? Mickie came in after me. My heart pounded against my rib cage. The porch boards creaked, then, after a pause, soft footfalls on the porch steps. Whoever it was, was leaving. I crept across the back porch, down the steps, and around to the side of the cabin, just as a man's shadowy form, pulling a kid's red wagon, reached the macadam road in front of the cabin. He turned left, and, with a slight limp, favoring his left leg, began walking up the road. I leaned around the mountain laurel bush. The white on his ball cap glowed in the moonlight. Steve! What was he doing here? He stopped, turned around, and faced the cabin. The moonlight filtering through the pine boughs cast shadows on his face. After a few seconds, he turned and headed back up the road. I waited until he was out of sight then climbed the front porch steps. A cardboard box, its lid taped shut, rested on the floor beside the door. I jiggled the front door knob—it was unlocked. Bending from my knees, I lifted the box and lugged it to the kitchen. I took one of the sharp knives from the knife block on the counter and carefully sliced through the packing tape.

When I pulled back the bubble wrap, I gasped. The two bird feeders were even more exquisite than I remembered. I lifted the gundog carving and unwrapped it. The faint scent of linseed oil caressed my nostrils. I smiled, delight coursing through me. I wouldn't wait for Christmas to give this to Gabe. His birthday was October 5th. I'd give it to him then. I couldn't find the invoice, though. I lifted out both bird feeders and set them on the table. I shook out the bubble wrap, but no invoice.

"What's all the racket?"

Mickie leaned against the doorframe, blinking against the bright ceiling light, red silk pajamas askew.

"I'm sorry I woke you," I said. "I couldn't sleep, so I made a cup of tea and went out to drink it on the back porch when I heard someone come up to the cabin and leave. When I went out front to check, I found this." I pointed to the empty box. "Seth brought the woodcarvings I bought today—"

"*Who?*"

I looked at her. "Steve. Who else?"

She looked at me curiously. "You said 'Seth.'"

"I did?"

She nodded.

"Well, I meant Steve. Both names begin with 'S.' Slip of the tongue."

She stepped to the table, pulled out a chair, and plopped down. "Water still hot?"

"What kind?" I asked, lighting the burner and putting the kettle back on to boil.

"Chocolate hazelnut."

After putting a teabag in her cup, I showed her the bird feeders and the gundog carving.

"Nice," she mumbled, running her fingers through her tangled curls and yawning. "But I didn't get up to fawn over Steve's woodcarvings at three in the morning."

"Then go back to bed."

She shook her head. "Why couldn't you sleep, Vange?"

"The water's boiling," I said, pushing my chair back and hurrying to the stove. I poured the tea then put our cups on the table.

"I dreamed of Seth," I said, placing the bird feeders back in the box. "It was . . ." I took a deep breath and sat down. ". . . like he was in the room with me, Mick. I've never had a Seth dream like that."

She swirled the teabag around in her cup, dipped it up and down a couple of times, then placed it, dripping, on the table beside her cup. I pulled a napkin out of the holder and slid it across the table.

"In the dream Seth turned into Steve." A shiver raced through me. "It scared me."

"Then Steve shows up, what, a half hour later? It'd scare me, too." She stirred her steaming tea. "You don't want to move on."

"Yes, I do. I made up my mind—"

"That's exactly it," she said. "You made up your *mind*. But your heart won't let go."

We sat in silence, the old wall clock tick-ticking away the seconds, the owl giving a hoot every now and then, the crickets' chorus fading. Finally, she drained her cup and stood.

I blinked back tears. "How can I get my heart to let go?"

"I don't know, Vange." She pushed her chair to the table. "Stop loving him."

"How do I do that?"

"Start hating him."

I stared at her. "There was nothing about him to hate."

"When Pops died, Mama was so angry, she'd shake her fist at his picture and cry, 'I'm so mad at you, Salvatore! Why did you leave me?'" Her bottom lip jutted out in determination, steel in her brown eyes. "Get mad. He left you, didn't he?"

The luau was to begin at six p.m. Hawaiian music was already blaring through the speakers, six black boxes set up outside the picnic pavilion, as we arrived around quarter to six. The aroma of a pig roasting on a spit over the open fire wafted through the evening air.

At first I thought we were at the wrong pavilion.

"These people are too old," I whispered to Mickie. Then I saw Patti Moore's laughing green eyes. As I looked closer, I recognized several friends from high school that I'd spent many a Friday night with, playing board games, experimenting with makeup, trying on each other's clothes, and sharing secrets. We squealed and hugged and laughed and squealed some more. Some of these people I hadn't seen since we graduated.

"Has it really been forty years?" I said, giving Dorothy a hug. "You haven't changed a bit."

As we chatted with classmates, I looked around for Steve. I'd taken a stroll to his cottage, just up the road from our cabin, before lunch—to see about the invoice—but he wasn't there. Everything was locked up.

Bill, wearing a Hawaiian shirt, white shorts, and sandals, was inspecting the food-laden tables while his daughter, Collie, followed at his elbow, making notes on a clipboard. She nodded, smiled at him, then headed for the caterer's van. Bill strolled over to the DJ, who handed him a microphone.

"Good evening, Class of 1967," his voice boomed over the speakers, "and welcome to Seneca Log Cabin Resort. I trust you are enjoying your stay thus far. In a few moments, Father Frank Thomas, one of our classmates, will say grace. Ladies, make sure you each get a grass skirt, lei, and flower clasp for your hair. And, for those of you who dare, we have coconut bras."

Guffaws and titters punctuated the evening air.

"Sorry, guys, you just get leis. Ah, here's Father Frank now."

After the blessing, Bill made his way through the crowd to us. By then, Mickie had brought back four grass skirts for us—"one for the front and one for the back"—and had donned a coconut bra over her tank top. Bill's hazel eyes gleamed when he saw her.

"You look . . . nice," he said, slipping a lei over her head and handing me mine. He fumbled with a flower clasp, trying to clip it in her mass of curls.

"Here, Dump," she said, gently pulling the clasp out of his hand. "I'll do it."

"Dad . . ." Collie approached us, all business.

"Ah, ladies," Bill beamed at her. "Have you met my lovely daughter, Colleen? Colleen, this is Mickie and Vangie, two of my closest friends in high school." He laughed. "Actually, my *only* friends in high school."

Collie gave us a frosty smile then turned to her dad. "The caterer wants to talk to you."

Bill nodded then turned to us. "I'll be right back."

"I have a feeling she's going to be a hard nut to crack," Mickie said.

I turned to my best friend, whose eyes followed Bill's retreating back. *She's in love with him.*

"I'm famished," Mickie said. "Let's get something to eat."

Bill joined us fifteen minutes later, balancing a plate of food and a drink, and eased himself between Mickie and me.

"Vangie wants to know where your caretaker is," Mickie said as soon as he placed his plate on the table.

"Steve?" He shrugged. "At the festival, selling his woodcarvings. Today's the last day, I think."

"I thought he was your right-hand man," I said, cutting a slice of pork. "This potato salad is delicious, by the way."

Mickie nodded. "So's the macaroni salad. Glad you opted for some good ol' country cooking in addition to the Hawaiian stuff."

"Thanks," Bill said, taking a sip of his bottled brew. "Steve got everything set up, then put his crew in charge. They know what to do. He's trained them well."

"Hey, Bill, do you remember the time . . ." someone began.

The table conversation turned to memories from high school days then what-are-we-doing-now. The DJ interspersed the Hawaiian music with songs from 1967.

"You might want to brush up on 1967," Bill said, collecting our empty plates and piling them on top of his. "We've planned a trivia challenge for tomorrow night's dinner."

"Like what was the top song in '67?" Mickie asked.

Bill smiled at her. "Something like that."

Mickie grimaced. "Sounds like fun."

"Excuse me, Dad?" A young man, in his mid-twenties, stood behind Bill. "Someone said you were looking for me."

"Ah, Will, I wondered where you disappeared to." Bill smiled up at his son, who, with his short brown hair, hazel eyes, and lanky build, looked like a young Bill with scruffy facial hair.

"Everything set for later on?" Bill asked.

Will nodded. "Yes, sir." His eyes shifted to Mickie, who sat close enough to Bill that their bodies touched. I couldn't tell his reaction. Collie, I thought, would have frowned outright.

Putting his arm around Mickie, Bill said, "Son, I want you to meet two of my good friends from high school—ha ha! my *only* friends in high school, Mickie Molinetti, also known as 'Mole,' and,"—he nodded at me—"Vangie Martin."

Will smiled—a warm smile that put a sparkle in his eyes. *He's got Roz's dimples,* I thought, returning his smile.

"Nice to meet you, ladies," he said then looked at Bill. "Dad, if you have a minute . . ."

Bill rose from the table. "Be right back."

"What's set for later on?" Mickie asked Bill when he returned.

He smiled. "Can't say."

"Aw, come on, Dump," Mickie said, a slight whine in her voice.

"Huh-uh." He shook his head and laughed. "You're not suckering me with those puppy dog eyes and sweet pout. You'll just have to wait until later."

Around nine-thirty, Bill grabbed a microphone and announced the surprise—fireworks. Mickie and I exchanged panicked glances.

"The fireworks will go off over the river and will be visible from here," he said. "They'll begin promptly at ten."

"Bill," I said when he returned to the table. "I can't stay for the fireworks."

"Neither can I," Mickie said.

His eyebrows shot up. "Why not?"

I was about to give the excuse that I didn't sleep well last night when Gary, an ex-Marine who was a Vietnam vet, provided the explanation.

"Because, Bill, they served in 'Nam."

Bill gave him a quizzical look. "So?"

"So, friend,"— Gary put a meaty hand on Bill's shoulder—"have you ever heard a missile explode at close range?"

Understanding dawned in Bill's eyes. "Oh, I'm so sorry . . . PTSD . . . I didn't think . . . after forty years . . ."

"It's all right, Bill," I said, patting his arm. "If you weren't there, you wouldn't know."

After assuring Bill we'd be okay, Mickie and I left. Gary and his wife, whose cabin was three doors up from ours, followed.

But I still huddled in bed, a pillow over my ears, trying to block out the sound . . . and the memories.

CHAPTER SEVEN

# REUNION

Dinner was an elegant affair in the spacious dining room of the lodge restaurant. Bill went all out. Steak and seafood, a live band. Maroon and gold banners—our school colors—hung from the wooden ceiling beams. Maroon candles flickered in golden holders on tables draped with white linen tablecloths and set with sparkling silverware. Folded gold linen napkins stood at each place setting.

I felt like a retread next to Mickie, who looked stunning in a sequined red chiffon halter dress that sparkled when she moved. A soft white shawl casually draped across her back and over her elbows. Against her loose brown curls, gold hoop earrings glinted in the soft light. Bill's eyes widened when he saw her. Suddenly I was invisible to him. And so was everyone else. He escorted her to a table next to the outside wall, after a "Hello, you look nice tonight, Vangie" to me.

*Bet he didn't even notice I'm wearing the same dress I wore on our date the other night.* I scanned the room for the "Friday night girls." An arm waved above the throng. They were seated at a round table next to the bandstand. I shouldered my way to them through the crowd.

"We saved you a seat," Dorothy said, taking her purse off the chair next to her.

We all were single—widowed, divorced, or just baching it for the weekend. At six-thirty we were herded into another room, where we posed for a class picture. Bill stood at the end of the second row, right behind Mickie, his hand resting casually on her bare shoulder. After jokingly harassing the photographer and smiling to the count of three too many times, we headed back to the banquet room, where Father Frank prayed for our "departed classmates" and said grace.

"I hadn't realized we'd lost ten classmates since graduation," I said to no one in particular while we waited our turn for the buffet line. Four had died in car accidents, two from cancer, one from AIDS, one suicide. Two died in Vietnam. Tommy was in jail, Suzie was hiding from an abusive husband, and no one had heard from Eddie in years. We pooled our knowledge of trivia to win Bill's "1967 Trivia Challenge"—a free massage at the spa. After dessert we headed for the restroom while the band livened up the evening with songs from our last year in high school. When we returned to the banquet room, the lights were dim, the disco ball sprinkling shards of colored light over the huddled dancers. Bill's arms were loosely wrapped around Mickie, while hers reached up around his neck. An acute sense of loneliness washed over me as I watched my best friend and my high school sweetheart slow dance.

Someone tapped me on the shoulder. I turned.

"Dance?" Steve asked, his shy smile peeking through his gray beard. He cleaned up nicely. A light blue short-sleeved shirt was tucked loosely into dark slacks that draped over his brown dress boots. The knot in his royal blue silk tie was slightly off center. His gray hair, neatly trimmed and combed back, was missing the ponytail. He'd made a trip to the barber.

I took the hand he had extended. "Love to," I said, following him out to the parquet dance floor. As I settled in his arms, I had a sense of *déjà vu*. The band's lead singer crooned the lyrics to "Can't Take My Eyes off You," sounding much like Frankie Valli.

"Thanks for dropping off the woodcarvings," I said. "But you forgot to put the invoice in the box."

"Would you like to go berry picking? I know where there are some fantastic blueberry bushes."

I leaned back and stared at him. "What does that have to do with the invoice?"

His shook his head, dead serious. "Nothing at all."

"I hardly know you."

"You could come to church with me tomorrow morning."

"Church?"

"I'll pick you up at nine. It's a little country church a few miles from here. Dress casual. Jeans. Those pants that come past your knees. No shorts."

I smiled at him. "I haven't said yes yet."

He smiled back, a slight dimple showing on his cheekbone below the left lens of his eyeglasses. "You just did."

We danced the entire slow set, then he led me back to my seat. I pulled out the chair next to me and gestured for him to sit down, but he shook his head.

"I have some things to get done before I hit the hay," he said with a lopsided grin that reminded me of Gabe. "See you tomorrow morning. At nine."

I spent the rest of the evening making rounds of the tables. By eleven o'clock, the crowd had thinned out. I wasn't the only old fogey who needed to be in bed before midnight. I stifled a yawn. I said my farewells, grabbed my purse, then headed for the door, where Mickie and Bill stood, chatting with those on their way out.

"Leaving so soon?" Bill asked, his arm casually draped around Mickie's waist.

I nodded. "Thanks, Bill. You outdid yourself. Everything was wonderful."

"Don't forget the picnic at one tomorrow," he said.

I *had* forgotten. Surely we'd be back from church in time.

"Here." Mickie pressed a set of keys into my hand. "Take my car back to the cabin." She smiled up at Bill. "I have another ride."

A little before nine the next morning, Steve's green truck, water dripping from the fenders, pulled into the driveway. I was waiting on the front porch swing. I tucked my daily devotional booklet into my Bible, zipped up the quilted cover, and picked up my purse. I felt like skipping down the porch steps, but didn't think it would look too dignified for a fifty-seven-year-old grandmother to act like a teenager on her first date. By the time I got to the truck, Steve was waiting by the passenger door. I'd decided on white cotton slacks and a lavender floral jersey. I'd thought about sandals but wasn't sure what kind of church he was taking me to. Some denominations frowned on bare toes. So I'd slipped on a pair of soft moccasins. His blue eyes sparkled as he opened the door for me.

"You'll do," he said with a grin.

"I better," I said, stepping up into the cab, which had a just-swept look and the smell of something spicy. "I'm not changing."

"I wouldn't ask you to," he said, shutting the door and leaning in the window, his face close to mine. "Never change because someone else wants you to. If they don't like you the way you are, it's their problem, not yours."

Something in the tone of his voice, the resolve in his eyes, sent a shiver through me. "Is that today's sermon, Reverend Steve?"

He grinned and tapped the door padding. "Roll up your window. You look cold."

Steve's church was a little white clapboard building set back from a winding country road a twenty-minute drive from the resort. Towering pine trees leaned protectively toward the steeple on the cemetery side. On the other side was a dirt parking lot with about a dozen cars. A couple, who looked to be in their twenties, had just arrived, and their young children raced across the lot, their parents calling after them not to run. They greeted Steve as we walked to the ramped entrance. The man, whose black shaggy beard made me think of Grizzly Adams, clapped Steve on the back.

"Hey, old man," he said, nodding his ebony ringlets in my direction, "See you finally took my advice and got yourself a woman!"

Steve's response was a deep blush, spreading from his cheeks to his ears in a flash.

"Hi," I said, extending my hand. "I'm Vangie."

"Evangeline Martin, this is Jonathon Goodwell and his lovely wife, Kate," Steve said. "Jon is our song leader and Kate's the pianist."

Kate smiled, her dimples igniting a sparkle in her green eyes. Pushing a strand of dishwater blonde hair out of her eyes with her wrist, she tugged at the tote bag straps on her shoulder then extended her hand.

"Nice to meet you. Welcome to Sunnyside Church." She elbowed her husband who, at six feet, towered over her. "Jon, the kids are running up the aisle again."

"Yes, dear," Jon mumbled with grin and a nod towards me. "Duty calls."

As he hurried into the church—the double doors were flung wide open—Kate turned to Steve.

"You're staying for the potluck, aren't you, Steve? I hope you brought your famous Bo Kho stew."

Steve's face reddened again as he turned to me. "I forgot to mention the potluck after Sunday school. I apologize. I'll take you back for the class picnic."

"You're having a dinner today here at the church?" I asked.

Kate giggled. "We like to party, so we have a picnic or potluck at least once a month."

I turned to Steve. "Is that what I smelled on the way? Your famous stew?"

I didn't think his face could get any redder, but it did. He nodded then put his hand in the small of my back.

"We'd best get inside," he said, shepherding me through the doors.

Curious eyes watched as Steve led me down a side aisle to a pew toward the front. Open double-hung windows on both sides of the sanctuary allowed the cool morning breeze to whisper through. *I should have brought my sweater*, I thought, eyeing the whirling fans hanging from the suspended ceiling. *Maybe it gets warm when everyone arrives.* Only a couple dozen people were scattered through the sanctuary. My own church in State College was packed ten minutes before the service began. If you were late, you didn't just lose your seat, you lost any available seat. Even the balcony was crammed. But then again, this *was* a holiday weekend.

Piano music reined my thoughts back to the little country church. Kate attacked the ancient, slightly-out-of-tune mahogany upright with emotion, her fingers flying across the keyboard as she played "Sweet Hour of Prayer." The old hymns resonated in my soul like nothing else. I closed my eyes, savoring every note. When she was done, a man of about sixty stepped up to the podium. He wore a gray suit, white shirt, and dark tie. His thinning salt and pepper hair was combed back, trim as his beard.

"That's Pastor Paul," Steve whispered to me. "He used to work in the mines before he was called into the ministry."

For the next hour, I enjoyed a casual but reverent worship service. Pastor Paul's prayer was simple, but heartfelt. His message, like his prayer, was delivered in a relaxed, conversational style, and was appropriately titled "Reunion." Sunday school, which followed the worship service, consisted of two classes: children and adult. Kate shepherded the kids—all five of them—to a basement classroom, while the adults stayed in the sanctuary. To my surprise, Steve was the teacher. The lesson was on the prodigal son.

Sunday school was over by eleven-thirty. As we headed up the aisle to the back door, Pastor Paul stopped us.

"You're staying for the potluck, aren't you, Steve?"

He shook his head. "Evangeline is a guest at the resort for the class reunion Bill's hosting. I have to get her back in time for the picnic."

I put my hand on his arm. "We can stay."

His blue eyes questioned mine.

"The class picnic doesn't start until one. No one will mind if I'm a little late. Besides, I have to taste your famous Bo Kho stew."

Steve's stew was delicious. Not too spicy, not too sweet.

"I want the recipe," I told him after my second serving. "The name sounds Vietnamese. You didn't serve in 'Nam by any chance, did you?"

His body stiffened. I changed the subject. We 'Nam vets understood each other.

He got me back to the cabin in time to change into denim capris and sneakers and meet up with the class at the pavilion where we'd had the luau Friday evening. I wasn't hungry after the country fare I'd enjoyed at the church, but I went through the line anyway. I scanned the crowd, looking for Mickie. She sat next to Bill at one of the picnic tables set up in the grove. When she saw me, she waved me over.

"Where have you been all morning?" she asked before I even sat down.

"I went to church with Steve."

She grimaced. "You mean you got up early to go to church?"

After we ate, we were free to enjoy the offerings at the resort and nearby Cook Forest State Park. Mickie took off with Bill, while Patti, Dorothy, Sara, and I skimmed through brochures and decided how best to spend the last few hours we had together as a class. The humidity of the past couple of days had lifted, and the temperature along the Clarion River hovered around a balmy seventy-five degrees. We paddled down the lazy river in canoes, zipped around a race track in tiny go-carts, bicycled down River Road on tandem bikes, belting out "A Bicycle Built for Two," and swam in the ice-cold outdoor pool. By early evening, only a few from our class of 1967 remained. After hugs and promises to keep in touch, Patti, Dorothy, and Sara checked out.

As I walked to my cabin alone, I thought back on the weekend. It certainly didn't turn out the way I'd envisioned. Bill and Mickie were an item, not Bill and me. Steve churned up emotions I hadn't felt since Seth—giving me hope that maybe I could put the past behind me. I stopped to watch a red squirrel scurry across the road. *All my life, with the exception of the time I spent with Seth, I've been looking for something.*

This morning, in that little country church, with their down-home hospitality and simple faith, with Steve beside me, I felt as though I'd finally found it. I'd come home.

CHAPTER EIGHT

# THE ACCIDENT

Mickie had already left for her day-long shopping trip when I pulled myself out of bed Monday morning and shuffled to the tiny bathroom. Stepping over a pile of damp towels and inside-out red silk lingerie, I opened the medicine cabinet and reached for my blood pressure medicine. The bottle was full—I'd just received a three-month mail order supply before I left. As I wrestled with the white plastic, child-resistant cap, it suddenly popped off and the bottle flipped out of my hands—and into the toilet. Mickie had left the top up.

I had no refills left. I'd have to call my doctor and ask for another prescription. Maybe he could call the online order place directly. *He* could tell them I dropped ninety pills in the toilet. I wondered if these places took calls from doctors like the hometown pharmacies did. Maybe my doctor could fax my prescription to Bill's office. I hated to think of the cost to have it sent overnight, but I couldn't afford to miss a dosage.

I glanced at the deer clock on the log wall. Half past nine. The doctor's office should be open. After four rings, an automated voice picked up. "We're on vacation this week. If this is an emergency . . ." I hung up then called Bill and told him what happened. I didn't appreciate his chuckling.

"I won't be around today, Vange. I have to go to Pittsburgh on business, but give me the name of the medicine and the dosage."

That information was still in the toilet.

"I'll have to call you back," I said.

Muttering under my breath, I pushed back the sleeves of my robe and gingerly fished out the bottle with my index finger. After drying it with a paper towel and dropping it in a snack bag, I slathered antibacterial soap over my hands and arms then called Bill.

"I'll get back to you in a few minutes," he said, hanging up.

Five minutes later, the phone rang. "You're all set. I've taken care of everything. Steve will pick you up in an hour and take you to a drugstore in Marienville. It's the one I always use. I know the pharmacist. He'll fill your prescription, but you need to take the empty bottle to show him."

A few minutes after ten, tires crunched to a stop on the loose gravel in the driveway. I watched out the front window as Steve stepped out of his truck and carefully shut the door behind him. He wore a pair of clean Levis and a white polo shirt, dressed up from his usual T-shirt and faded work jeans. Using the side mirror, he adjusted his Pirates ball cap. I smiled. The gesture reminded me of Seth. He'd always used both hands, one on the front of his cap and one on the back, to pull his military cap down to just above his eyebrows. *Forget it. Let it go.*

An hour later we were settled in a booth in an old-fashioned drugstore in the small town of Marienville, sipping cherry colas.

"I didn't know these kinds of places existed anymore," I said, dabbing my lips with a napkin. "In grade school, Mickie and I would save five cents from our lunch money every day until we had enough to stop at the corner drugstore. Back then they pumped cherry syrup into the glass of cola."

Steve smiled and nodded.

I folded my arms and leaned on the Formica tabletop. "Where did you grow up, Steve? Around here?"

Using his index finger, he pushed his eyeglasses to bridge of his nose, his gaze shifting from me to the tabletop. "I grew up on an Amish farm a few hours from here. Near Smicksburg in Indiana County. I left the community—ran away—when I was in my mid-twenties. Too confining."

"Did you have any brothers and sisters?"

He shifted in his seat, fiddling with his straw. "If you don't mind, Evangeline, I prefer not to talk about it."

My cheeks grew warm. "I'm sorry. I just—I was just trying to make conversation. I didn't mean to intrude."

His blue eyes softened. "No offense taken."

"Martin!" a voice called.

Steve raised his arm in a wave.

"Your prescription is ready."

He slid out of the booth and dropped a dollar bill on the table. I pushed my empty glass to the middle of the table and followed him to the "Pick up your prescription here" sign. He walked with a slight limp, favoring his left side. Maybe he had an accident on the farm.

I pulled my wallet out of my purse. "How much do I owe you?" I asked the checkout girl, a slender brunette who looked to be in her late teens.

She pointed to the clipboard on the counter. "Sign on the line by the X."

There wasn't much room, so I wrote, "E. Martin."

As I handed my debit card to her, I glanced at Steve. He stared at the paper I'd just signed, his face ashen. Thanking the girl, I tucked the receipt in my wallet, plucked the bag from the counter, and followed Steve to the truck. He drove slowly down the main street through town then turned on the highway just outside of Marienville. The truck gave a little shudder as he shifted and the gear took hold. His color had returned. Maybe it was the lighting that made him look so pale in the drugstore. He had a strong profile. Firm chin, ruddy cheeks above his graying beard. A faint scar ran down his neck, from his right ear, disappearing below his collar. I wanted to ask him about it, but from his reaction to my innocent question about his family, I didn't dare. I watched him as he slowed, shifted, and turned onto a gravel road.

"The long way around," he said, grinning and shifting again. "Thought you'd like to see more of the countryside."

He pushed the window buttons, and the scent of freshly cut hay drying under the hot July sun wafted through the cab. A green and yellow tractor groaned slowly across a large hayfield on the right side of the road, pulling a rake that turned over the piles of hay heaped in neat rows. I leaned back and closed my eyes, inhaling deeply, enjoying the sounds of the country. Then something sounding like bullets broke the spell. My eyes flew open. Loose gravel spit across the road and hit the truck. I grabbed the handgrip on the door as Steve whipped the wheel to the right just as a small, black car skidded past us, out of control. It spun around then somersaulted into a group of young birch trees before flipping into a gully on the opposite side of the road.

Our own tires skidded on the loose gravel as Steve jerked to a stop and pulled his cell phone out of his breast pocket. All I heard was "rural route" and "car overturned." I had already snapped off my seatbelt, flung open the door, and was racing to the drop-off where the car had disappeared. A black coupé rested upside down on top of a boulder, its tires spinning uselessly in the air, gasoline pouring from a gouge in its tank.

"Help!" I heard a female voice. "Jeb, where are you? Oh, God! Somebody help!"

"Coming!" Steve rushed past me and bounded down the bank, pushing aside the bramble bushes as he went. I followed. "Stay calm," he called. "How many are in the car?"

"Two. No, just me. I don't know where Jeb is." She started to wail. "Jeb!"

We reached the car, and Steve yanked open the door. A teenage girl, wearing very short cutoff jeans and one of those skimpy spaghetti strap tops, tumbled out. Steve caught her and gently cradled her as he carried her to bank and lowered her to the ground. I knelt beside her and began taking vital signs. She pushed my hands away.

"Jeb!" she screamed. "Jeb! Oh, my God, I killed him!"

"Who's Jeb?" Steve asked, pushing her long blonde hair out of her face. I checked her pupils. She felt clammy. I looked around for something to cover her with. I remembered seeing a flannel shirt in the truck.

"Keep her warm," I said, climbing up the bank. "She's going into shock."

"I know." Steve was rubbing her arms. "There's a blanket behind the seat. And a first aid kit."

By the time I returned, Steve was kneeling on the side of the overturned vehicle. I wrapped the blanket around the girl and approached the wreck. A faint groaning came from under the car. The humid air reeked of gasoline.

"Steve?"

"He's pinned under the car. He's still alive, but we've got to get this thing off him. I'm going to lift the car. Can you pull him out?"

I reviewed in my mind the best way to move an injured person without causing more damage. "Yes."

The muscles in Steve's arms rippled as he lifted the small car. It rose an inch or two—not enough to free Jeb, who was moaning loudly now. Steve scanned the area then scrambled up the bank.

"It's going to be all right," I told the girl, hoping Jeb heard me, too. "Seth'll get him out."

Steve returned with a machete and swiftly chopped a thin birch tree down. He dragged it to the car and, using a rock as a fulcrum, angled one end of the tree under the car. He pushed down, using his whole body. The car rose.

"Now! Pull him out!"

I leaned in and grabbed Jeb under the shoulders and, as slowly and gently as I could, pulled him out. When Jeb was clear, Steve slowly let the car back down. A siren wailed in the distance, growing louder with each heartbeat. Then something I hadn't heard for a long time, a sound that made me cringe—the whomp-whomp-whomp of helicopter blades. My joints turned to water, my insides to ice. A cold sweat sprouted on my forehead. My heart banged in my chest. *Oh, dear God, please. Not here. Not now.*

Vital signs. I needed to get Jeb's vital signs. With trembling fingers I reached to take his pulse, but Steve was already doing it. I took a deep breath. *Get hold of yourself, Vangie.* Pulling the pencil-sized flashlight from the first aid kit, I lifted Jeb's eyelids and flashed the light on the pupil. No response. Not good.

"Jeb!" Steve placed his hands on the teen's cheeks. "Jeb! Can you hear me? It's going to be all right. Dust Off is on the way. Hang in there, buddy."

The girl, sobbing, threw herself across Jeb. I pulled her back. I was shaking all over.

"Your name," I said. "Tell me your name."

"Diane. Diane Hollington."

"Where are you from, Diane?"

"Marienville. Oh, God, is he gonna die? It's all my fault! I was driving . . ."

I pulled her in my arms and rocked her, asking her how old she was, who was Jeb, and how old he was, discreetly getting the information the EMTs would need and keeping her mind—and mine—occupied. Steve checked Jeb for broken bones.

The first responders—a young man and woman who looked to be in their mid-twenties—stepped down the bank, lugging their medical equipment. Steve stood.

"What have we got?" the man asked.

"Possible concussion, chest and leg injuries. The car was on top him." I listened in awe as Steve gave them the boy's vital signs—

pulse, respiration. This former Amish man had had some medical training somewhere, that's for sure.

"I'll check the girl," the woman said.

"She's all right, I think. Just bruised." I gave her the girl's vital signs, then added, "I'm a nurse."

More emergency personnel arrived. A fire truck. Another ambulance. And the chopper. *Oh, dear Lord, the chopper.*

"Let's go back to the truck." Steve grabbed my hand and helped me up the bank. I saw the chopper when I got to the top. It had landed in the hayfield across the gravel road. It sat in the hot midday sun, rotor blades turning, churning up the dust from the just-cut hay and my insides into a frenzy. Steve practically carried me back to the truck and lifted me onto the seat. I felt cool water in my mouth, trickling down my throat.

The state police arrived. We had to wait to give our statements. I wanted to get out of there. The heat. The chopper. The groaning of the teenage boy. I was back in 'Nam. Steve hoisted himself up beside me and wrapped his arms around me. I couldn't stop trembling.

"Oh, Seth," I whispered as he gently stroked my hair and rocked me. I don't know how much time passed before the state policeman came over and took our statements. I pushed myself away from Steve. His face was pasty white. Sweat beaded his forehead, rolled down his face. His pupils were dilated. His breathing was shallow, rapid. He looked like I felt.

We watched as the boy was trundled to the chopper and the girl loaded into the back of the ambulance. The chopper took off and disappeared from sight, its awful sound fading in the distance. Steve reached over and buckled my seatbelt.

He gently pushed my bangs out of my eyes. "You all right?"

I nodded. "Let's go. Please."

He drove slowly. Somewhere between Marienville and Cooksburg, he pulled off into the parking lot of an ice-cream place. He hopped out and, in a few minutes, returned with two giant cones, handing me the twisty one topped with chocolate and sprinkles. We went to the shaded picnic table and licked the cool, soft ice cream, letting it dribble down our chins. I grabbed a napkin and dabbed his beard. He wiped my cheek with his thumb and smiled.

Then he asked, "Who's Seth?"

I caught my breath. "What?"

"You called me Seth back there."

"I did?"

He nodded, watching me carefully. I glanced away, staring at the cars pass on the highway. "Seth is . . . *was* my husband. He . . . died in Vietnam."

"I'm sorry."

"He was a Dust—Wait a minute! You said 'Dust Off' back there. How do you know about Dust Off if you're Amish? They're exempt from military duty."

Steve's expression went blank. He shook his head. The eyes that met mine had as many questions in them as I had in my heart.

"I don't know," he said. "I've never heard of it before."

CHAPTER NINE

# DISCOVERY

The skies had clouded up, and it looked like rain by the time Steve dropped me off at the cabin around one. We were both pretty shaken up by the accident and our reactions to it. I thanked him, checked my purse to make sure my prescription was there, and pushed open the door.

"How about tomorrow around eleven?" he said as I slid out of the truck. A few drops of rain splattered on the dusty windshield.

"For what?"

"I promised to take you berry picking, remember? I checked the weather. It's supposed to be cloudy, but no rain."

"Do I need to bring anything?" I asked.

He shook his head. "Just wear comfortable clothes and shoes with a good tread."

He waited until I'd unlocked the door and turned around to wave before he backed out onto the road and headed toward the lodge. After the weekend, I was sure he had a job list a mile long—especially since Bill was gone for the day. I put the kettle on for tea then changed into a more comfortable pair of capris and a T-shirt. By then I heard the steady pitter-patter of the rain on the roof, dripping onto the soft ground beneath the eaves. Mickie wouldn't be back until late. I had the rest of the day to myself. With a novel in one hand and a cup of tea in the other, I headed for the back porch.

After an hour, though, the dampness drove me inside, where I started a fire in the fireplace. The wood had already been laid, so all I had to do was put a lit match to it. In no time the warmth from the crackling flames had permeated the little room. I propped my feet up on the ottoman and rested my head against the side of the chair. Closing my eyes, I replayed the accident in my mind.

How did Steve know about Dust Off? Other than Vietnam vets and their families, few people even knew about the medical evacuation choppers. And where had he gotten his medical training? Had he been an EMT or first responder at some time in the past? And why wouldn't he talk about it?

His eyes told me he was as confused as I was. There was something about his eyes . . .

"Vangie!"

Someone tapped my shoulder.

"Vangie, wake up." Mickie's voice permeated the fog of sleep. I blinked. Dusk filled the room. Embers from the fire I'd started earlier smoldered.

I pushed myself to a sitting position. "What time is it?"

"Close to nine—at night. Did you have supper?"

I shook my head.

Mickie grinned and brandished a large paper bag. "Let's eat then. I'm famished."

I sniffed the air and raised my eyebrows. "Chinese?"

Her bottom lip jutted out in a mock pout. "You're no fun. I wanted to surprise you."

Over sweet and sour chicken, stir-fry vegetables, and rice, we shared the events of our day. After browsing craft shops and making some contacts to sell her pottery, she'd driven over to the Clarion Mall, where she'd spent most of the afternoon.

"The mall is right by the Clarion Hospital," she said, dipping a piece of chicken in sweet and sour sauce. "I got there just as a chopper was landing on the helipad." She shivered. "I still get an adrenaline rush when I hear a chopper."

I stared at her. "What time?"

She glanced up at the wall clock. "It's nine fifteen."

I shook my head. "What time did you see the chopper?"

Her face wrinkled up for a few seconds. "Around noon. Why?"

"I'll be right back." I pulled my cell phone from my purse and headed for the front porch, where the signal was the strongest. I punched in the number for information.

"What was that all about?" Mickie asked when I returned.

I told her about the accident.

"I wonder if he made it."

"He did. I just called the hospital and was able to talk to the boy's mother. She said when the car hit the boulder, it made a diagonal dent in the roof. Jeb was lying in the dent, so the car's weight wasn't on him. She said other than being banged up and needing a couple of stitches in his elbow, he's all right. They're keeping him overnight for observation."

"What about his girlfriend?"

"She's just bruised—and scared."

"They're lucky you and Steve were there. Lucky you guys had medical training. What's the matter? You've got a weird look on your face."

I told her about Steve using the name "Dust Off" then claiming he'd never heard the term before.

"That *is* odd," she said.

"We're going berry picking tomorrow," I said, gathering the empty containers and stuffing them in the bag. "I'm going to see what I can pry out of him."

Mickie nodded, a look of concentration in her brown eyes. "And I'll pry what I can out of Bill."

Tuesday dawned cloudy and on the cool side. I was ready early, so I walked up the road to Steve's cottage. He was just getting into his truck to come pick me up. I slid into the cab, and we were off.

"I called the hospital last night. The boy is fine." I told him what his mother told me. "She said it was a miracle and to thank you."

He snorted. "I called, too, but I got the dad."

I raised my eyebrows. "What did he say?"

"That if anything is wrong with his son, he'd sue us for moving him."

I put my hand on his arm. "He's just scared, Steve. He's a parent. All parents panic when their kids are threatened."

He glanced at me. "How many children do you have?"

"Just one. A son. He's thirty-five now."

"What's his name?"

"Gabriel Seth. I named him after his father. We call him Gabe."

"You said your husband died in the war?"

I watched his face carefully. "My husband was a Dust Off pilot. He evacuated wounded soldiers from the battlefields and brought them to the hospital. That's how we met. We married while still serving our tours. I got pregnant on our honeymoon."

"What happened?"

"His chopper was shot down two months after our wedding. They never found him."

"I'm sorry, Evangeline. You've had a hard life."

"I wanted to ask you—"

"Here we are," he said, pulling onto a dirt service road. A yellow cattle gate stretched across the narrow road. "We'll park here and walk in."

"But there's a 'No Trespassing' sign."

He grabbed the ice cream buckets on the seat. "That's not a problem. I know the owner."

After a half-mile hike along the road, we came to a field, where a dozen or so blueberry bushes, at least six feet high, were scattered.

"Are these wild?" I asked.

He nodded. "Grew back after the land was strip mined." He handed me a bucket. "Do you think you could pick enough to bake a pie?"

I snatched the plastic bucket from his hand. "Just watch me."

We filled all four five-quart buckets. We chatted amiably about little things—he asked me a few questions about Gabe, my work as a nurse, where I was stationed in 'Nam, but he changed the subject or gave a vague answer whenever I asked him anything about his past.

"What are you going to do with all these?" I asked on the way back.

"Eat some, freeze most of them, and give you enough for that pie you promised to bake."

"But I don't have the ingredients to make a pie."

He grinned. "I do."

The next morning while Mickie got ready to spend the day with Bill, I baked two blueberry pies. One for us—we'd share with Bill, of course—and one for Steve. I waited until lunchtime, when the pies were cool and I thought Steve would be home for lunch, to walk down to his cottage and present him with his pie. Maybe I'd be able to pry some information out of him. Mickie hadn't been able to get any more information from Bill than we knew already.

Steve didn't answer when I rapped on the screen door, but his truck was in the driveway, windows open, and the cottage wasn't locked.

"Steve?" I called through the screen. The only sound I heard was soft music coming from his stereo speakers. Balancing the pie with my left hand, I knocked louder.

"Steve!"

Still no answer. Maybe he was in the garden. I followed the stone walkway to the backyard, but he wasn't there. The door to the shop was ajar, so I peeked in. Woodcarvings in various stages of progress lined the workbench. A table saw sat in the middle of the concrete floor. Music played from speakers mounted above the workbench, but no Steve. Maybe he was in the shop when I first knocked at the cottage door and didn't hear me. I went to the back door and knocked again. When he didn't appear, I stepped inside.

"Steve?"

Dishes were stacked in the kitchen sink, an empty coffee mug on the table by a folded newspaper and a couple of woodworking catalogues. I'd just have to leave the pie with a note. Putting the pie on the counter, I scanned the kitchen and living room for something to write on.

On the end table by the recliner, I spotted a spiral-bound notebook on top of his Bible. I stepped across the room and picked up the notebook. A blue pen, which must have been inside the notebook, dropped on top of the leather cover of the Bible, which was frayed, cracked, and held together with transparent packing tape. Putting the notebook under my arm, I picked up the Bible, sat in the recliner, and leafed through the worn pages. Notes had been scribbled in the margins, verses underlined. A pocket-size paperback devotional book, folded open to today's reading, was sandwiched between the pages. Today's verse had been underlined: *Do not consider his appearance or his height. The LORD does not look at the things man looks at. Man looks at the outward appearance, but the LORD looks at the heart.* As I went to put the Bible back on the table, the heavy volume flipped out of my hands and landed, upside down and open, on the hardwood floor.

*Great.* I whispered a quick prayer that the pages weren't torn or wrinkled, then bent over. As I carefully turned it over, a folded paper fluttered to the floor. It was yellowed, wrinkled, and limp. I reached to pick it up—and my heart stopped. I recognized the stationery. It was the kind I used in 'Nam. Suddenly I couldn't breathe—a giant, invisible hand squeezed my chest. *It can't be.* Time stood still. With shaking fingers, I unfolded the paper.

*67$^{st}$ Evac Hospital, Qui Nhon*
*Feb. 9, 1971*

*12:30 a.m.*

*Dearest S,*

*I miss you so much! It's hard to believe in eight days we'll have been married for two months. I wanted to make a special dinner for Valentine's Day. And to prove to you that I can make more than macaroni and cheese.*

*I've been put on call in case they need me in the OR. How I wish I worked ER! Then I would know right away when your chopper landed. Then I could hope for a few moments with you. Just to touch you. It's been so long . . .*

*Sometimes it feels as though it was all a dream. Then I look at my wedding ring and the necklace, and I know it was no dream.*

*I have some wonderful news, but I'll wait until we're together. I want to see the look on your face when I tell you.*

*Soon this will be over, and we'll be together again. Until then, my love, Vaya Con Dios.*

*I love you.*

*Always,*

*Your "E"*

*How on earth did Steve get this?*

Carefully I folded the letter and slipped it in the front pocket of my shirt. I stuffed the devotional booklet back into the Bible and placed it on the table. That's when I noticed a ring lying close to the base of the lamp. I picked it up and inspected it. Except for a few scratches, the plain gold band looked almost new—and exactly like the one I'd only recently removed from my finger. My insides turned to ice. *Get a grip, Vangie,* I scolded myself. *There were lots of wedding bands just like this. It wasn't like you had them special ordered or anything.* Generic though they were, our wedding bands had our initials and wedding date engraved on the inside. I tilted the ring to see if it was engraved. It was, but the engraving was too small for me to read. I looked around for a magnifying glass. At the base of the lamp was a flat, pocket-size, plastic magnifier.

Leaning toward the window, I held the magnifier over the ring and bent my head closer. "EJB to SGM 12/16/1970." *Evangeline Joy Blanchard to Seth Gabriel Martin.* This was the ring I'd slipped on Seth's finger on our wedding day. I closed my hand around it, pressed it to my chest, and shut my eyes, remembering as if it were yesterday the look in Seth's eyes as I vowed to love him "as long as we both shall live."

*Could Steve be Seth?* I pressed my wrists against my temples to stop the throbbing. Who was Steve, anyhow? People wrote important events in their Bibles. I had Seth's Bible, but maybe Steve had something in his that would give me some answers. I leafed through the front pages until I found what I was looking for: *Presented to Nguyen Van Anh Dung from Nguyen Sinh An, April 15, 1973.*

Vietnamese names, I knew, didn't follow the first-middle-last name format, but reversed the order, so that the family, or father's, name was first, followed by the middle name, then the given name. "Nguyen" was a common family name—almost half the population used it—and "Van" was a middle name frequently given to males. As for the given name, the Vietnamese gave their children names that had meaning, especially of the traits they wanted the child to have. "Anh Dung," if I remembered right, meant "heroism" or "strength." "An" meant "peace" or "peacefulness."

I turned the page and read that Anh Dung had married Nguyen Thi Ai' on December 31, 1973, and they'd had two children, Nguyen Huu Lanh, a boy, in 1974, and two years later Nguyen Huu Tuyen, a girl whose name meant "angel."

A snapshot was tucked between the pages. The man wore a straw, paddy hat pulled down to his eyebrows. His shaggy, sand-colored beard covered his lower face and neck. The beard and slightly hunched posture reminded me of a young Steve, but something wasn't right about his jaw. It looked off-center, like someone had punched him hard and it stayed that way. In the traditional, black-pajama-like shirt and pants, he looked thin, but was nearly a foot taller than the slender young woman standing beside him. Her long, black hair was swept over her left shoulder and cascaded to her waist. She held a little girl on her hip; he held a little boy, a couple of years older. The photo had been taken on a city street. I turned it over and read the handwriting on the back: "Lanh, Anh Dung, Ai', and Tuyen, Saigon, 1978"—three years after it fell to the Communists. I flipped the photo over and held the magnifier over the man's face. I tried to imagine what Seth would have looked like with a beard.

Suddenly a shrill whine drowned out the soft music. The table saw. I slipped the picture in the back of the Bible and arranged it on the end table, notebook on top, as I remembered seeing it when I came in. The wedding ring I dropped in my pocket with the letter. I scanned the area around the chair, making sure nothing was obviously out of place, then quietly slipped out the front door and down the steps to the path through the woods.

CHAPTER TEN

# SEMPER FI

I was too rattled when I got back to the cabin to do anything but pace. I wanted to confront Steve—whoever he was—with the letter and the ring and demand he tell me how he got them. But I had to calm down, plan what I'd say. What if Steve had stolen the letter and the ring from Seth's body? He'd been in 'Nam, of that I was sure. I'd treated enough Vietnam vets at the hospital for thirty years not to recognize the symptoms.

Who *was* Steve, anyway? A man who went to church, read his Bible, and taught Sunday school but hid his past. Could he be Seth? I'd felt inexplicably drawn to him from the first time I saw him standing behind his truck in the lodge parking lot. He knew about Dust Off. I pictured the snapshot of the Vietnamese family. Was he Anh Dung, who married Ai′ and had two children with her? *No! My Seth wouldn't have married someone else! The mind may forget, but the heart remembers—doesn't it?* Thoughts swirled around in my head, meshing together in a jumbled mass of confusion.

I needed to talk to Mickie. I punched in the speed dial number on my cell but disconnected before it rang. This wasn't something to talk about over the phone. Perhaps a long walk would clear my head. I slipped into a pair of jeans, laced up my hiking boots, grabbed a protein bar and a trail map, and took off.

I strode along the berm of the macadam road until I came to the lodge. Bill's SUV wasn't in the parking lot, but Mickie's car sat in the reserved spot next to his space. Cook Forest State Park was only a mile or so up the road. I had all afternoon, a lot to think about, and a bundle of nervous energy to burn. With my long strides, I reached Cooksburg, the little village that sat in the middle of the state park, in twenty minutes. I stopped at the bridge and pulled the map of forest trails from my back pocket. Seneca Trail was only nine-tenths of a mile long, but the hiking was rated "difficult." I read the description. "This steep trail . . . ends in the Fire Tower/Seneca Point Area . . . offers an excellent overlook view of the Clarion River as you pass through old growth forest and 1976 tornado-downed logs." I folded the map, slipped it in my back pocket, and looked for the wooden arrow that marked the beginning of the trail.

The difficult trail taxed my hiking skills. When I came to the area that had been hit by the tornado, I leaned against a towering hemlock to catch my breath. Tree trunks still lay on the forest floor, thirty-one years later, almost to the day. *The damage must have been devastating.* According to the marker, the tornado had hit July 11; today was July 9. Without help from man, though, the area was coming back. *If Steve were Seth, could we come back?* Tears pressed against my eyelids. *How could we bridge the gulf between what we were then and what we are now? But what if Steve isn't Seth?* I choked back a sob. These were troubled waters indeed. There was no bridge over them. Wiping the tears from my cheeks with my jacket sleeve, I turned and resumed the steep climb.

When I got to Seneca Point, I leaned on the steel fence, panting. I pulled the protein bar from my pocket and, with trembling fingers, tore open the wrapper and took a bite. As the shakiness subsided, I gazed out over the valley. Lush green forests climbed the mountainsides on both banks of the sunlight-dappled river. Cloud shadows chased each other across the treetops. A hawk circled overhead. I couldn't even see the area that had been damaged by the tornado. The Bible verse Steve had underlined came to mind: "Man looks on the outward appearance, but God looks on the heart." *You know Steve's heart, Lord. You know whether Steve is Seth. I know only what I can see, and what I see is confusing. Give me the courage and the strength to find the answers—and soon.*

Voices sounded on the path to the overlook. I was breathing normally now and wasn't so shaky—the protein bar had done the job. But my sweat had evaporated, and I felt chilled. Time to go. When I got back, I'd show Steve the ring and the letter and ask for an explanation.

I chose the fire tower road that snaked through the "Forest Cathedral" rather than the trail I'd climbed earlier. It was easier walking, and, at this point, I needed easier. The nervous energy that had fueled me earlier had been spent. I wasn't in shape for hiking. I hadn't hiked or walked since last fall. I'd been too busy with the move to the cottage. Now my feet cramped in my hiking boots. I was sure I'd find a blister or two when I peeled off my socks, which were regular crew socks, not the hiking socks I usually wore. My leg muscles ached. By the time I limped into the cabin, Mickie was in the shower, singing at the top of her off-key voice.

"How long are you going to be?" I called through the bathroom door. "We have to talk."

"Come on, baby, light my fire," she belted out.

I pounded on the door, then opened it and stepped in.

"Mickie!" I yelled through the steam.

She poked her lathered head around the shower curtain and grinned wickedly. "Steve left you a note."

"What?"

"I found it between the screen door and the doorjamb when I got back. He wants to take you out to dinner tomorrow night."

"You read my note?"

"Of course," she said. "What are best friends for? It's out on the breakfast bar."

I left her singing boisterously and hurried to the kitchen and picked up the folded sheet of loose-leaf paper. His handwriting was heavy and lopsided, but readable.

*Evangeline, Dinner tomorrow night? 6:00. Dress casual. I'll be gone tonight and tomorrow. Call my cell with your answer. Steve*

I marched into the bathroom, where Mickie was swabbing herself with a large bath towel.

"I think Steve is Seth."

She stopped mid-swipe and gaped at me, wide-eyed. "Whoa! Did I hear you right?"

I told her about the letter and the ring. "I was all ready to march right down there and confront him."

"Let me see them."

I pulled them out of my shirt pocket and showed her.

"Let's talk about this over tea," she said, pulling on her robe. "And chocolate."

"How old is Steve?" Mickie asked as we set the tea things on the kitchen table. Well, she did. I stood and watched her.

I shrugged. "I never asked him."

"He looks about sixty-three, right?"

"I guess so."

"How old would Seth be now?"

"Sixty-two."

"How tall is Steve?"

I imagined him standing in front of me. "I'm five-ten now, and he's about four inches taller than me—six-two."

"How tall was Seth?"

"Six-four, but we don't know how badly he was hurt when the chopper crashed. Injuries to his back —and age—would account for the loss in height. And his limp."

"True," she said, lifting the lid off the box of chocolates and popping one in her mouth. "What about his voice? Does Steve sound like Seth?"

I sighed. "Even after all these years, I thought surely I'd recognize his voice—the tone, the timbre, the inflection, the way he said my name. But, to tell you the truth, I can't even remember what Seth's voice sounded like. Steve's voice is raspy, like he's getting over a sore throat."

"Like someone who's had an injury to his larynx," Mickie said, stepping to the stove, where the kettle spit boiling water out of its spout. "What about his eyes? You always said you'd know Seth by his eyes."

She poured the steaming water into the teapot.

"It's hard to tell," I said. "They're blue, like Seth's, and they twinkle like Seth's did. Steve wears glasses. Seth didn't. . . . I don't know, Mick. There's something about Steve's eyes that draw me to him. I'm trying not to look for Seth in every man I see that I think might be him, but a thirty-six-year habit is hard to break. And people change. I didn't even recognize some of our classmates the other night, they'd changed in appearance so much. And Seth always wore his hair—which was sandy brown—in a crew cut. Steve's hair is gray and much longer than Seth's ever was. Plus Steve has a beard."

She dropped a potholder on the table and put the teapot on it, then sat down across from me. "So what are you saying, Vange? You came busting in the bathroom, screaming that Steve is Seth, and now you sound like you're talking yourself out of it. Make up your mind."

I shrugged. "I'm not so sure anymore, now that I've had a chance to think about it—and talk it over with you."

She pointed to the letter and the ring on the table between us. "What about those?"

"Maybe Steve found Seth's body and took them, hoping to use them to find out who he was. Remember they found Seth's dog tags in the field with the burning chopper, so there were no dog tags on the body."

She nodded, her brow furrowed, a faraway look in her brown eyes. "Or maybe Steve met Seth in a POW camp, and Steve made it out, but Seth didn't."

"Or maybe Steve *is* Seth," I said, staring past Mickie to the clock on the mantel in the living room. "There's one more thing."

Mickie plucked another chocolate from the box and bit into it. "What?"

I told her about finding the snapshot and the marriage record written in the Steve's Bible. "Who is Anh Dung? And why does the man in the snapshot look like a young Steve?"

Mickie's eyebrows arched. "He didn't look like Seth?"

I shrugged. "He had a beard, and his hat was pulled down so I couldn't see the eyes clearly. I was ready to look at his face closer, but the table saw started, and I got out of there. Besides, Seth wouldn't . . . he *couldn't* . . ."

"If Seth had a head injury, he could have amnesia, Vange," Mickie said, the excitement in her voice rising. "You and I both know that getting conked on the head again and regaining your memory is nothing but schmuck."

"So he wouldn't remember that he was already married?" I shook my head. "His wedding ring would have told him that. I . . . he . . . betrayed me, Mick."

"Stop being so emotional. We need to get more information," she said, plucking another chocolate and pointing it at me. "He's going to be gone tomorrow, right? So, we'll do a little investigating."

"You mean snooping."

"Call it what you want."

"And if I refuse?"

"I'll go by myself."

"You wouldn't." I stared into her steely brown eyes. "Yes, you would. I shouldn't have told you anything."

"Calm down, Vange." She lifted the teapot and poured the steaming amber liquid into my cup. "Drink this. It's chamomile."

"I *am* calm. And for the record, I knocked before I came into the bathroom. You didn't hear me. And I didn't scream. I had to speak up because you were singing loud enough to scare every country critter within a mile."

"Whatever." She squinted at the digital numbers on the microwave. "Heavens! Look at the time! I have to get ready."

"Aren't you going to have tea?"

She shook her head. "Bill will be here any minute, even by his tardy standards." She plucked my cell phone off the breakfast bar, where I'd dropped it, and plunked it down on the table in front of me, a wicked grin on her pixie face. "Now call Steve—Seth—whoever he is—and accept that date."

After a long soak in a bubble bath, during which my mind churned with all I'd discovered that day, I heated the rest of the chamomile tea in the microwave and tried to read my novel. I didn't know what Mickie thought she'd find, but I didn't feel right about snooping while Steve was away. She'd probably sleep until noon. Maybe Steve would return early, and I wouldn't have to risk arguing with my best friend. Not that we never argued. But this time, I decided, I wouldn't budge.

Around ten I took two sleeping pills and turned in.

Ten hours later my cell phone rang, waking me out of a drugged sleep.

"Vange?" Mickie all but shouted. "Get down here. *Now!*"

"Where are you?" I asked, pushing aside the covers.

"Where do you think I am? In Steve's cottage. I found something . . . you've got to see . . . Get down here! Now!"

"Mick—" But she'd disconnected.

I pulled on a pair of running shorts and slipped an oversized T-shirt over my pajamas, slid into my flip-flops, and headed out the door. Mickie was waiting for me on Steve's porch swing, a sketch pad on her lap.

"How did you get in?" I asked.

"I didn't break in, if that's what you think."

She'd filched a master key from the lodge office, but when it didn't work, hunted around on his porch for an extra key he might have hidden.

"Steve is too careful of a man to leave—" I began, then stopped when Mickie, grinning wickedly, brandished a key.

"Where'd you find it?"

She sighed. "Men are so unoriginal. Under the mat."

"Oh, for heaven's sake."

"I found the snapshot in the Bible, just like you said. You're right, the man looks like a young Steve. But if you look closer, he resembles Seth, too. I think Anh Dung is Steve. And I know Steve is Seth. And do you know how I know?"

I shook my head.

She flipped open the sketch pad and held it up. "This."

I stared at the pencil drawing of a young woman, her long hair billowing behind her, a thin chain around her neck. She looked familiar.

"It's you," Mickie said, her voice rising. "That's what you looked like when you were in 'Nam."

I looked closer. She was right. The pencil drawing *did* look like me. She shoved the pad into my hands.

"Look at the other sketches."

As I leafed through the book, my heart pounded in my ears. There, in black and white, were pencil drawings of Mom and Dad Martin, Seth's parents, as they looked when I first met them, when I first came back from Vietnam, pregnant, homeless, and alone.

I shivered. A car motored past. "Let's get out of here."

Mickie put the sketch pad back on Steve's dresser where she found it and locked up, sliding the key under the mat exactly the way she found it—so she said. Neither one of us spoke as we walked back to the cabin. I went straight to the kitchen and put the kettle on for tea.

"Oh, shucks!" Mickie said. "We should have taken a hair from Steve's hairbrush to send to a DNA lab for comparison. Let's go back."

"No."

"But that will give you irrefutable proof—proof he couldn't argue with." She pulled out a chair, its wooden legs scraping the wooden floor, and plopped down. "Okay, this is what we'll do. When you go out with him tonight, discreetly pluck a hair from his head or someplace. Then we'll get one of Gabe's and send them both away for analysis."

"You watch too many crime shows. Why don't I just ask him?"

"Think, Vange. How's he going to react when you tell him how you got the letter and the ring? And how you know about the sketches? How's he gonna feel about you snooping around his cottage? He's so private and all."

"I didn't snoop around his cottage. You did. I just took him the pie I promised him and happened upon the letter and the ring."

"What about identifying marks? Did Seth have any birthmarks or anything that would identify him?"

"Not that I—wait! Yes, he did. He had *Semper Fi* tattooed on his back left shoulder."

"*Semper Fi*? Seth was Army, not Marines."

"It was also the motto of one of the Army units he hung around with. The tattoo would be faded by now, but should still be visible—if I got close enough." I stared into Mickie's scheming eyes. "Don't even think it," I said.

That afternoon Mickie was napping when my restlessness drove me out the door for another walk to clear my head. I found myself on the road to Steve's cottage. I wanted to see those sketches again. I thought he wouldn't be back yet, but I was wrong. His truck was parked in the driveway, and voices came from the backyard. I followed the stone walkway to the garden, where I found Steve working, shirtless, his back to me. A baseball game blared from a radio on the windowsill of the shop. I stepped to the garden fence. He was humming and didn't hear me. In the late afternoon sun, the tattoo was faint, but I could still see the outline of the words: *Semper Fi*.

My head buzzed. My ears rang. The letters swam before my eyes. I blinked. They were still there. I backed away, slowly, holding my breath, until I came to the cottage. Then I turned and ran as fast as I could.

CHAPTER ELEVEN

# REVELATION

Mickie sat at the kitchen table, dipping a cookie into a cup of milk and reading a magazine, when I burst through the back door. I stumbled across the floor to the table, where, panting, I grabbed the edge of the table with trembling hands and leaned forward.

Her eyebrows shot up. "What now?"

"Steve . . . garden . . . tattoo . . . Seth . . ." I gasped.

"Slow down, Vangie."

I shook my head. "I saw it. The tattoo. There's no doubt. Steve *is* Seth."

"Look at this," she said, holding up the magazine she'd been reading and shoving it in my face. "You've got to read this! It's an article about heart cell memories."

I peered at the article title: "Does the human heart have memories?"

Pulling out a chair, I sat and read. According to the author, a transplant surgeon from Texas, several of his patients who'd received heart transplants had later reported behavior that was out of character for them, but consistent with the donor. One young man, a vegetarian who listened to heavy metal music, started craving meat and listening to fifties rock and roll after his transplant, both traits of the middle-aged donor. In another case, a woman who never chewed gum craved spearmint chewing gum after her transplant. She later learned that the teenage donor chewed spearmint gum constantly.

"Listen to this," I said, reading aloud. "In his book *The Heart's Code,* Dr. Paul Pearsall documents seventy-three cases. He writes, 'The heart thinks, feels, remembers, and communicates with other hearts. The heart, not the brain, conducts the energy that becomes the cellular symphony that is the essence of our being.'"

I put the magazine on the table. "Energy cardiology, cellular memory. I was a nurse for forty years. How did I miss this?"

"You didn't work in a transplant program," Mickie said. "Cellular memory would explain how Steve remembered Dust Off and how to treat an accident victim—and the sketches."

I picked up the magazine from the table. "May I have this? This article gives scientific evidence that the mind may forget but the heart remembers. I want to give it to Steve to read when I confront him with the ring and the letter tonight."

At quarter to six, I was sitting on the front porch swing, going over the list I'd compiled this afternoon of the evidence that Steve was Seth. I still couldn't believe it. Maybe I was hallucinating when I saw the tattoo. Maybe I *wanted* to see it, so in my mind, I did. I felt through my purse for the plastic sandwich bag where I'd put the ring and the letter. It was still in the zipped compartment where I'd placed it this afternoon. The magazine was also in there. When would be the best time to bring it up? Mickie suggested after dinner, after we got back to the cabin.

"You want him to be able to drive," she said. "Think about how this is going to hit him. Be careful, Vange. Don't rush it."

But I wanted to rush it. I'd waited thirty-six years—a lifetime—for this moment. Tires sounded on the gravel. Steve had arrived. I took a deep breath and stood. But it wasn't Steve's little green truck sitting in the driveway, but a shiny black, extended-cab, full-size pickup. It looked a lot like the one Gabe just bought. What would Gabe be doing here? I wondered. Maybe he brought the kids to surprise me. Well, if that was the case, he was the one in for a surprise.

But it wasn't my son who stepped out of the truck. It was my husband. Minus the ball cap. Wearing a light blue oxford shirt with the store creases still running down the front. Whose broad smile when he saw me sent tingles through my soul and a lump in my throat. It was all I could do not to race down the steps and into his arms.

I met him on the stone walkway.

"I hope this is all right," I said, indicating the white capris, floral knit top, and sandals. "You said casual."

His eyes sparkled. "Perfect."

The truck sat so high, I needed the chrome running boards to get in.

"Nice," I said when he slid behind the wheel. "It has a new car smell, so is it safe to assume this is new?"

"Yep. Car dealer wanted to make room for the new models coming out—so I got a good deal."

"That's what Gabe always does when he's ready to trade in his old vehicles."

"Who?"

"Gabe. My son. I told you about him—remember?"

He shook his head then chuckled. "Forgive me, Evangeline. I must have been in the sun too long this afternoon." He reached across the seat and laid his hand on top of mine. "Either that or the sight of you has chased everything else from my mind."

His fingers intertwined with mine. *After dinner. I'll tell him then.* An hour later, we pulled into a parking lot in downtown DuBois.

"I hope you like Italian food," he said, shutting off the engine.

"My favorite," I said, checking my purse for the plastic bag for the umpteenth time.

"Forget something?" he asked.

I stretched nervous lips into what I hoped were a smile. "My lip gloss."

I came close to pulling that little bag out several times during the meal. But I kept hearing Mickie's warning, "Don't rush it." I wouldn't ask a single thing about his past until we got back to the cabin.

"What made you buy the truck?" I asked, tucking my napkin in the front of my collar.

"I need it for the fifth-wheel I bought last spring," he said, using his fork and butter knife to cut up his spaghetti. "I still have to get the hitch installed."

"You bought a fifth-wheel?"

He grinned. "Always dreamed of seeing the country. You don't think I want to be a handyman until I die, do you?"

"You're not a handyman," I said, cutting up my lasagna into bite-size pieces. "You're a caretaker."

"Same difference."

"What about your woodcarving business?"

He shrugged. "It's not really a business. More like a hobby."

I thought of the woodcarvings I'd seen on display at the Groundhog Festival. "How long have you been carving?" I asked.

He scratched the side of his head with his fingertips. "As long as I can remember, which, these days, isn't very long." His chuckle sounded forced. "To answer your question, Evangeline, about thirty years."

"You aren't going to quit, are you?"

He shrugged. "Probably not. As long as . . . as long as . . . excuse me." He took a sip of his ice water.

"As long as what, Steve?" I asked, stabbing a stubborn chunk of lettuce with my fork.

He put his fork down, folded his arms on the table, and leaned toward me, a faraway look in his blue eyes.

"As long as I keep getting these pictures in my head. I carve to . . ." he took a breath ". . . to exorcise demons, you could say."

"What do you mean?"

The waiter appeared with a pitcher of ice water and refilled our glasses. "Everything all right? Can I get you anything?"

"I'm fine," I said, impatient with the interruption. I was finally getting somewhere.

"We're good, thank you," Steve said.

After the waiter left, I repeated the question. "What do you mean, exorcise demons? What demons?"

He shifted his weight in his seat.

"You mean the pictures you get in your head?"

He nodded. "I get them in flashes. Sometimes the image comes and goes. Sometimes it stays with me for days, weeks, until I have to do something about it."

*Like sketch it?* I took a sip of my water. "Like carve it?"

He nodded.

"So these images are wildlife?"

"No."

"But all your carvings are wildlife, except for the bridge over troubled water carving."

He took a sharp breath. "What did you call it?"

"Bridge over troubled water."

He seemed shaken. "Why did you call it that?"

"Because that's what it is. A bridge over troubled water."

"There's a song by that title."

I nodded. "By Simon and Garfunkel. I know. It . . . it was a favorite of my husband and me."

"Ever since I got the picture in my head of the bridge, the raging waters, and the woman, I can't get that song out of my mind."

Suddenly I couldn't eat another bite. I pushed my plate away.

"I'm upsetting you, Evangeline. I'm sorry. I'll stop."

"No," I said. "This serving was really too large for me." My empty salad bowl blurred. "I had too much from the salad bar then filled up on the fresh bread."

He signaled the waiter for take-home boxes and our check.

"I'm sorry," I said as we pulled out of the parking lot. "I've just had a lot on my mind today. We're leaving tomorrow, you know."

He reached across the seat and took my hand again. "I wish you weren't. Will you give me your home phone number and address so I can call you or come and visit?"

*I'll do more than that.* "Of course," I said.

We rode in silence the rest of the way. When we got back to the resort, however, he pulled into the driveway of his cottage, not the cabin.

"I want to show you something," he said.

My heart was pounding. I fingered the plastic bag. *Now's the time. God, be with me.*

He came around and opened the passenger door and helped me slide out of the truck. Then he steered me to his workshop. Reaching above the doorframe, he retrieved a key and unlocked the door, then flipped a switch inside. Light flooded the interior.

"Go on in," he said.

I stepped over the threshold. The smell of wood shavings and new wood mingled with the odor of linseed oil and turpentine. The floor was swept, a barrel for the wood shavings in a corner. The handle of a shop broom rested against the wall next to a red and black industrial-style wet/dry vacuum. Trying to swallow the lump that had lodged in my throat, I walked over to the workbench, where several carvings in various stages rested—carvings I now knew he made from the sketches.

"May I?" I asked.

He nodded. I lifted each piece carefully, running my fingers reverently over the smooth wood, over Mom and Dad's features. Even the expressions were lifelike—and so like them.

"These . . . these are remarkable," I stammered. "Who are they?"

"I don't know. I just saw their faces in my head. I sketched them out first then did the carvings. Until I did, the mental images wouldn't leave. They haunted me day and night. That's what I meant when I said I carve to exorcise demons."

"I would hardly call these demons, Steve."

"They are when they get you up at night in a cold sweat, shaking like a junkie needing a fix."

I stepped over to the bridge carving. The wood was smoother, the woman's facial features clearer. I held in a gasp. It was me at twenty-one. And around the neck was the diamond cross necklace. I fingered the chain around my own neck and decided to leave the cross beneath the collar of the knit top.

"I see you've made progress," I managed to say.

"At first, the woman's face was hazy, but over the past week, since the festival, she's gotten clearer. And I was finally able to see the necklace that was just fuzzy before." He snapped his fingers. "Wait here a minute. There's something in the cottage I want to show you."

I knew what he'd come back with. He flipped the sketchbook open to the pencil drawing of the young me and held it next to the woodcarving.

"Do you have any idea who she is?" I asked.

"No, but she's been haunting me for more than thirty-five years. At first a lot . . . then she kind of disappeared for a while. But she's gradually come back. I see her more clearly than I ever have the past few days. She's like an angel who's constantly with me."

I reached into my purse for the snapshot Mickie had given me earlier, the studio headshot all officers got when they graduated boot camp. The likeness was unmistakable.

I pulled it out and held it up.

"Is this her?" I asked.

His face turned white. He took the picture from my hand and stared from the photo to the drawing to the carving. When he looked at me, his eyes were brimming.

"So, she's real," he whispered. "Who is she?"

I took the picture from his hand and held it next to my face.

"Me."

CHAPTER TWELVE

# STEVE'S STORY

"Let's go to the cottage," I suggested. I followed him along the stone pathway to the back door, through the kitchen and into the living room. We sat on the sofa facing the fireplace. I put my purse on the coffee table and turned to him.

"The carvings of the man and woman are images of my husband's parents."

He stared at me in disbelief. I rummaged through my purse and pulled out my wallet. I flipped through the photos until I found one of Mom and Dad Martin. I handed it to him.

"It was the last one they had taken for the church directory before they passed away. She died first, in '99, him a year later. They look older than when you saw them last, but they hadn't changed much. The resemblance is more than a coincidence."

He put the photograph on the coffee table beside the one of me and stared at it. "You said, 'when *you* saw them last.' I never saw them."

"Yes, you did."

"When?"

"Before you left for your second tour. In 1970."

He twisted to face me. "What are you talking about?"

I took a deep breath. "You're not Amish. And your name isn't Steve Michaels. It's Seth Martin. You're Seth Gabriel Martin. My husband."

He stared at me, his eyebrows knit together over the wire rims of his eyeglasses, his mouth in a tight line.

"I have proof."

I pulled the letter from my purse and unfolded it.

"Where'd you get that?" he asked. He sounded angry.

"When I brought your pie yesterday, you weren't around, so I looked for paper and pen to leave a note. I found a notebook under your Bible, and the letter fell out when I dropped the Bible. I didn't realize it was so heavy."

He snatched the letter out of my hands. "You had no business . . . no right."

Now I was getting angry. "I have every right. *I* wrote that letter. *I'm* 'E.' I took it because I thought *you* had no right to have it. I thought you stole it from my husband. That you knew what happened to my husband, and, by golly, I was going to get the truth from you."

"I didn't steal this letter from anyone."

"Where'd you get it?"

"It was in my back pants pocket when I came to."

"Came to?" I prodded gently.

It must have been a full minute before he spoke.

"I remember waking up in a Vietnamese villager's hut, in pain so bad I wanted to die. My life before that moment was gone. I didn't even know my name. I had nothing on me except the letter to tell me who I was."

Seth didn't carry his wallet when he flew missions. And he'd lost his dog tags in the second crash.

"Tell me about the villager," I prodded.

"Sinh An—the old man—told me in what little English he knew that he and his daughter had found me about ten yards from a burning American helicopter. At first they thought I was dead. When they realized I wasn't, they brought me back to the village and nursed me back to health."

"How badly were you hurt?"

"The damage was worse on the left side of my body, especially my face. That's why I remember in images, pictures in my head, not words. And even then, the images come in flashes, nothing I could hang onto. That's why I started carving them. My face healed up as well as it could under the conditions. I grew a beard to hide the . . . disfigurement."

"You had to know you were an American soldier," I said. "Why didn't you get back to one of the bases when you were well enough?"

"I did. With the help of Sinh An and Ai', his daughter, I made my way to Qui Nhon, the hospital compound that was written at the top of the letter. I was hoping that someone would recognize me or know who 'E' was."

"When? When did you come to Qui Nhon?"

He shrugged. "Two or three months after they found me."

I did the math. "You were shot down in enemy territory February 16, during Operation Lam Son. It took three days before they were able to get you out, but the rescue chopper went down. You were listed as MIA. Two months would make it April. I was still there. Three months would make it May. I left 'Nam at the beginning of May."

"There'd been a rocket attack. A building was burning," he said.

I shook my head. "There were no rocket attacks on Qui Nhon while I was there."

"I was told the nurses' quarters took a direct hit. That all the nurses had died in the attack."

I thought back. It hadn't happened after I left, while Mickie was there.

"Are you sure you went to Qui Nhon?"

He shrugged. "It doesn't matter now."

We sat in silence. Outside an owl hooted.

"I married her. Ai'. I thought my wife, 'E,' was dead." His blue eyes stared past me. "We had two children. A boy and a girl."

"Did you love her?"

"Yes."

Funny, but I didn't feel jealous. Which was strange. The Vangie of the Vietnam years would have been angry, hurt, and jealous. The Vangie Seth knew would have wanted to shoot them both. But this Vangie felt only sadness.

"What happened to them?" I asked softly.

His mouth tightened. "We managed to get on one of the refugee boats in '78. My wife and son died on the voyage."

*The Boat People. My Seth had been one of the Boat People!*

"What about your daughter?"

"I raised Tuyen myself. I found a nice, quiet little town in British Columbia twenty-five miles from Vancouver, got a job and settled down. Later I had reconstructive surgery on my face."

"What did you tell the doctors caused your injuries?"

"Farming accident. After Tuyen got married, I traveled around until I came here and started working for Bill. When I applied for a Social Security card, I just told them I was raised Amish and had no idea exactly when I was born. All I knew it was somewhere in Pennsylvania on a farm. Told them I left the fold, so to speak."

"When did you start going by Steve Michaels?"

"When I got to Canada. Until then, I was Nguyen Van Anh Dung, the name Sinh An gave me. When I got to Canada, I needed an English, or American, name, so I used the initials engraved inside the ring I had on when I came to."

He went to the recliner and rifled through the assortment of papers on the lamp table. I knew what he was looking for. I pulled the ring out of my purse and held it in my open palm. "This one?"

He snatched the ring from my hand.

"You had no right!" he said through clenched teeth.

I pulled my own wedding ring from my purse and held it up. On an impulse, I'd retrieved it from my Seth box before we left for the resort.

"I had every right," I said. "I put it on your finger. I thought you stole it from my husband."

He shook his head, but I didn't know if he was denying what I was telling him or shaking the cobwebs from his brain.

I continued. "The initials inside your ring are EJB to SGM. Evangeline Joy Blanchard to Seth Gabriel Martin. And the date engraved is 12/16/1970, the day we were married. Look inside my ring. See the initials engraved there? Now do you believe me?"

"I never said I didn't believe you, Evangeline."

*Then why aren't you taking me in your arms and kissing me? That's what I want to do to you.*

"Evangeline."

He took my face in his rough, dry hands—those beautiful hands that once wound themselves through my long, black hair—and gazed into my eyes with eyes full of pity, not love.

"Seth died in Vietnam," he said.

His words slashed my heart. I grabbed his hands and squeezed. Maybe if I squeezed hard enough he'd remember.

"How can you say that?" I cried. "You *are* Seth! Haven't I given you enough proof? Well, here's more: Seth had *Semper Fi* tattooed on his back left shoulder! I saw you working in the garden today. You had your shirt off! I *saw* that tattoo! And look—" I lifted the cross from under my collar. "This is the cross you gave me the night you proposed. Just like the one you carved."

His thumbs caressed my cheeks—like so long ago. Surely he remembered!

"The man in front of you now is not the man you fell in love with in Vietnam thirty-seven years ago."

"DNA." I grasped his shirt with both hands. Maybe I could shake some sense into him. "We can get DNA proof. Will that convince you?"

He shook his head slowly, a profound sadness in his eyes. I pulled the magazine from my purse.

"You have amnesia," I said. "Here's scientific evidence that even though the mind may forget, the heart remembers. That's how you remembered Dust Off. Why you have Seth's memories. Your heart is telling you the truth. Listen to it, Steve!"

He pulled the magazine out of my hands and dropped it on the coffee table.

"Let's go outside," he said.

He led me to the porch swing and pulled me down beside him. Putting his arms around me, he drew me to him. I lay my head on his shoulder, inhaling the sweet wood scent that still clung to his shirt. I could hear the beat of his heart.

"Oh, Seth."

"I'm Steve."

The tears started then.

The swing rocked gently, soothingly. He caressed my back, his lips against my forehead. I began to calm down. I felt safe, cuddled in his arms. He ran his fingers through my hair. I sat up abruptly.

"My hair was long and black the last time you saw me," I said. "I could dye it, or get a wig—"

He shook his head. Those beautiful blue eyes held only sadness. "Evangeline, in nearly forty years I haven't remembered anything except a few images. And until now, they made no sense. I doubt if I'll ever remember anything else."

He pulled me closer, and I nuzzled my nose in the V-neck of his shirt. I loved the smell of him. Something I thought long dead stirred in me. "We're still married, you know."

"Don't go there."

I pulled away and sat up. "Why not? You're Seth. In the flesh. I had you declared dead, but we can change that. I never divorced you. You never divorced me. So what if you were a bigamist—unknowingly, of course—for a few years? I never stopped loving you."

"Leave him dead, Evangeline."

The night was warm, balmy, but I shivered.

He kissed the end of my nose. "I haven't been able to get you out of my mind from the moment you slammed me with the car door. There you were with your violet eyes. I didn't know how to act. What to say. What to feel. I was drawn to you."

Hope, like a phoenix, rose in my soul. "Heart memories," I said.

He shrugged.

"You love me, Seth," I whispered. "You remember. I know you do."

He held my face in his hands. "Steve. I'm *Steve*, Evangeline. Attribute it to heart memories, if you want, because I am drawn to you. But as Steve."

My thoughts tumbled around in my brain, my heart seething with pain and confusion. I couldn't separate the two. Steve was Seth, no matter what he said, and Seth was Steve. And we were already married. Why couldn't he see that?

I stood.

He looked up at me, his face full of hope.

I searched his eyes. "I love Seth. You are Seth. But you refuse . . . I . . . I have to think. . . . I need to be alone."

I went into the cottage and picked up my purse. I left the magazine and the photos of me and his parents on the coffee table. Maybe he'd read the article after I left. When I stepped out the door, Steve grabbed me by the shoulders and pulled me to him. Emotion—love, pain, anger?—contorted his features.

"Evangeline . . ."

"Thank you for dinner," I whispered, kissing him softly on his lips. "I'll walk to the cabin. Good night . . . Steve."

I left him standing on the porch in the moonlight.

CHAPTER THIRTEEN

# SECOND THOUGHTS

It was the longest walk of my life. It was all I could do not to turn around and run back. I listened for the sound of his boots on the pavement behind me, or his truck door slam shut, an engine starting. Was he having second thoughts? Maybe he'd change his mind and rush to my cabin and tell me he was wrong. That he'd take my love anyway I wanted to give it—even if I insisted he was Seth, not Steve.

But the night was silent—even the owl and the crickets were quiet. I unlocked the door and let myself in the empty cabin. Dropping my purse on the chair by the front window, I stumbled across the dark room. I didn't bother to switch on the lamp—the moonlight poured through the side window, giving the room a ghost-like aura.

"I know all about ghosts," I muttered. "I've been living with one for thirty-six years."

It wasn't fair. After all this time, hanging on, sticking to my guns when everyone else told me to give it up, refusing the attentions of many attractive men—when I yearned for companionship, love, and intimacy. And then, just when I can't take being alone anymore and have him declared dead, he shows up. If only Steve would just admit he was Seth.

"Why is he being so stubborn?" I asked the empty room.

Deciding a nice, long bubble bath would help me get to sleep, I headed for the bathroom. While the water ran, I rummaged through the bottles of bath stuff I'd brought. Lavender, with its soothing and calming effects, was just what I needed. That and a nice, big hunk of chocolate with almonds.

I poured in two more capfuls than the directions called for, turned the water up, and watched as the bubbles frothed. I dropped my clothes on the floor and dipped my toe in.

"Ouch! That's *hot!*"

I jerked my foot back and turned up the cold water.

"A candle," I muttered. "Now where did Mickie put those 'Relaxation Therapy' candles she just bought?"

Wrapping a bath towel around my middle, I stepped into the living room on my way to Mickie's bedroom in search of candles. And stopped. There, on the porch swing, sat Steve. I could see him through the front window but wasn't sure if he could see me. I stood still, afraid to even breathe. What was he doing out there? I hadn't even heard him come. Why hadn't he knocked?

The longing that hit me in that moment nearly knocked me over— to invite him in and shed my towel. It wouldn't be a sin. After all, this man was my husband.

A rush of memories swept through me. Our honeymoon. The trysts in my hooch. The moments sandwiched between duty and exhaustion. The long, whispered talks. For thirty-six years I'd felt cut in half, still bleeding under a bandaged wound. Now I could feel complete again. Could we get back what we had so long ago? I wanted so much to try. *Remember?* I'd whisper. *Remember?*

Steve glanced in the window. In the moonlight his eyes met mine. Something sparked in them. Recognition? A memory? We stared at each other for what seemed like an eternity. Then I stepped forward, one hand clasping the towel, the other reaching out to him. He gave me a sad little smile, shook his head, stood, and turned away. *Don't go!* I wanted to shout. *Come back!* A door slammed and an engine roared to life. Tires crunched on the gravel driveway.

Tears splashed down my cheeks and onto my feet. Wait—it wasn't tears on my feet. *The bathtub! I left the water running. Oh, nuts!* I groaned and raced across the bathroom floor, slipping and sliding into the side of the overflowing tub, losing my towel in the process.

"What's all that racket?"

Mickie.

"Nothing," I called, reaching over the curved edge of the claw-foot tub and shutting off the water. "I just flooded the bathroom floor. Please tell me you're alone."

Mickie appeared at the door—alone. I breathed a sigh of relief.

"Evangeline Joy Martin!" She burst out laughing. "That must have been some hot date! I just saw Steve leave. Here—" She tossed me a dry towel. "Leave the mess and come tell me all about it. I'll put the kettle on. What we need is a nice, long girl talk with a pot of herbal tea."

"And chocolate," I said, grabbing the side of the tub and pulling myself up.

"Gotcha," she said, giving me the thumbs-up and turning to the kitchen. I looked down at the floor and sighed.

"Just let me get this mess cleaned up first. Do you know where there's a good mop around here?"

Mickie poked her head in the doorway, brown eyes sparkling.

"No," she said with a wicked smile and a wink, "but I'm sure the caretaker does."

"Don't even think it," I said. "Besides, he's not interested."

Over two pots of herbal tea and a two-pound box of expensive chocolate-covered nuts, I told her all that had happened.

"You're crazy," she said, shaking her head. "For decades you've hung on to this dream that someday you'd find Seth." She took a sip of her tea. "Frankly, I thought you were wrong, but, hey, it wasn't my life. Now you finally find him—I can't believe you're even thinking about it."

I sighed. "You don't understand."

"Oh, I understand, all right. I'm just not sure you do."

I plucked a chocolate-covered cashew from the box and bit into it. The sweet milk chocolate melted on my tongue.

"You're trying to change Steve into Seth," she said, shaking a piece of candy at me. "It's not gonna work, Vange. He's made a life for himself as Steve Michaels."

"I'm not trying to *change* him," I said. "I just need to convince him that he's Seth Martin."

Her tangled curls jiggled as she shook her head. "I don't know how you expect the guy to give up the only identity he's known and become someone he doesn't know."

"I can't pretend," I said. "And I won't live a lie."

"Well," she said, draining her cup and pushing away from the table. "I think you're a stubborn fool. We're leaving tomorrow. If you refuse to accept him as Steve Michaels, you're never gonna see him again."

After a night fraught with broken sleep, I rolled out of bed at six. No tea this morning. I needed strong coffee. While it brewed, I packed for the trip home. I wanted to be on the road right after lunch. The drive would take only a couple of hours, but I wanted to get back to my own little cottage.

I needed time alone to figure out where to go from here. Now that I'd had Seth declared dead. Now that I'd found him. Was I still married or not? If Steve wouldn't accept himself as Seth, what then? Was I free to date, to find a companion for my golden years? Did I even want to?

The aroma of hazelnut drew me to the little kitchen, where I filled the biggest mug I could find, then headed for the back porch glider, Bible in hand. The morning was cool and misty, the scent of pines heady, as I settled on the quilted glider and sipped my coffee. Perfect. My favorite time of the day—when the world isn't quite awake yet. The rising sun filtered through the trees, igniting hundreds of diamond dewdrops glittering in the grass. Chickadees took their turns at the bird feeder, ignoring the squawking blue jay on a nearby branch. Putting my mug on the wicker table, I opened my Bible, where I'd stuffed my daily devotional booklet, to the day's Scripture. *Forgetting what is behind,* I read, *and straining for what is ahead* . . . the page blurred.

"Not today." Two drops splashed on the worn black cover. "Tomorrow. At home. I'll have the rest of my life to cry. But I can't deal with this today."

Suddenly the morning wasn't perfect and peaceful. The restlessness that had haunted me since that awful moment in Vietnam when they told me Seth was missing rose up inside my soul like a big, black monster. Leaving my Bible and coffee on the back porch, I hurried to the bedroom to change.

Half an hour later I was walking along one of the forest trails, which one I didn't know. All I knew was that I wanted to run. From the past. From the present. From the future. From my own demons that had chased me since I'd come home from Vietnam alone. I walked until my throbbing knee—the one that took the brunt of my crash into the tub last night—protested. I leaned against a tree and scanned the forest around me. The trail curved through the trees to a bare rock surrounded by a wire fence. Seneca Point. The panoramic view of the Clarion River winding through emerald mountains rising from its banks had brought me peace and perspective yesterday. Perhaps I'd find the solace I needed today too.

I leaned on the fence, watching the water ripple along. *Forgetting what is behind, and straining for what is ahead . . .*

"I can't forget, Lord," I whispered. "And without Seth what's ahead is only emptiness."

*To everything, there is a season . . . a time to keep, a time to cast away. . . .* What time was it now? Time to keep or time to cast away? Was I wrong to insist that Steve give up the only identity he knew and, like Mickie said, become someone he didn't know? Could I forget the past? When I looked at Steve, who would I see—Steve or Seth? Could I ever love Steve as Steve?

*I think so, Lord. I was falling for him even before I found the letter and the ring.* I'd stop at his cottage on my way back to the cabin. Maybe he'd read the article. I'd say I stopped in to say hello. Good morning. I'm leaving today. Here's my address and phone number. Let's get together sometime. I'm sorry I ran off last night. But the cottage was closed up when I stopped by. So was the woodshop. No truck was in the driveway.

Back at the cabin, I took a shower, then drove Mickie's car to meet up with her and Bill for lunch at the resort's restaurant. From my seat at the table, I could see the parking lot. Steve's truck wasn't there, either. He was probably fixing something in one of the cabins.

"Vangie?"

I turned my head. Bill looked at me with an indefinable sadness. Next to him, Mickie studied the menu.

"What will you have to drink?" he asked.

"Um ... just water."

"You have a glass of water right in front of you." He leaned toward me. "You okay? You look a little pale."

Mickie's eyes met mine.

"Yes, I'm fine. I'm a little tired. I just came back from a morning walk up the mountain and down, and I didn't sleep well last night. Full moon."

He nodded. "Ah, full moon insomnia." I could've sworn he winked at Mickie.

The waitress bustled up to our table, pad and pencil in hand.

"Have you folks decided what you want?" she asked.

"I'll have ... uh ... just iced tea, please," I told her. "No sugar."

Bill ordered a chicken salad, and Mickie a Seneca-burger and fries. After the waitress gathered up the menus and left, Bill turned to me. "Steve's gone."

Mickie slipped her arm through Bill's. "You'd better tell her now," she whispered in his ear. Loud because that was Bill's deaf ear. So I heard.

A sick feeling grew in the pit of my stomach. "Tell me what?"

Bill took a deep breath. "Steve gave me his notice a month ago. He's retiring. He stayed on these past few weeks as a favor to help me with the reunion. He called me late last night. Said he was leaving early in the morning. Not to worry. His crew would take care of everything."

I was stunned. "Where—"

He shrugged. "Who knows? His plan was to pick up his fifth-wheel and tour the country."

Panic-stricken, I looked at Mickie. Her brown eyes glistened.

*THINK, Evangeline. Calm down and think!* I took a sip of my water, trying to appear nonchalant. My insides were churning. How long did it take to put a hitch on?

"Vangie, I told Bill everything."

Bill's hand caressed hers.

"What about your cell phone, Vange?" she asked. "Wouldn't you have his number there?"

Of course! Hope welled in me as I fished the phone out of my purse and found his number on my recent calls log. His voice mail picked up. "This is Steve. Leave a message. Thanks."

"Steve? This is Evangeline. Call me. Please. I . . . I have to talk to you."

I disconnected and put the phone on the table. What if he didn't call?

By the time Mickie came back to the cabin, my packed bags were in the car, and I was fretting.

"Where have you been?" I fumed when she finally waltzed in at three. "I wanted to be home by now."

I knew what a mess her room was.

"I'm not going back with you," she said.

I put down my book and stared at her. I couldn't remember when I'd ever seen her so *radiant*. She smiled and plopped on the sofa beside me.

"Bill asked me to marry him."

"Wow! That was fast! A week ago I thought he was going to pop the question to me. And a week ago I was ready to say yes."

"Oh, I know it's fast. But at our age, we can't waste time."

I hugged her. "I wish you the best, my friend. All the love you've ever dreamed of and more."

She dabbed her eyes. "Oh, we haven't even mentioned love. But we feel comfortable together, like a couple of old shoes." She giggled. "If love happens along the way, well, that'll be just fine."

"But you love him." I didn't have to ask.

She nodded. "I've loved him since high school."

I stood. "This calls for a pot of herbal tea and chocolate. Come on."

In the kitchen, she told me their plans. They'd marry as soon as possible.

"It'll be a small wedding," she said. "Just me, him, and the preacher. Our kids, too. And you, as matron of honor. You *will* come, won't you, Vange?"

I reached across the table and squeezed her arm. "I wouldn't miss it for the world. Oh, I just thought of something. If you're staying here, how am I going to get home?"

"You drive my car back. We'll come for it this weekend."

I'd miss her company—not just on the way home, but for the rest of my life. For most of our lives we'd been "single"—me for reason of a missing husband and her because of divorce.

She sensed my sadness. "Did Steve call?"

I shook my head. "I'll get his contact information at the office in the morning when I check out."

"No, you won't. The only address Steve left was an old email address. I tried sending him an email on Bill's computer, but it bounced back. Bill thinks he doesn't want to be bothered."

"What about his paycheck?"

She shook her head. "Direct deposit."

It was going to be a long ride home.

CHAPTER FOURTEEN

# FIRE

In August Mickie and Bill got married, and my shed burned down.

As planned, the wedding was small, only four of us and the minister in a late afternoon ceremony in the nearby village of Sigel. Will was his father's best man. Mickie's girls couldn't make it because they'd committed themselves to helping with a girls' boot camp somewhere in upstate New York, and Collie, Bill's daughter, refused to come.

Although Mickie had confided this was a marriage for companionship, not love, Bill's eyes told me different when she walked down the aisle of the little country chapel.

Dressed in a simple ivory brocade dress, her curly brown hair framing her pert Italian face, she stepped to the altar alone—"I don't need anyone to give me away," she'd told me. "I'm giving myself away."

Mushy me—tears welled in my eyes when they said their vows. *Give them the love of a lifetime,* I prayed, blinking away the tears and sniffing discreetly into my bouquet of red roses. Afterward we had dinner at the resort in the private dining room.

"I envy you," I told Mickie during the prime rib dinner. "A month-long honeymoon cruising the Mediterranean."

She giggled. "Bill booked the twenty-day Mediterranean Adventure. I've lost track of all the ports of call—Florence, Naples,

Rome—*Rome!* Think of all the history, the art! Do you think we'll get to see the Pope?"

I chuckled. I hadn't seen her this animated for a long time. But then love had been a long time coming for my best friend.

". . . Greece, Spain, Turkey. Monte Carlo," she said, counting off with her ruby red-nailed fingers. "Bill booked us in a deluxe suite—top of the line. I may not want to come back."

I grinned. "Who would blame you? And don't worry about your house. The realtor has my number. I stored your paintings in my spare bedroom. I had to move some stuff out to the shed, but it all worked out."

What did you do with your 'Seth' box?"

I sighed. "It's in my bedroom closet. I still haven't decided what to do with it. The journals are too personal to put out for the garbage man, and I can't bring myself to burn everything. Maybe Gabe or the grandkids will want them someday."

She twisted her ruby red lips in a wry grin. "Do you really think so?"

I shrugged. "You never know."

"What about all the pictures?"

"You mean the ones we took in 'Nam?"

She nodded.

"They're in the box, too—along with the snapshot you took of us on our wedding day. Maybe I should take that one out. But right now, I don't think I could handle seeing it."

"Haven't heard from him yet, huh?"

I shook my head. "I don't want to."

Her lightly shaped eyebrows arched.

"You were right," I said, taking a sip of my iced tea.

"Aren't I always? What was I right about this time?"

"You told me getting angry would help me to move on. The more I thought about the way he snuck off, the madder I got. He was right—

he's not the man I thought he was. Seth was brave, a take-charge man. Steve . . ." I took a determined breath. ". . . is a sniveling coward."

Mickie fingered the rose gold necklace around my neck. "Where's the cross?"

"With the wedding ring. Tucked away in a drawer of my jewelry box. Out of sight."

"Not in your 'Seth' box?"

I shook my head. "Someday I'll give them—or will them, whichever is the case—to Evie."

"Who's Evie?" Bill asked. "Your daughter?"

"My granddaughter." I thought of all the love I'd poured onto those pages. I swallowed. "I never want to see those journals again."

"Wow," she said, her eyes wide with surprise. "You really *are* mad."

When I got back from the wedding, I sealed the box with packing tape then lugged it out to the shed. It was time to forget what was behind and reach for what was ahead, although "ahead" still seemed as empty as ever.

The following Saturday I decided to tackle the shed project. When I'd moved in the spring, I'd simply stacked boxes and boxes of "stuff" I couldn't decide what to do with in the small wooden building about fifty feet from my cottage. Every time I pulled my lawn tractor in, I worried that I'd hit something. I couldn't store my garden tools the way I wanted. Now that the house had been given a thorough cleaning, with a fresh coat of paint inside and out, and new window dressings and scatter rugs, it was time to address the cluttered shed.

The first thing I did—before the day got too muggy—was empty it out. Then, after lunch, I planned to hose it out and cool myself off at the same time. While I was lugging the umpteenth plastic bin out to the lawn to put in one of three piles—keep, pitch, and not sure—a black, late-model pickup pulled into my driveway. My heart leapt to my throat. But the short, stocky man who jumped down out of the extended cab wasn't Steve. Carlie, my new Brittany spaniel puppy, pranced along the clothesline I'd clipped her to, yapping and hopping, stubby tail chugging away. *Some guard dog,* I thought, cupping my hand over my eyes to watch the mustached stranger approach.

"Hey." He trotted over to me. "You Evangeline Martin?"

"Who wants to know?" A woman alone has to be cautious. The local news had reported scam artists in the area. One would come to the door and distract the homeowner, while another two snuck in the back door and helped themselves to valuables. The man, who looked about my age, extended his hand and grinned. The waxed handlebars on his black mustache twitched. "Jonas Kramer. I live up the road in the stone house."

I nodded, taking his hand. "Evangeline Martin. Nice to meet you, Jonah."

"It's *Jonas.*"

My hearing was getting worse. Maybe I'd have to see about getting a hearing aid after all.

I studied the man standing in front of me. So this was the guy who owned the house I passed when I went to town. I admired his place, especially the in-ground pool in the backyard. His grip was firm, but not bone crunching, which I appreciated. Lately my hands—my fingers especially—hurt at night and when there was a storm moving in.

"Nice to finally meet a neighbor," I said, stepping back and wiping my brow. "Even if your place is half a mile away."

"Four-tenths of a mile, to be exact," he said, lifting his golf cap and scratching the top of his sunburned head. You tend to notice things like that when someone is six inches shorter than you.

"I have a package that belongs to you," he said, pointing his thumb over his shoulder at his truck. "Delivery guy brought it to my place yesterday. You weren't home. Everything was all locked up, and he couldn't find any place to leave it so it'd be out of the weather, so he left it with me."

"Thank you."

"I hope that was all right. I could've refused it."

"No," I said, studying my neighbor, who frowned. "I mean, no, I wouldn't have wanted you to refuse it, and yes, it's fine. I thought no one lived in the stone house. I've never seen any lights at night, and it always looks closed up when I go by."

"Been away. When d'you move in?"

"The end of April." I suddenly felt awkward. "You said you have a package for me?"

"Oh, yeah," he said, a boyish grin spreading across his ruddy cheeks. "I'll get it."

As he trotted back to his truck, I noted the casual way his mesh shorts draped from his waist, the calf muscles rippling with every step, the firm, straight back. *A runner.*

"Thank you," I said when he returned lugging a package about eighteen inches square.

"Careful," he said, handing it to me. "It's a mite heavy."

I frowned. I hadn't ordered anything and wasn't expecting anything from Gabe or Mickie. Who else would send me anything? I took the box, scanning the return address label. Just a PO box in Cooksburg. My heart leapt to my throat. Was Steve back?

"Thank you," I said again, hoping Jonas would take the hint and leave. He didn't. He stood, staring at my eyes.

"Sorry," he said, a blush spilling across his tan face to his ears, making the freckles on his nose stand out. "I just never seen anyone with purple eyes before."

"Violet," I said, shifting the box in my arms for a better grip. "My eyes are violet." *And the word is* saw, *not* seen.

An awkward moment passed as a jet scraped the summer sky overhead.

"Yeah, well," he grinned. "I best get going. See you around, Evangeline."

"Vangie," I called to his retreating back. "Call me Vangie."

He gave me the thumbs-up as he strode to his truck. I watched while he backed out onto the road, then pulled back into the driveway. The passenger window slid down.

"Hey," he yelled, leaning across the seat. "D'you want any help with them boxes? They look heavy."

I waved him away. "Thanks, but no."

"You know where I am if you change your mind."

His tires squealed on the hot pavement as he backed out a little too fast then headed for his place. I realized then how clearly I could see his house—and how clearly he could probably see mine. *Maybe I could plant some fast-growing bushes,* I thought as I headed for the cottage.

In the kitchen, I put the package on the table while I poured myself a glass of ice cold water and pulled the box cutter out of the utility drawer. After checking the package to determine the best way to open it, I carefully drew the razor edge through the tape, along the edges.

As I pulled open the top flaps and placed my fingers around the bubble-wrapped item, I gasped. *No! It couldn't be!* I lifted it out. Yes, it was—the "Bridge over Troubled Water" woodcarving that I'd wanted so badly, but Steve wouldn't sell. I stumbled into the nearest chair, put my head in my hands, and wept.

After a light supper of chicken salad and fresh blackberries in milk, I headed back out to finish my project. After lunch I'd hosed the shed, inside and out, and while it dried, transferred all the "keep" items to plastic storage bins—all the same size, of course. Now I pressed white labels on the tops and sides, marking with black permanent marker the contents. By eight o'clock the only thing I had left was my Seth box.

I stared at it. Where to put it? On the pile at the end of the driveway for Monday's garbage pickup? The pile behind the shed to be burned when it rained enough for the no-burning ban to be lifted? Or back in the shed? I sighed. I was hot, sweaty, and tired. My whole body ached. I overdid it, for sure. But I wanted to make the decision, once and for all.

I put it back in the shed—for now—then parked the tractor in its nice clean spot and headed to the cottage for a long soak in an Epsom-salt bath, a cup of warm milk, and bed. I'd deal with the Seth box another day.

I'd been dreaming—that Mickey Rooney, not Jonas, lived in the stone house and had just invited me over for a swim—when Carlie's urgent barking jolted me up out of dreamland.

"What is it, girl?" I mumbled, rolling over and reaching my arm out to pet her. But she paced between the bed and the window frantically, her sharp yaps piercing the night. A strange orange glow flickered outside the window. The acrid smell of smoke hung in the air. *Fire!*

The next thing I knew, I was wrestling with the garden hose, fighting to get it unwound, yanking it across the yard. I aimed it at the blaze. Nothing. *Water. Turn on the water!* I raced to the spigot, the spiky dry grass like tiny shards of glass against my bare feet. The faucet was stuck. Putting both hands on the valve, I leaned and turned with all my might. It gave. I turned until it stopped, then raced back to the hose.

Hissing steam and angry flames licked the night. Sparks popped around me. I sprayed back and forth, back and forth, my arms aching with the effort. Suddenly an earsplitting explosion threw me backwards—I flew through the air and landed on my back, hitting my head on the hard ground. Instinctively I rolled onto my stomach and curled up, knees under me and arms over my head. I was back in Pleiku, huddled in the bunker, scared to death the next mortar round would be my last.

"Vangie!"

Arms lifted my shoulders, held me close. *Steve. Oh, thank God! Steve's here.*

"Are you okay?" The arms cradled me, rocked me.

I opened my eyes, expecting to see a soldier with a helmet. Jonas's dark eyes exuded concern. My hands flew to my head. The shed! My Seth box! I shoved Jonas away and raced to the burning shed. I could still get it. But the arms that lifted me yanked me back.

"Let go!" I screamed, clawing at the hands that held me tight. "I can still save it!"

"It's too late," he said. He gripped me then shook me, hard. "Listen to me! There's nothing in there worth dying for."

I twisted around. The ravenous flames engulfed the entire structure, consuming the walls, studs, boxes—everything. My knees buckled, but Jonas's arms led me across the lawn to his pickup. He hefted me up onto the seat. Something was draped over my bare shoulders. In the distance, sirens screamed in the night, getting louder, closer.

"Wait here, Evangeline," Jonas said. "I've got to water down the cottage roof. The sparks . . ."

Stunned, I watched my shed burn. My Seth box—not worth dying for? Then it hit me: *Who cares?* Who'd take time to read the pages I'd so painstakingly, lovingly, and faithfully written? *Forgetting what lies behind and reaching for what is ahead. . . .* A heavy, invisible burden lifted, vanished into the smoky night. As I watched the firefighters, a calm settled over me—I was, finally, free.

CHAPTER FIFTEEN

# THE WORLD ACCORDING TO EVIE

"Sure hope you didn't have anything valuable in there." Jonas reached in the passenger window and adjusted whatever it was that draped my shoulders. I looked down. A man's plaid flannel shirt.

"Looks like your shed's a goner."

I raised my head and opened my mouth to answer. Fine, white ash sprinkled across his bald head and bare shoulders. A few gray hairs teased his muscular chest. In spite of the muggy August night and the blistering heat from the blaze, I shivered.

"No." I clutched Jonas's shirt tighter around me. "Nothing that can't be replaced."

He leaned in, the faint scent of either aftershave or deodorant mingling with the acrid stench from the fire.

"You all right?" His eyes met mine.

I nodded. I was glad he was here. For once I could sit back and let someone else take charge. My insides were ice, and my knees felt as though the lackadaisical Clarion River sloshed through them. And my head hurt something fierce.

"Carlie!" I bolted up and reached for the door handle. "My dog!"

"Easy, Evangeline. She's right here."

I leaned out the window. Yep, there was my precious Brittany—sitting patiently beside Jonas, the dog's pink nose nudging his dangling hand.

"She must like you," I said, an odd shyness creeping into me.

He grinned. "Why shouldn't she?"

"She doesn't like men," I said. "The poor UPS guy's scared to death to get out of his truck."

I peered over his shoulder. Hoses snaked from the tanker truck across my lawn to the burning shed. Flames shot high into the night sky. Steam hissed. Smoke roiled. My life burned. And I didn't feel sad.

The next morning I slept in. An insistent, annoying mechanical tune pierced through the grogginess and dragged me up out of dreamland. This time it was Chuck Norris who'd asked me over for a swim. I fumbled around the top of the nightstand for the phone before the answering machine picked up.

"Hi. This is Vangie. Leave a message." *Beep. Beep.*

"Vangie? This is Margot. I heard you had a fire last night, and you weren't in church. I just called to see if you needed anything. Actually, I called to see if the answering machine would pick up because then I'd know your house didn't burn down. Call me if you need anything. You have my number. It's on the Bible study group list."

I heard the click as Margot hung up and glanced at the red numbers on my alarm clock. *Good grief! It's almost one!* I pushed back the top sheet—and noticed I was still wearing Jonas's shirt. I pulled the collar to my nose. A faint odor of sweat mixed with deodorant and aftershave. The smell of a man. And just like that the longing hit me—the same yearning that swept me the night I saw Steve sitting on the swing in the moonlight. *Steve.*

I'd call Margot back later, thank her for her concern and assure her all was well at the Martin house. *And it is,* I thought, heading for the bathroom. *It really is.*

While I sipped hot tea and nibbled on rye toast, I scanned the Sunday paper. The Atlantic hurricane season wasn't supposed to be as bad as originally predicted. Lake Superior was shrinking and heating up. *Wish I could say that about me.* . . . Gas prices were predicted to climb to $3.16 in 2008, to $5.53 by 2016. *Gas.* I'd had a can of gasoline in the shed for the lawn tractor. Was that what started the fire?

A rap at my back door set Carlie off, barking and prancing with excitement.

"Just a minute," I called. I still wore Jonas's shirt over my nightgown, so I hurried to the bedroom and slipped into my kimono. "Coming."

On my way to the door, I glanced out the front bay window. Jonas's truck sat in the driveway.

"Just checking to see how you're doing," Jonas said when I opened the door. Carlie, her entire rear end bouncing back and forth, pushed her nose against the screen. A camouflage boonie cap with a fishing license pinned to it covered Jonas's head.

"Thanks." My face heated up. Jonas had walked me to the house and made sure I was safely tucked in bed after the firemen left around three in the morning. "Come in. Please." I opened the screen door to let him in. He rubbed Carlie behind her fluffy ears then stepped into the kitchen, a whiff of aftershave trailing him.

"Would you like some coffee?" I asked, tightening the sash on my kimono. "I could make some."

"Nah," he said. He pulled out a chair and plopped down. "Something cold, though, would hit the spot."

"Iced tea?"

He grabbed the newspaper. "Sure."

My hands trembled as I pulled the pitcher from the refrigerator and leaned the spout on the rim of the glass. Tea sloshed on the counter. I swabbed it with a dishcloth, wrapped the glass with a paper towel, placed it on the table in front of him, then sat down, glad to have some support under me. Why was I so shaky?

"Mmmm . . . perfect," he said, smacking his lips. "What's the paper towel for?"

"Condensation."

He wiped his lips with his bare wrist. "Doing okay?"

I sipped my tea. "Yes. Thanks for calling 911. All I could think of was putting out the fire."

He shoved his cap further back on his head. "You took a chance, getting so close. You're lucky you weren't hurt when that gas can blew."

"Is that what exploded? I thought—" I bit back the next words: *it was a mortar round*. "My head must have hit the ground pretty hard. I don't remember much after that. Bits and pieces. I appreciate all you did."

"I thought about staying and waking you up every two hours, but you weren't concussed."

Feeling awkward, I gave him a shy smile. "Thanks for your shirt. I'll wash it and get it back to you."

"No hurry. Tom—the fire chief—said your lawn tractor might be the cause. What kind of tractor was it?"

"My lawn tractor? But I made sure it cooled off before I parked it in the shed. And I took the key out."

He shook his head. "A certain type of tractor has a faulty ignition system. Could start a fire. Without the key in. What kind did you have?"

I told him.

"Yep. That's the one. The manufacturer issued a recall last month. It was on the news. Advised folks who owned them to park them away from structures until they got the system replaced. Didn't you get a letter?"

I shook my head. "I bought it used. All I have is the owner's manual."

"It was all over the news last month."

Last month I had other things on my mind.

"You have insurance?" he asked.

"Yes. I took pictures of everything in the shed after I finished cleaning it out yesterday. They're all on my digital. I'll download them later and put them in the insurance file."

He whistled. "You are one organized lady."

I smiled. "I try."

We sat quietly for a few minutes. Carlie had settled down under the table—at Jonas's feet. I finished my toast and tea, both now cold.

"Who's Steve?"

"Huh?"

"You kept mumbling his name last night."

Sudden tears threatened to ruin my carefully crafted composure. I focused my attention on the chickadee pecking at the bird feeder outside the kitchen window. And wondered where the woodcarver was. Jonas reached across the table and placed his hand on mine. I pulled it away. In the silence the ticking of the old clock on the mantel in the living room sounded like a bomb getting ready to go off. Jonas nodded curtly, gulped the last of his iced tea, and stood.

"If you need anything, Evangeline, I'm right up the road."

"It's *Vangie*," I called after him as he shut the door behind him.

Gabe and the kids showed up around two. I'd just gotten out of the shower and was brushing my teeth when I heard the front door slam and footsteps running across the hardwood floor.

"Gram? Grandma! What happened to your shed?"

"I'm in the bathroom," I called. "I'll be right out."

"Who's the guy?" Gabe stood at the bathroom door, which I'd opened after I stepped out of my hot shower to clear away the steam. Living alone you can do that.

"What guy?" I asked, running my fingers through my wet hair.

"The one hosing down what's left of your shed."

I walked to the back door. Jonas, now wearing a ball cap backward, sprayed the smoldering remains.

"My neighbor. Jonas . . . something. I just met him yesterday afternoon. He's the one who called 911. He was a big help to me last night. What's he's doing?"

"Jonas!" I called through the screen. "What are you doing?"

"Hosing down the hot spots."

I turned to Gabe. "He's hosing down the hot spots."

He gave me a wry smile. "I heard."

"He's cute, Gram."

This from my precocious twelve-year-old namesake, whom we call "Evie" to keep things straight. Evie, with her tall, slender form and violet eyes, took after the Martin side of the family.

"Do you have any cookies, Grandma?" asked seven-year-old Sammy.

Sammy was short for his age and on the chubby side. I knew Cammie, my daughter-in-law, didn't allow Sammy too many sweets. I raised my eyebrows at Gabe.

"Just two, son. And don't tell your mother."

While the kids settled in front of the TV with a plate of peanut butter cookies, Gabe and I headed outside. I introduced the two men, noting that Gabe, at six-four, was a foot taller than Jonas.

"Mom tells me you live up the road," Gabe said after shaking hands.

"Yep."

"Well, thanks, Mr . . ."

"Kramer, but call me Jonas."

"Thanks, Jonas."

In the afternoon sun a miniature rainbow glistened in the spray. I loved rainbows. Something good always happened to me after I saw one.

"That'll do 'er for now," Jonas said, dropping the hose on the ground. I bent over to roll it up and put it back on its hanger.

"Leave it, Evangeline," Jonas said. "I'll be back later on, after supper. Want to make sure all the hot spots are out. Everything's so dry, you know. Wouldn't take much for it to rekindle and spread."

"How long before we can be sure it won't flare up again?" I asked.

He shrugged. "Don't worry about it. I'll keep an eye on it."

After he left, Gabe and I settled in the Adirondack chairs on the patio with our iced tea. The kids, having finished their snack and complaining there wasn't anything on TV, snooped around the remains of the shed.

"What all did you have in there?" Gabe asked.

I told him.

"The journals?" he sputtered, choking on the tea he'd just sipped. "Oh, Mom, I'm sorry."

"I'm not."

His sandy brown eyebrows shot up.

"Gabe, who'd read them? You?"

"Truthfully, no." He looked relieved.

Should I tell him? The lazy sounds of the humid afternoon buzzed around us. *Your father's alive, Gabe. But he doesn't remember me.* I watched Evie and Sammy. *He had another family.* No. What good would come out of telling him? I didn't even know where Steve was. Or if I'd ever see him again.

"It's just as well," I said softly, mostly to myself. "It's time to move on. Put the past behind me."

When the adjuster came on Tuesday, I was ready for him. I'd made copies of everything in my insurance file, downloaded the pictures, and printed them out.

"I'm impressed," he said, leafing through the papers. "This should speed up the process quite a bit. Good thing your house didn't catch."

"When can I expect a check?"

"I'll turn in all the information," he said, pulling an index card out of his shirt pocket, scribbling something on it, then clipping it onto the file folder I'd given him with a paper clip he'd dug put of his pants pocket. He pressed the file into his briefcase, zipped it shut, and stood. "That's it, then."

After he left, I decided to go shopping, get some prices on lawn tractors, so when the check came in, I'd be ready. It would help to burn up the restless energy. I spent the afternoon pricing tractors, rototillers—something small that I could handle for the vegetable and flower gardens I planned for next year—and snow blowers. I arrived home hungry, my purse stuffed with brochures and my head spinning with information. Stopping at my mailbox, I glanced up the road, to Jonas's house. Maybe I could ask him about lawn tractors. And rototillers. And snow blowers.

*Silly!* I scolded myself, stuffing my mail into my purse and pulling onto my gravel driveway. I'd talk to Gabe. That's what sons are for.

"Gram, do you ever think about getting married again?"

I'd promised Evie a sleepover since I moved in, and the night before the family reunion seemed perfect. So, on the Friday evening after the fire, she was helping me with my offering for the reunion—Bo Kho, the Vietnamese beef stew dish that Steve had made. I looked up from the recipe card.

"Why do you ask?"

She shrugged. "Just wondering. Well, do ya?"

"Sometimes."

"I heard Mom and Dad talking. They don't like you living way out here in the sticks all by yourself. Dad said you made a big mistake when you bought this place."

"He did, did he?"

"Mom said you need a man."

"She did, did she?"

"That Jonas guy's kinda, like, cute. Even if he is, you know, short."

*So,* I thought, attacking a tomato with my knife, *my son thinks I'm a worrisome old lady. Forget asking HIM about a lawn tractor.*

"I've only just met him, sweetie. I'll be fine. I've been on my own my whole life. Here." I put a mixing bowl and the recipe card on the counter in front of her beside the spices I'd gathered earlier. "Do me a favor and mix these ingredients together. I have them highlighted, see? The measuring spoons are right here."

As she worked, I cubed the beef.

"Gram?"

"Hmmm?"

"Do you ever think about Grampa?"

My hands stopped. I blinked, trying to make the image of Steve's rugged face disappear.

"Yes," I said softly.

"Are you, like, still married to him?"

*I don't know the answer to that myself.* I sighed.

"Mom said you'd had him 'clared dead.' What's that mean?"

I smiled. "My, that must have been a long conversation. How did you stay still for so long?"

She giggled. "They were outside on the porch swing, which is, like, right under my bedroom window. They thought I was asleep. But I'd been texting my boyfriend. We had a fight, see, and he wanted to make up." She gave me a knowing look. "I was playing hard to get."

I shook my head. "Tsk, tsk. You're too young for boyfriends."

"Gra-am!" She rolled her violet eyes. "I am not! Trixie—she's, like, my very best friend in the whole world—Trixie's been goin' out with Doug for, uh, let's see—six weeks now."

"Going out? Her parents allow her to date? How old is she?"

She shook her head. "She doesn't go out go out—they just, like, hang out together, text each other, and all that kind of stuff."

"Oh, I see. Is the marinade ready? Good." I dumped the beef cubes in the bowl while she stirred, using my big rubber spatula. "That's good. Now take that plate and cover the bowl. While the meat marinates, why don't you and I grab a glass of iced tea and go sit on the patio?"

The August evening was warm. Maple leaves rustled in the soft breeze as we settled on the glider.

"Look, Gram," Evie said, pointing to the deepening sky. "A fingernail moon."

A sliver of moon hung just above the purple horizon. I smiled. "It does look like a fingernail, doesn't it?"

We sipped our tea, listening to the crickets begin their night song, watching the last of the swallows swoop through the sky heading for their nests, and savoring the pine scent riding on the whisper of the wind. The glider creaked gently.

"Is Grampa dead, Gram?"

*No. Yes. Yes and no.* I sipped my tea.

"I mean, I know he got shot down and all that, and kinda, like, disappeared."

I explained what MIA/BNR meant. "The chances of him showing up after all this time are slim to none. The government will send me a paper that says he's officially dead."

"Do you think you'll ever, like, fall in love again, Gram?"

I thought of Steve—his face, his hands, his smile, his eyes—the slight limp when he walked, his beautiful woodcarvings.

"I . . . don't know."

"You could marry Jonas. Then you wouldn't, like, be alone. And we wouldn't have to worry about you."

I gave her a hug. "You don't have to worry about me, sweetie. I'm not alone. Not really. I have you, your brother, your dad and mom, and lots of friends."

"Yeah, but we're not around all the time, you know? Don't you get lonely?"

Such deep questions for a twelve-year-old. But kids grow up fast these days.

"Sometimes," I said with a sigh, "sometimes I just want someone to play Scrabble with. Or take a walk in the woods with. Or make a good meal for. Or—"

"I play Scrabble."

I jumped.

A man's voice came out of the dusk, around the corner. "And I love home-cooked meals."

Jonas stepped out from the shadows and across the stone patio. He wore running clothes and a sweatband across his forehead. How long had he been there?

"Sorry. I didn't mean to startle you. I was taking my nightly jog when I decided to stop in and see how you're doing."

Evie winked at me.

"You've met my granddaughter, Evie?"

Jonas nodded.

"Hi, Jonas," she said with a little wave and a big grin. "Hey, what are you doing tomorrow?"

I gaped at her. *No, Evie. Don't.*

He shrugged. "Haven't decided. Why?"

She took a deep breath. "How would you like to go to a picnic with us? Gram and I are making a new dish—what's it called, Gram?"

"Bo Kho. It's a Vietnamese beef stew." I was aghast.

"Yeah—that. Anyway, my mom's family—they're Italian, you know—has, like, this huge thing every year—"

"Family reunion," I explained, feeling my face heat up.

"Yeah, that. Would ya like to come?"

Jonas grinned. "Sure," he said. "Why not?"

"Great!" she said, jumping up and nearly dropping her glass. "I think I'll go in and, like, check on the meat. See ya!"

My heart sank. I turned to my neighbor. "You don't have to go if you don't want to. Evie is, well, impulsive. It's her age."

"Actually, I'd like to go. Sure beats Saturday chores. What time are we leaving?"

Later, while the stew simmered on the stove, Evie and I chomped on popcorn and watched a movie.

"Evie," I said, pausing the DVD for a bathroom break, "why did you invite Jonas?"

She grinned. "Gram, sometimes you just gotta take the chance, ya know?"

"I'm too old for chances. Besides, take the chance on what?"

"On love, Gram. Sometimes you can't wait 'til it, like, comes to you. You gotta go after it."

CHAPTER SIXTEEN

# FAMILY REUNION

I don't know which was a bigger hit at the reunion—my Bo Kho stew or Jonas. All eyes were on my "date" as we piled out of Jonas's truck, which he insisted we take instead of my car. Evie hovered over our offerings—Jonas brought homemade pizza—in the backseat of the extended cab and peppered the poor guy with questions the entire hour it took to get to the county park.

"Where you from, Jonas?" "Ever been married?" "How long have you lived in the stone house?" "Don't you ever get lonely in that big place all by yourself?" "Do you swim in your pool a lot?" "How come every time I see you you're wearing a different hat?" Today he wore a white pit helmet.

Thanks to Evie, I learned that Jonas was retired, had just bought the property last winter, had never married, swam every day, collected hats, and was from all over.

"I'm an Army brat, Evie," he told her. "Do you know what that is?"

She giggled. "Of course. I'm not, like, stupid, you know."

And thanks to Evie's all-too-obvious matchmaking, Jonas learned that I was a retired nurse, a "widder," and "the best cook ever." She described in agonizing detail who all he'd meet at the reunion and how everyone was related. I doubted he'd remember any of it, but he surprised me.

"That your new man?" Cammie's brother, Rocky, asked me while I measured coffee grains into the crowd-size stainless steel urn.

"No," I said, snapping the lid in place and looking around for an outlet. We'd rented this same pavilion every year for the past I don't know how many years, and I never could remember where the outlets were.

"Here, Aunt Vangie, give me that," Rocky said, snatching the plug from my hand and pushing it into a thick, orange extension cord. I wasn't his real aunt, but all of Cammie's brothers and sisters—there were eight of them—called me "Aunt Vangie."

"Anyway, as I was saying," Rocky said, "that new man of yours is pretty impressive."

I scanned the crowd of men standing around, jawing away while the women set up the tables, and spotted Jonas and Gabe in what looked to be a serious conversation—about baseball from the arm motions my son made.

"Why's he so impressive?" I asked Rocky.

Rocky grinned. "He can remember names."

As I helped set up the tables, it was my turn to get peppered with questions.

"Listen up, everybody," I said, straightening up from smoothing a red-checkered plastic tablecloth on one of the wooden picnic tables. "He's my neighbor. I just met him a week ago. Evie invited him to come."

"Well, if you ask me," Cammie's Aunt Belinda said in her nasal whine, "something's not right. How come he never married? If you want my opinion, that says something—if you know what I mean. And that hat is just weird."

I bit back a sarcastic remark. It was pointless with Belinda. "I have no idea why he's never married," I said as calmly as I could, unfolding another tablecloth. "That's none of my business."

"Or yours, Belinda."

I bit back a smile. Mama Rose. The matron of this clan. Mickie's mother. With all the time I spent with the Molinetti family, it came as no surprise when my son announced he was marrying Cammie, Mickie's brother's daughter, and Mama's favorite—and only—granddaughter.

"Yes, Mama," a meek Belinda muttered.

"Come here, Evangelina," Mama said, opening her arms. I stepped into them. Mama's hugs soothed everything from my banged-up knees when I wrecked my bicycle to my broken heart when I returned from Vietnam.

"So, who is this neighbor of yours that he comes to a crazy gathering like this without knowing anyone? We'll talk later, Cara Mia. Now we eat. I hear the men's stomachs rumbling."

After Mariano, Mama's oldest son, said grace, the children raced to be first in line. Jonas grabbed my arm.

"Let's wait on the swing until the line goes down," he said, heading for the wooden swing in the copse of pine trees surrounding the pavilion.

"I hope there's something left," I said, easing down beside him. He stretched his arm across the scalloped back. His arm brushed against my shoulders, so I leaned forward.

"Relax, Evangeline," Jonas said, chuckling. "I just need to stretch my arm out."

I turned to him. "Why do you keep calling me 'Evangeline'?"

He grinned—that wide-mouthed, toothy grin that chased silent laughter across his ruddy face. "I like it. Always liked the poem, too. The ending's a bummer, though."

I gave a mock frown. "You mean to tell me you actually remember it?"

"Yep. I did a report on it for Senior English. Rewrote the ending. I had them meet up with each other five years later and, of course, they lived happily ever after."

I rolled my eyes. "Only in fairy tales."

"Happiness isn't just in fairy tales, Evangeline."

I opened my mouth to answer but didn't know what to say. I didn't want to sound like a bitter old lady, soured on life and given up on love.

"My mother loved the poem, too," I said softy, watching the lines move slowly down both sides of the food table.

"So she named you after the hapless heroine."

"Hapless? I don't know about that. She was loyal to Gabriel all her life. She never gave up the hope that someday she'd find him."

"Hey, you two on the swing!"

I turned my head. A grinning Evie pointed to a vacant spot big enough for two beside her at the table with Gabe, Cammie, and Sammy. "I'm saving your seats!"

Jonas waved at her then stood, holding out his hand to me. I stared at his broad palm for a moment, then put my hand in his—and kept it there after he'd pulled me to my feet.

Unfortunately there was also enough room at our table for Belinda.

"What about that Mickie," she said as soon as she settled across from us. "Going off to a class reunion and getting herself a husband. And your old flame, to boot. You know, she always had a crush on him. So did I. But he only had eyes for you. Frankly, I thought you were nuts when you dumped him right before you went off to war."

"Why, Aunt Binnie," Cammie exclaimed, "I never knew that! Too bad Bill didn't run right into your waiting arms! Then Aunt Mickie would be here today instead of somewhere in the Mediterranean on her honeymoon."

Binnie squirmed on the hard seat. "Harrumph. Mind your manners, young lady. I am still your aunt—your *elder*. Didn't your mama teach you anything?"

I suppressed a smile and silently thanked my daughter-in-law, focusing on cutting into my lasagna with a plastic fork—which snapped in two. Jonas gave me his. I nodded my thanks as Binnie launched into another monologue.

"Jonas, did you really make this pizza all by yourself? From scratch? You did? Even the dough? Where'd you get the mushrooms? They aren't wild mushrooms, are they? Wild mushrooms are dangerous, you know. You have to know what to look for when you go picking. The poisonous ones look just like the good ones. Why, a friend of the uncle of a friend of mine died after he ate a poisonous mushroom. His daughter picked it in the woods and put it on a pizza—just like this. She felt just awful, causing her own father's death. His system shut down—kidneys, liver, all that kind of stuff. They put him on a transplant list, but—" She sighed—loudly—and shook her head, her gray-streaked red curls bouncing around her gaunt face like a rusty spring. "He died only two days after he ate it."

Later, while the men tossed horseshoes or snoozed in canvas foldout chairs, Mama and I settled in the wooden swing. I caught her up on the events of my life since we last talked in the spring.

"I love my cottage," I told her, watching Jonas easily score a ringer. "No matter what Gabe says. I needed a new start."

She nodded. "Change can be good. So tell me about this Johnny."

"Jonas. I don't know much about him except he bought the big stone estate house up the road from me. He's the one who called 911 when my shed caught fire."

Mama's brown eyes widened. "Fire?"

I told her. "I had the box with all my journals in there."

She nodded. "Perhaps God is telling you it's time to let go."

I took a deep breath. "Mama, I found him. I found Seth."

She stopped the swing, her wise eyes full of questions.

"I haven't told anyone. Mickie knows. It was at the reunion. He was the caretaker." Tears pressed against my eyelids; a lump lodged in my throat. "He . . . didn't remember me."

"Where is he now?"

I dabbed my eyes with a crumpled napkin. "I don't know." I told her about the night I confronted him and his empty cabin the next day. We sat in silence, the creak of the swing protesting having to work on this muggy summer day. The men finished their horseshoe game, and we watched as a grinning Jonas, obviously a winner from the claps on his back, loped towards us, hopping gnarled tree roots.

I heard her sigh. "This complicates things, eh, Evangelina?"

"It sure does," I said, rising to meet him. "It sure does."

"Thanks, Evangeline," Jonas said later as he pulled into my driveway. "I had a lot of fun."

"Don't thank me," I said, laughing, as he coasted to a stop behind my car and shut off the engine. "Thank Evie. She's the one who invited you."

He turned to me. The early evening shadows fell across his face, making him look old and tired—and sad. I regretted my flippant remark about Evie's inviting him.

"I'll accept your thanks," I said, my natural shyness creeping up in me, "if you join me on the patio for some iced tea."

His face beamed with a toothy grin. "Thanks. I will."

Fifteen minutes later we were ensconced in the Adirondack chairs, watching the orange sky fade into a deepening purple.

"I love sunsets," I said, sipping my tea. "That's one of the things I liked about this house—the view of the western sky."

"Sky watcher?"

"I love to watch the sky in all of its moods—especially when a storm is coming."

"I always wanted to be one of those storm chasers." He sighed. "Didn't work out."

"Why not?"

He gulped down the rest of his iced tea then put the empty glass on the arm of the chair.

"It was always assumed I'd follow Dad into the Army. I wanted to go to college, but Dad had pulled some strings to get me an appointment to West Point. I inherited his stubbornness. In the end we compromised. I went to college, but owed Uncle Sam four years after I graduated. I figured by that time, the war would be over."

It was strange, talking about Vietnam. It had been taboo for so long. Except for Mickie, there hadn't been many people I could talk to about it. It was a war best forgotten.

"The Army put me through nursing school," I said. "I'd always wanted to be a nurse, but my dad died when I was a senior in high school, and there was no money. I thought I'd have to go only if I volunteered."

He grunted. "Where d'you serve?"

"Pleiku and Qui Nhon."

He nodded. "The good ol' Seventy-First. Spent some time there before I was shipped back to the States."

I reached across the space between our chairs and put my hand on his arm.

"You must have been wounded pretty badly to be sent home," I said softly.

"Thanks."

"For what?

"For not telling me I was lucky."

Suddenly I didn't want to talk about it anymore.

"What are you doing Friday evening?" I blurted.

"Haven't thought that far ahead yet. What d'you have in mind?"

"I haven't played a decent game of Scrabble in ages," I said, raising my eyebrows in a mock challenge.

His eyes sparkled. "You're on. How about I bring my famous homemade pizza?"

"You're on."

For an awkward moment we gazed at each other. Then he stood. "I'll be on my way, then."

"I'll walk you to your truck. I have to get my mail."

*He's nice,* I thought, as I watched him drive up the road in the deepening dusk.

Later in the kitchen, after I'd showered, I put on the kettle for a cup of herbal tea and sat down at the table to open the mail. An official-looking envelope lay on top of the pile. I picked it up and read the return address: U.S. Department of Defense. My heart thudded and my fingers trembled as I slit it open and pulled out the document.

Seth Gabriel Martin was officially dead.

CHAPTER SEVENTEEN

# ANGELA

"Next year I'm going to have a gazebo with a built-in picnic table," I said, as I helped Jonas carry the old, heavy picnic table that came with my property from the patio to beneath the canopy I bought for the annual Martin Labor Day cookout.

"I hope you plan on a big one," he said, puffing in the hot morning sun. "Why do you need two tables anyway? Four adults and two kids don't take up that much room."

"I told you. One for the food and one for eating. I can't enjoy my food if I have to balance a disposable plate on my lap."

We set the table on the grass in the center of the canopy, which took only forty-five minutes to erect after Jonas went home for a length of rope to take the place of the one missing from the box.

"How's that?" he asked after we'd adjusted it once too many times for his liking.

I surveyed the ten-by-twenty-foot space. The table, with attached seats, was a smidgeon off-center, but the look on my neighbor's face told me I'd better act satisfied. I could always move it after he left. It only needed to be shifted a couple of inches.

"It's perfect," I said.

He pointed to the silver plastic covering above our heads. "You know this cheap thing ain't gonna last, don't you? You can see daylight through it."

"It was ten dollars less expensive than the ten-by-ten. I have twice the space for less. Plus, it was in the clearance bin, so I got an eighty-dollar canopy for seventy-five."

"You can always use it for a carport until the first windstorm of the season blows it away," he said, laughing. "Maybe you'll get your money's worth out of it."

He walked around the rectangular canopy, checking the poles, guide wires, and stakes.

"Looks good," he said when he was done. "What's next?"

"The food table."

He tightened the red paisley bandana around his head and hopped up onto the truck bed. Lowering two wooden sawhorses to the ground, he barked, "Put them where you want. I'll get the plywood."

I frowned. The four-by-eight sheet looked a bit much for a man of his stature, even if he was in shape. "Do you need help? It looks unwieldy."

He snorted. "Unwieldy? Don't use that high-falutin' language with me, woman."

I grinned. "I beg your pardon, kind sir. When you've effortlessly carried it to the other side of the canopy, where I'll set up the sawhorses, I'll magically transform it into a food table. It *is* thick enough, isn't it? You've never been to a Martin cookout. We like to eat. There'll be a lot of weight on top."

"It's a quarter of an inch thick," he said after placing it on top of the sawhorse and adjusting it. "If you're worried about it, I'll go get another sawhorse and put it in the middle. That'll keep it from bowing in the center."

"That's a good idea," I said. "Let's do it."

While he made one more trip up the road, I opened the packages of red, white, and blue disposable tablecloths I'd bought, leftovers from the Fourth of July, another find from the bargain bin. I placed red and blue jar candles on top to hold them down, then added the white wicker basket containing the plasticware and napkins. I was stacking the disposable plates on the table when he returned with the extra sawhorse, which was dripping wet.

"Had to hose it off first," he said.

I eyed my set-up table warily. "Why don't I lift the plywood while you slide it under?"

"Good idea," he said with a grunt.

"If there's nothing else, I'd best mosey on up to my little kitchen and get my contribution thrown together," he said when we were done. "What time are they coming?"

"We eat at one," I said, adjusting the candles that had slid.

"Gotcha."

Gabe, Cammie, Evie, and Sammy blew in around half past noon, backing their SUV right up to the canopy. Evie burst out of the backseat.

"Hey, Gram! We brought the badminton set. Be my partner?"

"Sure," I said, smiling.

"No fair!" Sammy wailed, slamming his door. "She always gets to go first."

Evie smirked. "That's because I'm older, smarter, and faster than you, squirt."

"Enough, you two!" Cammie lifted the SUV's back door. "Help me get this food on the table. Everything looks great, Mom. The canopy's a good idea. Food table over there?"

I helped them lug countless bowls and casseroles and one slow cooker to the food table.

"Do you think you brought enough?" I asked, handing the last dish to Evie.

"She's been in the kitchen all weekend," Gabe said, planting a kiss on my cheek.

Cammie grinned. "Working full time, running two kids to and from soccer practice and ballet lessons, plus keeping up with household chores and family duties doesn't leave me much time for what I love to do most—cook. So I put the kids to work cleaning the house and folding laundry while I cooked and baked to my heart's content."

"Good thing we have the extra fridge in the garage," Gabe said, dipping a tortilla chip into a bowl of cheese.

"Did I see your famous chocolate-zucchini cake?" I asked Cammie.

"I helped make it," Evie piped up. "While Mom grated the zucchini, I measured and mixed the dry ingredients."

"She was a big help," Cammie said, smiling at her daughter. "Thanks to a grandmother who took the time to show her how to read a recipe and measure ingredients."

"She's a delight to work with," I said, wrapping my arm around my granddaughter and giving her a quick squeeze. "If you don't mind, I'd like to have the kids stay with me one Friday night a month. On separate Fridays, of course. Now that I live out here, I won't get to see them as often as I did when I lived in town."

Evie squealed. "Say yes, Mom. *Puh-leeze*?"

"When are we gonna eat?" Sammy whined. "I'm hungry."

I laughed. "As soon as Jonas gets here."

At five minutes to one, Jonas's truck pulled in the driveway. Evie ran to meet him. "What'd you bring, Jonas?"

Blue and yellow oven mitts on his hands, he carried a rectangular glass baking dish covered with aluminum foil across the lawn to the food table.

"Holy banquet!" he said, looking up and down the crowded table for a place to put his contribution. "Are you planning to feed Coxey's Army?"

Cammie made room on the table for Jonas's casserole. "What smells so good?" she asked.

He peeled back the foil. The aroma of melted butter and onions wafted with the steam that rose from it. "Pierogi lasagna. It's really very easy."

"What about your pizza?" Evie asked.

He grinned. "Be right back." He jogged back to the truck and returned with two round pans of his now-popular, made-from-scratch pizzas. Cammie and I shuffled the dishes on the table to make more room.

"Oohhhh," Sammy breathed, his blue eyes wide with pleasure. "Jonas's pizza. Can we eat now? I'm hungry."

We all laughed. "Gabe," I said, nodding to my son. "Will you say the blessing?"

"I helped make the zucchini cake," Evie proudly told Jonas as they made their way down the food table. She was, of course, next to him.

"Where is it?" he asked.

She pointed. "There."

"I'll make sure I get a piece," he said. "What's that on top?"

"Chocolate chips," she said. "What's the matter? Don't you like chocolate chips?"

Her countenance fell as he shook his head. Then his too-big-for-his-face mouth spread in a wide grin. "That's okay, Ev, I'll just pick them out."

"What's the cocky army?" she asked him when they sat down. She made sure she sat next to him.

"Coxey's Army—C-o-x-e-y—was a group of jobless men who marched to Washington, D.C., during the depression in the late 1800s to protest unemployment. A hundred men started the march in Ohio, but by the time they got to D.C., there were about five hundred. A man by the name of Jacob Coxey led them. Hence the name, Coxey's Army."

"Gee," Evie said, biting into her pizza, "they must have really been depressed."

Cammie, who sat across from me, waved her plastic fork at me. "Mom, I have a favor to ask."

I cut through a chunk of potato in my potato salad. "If it involves spending time with my grandchildren, do you even have to ask?"

"Did Gabe tell you about my promotion?"

I stopped cutting and looked up at her in surprise. Cammie started working as a bank teller when she and Gabe first got married, at twenty, to help put him through school. She'd worked her way up to loan officer in one of local branches. "No, he didn't. Shame on you, Gabe, for not sharing the good news."

He grinned, his blue eyes on Cammie, sparkling with pride. "It's her news to tell. Besides, my dear mother, I haven't seen you since the family reunion. Every time I call, you're not home. I hear your neighbor has been keeping you busy, luring you to his place with that in-ground swimming pool of his."

Cammie pierced a pierogi with her plastic fork and lifted it, dripping with butter, to her lips. "I'm going to head up the loan department at the main office downtown. I found out for sure two weeks ago. I start tomorrow."

"Congratulations," I said. "I'll hug you later. What's the favor?"

"I'll be putting in another five hours a week, staying until five-thirty Monday through Thursday and working until seven on Fridays. Can you pick up Evie after school on Tuesdays and Thursdays and take her to her ballet lesson? Same time both days: four-thirty to five-thirty. We have everything else worked out."

Everything else being Gabe's coaching baseball at the university until six, Sammy's scout meetings and soccer practices, supper, and everything else that goes with raising a family these days. It made me glad I'd had only one.

"I'd love to," I said. "Am I to stay and take her home, or will someone pick her up afterward?"

Cammie gave me a pleading look. "If you could hang around and bring her home after she's done, we'd really appreciate it."

"No problem," I said. "Isn't the dance studio close to the mall with all the craft shops?"

She shook her head. "Evie's changing ballet schools this year. She needs more of a challenge. Joan's taken her as far as she could."

"Where's the studio?" I asked, hoping it wasn't too far a drive. In the winter, roads could get bad fast in these central Pennsylvania mountains.

"In Bellefonte."

"Why that's just up the road!" I said, relieved. "Closer than State College."

"It's settled, then?"

"Of course," I said. "I'll take along some reading or crocheting."

It didn't work out the way I'd planned. When I walked Evie to her class on Tuesday, I noticed the school also offered classes in a variety of dance styles, including ballroom dancing. I'd been wanting to take ballroom dancing for years. I studied the brochure. The class was offered Tuesdays at the same time as Evie's class. I checked the classes offered on Thursdays at four-thirty. Water aerobics. This place had a swimming pool? The ballroom dancing didn't start until next Tuesday, and the water aerobics began a new session Thursday. I called Jonas and asked him if he'd like to take the ballroom dancing with me.

He burst out laughing. "What? With my two left feet?"

I signed up anyway. The nice young blonde in the office told me that the instructor would pair me up with someone. After I wrote a check for my tuition and dance shoes and gave them my shoe size, she asked if I had any questions.

"Who's the instructor?" I asked.

She reached into a file folder on the counter and pulled out a sheet of glossy paper.

"Angela Woods." She tapped the photograph on the one-sheet. "She's just joined us this year after traveling around the country."

Angela Woods appeared to be around thirty, a slender, dark-haired beauty with Asian features.

"As you see from the bullet list, Ms. Martin, Angela comes to us highly qualified. She can teach anything from ballet to ballroom dancing to water aerobics. We were lucky to get her."

Her credits included training at an internationally renowned dance institute in Vancouver, several first place finishes in national and international competitions, both in ballet and ballroom dancing, guest teaching stints at a variety of dance studios in the United States and Canada, and performing on the stages of America, Europe, and Asia.

"Wow," I said, ignoring the "Ms. Martin." I couldn't wait to get started.

My concerns that Angela Woods might be too performance-oriented to be a good teacher were banished within minutes after the first class began. She had a calm, gentle nature, sparkling dark eyes, a sweet smile that reminded me of someone, and possessed more patience than I thought possible in someone whose excellence demanded perfection. She paired me up with Gene, a tall, sixty-something man with thick white hair and a trim mustache, who was taking the class to surprise his wife.

"She's been taking ballroom dancing for years," he told me during our get-acquainted time. "Every year she asked me, and every year I said no. The classes have done so much for her. She has more stamina than she's had in years. She runs circles around me." His gray eyes gleamed. "And she looks like a million bucks. So I thought I'd surprise her for our fortieth wedding anniversary next summer."

"Where does she think you are?" I asked, thinking what a sweet man he was.

He grinned. "Playing poker at the firehouse. Perfect cover. She knows I don't take calls when I'm playing poker. What about you?"

"My granddaughter's taking ballet here at this same time, and I've wanted to do this for years."

Before we started learning dance steps, Angela led us through a series of stretches, bends, and lunges.

"Wear comfortable clothes," she said. "We don't dress up until we practice for the recital."

Recital? I glanced at Gene, who looked as aghast as I felt.

"As for the dance shoes you received before class, wear them around the house to get used to them and break them in. You won't need them for class until after the first of the year. Until then a good pair of sneakers—with adequate support—will do."

By the time our first class was finished, I'd already made up my mind to sign up for summer classes. I was changing my shoes—we weren't to wear the shoes on the dance floor that we wore outside—when Evie burst into the room, pulling a slim, dark-haired girl behind her.

"Gram, Gram! Meet my new best friend, Ali," she said, out of breath.

Ali smiled shyly, a nervous glance at Angela, who was striding purposefully in our direction.

"Nice to meet you, Ali," I said, extending my hand. She laid her dainty hand in mine. "I'm Vangie Martin."

"You can call her Gram if you want," Evie said.

"You will call her Mrs. Martin," Angela said, stepping beside Ali and wagging a slender finger in Ali's pixie face. "How many times, daughter, do I have to tell you to wait for me outside the classroom until I'm finished?"

Ali's face fell. "I'm sorry, Mama."

"It's my fault," Evie said. "I wanted her to meet my gram. She didn't want to come in, but I made her. I'm Evie, by the way. Ali's my new best friend."

Angela smiled and shook her head gently. "As I tell Alisia, no one can make you do anything."

"Even if they drag them into a room, kicking and screaming?" Evie asked.

"You didn't drag her, you pulled her by her arm." Angela's quiet voice had a hint of amusement. "And I didn't see her kicking or hear her screaming. In fact, she seemed quite willing. But from now on you will remember that you wait outside the door, right, Evie?"

Evie's face grew serious. "Yes, ma'am."

Angela's sweet smile ignited the sparkle in her deep brown eyes. "Angela," she said, looking from me to Evie. "You can call me Angela."

CHAPTER EIGHTEEN

# JONAS

Life settled into a comfortable routine. Evie's night for a sleepover was the second Friday of the month. Sammy stayed on the fourth Friday. The other Friday evenings became date nights for Jonas and me. We played board games, worked on jigsaw puzzles, watched movies, and occasionally went out to dinner and a movie. When we stayed in, he brought his homemade pizza and I made a salad.

One Friday evening in the middle of October, we bundled up and sat by a campfire in the backyard. Carlie lay with her head on her front paws between our canvas fold-up chairs.

"Have you figured out how to use that snow blower you bought?" he asked as we held our mountain pie irons in the glowing embers. "You realize you might be needing it in another couple, three weeks."

"I read the manual," I said. "It'll be fine. It's like with anything else—you learn as you go."

He chuckled, his breath a frosty vapor. "Hope you're a fast learner."

Jonas and I both had fireplaces, so we spent several glorious fall days in the woods on our properties, cutting and hauling firewood. I asked him about his chainsaw.

His laugh rang through the golden woods. "You *are* an independent cuss, aren't you?" he said. "First the blower and tiller, and now you want to pack a chainsaw? I don't think so. It's too dangerous. As long as I'm around, Evangeline, I'll cut your firewood. Don't you worry your pretty little head about it."

*And how long are you going to be around?* I wanted to ask.

We stacked the firewood in neat rows on my patio and covered it with a blue tarp. His firewood he just tossed in a pile in his barn.

"Doesn't it take up more space that way?" I asked.

He shrugged. "Who cares?"

My life was almost busy enough to keep my mind off Steve. But I wondered where he was, what he was doing, every time I walked by my fireplace. I kept the bridge woodcarving on the mantel. One Friday evening, Jonas pointed to it.

"That's one of the most beautiful woodcarvings I've ever seen. Where'd you get it?"

"I ordered it from a woodcarver when I was at my class reunion this summer," I said, trying to figure out the best way to use my letters on the Scrabble board. He was ahead by twenty-five points. "It was in the package you brought over the day before my shed burned."

"I wouldn't mind having something like that. He do anything else?"

"Wildlife," I said, placing my "Q" on a triple letter square and the rest of my letters for "EQUAL" on the board so that I had enough points to pass him.

"Ouch!" he said, grinning. "You don't mess around, woman!"

I smiled and sipped my hot chocolate. "I learned from the best."

"And who's that? Your English teacher?"

I laughed. "No, my husband. We played a lot in Vietnam. It helped to take our minds off the war."

"Steve?"

My head jerked up, my hand flew to my chest, which suddenly felt tight, knocking my letter tiles onto the floor. Embarrassed, I plucked them from the carpet and arranged them on my wooden tile rack in alphabetical order while Jonas added "T-R-I-A" to the "L" in "EQUAL."

"My husband's name was Seth," I said quietly. "He died in Vietnam."

Which wasn't a lie. The man I fell in love with and married died in a paddy where Sinh An and Ai′ found a broken body that was once my Seth.

"He was a Dust Off pilot," I said. "You know what Dust Off was?"

He nodded, his dark eyes intent, studying me. I'd never noticed before, but his eye color was almost black.

"We married four months after we met, while we were still on our tours. He was shot down two months after that. They never found him."

*I did. But he wasn't Seth anymore.*

Jonas reached over the board and put his broad hand on mine. "I'm sorry, Evangeline."

I pulled my hand away. "My turn," I said, trying to smile. But my lips refused to cooperate. The best I could manage was a half smile that I was sure looked like a snarl. I studied my letter tiles. I had an "E" and the "X." If I added them to the "S" at the end of "MONKEYS," I could put the "X" on a double word score. But I didn't want to give him any ideas. I added the letters "A," "X," and "I" after the "T" in "TRIAL."

"What?" he gasped in mock surprise. "Not using any triple or double letter or word scores? You're either getting soft or slipping."

Later as we packed the game away, he pointed to the bridge carving again.

"You never did tell me the name of the woodcarver," he said. "Someone you know?"

"Why do you ask?"

"Because that face—that woman's face in the background—looks an awful lot like you."

"Steve," I said, my heart thumping in my chest. "His name was Steve."

I'd gotten to know Angela a lot better than the other people in both my ballroom dancing and water aerobics classes because I was the only student she had in both classes. We often waited together for the girls, whose class had been extended half an hour in preparation for their upcoming Christmas recital. They were going to be performing sections of *The Nutcracker.* Angela shared little personal information, but one November evening, she let down her guard and let it slip that she was divorced.

"I'm so sorry, Angela," I said, squeezing her hand.

"I'm not," she said, a flash of anger clouding her brown eyes. "He was my dance partner."

"What happened?" I asked gently.

She looked away and shrugged. "He found another partner."

"How long were you married?"

"Ten years. We danced together in competitions and in performances when I was in high school. He was five years older than me. My father didn't like him, but he saw I was in love and stubborn. When I graduated from high school, I was scheduled to go on tour with him. Papa said no." She sighed. "So we got married. That was the only way Papa would let me go."

"Fathers are protective of their daughters."

Her gentle smile accented the sadness in her eyes. "He raised me alone after my mother died. I never knew either of my grandparents. I have some foggy memories of my mother's parents back in Vietnam—"

"You were born in Vietnam?" I asked.

She nodded. "In the Kon Tum Province in the Central Highlands. It borders Laos and Cambodia. We left Vietnam when I was five. My father was an American serviceman."

I put my hand over hers. "I served in Vietnam as an Army nurse. In the Central Highlands. Most of the GIs who took up with the local girls left them there. Your father must be a man of honor, not to leave you and your mother behind when he came home."

She cocked her dainty head to one side. "A man of honor. I never heard it put that way."

"What's his name?" I asked. "Perhaps I knew him."

Just then the girls ran up to us.

"Gram, could Ali stay overnight with me Friday night?" Evie asked.

I glanced at Angela. "If it's all right with her mother."

Angela stood, grabbed the straps of Ali's ballet bag, and pulled them over her shoulder. "Only if I send supper," she said.

"What'll you make, Mama?" Ali asked, blue eyes shining.

"What do you want me to make?" Angela asked.

"BK stew. It's my favorite in all the world," Ali said.

Angela smiled. "Then BK stew it will be."


Cammie and Gabe traditionally held Thanksgiving dinner at their house, unless it was her father's turn to host Mama Rose. This year was Mickie's turn, and Mickie and Bill had invited the whole family—Mama Rose, all Mickie's brothers and their wives—to dinner at the resort. She'd also invited me, but I declined. I didn't like traveling that time of the year—the weather was so iffy. I wanted to spend the day with Gabe and his crew.

"I'll see you Monday for our annual Christmas shopping trip," I told her.

This year we set three extra places at the table—for Jonas, Angela, and Alisia. Evie, of course, had invited all of them, then told Cammie. Jonas brought his pierogi lasagna, I brought pumpkin pie and a big salad, and Angela brought Bho Ko stew, which Evie said "tastes just like Gram's."

"I'd like to do something different this year," Evie said as we joined hands to say grace. "Let's go around the table and each person say one thing you're thankful for this year."

Cammie was thankful for her family, Sammy that his soccer team won the championship, Gabe was thankful for his health, Angela for "the Martin family who eases my loneliness," Ali for being selected to dance a solo part in the upcoming ballet performance, Evie for her new best friend "who's like the sister I never had." Jonas said he was thankful he had a chance to get away from the snow and ice and winter in Arizona. I was going to say I was thankful for good neighbors, but Jonas's bombshell left me dumbfounded. So I said the first thing that popped into my head: "I'm thankful for Steve."

"Who's Steve?" Gabe, Cammie, and Evie chorused.

My face, I knew, could give the cranberry sauce competition in the color department. I forced my horrified lips into a smile.

"Long story," I said. "I'll tell you about it sometime."

"Can we say grace now?" Sammy piped up. "I'm hungry."

We bowed our heads as Gabe began the traditional Thanksgiving blessing and we joined in: "We thank you, Father, wise and good, for homes and friends and daily food. Bless to our use this food we take, and keep us all for Jesus' sake. Amen."

I silently added one more praise: *Thank you, God, for Sammy and his face-saving appetite.*

"When were you going to tell me?" I asked Jonas on the way home that evening.

Jonas flicked the windshield wipers up a notch. The wet snow that had begun late in the afternoon had gotten heavier. I was glad we'd brought his four-wheel-drive truck instead of my front-wheel-drive car. I was beginning to regret my decision to forgo the SUV and buy a car as we came up behind an ashes-spewing state plow truck.

"Sorry, Evangeline," he said as he downshifted. The pickup shuddered slightly as the transmission took hold. "I didn't even think about it. Chas, an old Army buddy of mine, called yesterday and invited me out for the winter. I haven't made up my mind yet."

"It didn't sound that way at the table," I said, turning up the heat and the fan.

He sighed and dropped his camouflage outback hat on the leather seat between us. "It's gonna be a long, hot ride home."

"You could come with me," Jonas said later that evening over pumpkin pie and decaf coffee.

I put my mug on the kitchen table and stared at him. A sheepish grin spread across his ruddy face.

"Ever been to Arizona?"

I shook my head. "I don't care for deserts and hot climates. I love Pennsylvania, with its trees and mountains, and change in seasons. I could never live anywhere else. Besides, we're not married."

His eyebrows shot up as he tapped his forehead with his palm. "What were you thinking, Kramer? A church-going lady like Evangeline would never live in sin."

He looked at me and grinned, his deep, dark eyes laughing. "Then we'll get hitched."

My jaw dropped. "Is that a proposal?"

He shrugged. "If you want it to be."

"But . . . you've never said you love me. You've never even kissed me, except for a peck on the cheek when you come and when you go."

"We're comfortable together, and we enjoy doing the same things, playing board games, cooking, putting together puzzles, swimming. We get along well, don't you think?"

I thought about it for a moment. "Yes."

"In my book, companionship and friendship are what make a good marriage."

"What about love?" I asked.

He snorted. "Evangeline, love is for the young. Romantic love, that is. People our age just don't fall in love."

I thought about the way Bill and Mickie looked at each other, and the way Gabe and Cammie snuck in quick kisses when they thought no one was looking.

"I disagree," I said. "Love is the single most important ingredient in a marriage. You can't have a real marriage without it."

"Evangeline, I could never love you the way a husband loves a wife."

I stared at him.

"I could never be a lover—to you or anyone else. A Bouncing Betty took care of that."

In Vietnam, a "Bouncing Betty" was what we called a land mine that detonated at waist level.

He blinked, swallowed, then continued. "I got engaged right before I left for 'Nam. The wedding was planned for when I got back. She still wanted to go through with it after I got hurt. But I said no. I couldn't give her the family she wanted—she wanted six kids. I couldn't even please her the way a man . . ." He raised his hand, using his bent knuckle to dab his eyes.

"I sent her away. A year later I heard she'd gotten married." He sighed, his deep eyes a million miles away. "I saw her at our twentieth-year class reunion. She got her six kids. They struggled to make ends meet, she told me, but I could tell they were happy."

I reached across the table and grasped his hand. "Oh, Jonas, I'm so sorry."

He pushed his chair out and stood. "I'll be at camp for the next couple of weeks for deer season. When I come back, I'll need your answer."

I looked up at him. "When do you leave for Arizona?"

He slid his arms into the sleeves of his black leather jacket. "Right after Christmas."

He positioned his black fedora on his head, then bent down and kissed me lightly on the forehead.

"I can give you financial security, companionship, and never a dull moment. Think about it, Evangeline."

CHAPTER NINETEEN

# A DECISION AND A CONFESSION

"Jonas asked me to marry him," I told Mickie over lunch the following Monday.

Her head jerked up, as the manicured hand that held her Philly cheese steak sub stopped midway between her plate and her gaping mouth.

"Close your mouth or take a bite of that enormous thing. We're in public," I said, fighting the melted cheese in my French onion soup. "Aren't you going to congratulate me?"

She put the sandwich back down on her plate. "Did you say yes?"

I avoided the eyes that I felt boring through me from across the table. "Not yet."

A loud sigh escaped her lips. "You haven't decided then."

"I'm supposed to give him my answer in two weeks when he comes back from a hunting trip," I said.

"Do you love him?" she asked.

"We enjoy being together."

"That's lame. Answer the question."

I thought about the way I felt when I was with Steve—and pushed the thought away. "We're comfortable together."

"*Now* you are. You're both healthy. But what if one of you gets cancer or Alzheimer's? Or has a stroke? Are you willing to play nurse to someone you don't love? And what if you're the one who gets sick and he deserts you?"

I stared into my soup. Would Jonas stick with me if I were bedridden? Change the sheets? Empty the bedpan? I remembered how he took care of things when my shed burned down. And the firewood was his idea. Since I'd met him, he'd been there for me every time I needed him. And I told Mickie so.

"Has he told you he loves you?"

I fidgeted on the leather seat and scooped a soggy crouton out of my soup bowl.

"I thought as much," she said, a smirk in her voice.

"We enjoy doing the same things," I said, repeating Jonas's words. "Companionship and friendship are important in a marriage."

"So is love."

I sighed. "I had my chance, Mick. Love like that doesn't come around a second time."

Mickie dug into her purse, pulled out a slip of paper, and slid it across the table. "Here."

I unfolded it. It was a phone number.

"It's Steve's," she said, a smirk playing at the edge of her lips.

I shook my head and slid the paper back across the table, trying to stir up the anger I'd felt when I returned home alone four months earlier. "Steve left me, remember?"

She slapped the table with her palm. "Doggone it, Vange! Why do you have to be so stubborn?"

"He's the one who's stubborn. But why are we arguing? It doesn't matter anymore."

"Of course it matters. How are you going to marry Jonas when you're still married?"

I stared at her. She chuckled.

"This isn't funny, Mick. I . . . I never thought . . . Oh, for heaven's sake, I'm still married, aren't I?"

She nodded, her triumphant grin igniting the sparkle in her brown eyes.

"I'll see my lawyer about a divorce," I stammered.

"And tell her what? That you want to divorce a dead man?"

"But he's not dead."

"You've got a death certificate saying he is."

"But I can prove he's still alive."

"And that would help only you. You're not thinking of Steve." Mickie placed the slip of paper in my hand and closed my fingers over it. "It's your decision, Vange. But do yourself a favor and call Steve before you give Jonas your answer. Don't settle for less than love."

I slipped the paper in my jeans pocket. "Look at the time. And I've got to get my Christmas decorations yet. Did I tell you I lost all my old ones in the fire?"

As I checked my pockets before dropping my jeans into the clothes hamper that evening after my shower, my fingers found the slip of paper with Steve's phone number.

*Should I or shouldn't I?* I didn't love Jonas. He didn't love me. How long would "like" last? Could we truly be committed to one another without the love that bonded people together in the tough times?

I slipped the paper in the pocket of my robe and walked out to the living room, where the fire I'd started before my shower crackled and popped in the stone hearth. I lowered myself onto the sofa and stared at the flames licking the logs that Jonas and I had cut and gathered and stacked. My eyes were drawn to my gardenia plant three feet from the fireplace—the plant that Sammy nearly killed when he poured the wrong water on it. The plant that I'd nursed back to health. *Why didn't I just let it die?* I'd gotten it when I first moved into my own place when Gabe started kindergarten. I'd nursed it and babied it and kept it around because it reminded me of my missing husband. As long as it was alive, I reasoned, so was Seth, somewhere, and so was my hope.

But now I knew the truth. My husband was no longer missing in action involuntarily. He was missing in action because he chose to be.

"It's so unfair, God," I whispered, tears coursing down my cheeks. "I hung on all those years, always believing I'd be rewarded for my faithfulness and someday I'd find him. And now I've lost him all over again. How could you let this happen?"

*Call Steve before you give Jonas your answer. Don't settle for less than love.* Mickie's words reverberated in my brain. I picked up the phone, punched the numbers, and counted the rings . . . one . . . two . . . three . . . On the fourth ring, a woman answered. I disconnected.

I sat there, numb, staring into the fire and holding back the tears. *He didn't waste any time.* Kneeling on the stone floor in front of the fireplace, I carefully dropped the paper with Steve's phone number into the flames and watched as it turned to ash.

My phone rang. I checked the caller ID. The number I'd just dialed. Steve. I let my voice mail pick up then waited a few minutes before I went through the rigmarole to get to my voice mail. I didn't even listen to the message before I deleted it. Then I erased my call log.

Jonas called half an hour later to tell me he'd bagged his buck and would be home Friday. *Have your answer ready*, I heard in his voice. As I hung up, I knew what that answer would be.

The girls danced beautifully in their recital on Friday evening, and afterward I gave both Evie and Ali a single red rose. Evie wanted to celebrate by going out for pizza, but Ali was eager to get home.

"Mama, can't you hurry any faster?" she demanded, pulling on her red fur-lined parka over her costume.

"Patience, Alisia," Angela said. "You know the director is always the last one to leave."

Ali turned to me, her blue eyes gleaming. "My grandpa's here this week! He was at the recital tonight—I saw him, Mama! He was sitting in the back row by the door."

I turned to Angela. "Your father's in town? How wonderful! Why don't you leave now? I can close things up here. After all, that's what backstage help is for."

Angela's perfectly shaped eyebrows arched; then she shook her head. "I have to make sure everything is cleaned up tonight. We're leaving with Papa after church tomorrow to spend Christmas with him in Vancouver."

"I'll be right back." I hurried out to explain the situation to Cammie.

Angela's eyes widened when I returned with Cammie, Gabe, Sammy, and Evie behind me.

"Tell us what needs done," I said.

Jonas banged on my back door Saturday morning, lugging a box of frozen meat.

"Venison," he said, stepping past me into the kitchen, where he laid out a dozen white packages. "Chipped and ground. One-pound packages, except the two roasts. They're two pounds."

"What if I don't like venison?" I teased.

Jonas shrugged off his hunting parka and hung it on the back of a kitchen chair with his orange Mad Bomber rabbit hat. "I'll give you some recipes. You'll love it. Trust me." He looked around my kitchen. "How about some coffee, woman?"

I spent the next half hour listening to tales of Jonas's hunting trip and rearranging my freezer. I just barely got all the meat in. *Next year I'll have to buy a small deep freeze for all my garden vegetables.*

"Have you had breakfast yet?" I asked him. "Would you like me to make you some eggs?"

He shook his head. "Not hungry. Thanks."

I put the kettle on for more tea then sat opposite Jonas at the kitchen table. His dark eyes gazed into mine with intensity. "Well, Evangeline, what's your answer?"

I looked past him into the living room, where my gardenia plant reached for the sunlight streaming through the window.

"You're a wonderful man, and I know we could have a good life together," I said, returning my gaze to his wind-chiseled face. "But I can't marry you."

The intensity in his eyes softened. "I understand. I kind of expected it."

I reached across the table and grasped both his hands. "I do love you, Jonas. You're like the brother I never had."

He got up, stepped around the table, and pulled me to my feet. Holding my face in his hands, he kissed me lightly on the lips. "Evangeline, Evangeline," he whispered in a husky voice. "May your story end happily ever after."

Then, releasing me, he grabbed his jacket and hat, and slipped out the door.

I spent the rest of the day figuring out how to put together the artificial tree I bought when Mickie and I went shopping. At one point, I was so frustrated with the directions that came with it that I almost called Jonas. I called Gabe, but when the answering machine picked up, remembered they were shopping and wouldn't be back until late.

"Aw, phooey with it," I said, tossing the sheet with the directions back into the box. I put the kettle on for tea; then, pulling on a hooded sweatshirt and boots, I stomped through the snow to get my mail. Among the flyers and Christmas cards was a long, white envelope. My name and address were scrawled on the front in blue ink in handwriting I didn't recognize. I scanned the return address. No name. Only a room number in the VA Medical Center in Loma Linda, California.

Back in the kitchen, I poured my tea; then using the letter opener I kept in a basket on the kitchen table, I slit the business-size envelope open. I pulled out a folded sheet of loose leaf paper and opened it, checking the signature first. "Bubba, former Sgt. First Class Robert Wilcott" was scrawled across the bottom, barely readable. The handwriting looked shaky in a few places, the lines slanted upward across the page, and several dried water splotches smeared the blue ink. It was dated December 1, a week ago.

*Dear Vangie,*
 *I'm dying. I don't have long. I'll probably be gone by Christmas.*

Something in my gut tightened.

*I'm writing to ask you to forgive me, but I'll understand if you don't.*
 *Seth came back the day the villa burned down. I was on guard duty. I didn't recognize him at first. He was dressed in those black pajamas and cone hat the villagers wore. He'd lost a lot of weight and had a beard. The bottom half of his face looked funny, like somebody punched him hard and his jaw stayed that way.*
 *He was holding a sheet of paper. He asked if this was Qui Nhon. His voice was weak, raspy, like there was gravel in his throat. I asked him why he wanted to know. He held out the paper. His hands shook like he had palsy or something. I recognized your handwriting. I demanded to know his name, where he was from, what he was doing there. He gave me a blank look. I knew then he probably had amnesia. I accused him of being a traitor—I made up some story about someone going AWOL who they thought was giving away our secrets to the VC. I told him he was under arrest for suspicion of treason. And murder. I told him all the nurses had been killed in the fire. He looked at me like I was speaking another language. Then he turned and ran,*

*lop-sided like. I lifted my rifle and aimed. My finger was on the trigger. I was ready to squeeze. But I couldn't. Something stopped me.*

*Now I know what it was. It was God.*

*Last week I asked Jesus to forgive me. And, you know what, Vangie? He did! Amazing grace, how sweet the sound that saved a wretch like me! I read Psalm 51 over and over and cry. I've been crying for a week. Not because I'm going to die soon. But because God can forgive even me. I feel so clean.*

*I got your address from a buddy high up in the VA. I also asked him to try to find out about Seth. I'm so sorry, Vangie. God only knows how many years you could have had together. God forgave me. I only hope and pray you can, too.*

*Sincerely,*

*Bubba*

*(Former Sgt. First Class Robert Wilcott)*

The blue ink blurred. I was stunned. Numb.

"Oh, God." A lump thickened in my throat. "No wonder he disappeared when I told him who he was. He thinks he's a traitor."

Letting the page flutter to the floor, I covered my face with trembling hands. My fingertips were icy. I was surprised to feel the wetness on my cheeks. My insides quivered as something in me built up like a reservoir ready to overflow with the chilling monsoon rains I remembered so well from my own time in hell.

Then the dam broke.

CHAPTER TWENTY

# GABE

Christmas came and went. I left my decorations up through January, since it's such a dark month. The electric candles in the window helped to dispel the long winter nights. But I had to keep changing the bulbs because the cat I'd gotten from the animal shelter kept jumping up on the windowsills and knocking the candles to the floor. I would have gotten rid of Rascal, which I named the soft gray and white kitten, but he was a good mouser. I hadn't seen any signs of the pesky little creatures since Rascal took up residence and started torturing Carlie, who knew better than to mess with a hissing, clawing feline a fraction of her size.

January also brought a series of snowstorms that made me regret buying a car instead of a four-wheel-drive, a snow blower that didn't attach to the front of my lawn tractor, and a house without a garage. My lack of experience driving a front-wheel-drive vehicle sent me skidding into a snow bank more than once. Although I limited my trips to town, I missed my dance class once and my water aerobics class twice—only because the classes were canceled due to the bad weather. On the first of February I braved the roads and took Angela, Ali, Evie, and Sammie to Punxsutawney for Groundhog Day. Standing on the frozen ground on Gobbler's Knob for hours with thousands of people who came from all over the world would have been fun if I hadn't been so cold. I'd borrowed Gabe's hunting pants and coat, bought wool socks, and layered my clothes, but still I froze. And I couldn't move—both because of the standing-room-only crowd and because I was bundled up so much I couldn't even turn my head. Phil saw his shadow. Six more weeks of winter.

I gave up blowing out my driveway after the first snowstorm. I limped in and headed straight for an Epsom-salt bath. My arms, legs, and back ached for a week. All that pain was in vain—the snowplow pushed the snow from the road back onto the driveway, creating a foot-high snow bank at the end that got higher with each pass it made. Gabe had wanted me to buy a blower that attached to the front of the tractor, but that meant he—or someone else—would have to put it on every fall and take it off every spring.

"I'll have to come over to make sure it's in good running condition anyway," he had argued.

"This walk-behind model is fine," I had argued right back. "My driveway is only twenty feet long. It'll give me some exercise. How hard can it be?"

"Fifty feet." He grunted. "Just don't say I didn't warn you."

He was right. The driveway *was* fifty feet long. When he dropped in after I used the blower for the first time and found me hobbling around, he had "I told you so" written all over his wise-son face. One look from me, though, and he didn't dare say it.

And I missed having a garage. I used the canopy I bought for the Labor Day picnic until a windstorm blew it up the road to Jonas's place. He was nice enough to dispose of it without telling me "I told you so." It broke my frugal heart, but starting the car with the remote starter ten minutes before I planned to leave was a lot better than showing up looking like the abominable ice woman after scraping the windshield and back window and side windows to get wherever I was going.

But I made it through that first winter without totaling my car or burning the house down when I piled on the logs in the fireplace and the wind pulled the flames up the chimney and started the flue on fire.

The rumbling scared me witless, but at least it cleaned out the creosote from inside the chimney. I didn't tell Gabe about that one. He probably would have packed me up and moved me back to town.

By the time May rolled around, I'd crocheted afghans for Evie, Sammy, Ali, and Angela. Of course, I had to up my intake of vitamin B6 and go back to wearing the wrist splints at night to rein in the carpal tunnel syndrome that flared up. But by mid-May the buzzing in my hands and arms that woke me up at night calmed down enough for me to run the rototiller. Gabe brought his plow and harrow and worked up a twenty-by-twenty-five-foot section at the edge of the backyard, telling me in his wise-son voice that I'd gotten carried away.

I'd planted onions, peas, carrots, beets, green and yellow beans, red potatoes, six green pepper plants, and a dozen tomato plants. Because we can get frost as late as May, I had to wait until the full moon was past before I put in the pepper and tomato plants. Which was what I was doing the Saturday morning before Memorial Day when Gabe, Cammie, and the kids dropped by on their way to a ball game.

"We have an extra ticket, Mom. Sammy's friend canceled at the last minute. Why don't you come with us?" Gabe said.

I was on my knees, mixing lime and fertilizer in the loose soil before putting the last tomato plant in. I looked up. Gabe's back was to the sun, his hands resting casually on his hips. I caught my breath. His silhouette was remarkably like his father's.

"You okay?" Gabe asked, reaching down to help me to my feet.

I waved him away. "I'm fine," I said, pushing myself up from the ground and adjusting my sun visor. "For a second I thought . . . oh, never mind."

So many times over the past year I'd almost told him about finding his father. But I couldn't see what good it would do. In rejecting me, Steve had also rejected our son. And we mothers do all we can to protect our children from hurt, even if that child is thirty-six. After I got Bubba's letter, I'd tried, without success, to get in touch with

Steve. But where do you look when someone doesn't want to be found? And Steve had spent thirty-seven years learning the techniques of hiding. I even Googled his name and checked all the woodcarving sites I could find. Mickie told me Bill had no clue where Steve was or how to contact him. She no longer had the phone number she'd given me.

Evie's voice broke into my thoughts. "Who's at Jonas's house?"

I cupped my hands over my eyes. Dirt fell from my garden gloves onto my sunburned cheeks as I squinted in the late morning sun.

"I don't recognize the car," I said.

We watched as a man in a light-colored business suit strode up to the front door, put a key into the lock, and let himself in.

"When's he coming back?" Evie asked. "I miss him."

"I don't know, sweetie," I said, pulling off my gloves. "I miss him too."

"Go hop in the shower, Mom," Gabe told me. "I'll put in this last plant and clean up."

"My garden tools—"

"Got it covered. Go get ready. The game starts at one."

Half an hour later we piled into his SUV. When we drove by Jonas's house, the man was outside taking pictures. The sign on the door of his SUV read "Acre Real Estate."

"Doesn't look like Jonas is coming back," Cammie said.

Tuesday morning I called Gabe.

"Something's eating my plants," I said.

He sighed. "I'll be by after supper with a roll of chicken wire."

At six o'clock that evening my phone rang.

"Mom?" Cammie's voice sounded strained. "Something's wrong with Gabe. I'm taking him to the emergency room. Can you come over and stay with the kids?"

I drove as fast as I could, praying the entire way. Cammie wasn't one to rush to the ER at every little thing. Twenty minutes later, I arrived at Gabe's house.

"What's wrong?" I asked Cammie, who was trying to get Gabe off the sofa. A plastic ice cream bucket and a bath towel sat on the coffee table. The room reeked of vomit.

"How long has he been throwing up?" I asked.

"Since he got up this morning. He went to work but came back at noon. His temp is 103.4. Oral."

I checked his pulse. Rapid. Breathing shallow. His skin was clammy and way too pale.

"Diarrhea?" I asked. Evie and Sammy stood wide-eyed in front of the TV.

Gabe nodded weakly.

"When did you first start having symptoms?" I asked Gabe, checking his pupils. I didn't like what I saw.

"Yesterday morning," Cammie said. "He complained of an upset stomach when he came down for breakfast. We thought it was something he ate at the baseball picnic Sunday."

Gabe and Cammie usually host the team for a picnic when the season is over. Since they hadn't gone any further in the playoffs, their season had ended at regionals.

"Can you remember what you ate?" I asked Gabe. He shook his head weakly.

"One of the boys brought a pizza that tasted awful," Sammy said.

"It *was* yucky," Evie said, wrinkling her nose. "I took one sniff and threw my piece away. I think everybody else did, too. Dad ate a whole slice because he didn't want the kid to feel bad."

"Did anyone else get sick?" I asked. "Cammie, can you get me a list of everyone who was at the picnic? And their phone numbers?"

"On Gabe's desk in his study," she said. "There's a check mark beside the names of those who came."

I helped her get Gabe into the SUV then started calling with my cell phone. An hour later, Cammie called.

"They're running some tests," she said. "They think it might just be a stomach virus."

I told her what I'd found out.

"Three of the boys were up all night vomiting, but they're okay now. They were the ones who said they'd eaten—meaning swallowed—at least one bite of that pizza. Everyone else said they either didn't have any of it or spit it out when they tasted it. I haven't been able to reach the boy who brought the pizza. I'll keep trying, though."

"Is Dad going to be all right?" Evie asked when I hung up. Sammy stood beside her, solemn faced.

"They're still running tests," I said. "They think it might just be a nasty stomach virus."

"When will they know for sure?" Evie asked.

I shrugged. "I don't know, sweetie. Soon, I hope. Why don't we play a game or something while we wait?"

We were playing our second game of *Sorry* when my cell phone rang. It was the grandmother of the boy I couldn't reach. What she told me turned my blood to ice.

"I'll be right back," I told Evie and Sammy. "I have to make a phone call."

They looked at me, alarmed. "Is it Dad?"

I tried to act calm. "No. It was . . . someone returning my call. I need to call your Mom with some info. Sammy, take my turn for me until I get back."

"Cammie?" I said when she answered. "The boy who brought the pizza? He bought it ready to bake from a grocery store, then added pepperoni and fresh mushrooms that he picked that afternoon. Cammie, he's in the ICU at the hospital in his hometown in a coma. He . . . he got sick late Sunday night. Same symptoms as Gabe. His body systems are shutting down. Cammie, tell them to test for alpha-amanitin. It's a mushroom toxin."

"Please, God," I prayed after I hung up. "Don't let my son die."

Alpha-amanitin came from *Amanita virosa*, also known as the destroying angel, one of the most poisonous of all mushrooms. Its deadly toxin damaged the liver and kidneys, often fatally. There was no antidote.

An hour later, Cammie called on the house phone.

"Bring the kids," she said, crying. "Gabe tested positive for a-amanitin. It looks like his kidneys are damaged."

*How do you tell your grandchildren their father, your son, is dying?* I wondered as I hurried back into the house. I strode into the den and shut off the TV.

"Get whatever you want to take," I said. "We're going to the hospital. Your father is very sick."

While the kids packed their backpacks, I called Mama Rose and told her. She would call the rest of the family. Next, I called Mickie, who said she and Bill were on their way. Then I called Margot to get the church prayer chain started.

*Oh, God,* I prayed as I drove to the hospital, *I know I haven't been faithful to you. I've been avoiding you since . . . since Steve left me. I blamed you. I've been mad at you. But I need you more now than ever before. My son . . . oh, please, God, don't let Gabe die! And please, please, help me to find Steve. I need a miracle, Lord. No, make that two. I need two miracles.*

CHAPTER TWENTY-ONE

# STEVE

My cell phone rang as I pulled into the hospital parking lot. I checked the caller ID. Angela.

"Vangie? Is everything all right?"

I pulled into a spot a million miles from the emergency entrance. *How did she know?*

"You missed dress rehearsal tonight."

I'd forgotten all about it. Our ballroom dancing recital was coming up Friday evening. Both Tuesday and Thursday classes were slated to be dress rehearsals.

"Oh, Angela, I'm so sorry," I said. "Can you find Gene another partner? I think I'm going to be tied up for a while." I told her about Gabe.

"Where are you?" she asked.

I told her.

"Do not worry about the recital," she said. "We can reschedule it if we have to. That's one of the benefits of having it at the studio. Is there anything I can do for you?"

"Outside of finding a kidney for my son, just pray," I said. The kids had shot out of the car as soon as I'd stopped and were halfway across the parking lot.

"I have to go, Angela. Thanks for caring."

Gabe was in ICU, wires and tubes snaking from his feverish body to machines that clicked and hissed and dripped and hummed. After my five minutes were up, I joined Cammie in the ICU waiting room.

"The only thing that will save him is a transplant," Cammie said, her voice breaking. "And the best chance we have for a match is from a relative. With my diabetes, I can't be a donor, the kids are too young . . ."

A commotion outside the door spilled over into the little waiting room. Mama Rose, wearing a blue flowered dress and blue babushka over her gray hair, strode purposefully to the overstuffed sofa where Cammie and I sat. Six elderly ladies carrying rosaries followed in her wake. The Rosary Society. Cammie brought her up to date.

"Only a kidney transplant will save him," she said. "Outside of Vangie and the kids, he has no living blood relatives."

"We will pray," Mama said. "God is the one who made our bodies. He understands more than the doctors do."

"I'm going to see if I can donate one of mine," I said. "Time is running out to find a suitable donor."

As Mama and the rosary ladies left to find the chapel, I followed the nurse for the tests that would show whether one of my kidneys would be suitable for my son. I purposely didn't tell them about my high blood pressure. It had been back down in the prehypertension stage when I went for my annual physical in April. I'd talked my doctor into taking me off the blood pressure medicine. I was to continue taking the diuretic, watching my diet, and exercising regularly. My blood pressure had been normal when I took it that morning.

"I'm sorry, Mrs. Martin, but the cross matching test was positive," said Dr. Langhorne, the head of the transplant department, told us an eternity later.

"That's good, isn't it?' Cammie asked, hope sparking in her hazel eyes for the first time that night.

He shook his head. "When we do a cross match test, which is a very sensitive test and the last of three we perform, we mix the donor's and the recipient's blood cells to see if the recipient's cells will respond to the donor's. This will indicate whether or not the recipient will respond to the transplanted kidney by attempting to reject it. A positive cross match means that the recipient has responded to the donor—in this case, Gabe's cells have attacked and killed Vangie's white blood cells—so the transplant should not be done because the organ will be rejected."

"But what about anti-rejection drugs?" Cammie asked.

The doctor shook his head. "With Gabe's blood type, AB, a donor with O or AB blood type would be ideal. Vangie's blood type is A. Two out of three tests show she is not a compatible donor." His gaze met mine. "In addition, her blood pressure has been erratic, according to her doctor. In the meantime, we're checking all the donor banks and keeping our fingers crossed."

A gentle voice spoke up. "What about me?" I turned. Angela! What was she doing here? "My blood type is AB. I'm in good health. I'd like to be tested, please."

I was dumbfounded.

"Are you a relative?" Dr. Langhorne asked her.

She shook her head.

"A relative is our best bet," the doctor said. "But we'll test you on the off-chance that you can be a donor. The matches don't have to be exact, but they should be compatible."

While Angela went to be tested, I took a walk to the chapel. Evie and Ali were huddled together on one of the sectionals, watching one of the Disney channels and whispering together. Sammy was curled up on the recliner, his head resting on his arm, fast asleep. Cammie had gone back to Gabe's bedside.

As I stepped into the chapel, I was astounded. It seemed that every pew was filled. Murmured prayers filled the dimly lit room—Mama and her Rosary Society ladies, Margot and half a dozen ladies from my church Bible study group, just about the entire Molinetti clan, including Mickie and Bill, young men wearing Penn State baseball jerseys. Catholics and Protestants huddled together, young and old, praying for my Gabe. Tears splashed down my face as I stumbled into a back pew. I would never again treat Margot like a busybody. Here it was, after midnight, and instead of being home in bed, she was kneeling in one of the front pews, praying. One of the boys came back and introduced himself as the captain of Gabe's team.

"Any news?" Justin whispered.

"They're still looking for a donor," I said.

"How old does a donor have to be?" he asked.

"Eighteen."

"Can I get tested?"

"If you're older than eighteen and in good health, yes," I said.

His eyes filled with tears. "Marty didn't make it," he said, swallowing hard. "You know, the one who brought the pizza."

"I'm so sorry."

I watched him stride back to the front, where the rest of the team waited. They watched him with interest as he spoke, gesturing, then as a group, left the chapel. Justin nodded to me on his way out. I knew where they were headed.

Mama Rose made her way back to me. Putting her arms around me, she pulled me to her.

"Mama," I whispered, "we need a miracle."

She ran an arthritic hand over my hair. "Then, Cara Mia, a miracle is what we will pray for."

*What are the chances?* I thought, resting my head on her shoulder as she rocked me.

Sometime during the night we got our miracle. Dr. Langhorne strode into the ICU waiting room, his face beaming like the soon-to-be rising sun.

"We have a match," he announced.

"Oh, praise God," Cammie said, her voice breaking. "The donor bank came through."

Dr. Langhorne shook his head. "Not the donor bank. Her," he said, pointing to Angela. "Blood, tissue, and cross match tests show that she's more than compatible. On a hunch I ran a DNA test. You, Angela, and Gabriel Martin are blood relatives, most likely half-siblings."

Bits and pieces of what Angela had told me about her past meshed with another person's life story I'd heard in the not-so-distant past. *My father was an American serviceman . . . We settled in Vancouver . . . My wife and son died on that voyage. . . I raised my daughter alone . . . He raised me alone . . .*

"What . . . what is your father's name?" I asked, my voice a mere whisper. I knew what the answer would be.

Angela's shocked eyes met mine. "Steve Michaels."

"I . . . met your father this summer. He was the caretaker at the resort where the class reunion was held. I . . . we . . . enjoyed spending time together. He's the one who did the bridge woodcarving on my mantel."

"Is he the Steve you mentioned last Thanksgiving?" Evie asked.

I nodded.

Angela pulled her cell phone out of her jeans pocket. "I have to call my father."

"Wait," I said. "I thought Steve's daughter's name was Tuyen."

"*Tuyen* is my Vietnamese name. It means 'angel,'" Angela said, putting the phone to her ear. "When we moved to Canada, Papa changed it to Angela."

Where was he? Vancouver? What time was it there? Midnight?

"Papa?" Angela's gentle voice said, "I'm sorry to call you so late. There is someone here you need to talk to."

She handed the phone to me.

"Steve?" I said, my insides quivering. "Don't hang up. Our son is dying."

It was so quiet on the other end, I thought he'd disconnected. Until he exhaled.

"What happened?"

I walked to the corner couch, away from the TV, the family, the shock as they dealt with the bombshell that just dropped on them.

"He ate a poisoned mushroom," I said in a low voice. "He needs a kidney transplant. Angela—she's my dance instructor—offered to be tested. That's how we found out. She's . . ." My voice broke as I told him his daughter was donating her kidney to our son. "She's a remarkable young woman. You raised her well."

"Where are you?"

I told him. "But Gabe and Angela will be taken to the Hospital of the University of Pennsylvania in Philadelphia for the transplant. I'm not sure when they're leaving. Soon, I think."

"I'm on my way. Evangeline?"

Hearing his voice, the way he said my name, calmed the beast of fear I'd been fighting since Cammie called.

"Yes, Steve?"

I thought I heard a sob. "Do you still have that cross necklace I gave you?"

"Yes," I whispered. "But I—"

"Put it back on."

Shortly after dawn, a medical helicopter took Gabe and Angela to HUP's Penn Transplant Institute in Philadelphia, where a team of transplant specialists would take one of Angela's kidneys and transplant it into her half-brother.

Twelve hours after Angela called him with the news that rocked all our worlds, Steve stepped off a plane in Philadelphia. I was there with Evie and Ali and Sammy, to meet him. His eyes were red-rimmed from traveling all night, and his limp was more pronounced than I remembered. He'd lost weight—his face was thinner, his shirt hung off his shoulders, and his jeans were cinched up by a belt. It had been nearly a year since I'd seen him. A duffel bag hung from his shoulder.

I wanted to rush into his arms, but I didn't know how he felt about me.

"Grandpa!" Ali shouted, breaking into a run. Evie stood, wide-eyed, watching while he lifted Ali off her feet and hugged her. After he put her down, she grabbed his hand and led him to where we stood by the baggage carousel.

"Grandpa, this is Evie—your other granddaughter—and Sammie, your grandson. Isn't it great, Grandpa? I have *two* cousins!"

Steve smiled at Evie, who stepped right up to him and gave him a hug. For once, she had nothing to say. But I saw the tears glisten in her violet eyes as he wrapped his arms around her.

"And this is Sammy?" Steve asked when Evie finally let him go.

He mussed Sammy's black, shaggy hair. "Hi, Sammy."

Sammy smiled shyly—until Steve pulled out a candy bar from his jacket pocket. "Hey, Sammy, you look like you could use this. I bought a few extra on my layover in Houston."

Sammy's eyes widened, his mouth opened in a wide grin. "Boy, do I ever!" Snatching the candy bar from Steve's hand, he wrapped his chubby arms around him. "Oh, Grandpa, I love you forever!"

We all laughed. Steve tossed a candy bar to Evie and Ali then dropped a couple of chocolate almond kisses in my hand.

"Luggage?" I asked when Sammy let him go.

He nodded to the duffel bag. "Just this."

"Let's go then. I hope I remember how to reprogram the GPS to give me the directions out of this place and to the hospital."

Steve grabbed my hand and smiled—and those tired eyes twinkled behind his eyeglasses. "You will."

The kids snoozed on our way back to the hospital. They'd been up all night. After we stopped in to see Angela, I turned to him.

"Are you ready to meet your son?" I asked.

He looked nervous but nodded. Taking his hand, I led him to Gabe's room. He stood next to the dialysis machine, staring at the pale form lying on the bed. After a few minutes, Gabe blinked then opened his eyes. Cammie and I had told him about Steve and Angela the night before, but I didn't know how much he'd heard or understood.

"Gabe?" I leaned over the metal rail on the side of his bed. "This is Steve Michaels—your father."

Gabe lifted his hand from the bed and reached for Steve. Steve grasped his son's hand in both of his.

"Hi, Dad," Gabe whispered, his trademark lopsided grin spreading across his face. "After I get my new kidney, we have some catching up to do. D'you play baseball, by any chance?"

We booked two rooms in one of the nearby motels—one for Steve and Sammy, and one for me and the girls. Cammie stayed at the hospital. The concierge told us, since we were relatives of an HUP patient, we'd get a discount.

"We have two patients," Evie told the concierge as I handed him my credit card. "Do we get a double discount?"

Behind me, Steve chuckled. The conceirge's eyebrows arched. I was about to chide Evie when he said, "You have *two* patients?"

Evie launched into the whole story, adding that her grandpa had just gotten in from British Columbia. He listened patiently then smiled.

"You most certainly do get a double discount, young lady."

The next morning we were at the hospital at six, in time to pray with Gabe and Angela before they were whisked away to the operating room. Because Angela's laparoscopic surgery meant less scarring, pain, and recovery time, she'd be able to leave the hospital after only three days and return to a normal work schedule in four weeks.

Gabe, on the other hand, would undergo open surgery, and would take longer to recover. But he was assured he could be back to work part-time in time for baseball tryouts when the fall semester started at the end of August, as long as he took it easy for a while.

The next five hours dragged on. At eight, Steve and I took the kids to the cafeteria for breakfast. Evie and Ali just wanted a bowl of cereal, but Sammy said he was starving. As we sipped our coffee, Steve and I chatted about safe topics—my garden, his woodcarving, which teams looked the most promising to go to the World Series. He chuckled when I told him about my winter woes. I didn't mention Jonas. He asked how Bill and Mickie were. So apparently he knew they were married.

On the way back to the waiting room, he grabbed my hand and held me back while the kids rushed to see who'd be the first to the elevators and thus got to push the button.

"We have to talk, Evangeline." He spoke in a low voice, his blue eyes searching mine. "There's so much I have to tell you. But let's get the kids home first. In the meantime . . ."

He glanced at the kids, who were pushing the up buttons on all the elevators. Taking my face in his hands, he leaned towards me and kissed me on the lips—a tender kiss that sent shivers through me.

We brought Angela and Gabe home on Father's Day. Bill arranged for a private plane to take us from Philly to State College—the same one that flew us to Philly from State College the night Gabe almost died. Steve spent his nights at Angela's, and his days mostly with me, Gabe and Cammie, and the kids. Evie and Ali were delighted to be cousins. Carlie, my fast-growing gundog, took to Steve better than she took to Jonas. Rascal hissed at him until he "accidentally" dropped a chunk of tuna on the floor while making a sandwich.

We had a family picnic on the Fourth of July in my backyard. After everyone had left, Steve and I settled on the glider on the patio. He put his arm around me.

"I'm sorry, Evangeline, for running off last year," he said. "All my life, I've been looking over my shoulder . . ." He took a breath. "There's something I need to tell you, then there's something I want to ask you."

He told me about coming to Qui Nhon.

"I didn't know if I was the traitor that guard said I was," he said. "I didn't remember anything. So I ran. I've been running ever since. I'm sorry, Evangeline. I'm a coward and I wasn't honest with you. That's why I left last year. Not because I was afraid. But because I was ashamed. You deserve so much more."

"What was it you wanted to ask me?"

He pulled me close to him. "I realized in the past year that I made a mistake. Will you forgive me?"

"Yes. Is that all you wanted to ask?"

He opened the sketchbook he'd brought out earlier and laid it on the wicker stand beside the glider.

"Look," he said, handing it to me.

Tears blurred the image of me—as I looked now, with short, white hair and eyeglasses—and wearing the cross necklace.

"After last summer—after you told me who I'd been drawing all those years—the images stopped. Those images anyway. In their place . . . well, you can see what replaced them. But no more demons, except the demon of regret. And I started remembering bits and pieces of our time together in Vietnam. Not a lot. Just little flashes of memories—happy ones. And I kept seeing that cross necklace. I read the article, Evangeline."

"Why didn't you call me?"

"Because I don't deserve you."

"Wait here," I said. "I'll be right back."

I went into the cottage and returned with Bubba's letter and a small box. I handed the letter to Steve. When he was done reading it, he wept. I held him and we cried together. When our tears were spent, I picked up the box, which I'd laid on the wicker stand beside the glider, and put it in Steve's hands.

"What's this?" he asked.

"Open it," I said, smiling.

His hands shook as he lifted the lid. He turned to me then, his blue eyes puzzled.

"Don't you know what that is?" I asked.

He shook his head.

"It's your Medal of Honor."

And the tears started all over again.

A month later I became Mrs. Steve Michaels. We had our wedding rings melted down and recast into new rings, engraved with our initials—EJM and SGM—and our wedding date, 9/2/2008.

One of the stops on our month-long honeymoon trip was the Vietnam Veterans Memorial Wall in Washington, D.C. We walked along the length of the wall, looking for names of those we knew, one in particular. When we came to it, we stood side by side in that quiet, solemn spot. As the sun came out from behind a puffy white cloud, the reflected faces of a man and a woman stared back at us, superimposed on the name etched in the polished black granite—Seth Gabriel Martin.

# ACKNOWLEDGMENTS

From the time an idea is born in a writer's mind and heart to the time it finally sees publication, many are the hands that help its birth and development.

My first thank-you goes to my husband, Dean, for believing in me, encouraging me, and not complaining when supper was late and when I'd hole up in my writing room on his only day off from work (besides Sunday).

Thank you to my cousin, Mary Ann Ayers, whose career as a Navy nurse and whose dedication to her patients inspired me to learn more about the nurses who served in Vietnam.

Thank you to my two online writers' critique groups, the ladies who both encouraged me and challenged me as they reviewed this manuscript in its roughest stages: Melanie Rigney (a.k.a. "Joy"), Virelle Kidder ("Cookie"), and Christa Parrish ("Ace") of the Novel Buds; and Kathy Bolduc, Kay Clark, Patty Kyrlach, and Robyn Whitlock of the Writing Academy's Writers Exchange.

Thank you to Vietnam veteran Bill Bishop, a former U.S. Navy Seal who read Part One of this manuscript for accuracy and suggested corrections.

Thank you to Bob and Judy Long, former missionaries to Vietnam, for providing information about the climate and locale and for suggesting websites to use in my research.

Thank you to Sandra Byrd, my mentor for the Christian Writer's Guild Craftsman Course, who encouraged me and challenged me to be a better writer of fiction.

Thank you to Marsha Hubler, my editor, writing colleague, and friend, whose suggestions helped to fine-tune the manuscript and ready it for publication.

Many thanks to Linda M. Au, proofreader extraordinaire, writing colleague, and friend, whose sharp eyes and knowledge of the craft of writing, as well as the nuts and bolts of publishing, helped to make this project truly professional and helped to calm me down in the final stages of production.

Not to forget Lynnette Bonner of Indie Creative Design, whose skill goes beyond merely putting fonts and pictures together. She is gifted at designing book covers that capture the heart of the story. You, too, have helped to make this book professional.

Thank you to my BFF, Sharon Cessna, who has been in my writing corner from Day One, cheering me on, picking me up, and dusting me off when I fell flat on my face, and believing in me even when I didn't.

Thank you to my big brother, Pete Maddock, for your faith in me and for your prayers.

And a final thank you to God, who blessed me with a love for stories and a love of words, and the opportunity to serve Him doing what I love to do.

# ABOUT THE AUTHOR

MICHELE HUEY is an award-winning author whose published books include several novels, as well as compilations from her award-winning newspaper column. Her favorite setting for her fiction is western Pennsylvania, where she lives with her husband, Dean, who provides her with much fodder for her writing. The mother of three grown children and the grandmother of five, she loves hiking, camping, swimming, and reading, and is an avid (and sometimes rabid) Pittsburgh Pirates fan. Visit Michele online at michelehuey.wordpress.com.

# BOOKS BY MICHELE HUEY

## FICTION

*The Heart Remembers*
*Mid-LOVE Crisis* (formerly *Before I Die*)
*Getaway Mountain: PennWoods Mystery Book 1*

## COMING SOON

*Ghost Mountain: PennWoods Mysery Book 2*

## DEVOTIONAL

*Minute Meditations: Meeting God in Everyday Experiences*
*I Lift Up My Eyes: Minute Meditations Vol. 2*
*God, Me & a Cup of Tea*

# CONTACT INFORMATION

Email: michelehueybooks@gmail.com

Website: michelehuey.wordpress.com

Blog: godmetea.wordpress.com


Dear Reader,

I hope you enjoyed *The Heart Remembers*. This is truly the story of my heart. Please consider submitting a review and/or rating on Amazon and on Goodreads (goodreads.com/michelehuey). Your feedback is greatly appreciated.

Blessings,
Michele